THE NINTH
BUDDHA

By the same author

The Last Assassin
The Seventh Sanctuary

THE NINTH BUDDHA

Daniel Easterman

GUILD PUBLISHING LONDON

This edition published 1989 by
Guild Publishing
by arrangement with Grafton Books

CN 8611

Printed and bound in Great Britain by
Mackays of Chatham PLC, Chatham, Kent

For Beth, with a silent purr

PART ONE
Advent

'. . . twenty centuries of stony sleep
Were vexed to nightmare by a rocking cradle. . . .'

W. B. Yeats, 'The Second Coming'

Hexham

1

Hexham, England, December 1920

Snow had fallen in the night, a stark white emblem of another world, purity lost and stranded in the depths of our humanity. Above Causey Hill, a white, bloated fog hung like a freezing shroud. The long, low lights of Advent huddled in the cold and gloom, extinguishing their flames in preparation for the mystery that was to come. In halls and cottages, the fires of Christmas were emblazoned with frost and rimmed with soot. In village squares, in the ancient gathering darkness, ice formed on newly erected monuments to ten million dead.

Night and the expectation of night to come, the great untrammelled dark barking and whispering beneath the eaves all winter long, the dull onslaught of mystery in the hard, silent heart of an unredeemed and unforgiving world. God and the expectation of God to come. The Lord of light and darkness would return as he had always done, born into the freezing flesh of the dying year. The Prince of Peace would come into a world freshly awakened from a nightmare of slaughter in which whole armies of innocents had died, a world at whose bloodletting even Herod might have blanched. It was harder now than it had ever been.

In the soft, candled interior of St Mary's, evening mass was reaching its climax. In view of the bad weather, it had been decided to hold a second mass that day, for those who had not been able to attend in the morning. The ancient liturgy unfolded its mysteries among the shadows. At the altar, the violet-coloured vestments of the priest enhanced the darkness as his voice enhanced the silence.

Holding the chalice in his left hand, the priest made the sign of the cross with his right.

Benedixit, deditque discipulis suis, dicens: Accipite, et bibite ex eo omnes.

He raised the chalice, blood mixed with water, wine transubstantiated.

11

Hic est enim Calix Sanguinis mei . . . for this is the chalice of my blood . . .

Christopher Wylam sat in the last row of worshippers, rising with them and sitting again, intoning the responses, telling his beads, inhaling the wafted incense. His son William sat beside him, tiny fingers echoing his father's, speaking what he knew of the responses. William was ten, but he carried himself like an older child, as though he already knew a little of what life held in store for him.

His father was something of an enigma to the boy. Until fourteen months ago, Christopher had been little more than a name to the boy. William still remembered the photographs in his mother's room at Carfax, the house just outside Hexham where they lived with Aunt Harriet and his three cousins, Roger, Charles and Annabel. He had never been able to relate the man in those faded prints to the shadowy figure he had last seen at the age of three, waving sadly to him and his mother as their crowded train pulled slowly out of Delhi Station.

But he remembered almost nothing of Delhi now, only little things, like snatches of dreams: an old ayah bending over him and singing softly into the throbbing night, a toy elephant on wheels that he had pulled along behind him on a length of string, great white mosquito nets suspended in the hot air above his cot.

Christopher had returned to William's world only to shatter it, a stranger in strange garb, claiming him for his own. The boy remembered his mother's feverish excitement as the hour of Christopher's return drew closer – the dangerously flushed cheeks, the sunken eyes bright with thoughts of his homecoming. He himself had hoped for a soldier coming home from the war at last, wearing a uniform and bright medals that would catch the sun. 'Bye, Baby Bunting, Daddy's gone a-hunting,' his mother had sung in the nights to him when he was small, exorcizing the fatherless dark. 'Gone to fetch a rabbit-skin to wrap a Baby Bunting in.' But he had been met at the gate by a quiet man in civilian dress, a man who had no tales of heroism to tell and no medals for his son to polish.

William's disappointment had been keen. His cousins had not helped: their father, William's Uncle Adam, had been killed at the

12

Somme three years before. His photographs, draped in black crêpe, took pride of place on the high mantelpieces at Carfax; his medals lay on velvet in a glass case in the hall; and a tablet to his memory stood just left of the altar at St Mary's.

Roger and Charles made William's life a misery. They mocked his father, who, they said, had never been a soldier at all; or, if he had, must have sat at a desk in India throughout the war – a sort of conchie, really. Once, they had left a white feather on William's bed, bearing a little hand-made label: 'For your father'.

All this might have been hard enough for a boy of nine to bear. But his father's return coincided with the beginning of his mother's last struggle against the illness that had been consuming her for the past eighteen months. 'The decline', people said when they thought William was not listening, and he could tell from the way they averted their eyes that they expected the worst. She had kept going for the past six months in anticipation of Christopher's return. He had seen it in her eyes each time he visited her in her cold bedroom: a violent craving that exalted and exhausted her.

Two months after Christopher's arrival, just before Christmas, when everyone seemed to be preparing for festivity, for new birth in an old world, his mother died in her sleep.

Though he knew it to be unjust, William blamed his father for her death. And Christopher himself carried a measure of guilt about with him that only served to reinforce his son's unspoken accusation. The truth was that he felt awkward with the boy and unable to come to terms with his wife's death. Explanations were beyond him. In the hard winter that followed, he would walk for hours across cold, infertile fields, seeking to resolve his guilt or at least pacify it for a while. He kept a painful distance between himself and the boy.

Spring had thawed the fields and laid the first flowers on Elizabeth's grave, but it had done nothing to bring father and son closer. It was decided that William should go to Winchester that autumn. And then, abruptly, all that had changed. One day, while Christopher was in Hexham with his sister Harriet, William went unobserved to his father's room and opened his desk. What was he looking for? He himself could not have answered that. In a sense, he was looking for his father. And in a sense he found him.

Inside a drawer in the top right-hand corner, he found a small red box among a pile of papers. On the lid was the royal crest, and inside lay a medal in the shape of a cross. William recognized it at once: the Victoria Cross. He had seen a reproduction of it in a magazine during the war. In an envelope next to the box was a letter from Buckingham Palace, in which Major Christopher Wylam was commended in the highest terms for 'exceptional bravery in service to his King and Country'.

For days William was torn between excitement at his discovery and guilt about the means by which he had come by it. On the Sunday, after church, he confessed to his father: by now he needed an explanation more than he feared any possible punishment. And that afternoon, for the first time, they talked in Christopher's study until the fire died down and turned to ashes.

Christopher told the boy that there was more to war than pitched battles or tanks or aeroplanes; that the war he had fought in India had been lonely and diseased and treacherous; and that what he now told William must remain an inviolate secret between them.

From that day, they had begun to draw close, each sharing the other's grief at last, as far as possible. It was agreed that William ought to stay at least another year at Carfax, after which they would decide whether he should go away to school at all. When summer came, there were roses on Elizabeth's grave.

They had reached the Paternoster. The priest recited the familiar prayer aloud, his lips moving with rich and practised smoothness. He must already have spoken those same words countless thousands of times in his lifetime. He was a young man, in his early thirties: he had served as a chaplain during the war. Christopher wondered what he thought of while he prayed: of Christ stretched out on the wooden frame of his consecrated life, nailed to him, hand to hand, foot to foot? Of the solemnity of these, his daily actions? Of his priestly role, ordained to bind and loose, to curse and bless? Or did he think of his dinner, of turnip and meat pie and roasted potatoes swimming in thick gravy?

To an astute observer, it would have been obvious at a glance that Christopher Wylam was an Englishman who had spent little time in England. He seemed ill-at-ease in his winter clothes, and his skin still retained much of the colouring that can only be

14

obtained in warmer climates. His fair hair had been bleached by the sun and was swept back from a high, mournful forehead. There were wrinkles at the corners of his eyes, finely etched lines radiating towards the temples like filaments spun from a spider's web. The eyes themselves were dark and heavy-lidded, yet touched by a depth and clarity that caught others unawares. One sensed – perhaps it was only a trick of the candlelight – that his eyes were closed to what was happening in the church and opened on to other, more alien vistas.

He looked round the small church. Not many had ventured out this evening. Men and women and restive children filled the front pews, some genuinely pious, others there from force of habit or a sense of duty. He himself came for William's sake and perhaps as a penance for his betrayal of Elizabeth.

The priest had broken the Host and taken the Body of Christ. He lifted the chalice and drank the consecrated wine, the blood of God, the blood of Christ, the blood of the world, red with redemption.

Christopher imagined how the wine must taste, imagined it transformed into blood, and he felt a sour bile rising in his throat. Father Middleton had preached of Christ's coming and prayed that the peace of Christmas might remain throughout the coming year; but Christopher had no welcome for the pale god-child of Christmas. There was no celebration in his heart tonight, only a dull anger that repined against God and His season of specious joy.

There was silence as the priest raised a fragment of the Host and held it high before the congregation.

'*Ecce Agnus Dei*, behold the Lamb of God,' he said, '*ecce qui tollit peccata mundi*, behold him who takes away the sins of the world.'

One by one, the congregation rose and made for the altar, weighed down with sins, all but the children. Christopher stood up and followed William to join the line of waiting sinners. An old man knelt and opened his mouth, tongue partly extended to receive God's body.

Corpus Domini nostri . . .

So many sins, thought Christopher, as he watched the silver paten flash in the candlelight. The Host touched the old man's tongue. Mortal sins, venial sins, the seven deadly sins. Sins of

15

commission and omission, the sins of pride and lust and gluttony, sins of the flesh, sins of the mind, sins of the spirit. Sins of the eye, sins of the hearing, sins of the heart.

Jesu Christi . . .

He knelt and opened his mouth. He felt the wafer touch his lips, dry, tasteless, forlorn.

. . . custodiat animam tuam in vitam aeternam. Amen.

When Elizabeth had died, something in him had followed her. He and William had visited her grave earlier that day, a little, snow-covered mound among so many behind the church. She belonged to the earth now. He remembered the funeral – the frost, the ground hard like iron, the spades futile, out of season, the black horses, their breath hanging naked and abandoned in the thin winter air.

He remembered her as she had been in those last two months: pale and feverish by turns, remote, her face turned to the wall, intensely conscious of death's approach. There was nothing sculpted or romantic about her passage from the world, nothing fine or ethereal: just a young woman racked with pain, just blood and sputum, and in the end decay. After her death, men had come and burned her clothes and the furniture in her bedroom and scraped the walls as though they harboured some deadly miasmatic force. She had been thirty-one.

For two months, he had sat by her bedside holding her hand; and for two months he had been conscious that they had become strangers to one another. She had died in his arms, but a nurse would have done as well. More than a war lay between them: in their world, love was as hard to come by as forgiveness. They had met in Delhi eleven years earlier, at the first dance of the winter season. She had come out with the 'Fishing Fleet' – the annual contingent of eligible young ladies in search of husbands – and had stayed behind as Mrs Wylam. He had not loved her – Fishing Fleet girls did not expect love – but he had learnt to care for her.

He sat down in his pew again. At the altar, the priest purified the chalice and began to recite the Antiphon: '*Ecce Virgo concipiet et pariet filium*. Behold a Virgin shall conceive and bear a son.'

In another month, Christopher would be forty, but he felt older. His generation – what there was left of it – was already old: young-

16

old men to rule a decaying Empire and heal the breaches left by war. He shuddered. There would be another war in Europe. A year ago, the thought would have left him cold. But now he had a son to fear for.

Unlike so many who had fought in the trenches in France and Belgium, Christopher's mind and body were intact. But his own war, that dark, secret and dirty war whose details he was not even permitted to speak of, had changed him. He had returned with his body whole and his spirit in tatters: cold, cold and lonely, and the dusts of India choking him, filling his throat and chest and nostrils with dry and bitter odours.

Elizabeth's death so soon after his return had made of that change a permanent and frozen thing, hard, calcified in the blood, ineradicable. It consisted in part of the obvious things that came through war and death: bitterness, a loss of joy, a certain coldness of the affections, grief written large, a deep sense of futility. But there were other feelings too, feelings that surprised him: a profound sense of human worth under all the tawdriness, compassion both for the men he had killed and for himself in his former ruthlessness, patience to accept what he had come to believe was inevitable. At times he dreamed of tall white mountains and cool, waveless lakes. And he spent a lot of time with William.

The priest read the last Gospel, final prayers were said, vespers were sung, and the service came to its appointed end. Christopher took William's hand and led him out of the glittering church into the darkness. It was the Sunday before Christmas, but he found it hard to believe that God would ever return to earth.

They did not notice the car waiting in the shadows further down the street.

2

'Christopher.'

He turned to see a figure approaching from the side door of the church. Father Middleton, still in his cassock, was making towards them.

'Good evening, Father. What can I do for you?'

'I'd like to talk with you, Christopher, if I may. Could I walk with you a little? Would you mind?'

The priest was shivering slightly from the cold. His thin cassock was more a spiritual than a physical garment. But he was a strong man who made a point of defying the elements when he could. Christopher liked him: he made no show of piety and had helped after Elizabeth's death by steering well clear of all talk of the blessed souls in paradise.

'Perhaps we could talk in the church,' suggested Christopher. 'It's cold for you out here.'

Father Middleton shook his head firmly.

'Nonsense, Christopher. I won't die. You've both got some way to go. And I only want a few words anyway: just along Hencotes past the Sele, then I'll leave you and get back to my little fire.'

Christopher nodded and they set off. He felt his son's small hand in his, warm and fragile, the frosted snow giving beneath his feet, the fog gathering force beyond the limits of the flickering gas-lamps. The presence of the priest made him self-conscious. Somewhere behind them, a car door opened and closed in the darkness.

'I've been thinking,' said the priest, 'that it may be time to put up a permanent memorial to our war dead. I thought perhaps a small chapel in their honour, dedicated to the Virgin. Nothing ostentatious. Just a quiet place near the front. Somewhere a widow can light her candle and be left in peace.'

Out of the darkness, muffled footsteps crossed the street and came in their direction. In another place, at another time, Christopher might have taken alarm. But it was Sunday and this was

England. Long months of inactivity had lulled his instinct for danger. The darkness thickened round him, like something solid moving against his flesh.

'How can I be of help, Father? You'll want a donation, of course. I'll be glad to contribute.'

'Indeed. I'll be grateful for anything you're willing to give. But I wondered if I could ask more of you. You're a military man yourself. I've heard . . .' – he hesitated – '. . . that you were decorated.'

They were nearing the end of Hencotes. A single light struggled against the dark, laying a yellow film across the firmly packed snow. Christopher stared ahead into the darkness. Who had told the priest? Not William, he was sure of that. His secret was safe with the boy. Perhaps Harriet . . .

'Yes,' he said. His breath mingled with that of the priest, white and listless in the clear air, like milk moving in water.

'I'd like to set up a fund,' Father Middleton continued. 'You're the man at Carfax now, ever since Major Ridley died. There's your sister, of course. But I'd like a man, a soldier, to head the appeal.'

'I was never a soldier.'

'No. But highly decorated. For valour. I ask no questions. You have military rank.'

'Father, I'm not sure . . .'

The footsteps were upon them now. Two men emerged from the shadows, their faces pallid in the thin light. They were dressed in heavy coats and wore shallow fur hats pulled down well on their heads. The first man had a narrow, sour face and eyes that looked as though he had not slept for nights. His companion was heavier and coarser-featured, with dark stubble on his chin.

What happened next took only a few seconds, but it was to remain etched on Christopher's memory for the rest of his life. The thin man nodded at his companion. Both men began to run at once. There was no time to skip or dodge. Christopher felt himself bowled over, then the thin man was on top of him, pressing him into the snow, crushing his chest, making it impossible for him to breathe.

There was a stifled cry. Twisting his head, Christopher saw the heavy man grab William from behind and begin to pull him, struggling, across the snow. The boy kicked out, trying to escape, but the man was too powerful for him.

Christopher pressed up, freeing his right arm in an attempt to grab for his assailant's throat and dislodge him. But the man twisted away from him, thrust a hand into the wide pocket of his coat, and brought out a large pistol. Christopher froze as the man raised it and held it against his head.

'I am ordered not to harm you,' the thin man said. His voice was soft, the accent foreign yet hard to place. 'But I do not always obey orders, and I have killed a great many men in my time. I intend to leave here without interference. Do you understand? So please lie still and let us do what we have come here to do. The boy will not be harmed: I promise you.'

William cried out, still struggling with his captor.

'Father! Help me! Help me!'

The thin man cocked the pistol and held it very hard against Christopher's temple. Beneath him, he felt the snow cold and precise against him, and a stone that stabbed mercilessly into the small of his back.

He had forgotten Father Middleton. The priest, stunned by the suddenness and violence of the attack, had remained standing in the middle of the road, a single arm raised, whether to ward off further attack or to bless his attackers it was not clear. But at the boy's cry, like a sleeper awakened, he stirred and began to stumble through the dragging snow.

Encumbered by the struggling child, the heavy man was finding it hard to make progress. He almost slipped as William twisted in an effort to throw him off balance. One arm was round the boy's throat, while the other desperately tried to pin William's flailing arms to his side.

The priest ran up, arms reaching for the boy's assailant. He cried out inarticulately, the same voice that had spoken Mass only minutes before, troubled now with fear and a grim rage. His finger's tore at the man's arm, dragging him from the boy. The two men slipped and slithered on the wet ground, their feet struggling for some sort of purchase. Suddenly, the heavy man lost his balance and fell, pulling the priest with him.

'Run, William!' Father Middleton shouted. 'Run like hell!'

William hesitated, then turned and ran back in the direction of the town, in search of help. On the ground, the priest rolled in the snow, fumbling for a grip that would allow him to overpower the kidnapper. He was a rugby player, but the man beneath him was stronger than him and was starting to recover from his fall. The priest got his arm across the big man's windpipe, hoping to crush the air from his lungs, but as he did so the other man succeeded in bringing up his knee hard into his groin.

Father Middleton grunted and bent with pain. The heavy man squirmed, pushing him away from him, wriggling out from beneath his body. But as he started to get to his feet, the priest recovered his breath and lunged at him in a low tackle, bringing him down heavily into a patch of virgin snow.

Suddenly, something glinted in the lamplight. As the priest threw himself across to pin him down again, the man lifted a knife and brought it up in a smooth arc. The knife-blade shimmered in the light, then disappeared as it entered the priest's chest. Father Middleton's body jerked backwards, trying to escape the pain of the blade, but the momentum of his leap kept him moving down on to the hilt. He fell on to the man, tearing the knife from his grasp, throwing blood across his face.

'Jesus!' he cried, writhing with pain. He reached for the knife-handle, but his hand had lost all its strength. It slipped on blood and fell against his chest. With his last strength, he traced a clumsy cross over his heart. His hand shook and fell away, his legs jerked, then he became still.

Christopher pressed up against the muzzle of the gun, but a hand pushed hard against his shoulder and forced him down again.

'You bastards!' he shouted. 'You murdering bastards!' But the man with the gun did not relax his grip or move the barrel. A light went on in a window across the street. There was the sound of a sash being raised.

'What's going on out there?' someone shouted.

'Get the police!' shouted Christopher. But the thin man struck him hard across the cheek and pressed a hand down heavily against his mouth.

He saw the heavy man wipe the blade of his knife on the priest's cassock and stand up. His face showed no sign of emotion, no hint of regret. He had killed the priest as he might have killed a sheep or a pig, and thought as little of it. Christopher wanted to kill him just as wantonly. At least William had got away. Whatever happened to him now, the boy was safe.

There was a sound of footsteps. Someone was coming up the street. People had heard their cries: someone was coming to help.

A man stepped out of the shadows, a tall man dressed in a coat and hat like those of the first two men, but of better cut and quality. In front of him, his hands pinned and a cloth tied tightly round his mouth, was William. The man was supporting the boy, forcing him to walk in front of him.

There was a rapid exchange of words in a language Christopher did not recognize. He guessed it might have been Russian, but the men said so little he could not be sure. He opened his mouth to call to William, to reassure the boy somehow that, come what may, someone would track him down and rescue him. But before the words could reach his lips, the thin man raised the gun and struck him across the temple. The world leapt at him then shrank away again as quickly as it had come.

He did not lose consciousness completely. There was a taste of snow in his mouth and he realized he had rolled over on to his face. As he struggled to move, he heard the sound of car doors slamming and a motor being started. Somewhere in the darkness, voices were calling. He saw lights weaving through the shadows and red blood on the snow and the dark shapes of men and women standing and staring at him. There was a roaring sound, then the headlights of a large car stabbed through the darkness at him. A second later, they were gone and he was in the darkness, sobbing into the bitter snow.

3

The clock on the Abbey tower chimed six times. It was Tuesday evening, and the market-place, recently filled with people buying geese and turkeys for the coming Festival, was deserted. Snow had begun to fall, gentle and bright against the uncertain halo of a street lamp.

Christopher was growing cold. Winterpole should have been here by now. On the telephone he had said he was taking the mid-morning train from King's Cross to Newcastle, then driving the rest of the way to Hexham. Even allowing for a quick lunch, he should have been here two hours ago.

It was two days now since the attack and William's kidnap, and still the police had nothing to report. A superintendent had grilled Christopher for hours, asking questions both men knew could not be answered. Scotland Yard had been notified, and an alert put out to watch every port; but nothing had been seen of three foreigners and a boy in a large car. The kidnappers themselves had remained silent: no message, no telephone call, no ransom note. It was as if they had vanished into thin air.

Christopher walked up and down in an effort to keep warm. Behind him, the coloured windows of the Abbey hung suspended in the blackness, dimly lit patterns from another age. A faint sound of singing could be heard: Evensong was almost over.

Out of the darkness, borne on the cold night air, all the smells of England came to him, whether real or imagined he neither knew nor cared. He smelled dead leaves beneath the snow on the Sele, and below that the fragrance of countless summer days, the odours of leather and resin and polished willow, grass trodden beneath the feet of running batsmen, the green turf cut away at the crease, the naked soil giving up its worms. And flowers in spring, and bonfires in autumn, and the dead rotting in ancient churchyards all winter long.

There was the sound of an engine coming down Priestpopple on

23

to Battle Hill. He heard it turn right into Beaumont Street, heading for the Abbey, and moments later its lights appeared. The car stopped on the corner opposite him and the driver extinguished the lights and the engine. Winterpole had come at last. Winterpole and all he stood for. Christopher shivered and walked across the street. The car door was already open, waiting for him.

There was just enough light from the nearest gas-lamp to confirm what Christopher had already guessed: Winterpole had not changed visibly since they last met. A little greyer on the temples, perhaps, a little tighter around the lips, but otherwise unchanged and unchangeable. As always, he reminded Christopher of nothing so vividly as an undertaker. He dressed in black whatever the season or the time of day, as though in perpetual mourning, though what or whom he mourned for no-one had ever been able to guess.

Briefly, as he entered the car and closed the door, Christopher caught a glimpse of Winterpole's eyes. Who was it had said, all those years ago, that they were like a doll's eyes? Perfect, blue, and shining, yet with no more life in them than pieces of cobalt glass. Splinters in the skin, grown hard over the years. It was rumoured that the only time he had ever been known to smile was when his mother died after a long illness. He had turned up late for a rugger match somewhere: 'Sorry I'm late,' he was reputed to have said, 'I've just been burying my mother.' And he had smiled.

'I'm sorry to have kept you waiting in the cold,' he said as soon as Christopher had settled in the soft passenger seat. 'I came as quickly as I could. The trains are running to time, but the road to Hexham is bad. I was lucky to get through.'

Christopher wiped a half-moon in the condensation on the window by his side and looked out. The lights were going out in the Abbey and the last worshippers were making their way home in silence. After Sunday, people were staying together.

'Yes,' Christopher murmured. 'You were lucky.'

Major Simon Winterpole was the head of British Military Intelligence's Russian and Far Eastern Section. Since the Bolshevik revolution of 1917, his had become one of the most powerful voices in the country, discreetly but firmly guiding British foreign policy with respect to out-of-the-way places most Ministers had never even heard of. Even before the war, he and Christopher had met regularly to discuss Russian intelligence activities on the northern borders of India.

'How long has it been now, Christopher?' Winterpole asked.

'How long?'

'Since we last met. Since we last spoke.'

Christopher did not have to think. He remembered their last meeting well.

'Five years,' he said. 'At the end of nineteen-fifteen. You came to Delhi after the Benares Conspiracy Trial.'

'So I did. I remember now. A lot has happened since then.'

Christopher did not reply. He hated meeting in the dark like this, like men who had something to hide. Like clandestine lovers. But Winterpole had insisted. Unlike Christopher, he loved the secretiveness of his trade, the little rituals that set him and his colleagues apart from other men.

'And how long is it now since you left the service?' Winterpole went on.

'A year,' answered Christopher. 'A little more. I thought you might come then. You or someone like you. But no-one came. Just a letter, signed by someone called Philpott. All about the Official Secrets Act. And my pension.'

'We thought you needed time,' said Winterpole.

'Time? Time for what?'

'To mull things over. To get away from things.'

'What was there to mull over? I had made my mind up.'

'Dehra Dun. The war in general. Your wife's death. Whatever mattered to you. Whatever still matters to you now.'

Several of Christopher's best agents had died in Dehra Dun because of an administrative blunder by the Delhi Intelligence Bureau, to which he had been attached. He still felt a sense of responsibility for the deaths, though he had been in no way to blame for them.

'I was surprised,' Christopher said at last.

'Surprised?'

'That you let me go so easily. Just that letter. That letter from Philpott; whoever Philpott is.'

Winterpole took a silver cigarette-case from his pocket and snapped it open. He offered a cigarette to Christopher, but he declined. Delicately, Winterpole extracted a single cigarette for himself, closed the case, and put the cigarette between his lips. He paused briefly to light it. Christopher remembered the smell from the old days. The match flared briefly and died.

'How can I help you, Christopher?' Winterpole asked. 'You say your boy was kidnapped. I'm sorry to hear that. And I understand someone was killed; a priest. Have the police discovered anything?'

Christopher shook his head.

'You know they haven't.'

'Have you no idea at all who was responsible?'

'I was hoping you might tell me that.'

There was a nervous silence. Winterpole drew on his cigarette and exhaled slowly, through the corners of his mouth. The car filled slowly with a perfumed smoke.

'Me? Why should I know anything about this?'

'You didn't travel all the way from London to tell me you know nothing. A telegram would have done. A telephone call. A messenger-boy.'

Winterpole said nothing. He was watching the snow fall against the windscreen.

'Let me tell you exactly what happened,' Christopher went on. Carefully, he described the events of Sunday night. When he had finished, he turned to Winterpole.

'I am not a rich man,' he said. 'In any case, there has been no ransom note. The men who took my son and killed Father Middleton were Russians – I'd stake my life on that. If they were, there must be a link with you: whether they are Whites or Reds or some other colour, they could not be in this country without your knowledge. And if you are involved, that establishes a sufficient link with me.'

'I assure you, Christopher, I am not involved.'

'I'm sorry,' Christopher said. 'Perhaps "involved" is not the correct word. "Connected" – is that what I should have said? Or "informed" – would that express it better?'

Winterpole was silent. So much depended on how he phrased himself. In this business, the right choice of words was often more important than the right choice of weapon. A man's life could hang in the balance. Several lives. Winterpole thought of himself as a general, though his troops were few and easily wasted. He disposed them like tiny chessmen on a vast and tilted board, little glass

26

pawns clinging precariously to the surface: an army of glass, brittle, betrayed, and dreaming.

'I think,' he said slowly, 'that I may be able to help you. And you, in your turn, may be able to help me.'

'You mean that's the price I have to pay if I want to see William alive again?'

Winterpole said nothing. He pulled deeply on his cigarette, wound down the window, and tossed it half-smoked into the darkness. Slowly, he wound the window up again. It was suddenly cold in the car.

'Tell me,' he said. 'Have you ever heard of a man called Zamyatin? Nikolai Zamyatin?'

4

'Zamyatin,' Winterpole began, 'is probably the most dangerous Bolshevik agent currently operating in the Far East. He's a leading light in Comintern, the Communist International set up by the party in March last year to co-ordinate the work of worldwide revolution. In Moscow, he is Trotsky's *éminence grise*. In the East, he is almost independent. Without Zamyatin, it's safe to say there would be no Bolshevik policy in the region. To be honest, if it weren't for Nikolai Zamyatin, I would sleep a lot more easily in my bed at night.'

And if it weren't for Simon Winterpole, thought Christopher, *a lot of other people would sleep better*.

'Exactly what has any of this to do with me or my son's disappearance?' he asked. 'I don't know this Nikolai Zamyatin, I've never heard of him, and I assume he has never heard of me.'

Winterpole glanced at Christopher.

'Don't be so sure about that,' he said.

There was something in Winterpole's tone that unsettled Christopher. Like a swimmer who senses the first pull of the undertow plucking him down, he could feel the past tugging at him. He wanted to cry out, to struggle against drowning in waves that might be of his own devising; but his limbs felt tense and his throat was raw with the cold night air.

'Go on,' he said quietly.

'Zamyatin is half Russian, half Buriat Mongol. His father was Count Peotr Zamyatin, a wealthy landowner from Cheremkhovo to the north of Lake Baikal. His mother was a Buriat woman, one of the peasants on his father's estate. They're both dead now. Nikolai was born about 1886, which makes him roughly thirty-four.

'He had a little money as a child, enough to get what passed for an education in Irkutsk, but he learned soon enough that he had no hope of inheriting a penny from his father. By the age of sixteen,

28

he was an active member of the Communist Party in the region, and before he turned twenty he had been sent to Moscow. He was about thirty when the Revolution started. Sovnarkom, the Soviet of People's Commissars, sent him out to help organize the new order in Transbaikalia. From that point on he led a charmed life. In Moscow, the Russians accepted him: he was the rebel son of an aristo claiming his own on behalf of the people. And in Transbaikalia he was a local boy made good. What had been a disadvantage – his mixed parentage – now became his passport to power.

'He was Moscow's chief man in Transbaikalia throughout the Civil War. Now he talks with Lenin and Trotsky and Zinoviev about an empire beyond Siberia, a people's republic stretching to the Pacific. China, Mongolia, Manchuria, Tibet. They can all see that Europe's hopeless now, that it may be hopeless for another fifty, another hundred years. But they need to dream, you see, and so they dream about the East. And all the time Zamyatin stands there whispering in their ears like a mesmerist, telling them that he can make their dreams reality.'

Winterpole paused for a moment, staring into the darkness beyond the windscreen, as though he could see a second darkness gathering there, discrete, intact, waiting. He shivered. It was cold: cold and empty.

'About a year ago,' he went on, 'Zamyatin dropped out of sight. One minute, my people were sending me almost daily reports about him, the next he was gone. There were sightings at first, but they all proved negative. The internal pogroms had already started, of course, so my first thought was that he had fallen victim to his erstwhile friends in the Kremlin. Stalin is the coming man in Russia, and he wants socialism in one country. Zamyatin could have been a sacrifice, a reassurance that the others are not dreaming too hard.

'But time passed and Zamyatin's name wasn't mentioned, and I knew he must still be alive. They have to denounce their victims, you see – it's no good just doing away with them some dark night. Their deaths are a sort of atonement, you understand, and their sins must be expiated in public. *Pour encourager les autres.*

'Then, about four months ago, I had a firm sighting. One I could rely on, from one of my best men.' He hesitated. 'He was seen in Tibet, in the west, near Mount Kailas, near a monastery called Phensung Gompa. He was alone, and he seemed to have been travelling for a long time. In Tibet, Christopher. Nikolai Zamyatin. I didn't believe it at first. But my man managed to take some photographs. There's no doubt about it. He was there. Am I making sense to you?'

Christopher nodded. Winterpole was making a sort of sense. Tibet was Christopher's territory, one of his special sectors. The agent who had sent the photograph had probably been one of his own men, recruited and trained by him. He followed the other man's gaze into the darkness beyond the windscreen. More strongly than before, he felt that he was being sucked down beneath heavy waves. Thin hands above the water; the taste of salt on his lips; and a cold wind coming from the shore, driving him out to sea.

'You were in the Kailas region back in 1912, weren't you, Christopher?' Winterpole asked.

'Yes,' said Christopher dully.

'What were you doing there?'

'I was looking for agents. Russian agents. We had received a report, a reliable report. I was sent to investigate.'

'And what did you find?'

Christopher shrugged.

'Nothing,' he said. 'I spent a month up there, on the slopes of Mount Kailas itself and round Lake Mansarowar. It's a sacred region. I made excursions to several of the monasteries. I spoke with pilgrims. If there were Russians, they must have been invisible.'

He saw Winterpole shake his head.

'Not invisible,' he said. 'Dead.'

Christopher realized that, with one hand, he was holding tightly to the door-handle beside him. Drowning men never let go: that is an axiom. He tightened his fingers on the cold metal.

'There were two of them,' Winterpole went on. 'Maisky and Skrypnik. Maisky was a Jew, the son of a watchmaker from the *stetl*. I met him once in Petersburg. A small man with bad teeth.

'There was a third man with them, a Mongol guide. He made his way back to Russia after they died and managed to make a report. Badmayeff was their expert on Tibet then. He interviewed the man and wrote the report himself.

'Now, Maisky and Skrypnik had gone to Tibet officially as explorers, so heavily edited versions of the report were deposited in all the proper places – the Institute of Oriental Languages at the Ministry of Foreign Affairs, the Oriental Section of the Imperial Archaeological Society, and the Imperial Academy of Sciences. One or two articles were even published in journals. I read some of them myself.'

He paused and fingered the steering-wheel again. No-one passed in the street. It was Tuesday night, and it was cold, and children were in bed at home, dreaming of fat Father Christmases and dining off brandied pudding in their sleep.

'The real report, the unedited version, was locked away in a file in the Secret Service archives and promptly forgotten. The Mongol disappeared – almost certainly killed because of what he knew.'

'What did he know?'

'Be patient, Christopher. I'll come to that. I think Badmayeff planned to act on the report, but first of all he needed funds and the backing of the right people. However, it was already 1913 and circumstances were far from propitious for an undertaking in Tibet. The file stayed where it was, gathering dust. I had no idea of its existence, of course. No-one had any idea.

'I only discovered what I have just told you this year, after I received the report about Zamyatin being sighted near Mount Kailas. My information was reliable. There were photographs, as I said. So I believed Zamyatin had really been there. And I asked myself what could possibly bring a man like Nikolai Zamyatin to such a God-forsaken place. A man on his way up. A man with access to the corridors of power.

'It was then I remembered that you had been there in 1912. Looking for Russian agents. Perhaps, I reasoned to myself, you had been mistaken. Perhaps there had indeed been agents, or at least one agent. If so, I argued to myself, there must have been a report, there must still be a report somewhere . . . and Nikolai Zamyatin must have found it and read it.'

Abruptly, Winterpole reached out a hand and cleared a space where fresh condensation had fogged the windscreen. Outside, the snow still fell, its faint flakes drifting down past the street-lamp, remote and colourless, like shadows falling from another planet.

'I instructed my best agent in Moscow to look for the report. It took him a week to find it. Or, to be precise, to find the file it had been in. The report itself was missing – Zamyatin had either kept it or destroyed it, there was no way of knowing which. There was, however, a second file in Badmayeff's hand. It contained a synopsis of the full report, intended for the eyes of the Tsar himself. The synopsis is less than a foolscap page in length and it tells us very little. But it does make one thing clear: Maisky and Skrypnik were sent to Tibet expressly to search for something. And whatever it was, they found it.

'What is also clear is that their discovery did not go back to Russia with their Mongol guide. It was left in Tibet. Badmayeff's synopsis ends with a request for further finance in order to kit out an expedition to bring it back. But war broke out in Europe and everybody started waving flags, so no expedition was ever sent. Until this year. Until Nikolai Zamyatin appointed himself to the task.'

Somewhere, footsteps sounded on hard ground and faded again. Someone was reclaiming the streets from Sunday's violence. A light went on in a room opposite and was extinguished a few seconds later. A dog barked once and was silent. The night continued.

'What has any of this to do with me or my son?' Christopher asked again.

Winterpole leaned his forehead against the cold rim of the steering-wheel and breathed out slowly.

'I don't know,' he said. 'I wish to God I knew, but I don't. I swear that's the truth.'

'Then why . . .'

'Go through all this? Because, Christopher, although I cannot begin to explain it to you, I know that there is a connection. So far, all I know is that you were in the Kailas region eight years ago. And Nikolai Zamyatin was there four months ago.'

'You mean that's what brought you all the way up here? My son is kidnapped and you come here talking about coincidences. You tell me stories about a man I've never seen or heard of.'

Winterpole did not answer at once. Outside, the snowflakes danced as he came closer to the heart of the thing. They were all dancing: himself and Christopher Wylam, and somewhere far away, Christopher's son and a man called Zamyatin, all caught in a Dance of Death, turning round and round in the still darkness like figures on an old clock.

'There's something else,' he said at last, his voice flat and emotionless.

'Go on.'

'Last month,' he said, 'a Tibetan monk arrived in Kalimpong in northern India. He was dying: he'd come over the high passes during some very bad weather. Somehow – we're not sure exactly how – he managed to get a message to a man called Mishig. Mishig is a Mongol trader with his base in Kalimpong. He's also an agent for the Russians. Until the Revolution, he worked quite happily for the Tsarist regime. Now he's a messenger-boy for the Bolsheviks . . . and just as happy. He keeps them informed about traffic to and from Tibet. Low-grade information mostly, but from time to time it throws up pearls. So they've given him a small radio transmitter that he uses to communicate with a controller in Calcutta, whose identity is still unknown to us.

'We know that Mishig's control is able to get messages through to Moscow and Europe, but we haven't yet worked out his system. In the meantime, we go on monitoring all the signals that pass between Mishig and Calcutta.'

There was a pause. Winterpole took a deep breath.

'On the tenth of November, we intercepted a message to Calcutta from Mishig. It was marked "urgent" and had been encoded quite differently to any of his previous signals. And it was signed with the code-name "Zima". That's Russian for "Winter". It's the official code-name for Nikolai Zamyatin.'

Winterpole paused again. Christopher sensed that he was reluctant to get to the point.

'Exactly what did this message say?' he asked.

'You understand, Christopher,' Winterpole said in a quiet voice, 'that there can be no going back. Once I have told you, you won't be able to leave it alone. I can still spare you, I can still keep silent. It's your decision.'

'Tell me. I have to know.' He felt the tension in his stomach tighten into a knotted cord. Outside, the snowflakes danced and fell.

'He asked for information,' Winterpole said. 'Information about an Englishman called Christopher John Wylam, who had worked

33

for British intelligence in India. And about his son. A boy called William.'

The undertow had him firmly in its grip at last, and he could feel himself going under. Thin hands flailing, tearing the sunlight out of the sky. He said nothing.

'Three weeks after that,' the other man went on, inexorable now he had begun, 'we got hold of a signal from Calcutta to Mishig. It said they had tracked you down in a place called Hexham in England. There was a request for further instructions.'

He paused.

'I'm afraid that's where things went a bit wrong,' he said. 'We thought Mishig would send another message to Calcutta later the same day. He was due to despatch one of his routine signals. But he never made the broadcast. He took the next train from Siliguri to Calcutta. We're certain he carried the instructions to his control in person – either orally or in writing, it doesn't matter. That was six days ago.'

Christopher looked at Winterpole.

'You knew about this and you didn't notify me. You knew something might happen, but you kept quiet.'

'Try to understand, Christopher. We needed to know what Zamyatin is up to. We had to let them show their hand. I was afraid you might do something to prevent them if you knew. I'm sorry.'

'They might have killed him. For all I know, he's dead now. And they did kill Father Middleton. For what?'

'We still need to know, Christopher. What Zamyatin is doing in Tibet. What he wants with your son. I'd like you to go to India, to Kalimpong. And if it's necessary, to Tibet. I think that's where they're taking your son.'

'I know,' Christopher replied. He looked away from Winterpole. Outside, the shadows of night were descending on grey and mottled wings that troubled the snow-filled air. 'I know,' he said. And the snow stopped falling and there was only darkness.

5

Nedong Pass, southern Tibet, January 1921

He was cold. There had been more snow that morning, white,
blinding snow that had whipped at his face and hands. It had
blotted out everything: the road, the rocks, the footprints they left
behind. It was impossible to tell whether they were still in the pass
or not; he thought they might have lost their way. Tobchen was
frightened, he could tell. Once, the pony had almost slipped on a
ledge over a steep precipice. Since then, Tobchen had made him
walk, holding the animal's bridle, stiff with frost. The old man
went in front, repeating mantras endlessly, spinning his prayer
wheel like a madman.

Since early afternoon, the snow had given way to a fierce wind,
a wind so sharp it threatened to tear the skin from a man's bones.
It rose to gale force like this every afternoon. The day before, they
had passed a group of travellers wearing masks, dark masks of
leather painted with the features of demons. He had been frightened and had called out.

'Tobchen, Tobchen – who are those men? Why are they dressed
like that?'

The old man had looked up and shouted back. The wind
snatched his words away and he waited until the boy came
alongside him.

'Don't worry, my lord. They are only travellers. They wear the
masks to protect their faces from the wind. And they paint them to
frighten the demons.'

The men had gone past without a word, silent and incurious,
harried by the wind, dark figures driven remorselessly into the
void. He and Tobchen had been left alone again to battle on
against the elements.

They stopped just after sunset. The old man found dried yak
dung somewhere and lit a fire. There was tea and *tsampa* as always,
but Samdup did not complain. And if he had, Tobchen would not
have listened to him. He was a *trulku*, but he was still a child, and

35

Tobchen treated him with a mixture of awe and sternness that allowed for no lapses in discipline. He was worried that the old man was growing tired. He wondered how much longer the journey would last.

'How much farther to Gharoling?' he asked.

The old monk looked up, his tea cup clasped in frost-bitten fingers.

'Soon, my lord, soon.'

'But how soon, Tobchen? Tomorrow?'

The lama shook his head.

'No, not tomorrow,' he said. 'But with the help of your prayers and the grace of Lord Chenrezi, it will not be long.'

'Will it be the day after tomorrow, Tobchen?' the boy insisted.

'Drink your tea, *khushog*, and don't ask so many questions. When you have finished, I will light a lamp and we will study the Kangyur together. Your education must not be neglected just because you are travelling.'

The boy fell silent and sipped his tea, lifting out from time to time the balls of *tsampa* that provided the only real nourishment in his meal. The wind was still high, but they sat in the shelter of an outcrop of rocks, listening to it pass. The heavens were invisible behind acres of heavy cloud.

'Why are we going to Gharoling, Tobchen?' Samdup asked.

'I have told you before. To visit Geshe Khyongla Rinpoche. The Rinpoche is a great teacher, greater than I. It is time for you to study the Sutras. Then you will be ready to undertake the study of the Tantras. You must know both to fulfil your destiny.'

'But there are teachers at Dorje-la Gompa.'

'Yes, there are good teachers there. But none as great as Khyongla Rinpoche. Do you remember when we studied the *Lama Nachupa* together, how it described the duty of a disciple towards his *guru*?'

'Yes, I remember.'

'Now it is time for you to put all its counsels into practice. You have not come among us to learn. You have come to remember all you knew before. The Rinpoche will instruct you how to do that.'

There was a pause. Snow had begun to fall again. It would be a cold night. The boy's voice sounded faint in the darkness.

'Was there danger at Dorje-la Gompa?'

36

Unseen, the old monk stiffened.

'Why do you think there was danger, my lord?'

'I sensed it. When the stranger came. I sense it now. Am I right?'

There was silence for a moment, then the old man answered.

'You are not mistaken, *khushog*. There is danger.' He paused. 'Great danger.'

'To me?'

'Yes. To you.'

'Is that why we are fleeing to Gharoling? Is that why we left at night?'

The old man sighed.

'Yes. We will be safe there. Khyongla Rinpoche understands. If . . . if anything should happen to me, lord, make your way to Gharoling. They will expect you there. Do not attempt to return to Dorje-la. Do not go anywhere but Gharoling. Do not trust anyone but Khyongla Rinpoche and those he advises you to trust.'

Silence fell again as the boy digested what he had been told. The world was proving to be a harder place than he had once thought it. Then his voice broke into the old man's thoughts again.

'Is it my other body?' he asked. 'Is he responsible for this?'

Tobchen shook his head.

'No, my lord. I am sure he knows nothing of you. At least I think not. When it is time, he will be told.'

'Would he try to kill me if he knew?'

The lama did not answer immediately. So many incarnations, he thought. They began as children and grew old and died. And were born again. An endless cycle.

'Yes,' he said. 'I think so. I think he would have you killed.'

Kalimpong

6

Kalimpong, northern India, January 1921

Kalimpong dozed in the thin January sunshine. It dreamed of wool and cotton and bright Kashmiri shawls, of Chinese silks, deer antlers and musk, of Indian sugar, glass, and penny candles, of long, jangling caravans coming down from the Chumbi valley out of Tibet, of traders bringing their wares in gunny sacks from the plains of India. But on the high passes to the north, snow fell in easy splendour, thick and white, falling in a trance like the substance of dreams on rocks as cold as sepulchres. For two weeks now, no-one had dared to venture over the Nathu pass. Trade had been brisk with the arrival of the last caravan from Gyantse, but now it had fallen off again, and the tiny market town waited for word that the large consignment due from Lhasa was at last on its way.

Christopher Wylam let the clear air fill his lungs. He felt better in Kalimpong. The town itself was little more than a trading-post on the outskirts of an empire, an entrepôt for traders coming down from Tibet with wool and yak-tails to exchange for cheap manufactured goods and more expensive fabrics. But it stood on the edge of mystery. In the air, Christopher could already taste the snow and ice of the Himalayas. They lay on his tongue like a flavour remembered from childhood, at once familiar and exotic, conjuring up memories of silent journeys in the dim, falling snow.

He had only to lift his eyes to see the mountains themselves standing silently in the distance beyond green foothills. They rose up like ramparts barring access to the great Tibetan plateau beyond, a forbidden kingdom jealously guarded by its protector deities. And, more prosaically, by armed Tibetan border guards.

As he stepped down from his pony, the spices and perfumes of the bazaar brought back to him vivid memories of his father. He remembered walking here with him, followed by their *chaprassi*, Jit Bahadur. And behind would come his mother dressed in white, carried in an open *dandy* on the shoulders of four impeccably

41

dressed servants. That had been in the days when his father was stationed nearby as British Resident at the native court of Mahfuz Sultan.

Arthur Wylam had been an important man, appointed to his post by the Viceroy himself. The Wylams had been Anglo-Indians for three generations: Christopher's grandfather William had come out with the Company just before the Mutiny and had stayed on afterwards as an ICS District Magistrate in Secunderabad. Young Christopher had been brought up on stories of the great Raj families – the Rivett-Carnacs, the Maynes and the Ogilvies – and had been told repeatedly that it was his duty, as it would one day be that of his own son, to add the name of Wylam to that illustrious roll.

Kalimpong had scarcely changed. The main street, a rambling affair of little shops, rang to the sound of hawkers and muleteers as it had always done. Here, Bengali merchants rubbed shoulders with little Nepali Sherpas and fierce-looking nomads from Tibet's eastern province of Kham; pretty Bhutanese women with their distinctive short-cropped hair collected glances from young *trapas* making their first pilgrimage to Buddh Gaya; cheerful Chinese traders argued with sharp Marwari merchants and made a profit out of it. On a flat stone in the middle of the bazaar, a blind man sat begging, his eyes running sores, his fingers bent into an attitude of perpetual entreaty. Christopher tossed a coin into the upturned hand and the old man smiled a toothless smile.

Christopher's father had always preferred the bustle and anarchy of Kalimpong to the stiff formality of Darjeeling, the British administrative centre some fifteen miles to the west. How many times had he told Christopher that, if he was to live in India, he must learn to be an Indian? Arthur Wylam had in many ways despised his own caste – the Brahmins, the heaven-born of the Indian Civil Service and Indian Political Service – for their insularity and prejudice.

The Civil List, with its tedious enumerations of precedence, the clubs with their ridiculous rules of etiquette and protocol, the effective apartheid that made even high-born and educated Indians outsiders in their own country – all had at one time or another drawn his wrath. His love for the Indian people, for their languages, their customs, their religions, their foolishness and their

42

wisdom, had made him an effective and eloquent intermediary between the Government of India and the various native rulers to whose courts he had been assigned. But his scorn for convention in a society riddled by it the way a chest of drawers is riddled by worms had earned him enemies.

Christopher left his pony at a stable and took his bags to a small rest-house run by an old Bhutanese woman near McBride's Wool Depot. The rest-house was noisy and smelly, and it teemed with energetic little Kalimpong fleas whose great-great-grandparents had come to town in a particularly noxious sheepskin from Shigatse; but it was the sort of place where no-one would ask too many questions about who a person was or what he was doing in town.

He could have stayed in the Government guest-house, a small dak-bungalow just outside town, complete with potted plants and ice and servants. But that would have involved getting chitties in Calcutta and travelling as a Government official – the last thing either Christopher or Winterpole wanted. As far as the Government of India was concerned, Christopher Wylam was a private citizen visiting the hill country merely to relive some pleasant childhood memories and recover from his wife's death. If there was trouble and questions were asked, Mr Wylam would not officially exist.

When Christopher came downstairs, the rest-house was in turmoil. A party of Nepalese had arrived after a journey of almost three weeks from Kathmandu. They had come to find work in India, in the tea-plantations round Darjeeling. There were about a dozen of them, poor men in ragged clothes, farmers whose barley had failed that year, leaving them without enough food for the winter. They had come to the rest-house on the recommendation of a Nepalese trader whom they had met on their way, but now the bossy little landlady was telling them there was no room for so many.

There was little likelihood of the scene turning genuinely ugly – such outbursts seldom went beyond words or, at the most, some harmless pushing and shoving. But Christopher felt sorry for the men. He had lived with peasants just like them in the past, and had travelled widely in Nepal: he could understand what it was that had forced them to leave their homes and families at this time of year to make such a hazardous and uncomfortable journey, carrying their provisions on their own backs.

What a contrast there was with his own journey to India. Winterpole had arranged for Christopher to fly there in a Handley-Page biplane by way of Egypt, Iraq and Persia. While these men had been trudging through snow and ice, buffeted by high winds and in constant danger, he had flown like a bird across the world, his worst discomforts cramp and a little cold.

He felt an impulse to intervene, but checked himself just as he was about to step forward. Instinct gave way before training: the rules of his trade said 'do not draw attention to yourself, merge into the background and stay there, do nothing curious or out of character'. He had come to Kalimpong in the guise of a poor English box-wallah from Calcutta – a trader down on his luck and desperate for a new venture away from the scenes of his failure. No-one would give such a man a second glance: he was a common enough sight in the doss-houses of the big cities and the flop-downs of the frontier bazaars.

Christopher turned away from the shouting peasants and went into the rest-house's common room. This was the centre of the house's activities, where guests cooked their own food during the day and where those without bedrooms slept by night.

The room was dark and grimy and smelt of sweat and old food. In the corners, bales of wool and gunny sacks filled with rice or barley were stacked up high. By one wall, an old man and woman were cooking something over a small iron tripod. Near them, under a greasy-looking blanket, someone else was trying to sleep. A fly buzzed monotonously as it toured the room, out of season, dying, finding nothing of interest. A girl's voice singing came through the half-shuttered window. She sang in a dreamy, faraway voice, a Bengali song about Krishna, simple but possessed:

> *Bondhur bāngshī bāje bujhi bipine*
> *Shamer bāngshī bāje bujhi bipine.*
> *I hear my lover's flute playing in the forest;*
> *I hear the dark lord's flute playing in the forest*

Christopher imagined the girl: pretty, dark-eyed, with tiny breasts and hair pulled tight in long plaits, like the images of Radha that hung on the walls of so many homes. For a moment, he wondered what she was really like, singing in the alley outside as if her heart would break. Then he called out, breaking the spell of her voice, and a boy came.

'Yes, *sahib*. What do you want?'

'Tea. I'd like some tea.'

'*Ystrang?*'

'No, not bloody *ystrang!* Weak tea, Indian-style. And get me a *chota peg* to go with it.'

'No whiskey here, *sahib*. Sorry.'

'Then bloody get some, Abdul. Here, take this.' He tossed a grimy rupee to the boy. 'Step lively! *Juldi, juldi!*'

The boy dashed out and Christopher leaned back against the wall. He hated the role he had chosen to play, but he played it because it made him inconspicuous. That sickened him more than anything – that it was possible to be inconspicuous by being rude . . . and that politeness to a native would have made him stand out like a sore thumb.

The fly buzzed and the girl's voice continued outside, rising and falling as she went about her chores. Not since his arrival in Calcutta had Christopher had time to sit and think. The journey had been all rush and bustle: the hurried preparations for departure, the clumsy, rushed farewells, the staggered flight from staging post to staging post across the world, the hot, sleepless railway journey from Calcutta to Siliguri, and finally the trek by pony to Kalimpong. No time to reflect on what he was doing. No time to reconsider. Just the world rushing past beneath him, water and sand and silent green valleys where time stood still. And yet always a growing realization of what it was he had embarked on, a tight knot of fear in his chest that grew tighter and larger with every stage he travelled.

He had thought about William constantly, trying to understand how the kidnapping could possibly fit into Zamyatin's plans, whatever they might be. Apart from his own expedition to Kailas in search of Russian agents, he could see no link between himself and this man. Was William no more than bait, intended to bring Christopher to the Russian, for reasons he could not begin to guess? That seemed unnecessarily elaborate and clumsy. Not for the first time, he reflected that Winterpole might not be telling him the whole story, or even that what he had told him was largely fabrication.

The boy returned carrying a tray on which stood a cheap, battered teapot, a cracked cup, and a small glass of whiskey-coloured liquid that Christopher took to be anything but whiskey. There was a low wooden table nearby; the boy set the tray down and poured tea into the germ-laden cup. It was strong, the way all Indians imagined Europeans liked to drink it. Christopher shrugged: he would soon be drinking Tibetan tea made with salt and butter – why turn up his nose at Darjeeling's finest?

'It's quiet outside,' he said. 'Have the Nepalis gone?'

'Yes, *sahib*. Not nice people. Very poor. No room here for them.'

'Where will they go?'

The boy shrugged. What did it matter where they went? He had already consigned them to the nothingness his mind reserved for everyone of no immediate use to him. He turned to go.

'Just a moment,' said Christopher. 'Can you tell me how to find the Knox Homes – the orphanage?'

A shadow seemed to pass briefly across the boy's face, then it was gone and he was smiling again. Yet not really smiling.

'The orphanage, *sahib*? What would you want with the orphanage? There is nothing there, *sahib*, nothing but children.'

'Listen, Abdul, I asked for directions, not advice. How do I find the place.'

Again that curious expression in the boy's eyes, then he shrugged.

'It's very easy, *sahib*. Have you seen the tower of the church?'

Christopher nodded. It was the most prominent landmark in Kalimpong.

'The orphanage is a red building beside the church. A big building. With many windows. You will see it, *sahib*, once you are at the church. Will that be all, *sahib*?'

Christopher nodded absently, and the boy turned again to go. Then, in the doorway, half of his body caught in a pale shaft of sunlight, half in shadow, he turned back.

'Are you a Christian, *sahib*?'

Christopher hardly understood the question. Just as all Indians were Hindus or Muslims to the uninitiated European, so all white people were Christians to all but a few Indians.

46

'I'm not sure,' Christopher replied, wondering if it was the right answer to give. 'Should I be?'

'I don't know, *sahib*. You don't look like a missionary.'

Christopher frowned, then understood.

'You mean the orphanage?'

'Yes, *sahib*.'

Christopher shook his head.

'No,' he said, 'I'm not a missionary.'

'But you are going to the Knox Homes.'

'Yes. Do only missionaries go there?'

The boy shook his head.

'I don't think so, *sahib*. All sorts of people go there. It's a very important place. Important people go there.' Again that odd look.

'And you don't think I look important enough or Christian enough to go there – is that it?'

The boy shrugged. He felt he had spoken out of turn. It was never good to cross a European.

'I don't know, *sahib*. It's none of my business. Sorry, *sahib*.'

He turned and slipped into the waiting shadows.

'Boy,' called Christopher.

The boy returned.

'What's your name, boy?'

'Abdul,' the boy replied, mumbling the word as though it had a bad taste.

'No, it isn't. You're not a Muslim. And even if you were, Abdul's not a proper name. Even I know that. So what's your name?'

'Lhaten, *sahib*.'

'Laten, eh?' Christopher mispronounced the name deliberately. 'Very good, Laten. I'll call you if I need you.'

'Thank you, *sahib*.'

Lhaten glanced curiously at Christopher once more, then left.

Christopher sipped his tea. It tasted vile. He put the cup down and quaffed the *chota peg* in a single swallow. It wasn't much better. Outside, the girl had stopped singing. The sound of men and animals from the bazaar had grown duller. An afternoon silence had fallen over Kalimpong. Christopher sighed as he put down the chipped whiskey glass. He was back.

7

Mishig, the Mongol trade agent who had sent the messages to Calcutta, had disappeared. According to George Frazer, the British Agent, he had returned to Kalimpong briefly, then left without warning about ten days earlier. Frazer told Christopher what he could about the monk who had brought the original message out of Tibet.

He was called Tsewong. It semed that he had battled his way over the Nathu-la pass, down through Sikkim, and almost to the outskirts of Kalimpong before collapsing from exhaustion. According to the report received by Frazer, he was found on the roadside by a passing farmer on the fourteenth of December – feverish, delirious, and near to death.

The farmer had brought him on his cart to the orphanage, where the Reverend John Carpenter and his wife had cared for him until the Mission doctor returned from a visit to a nearby village. The doctor had advised against Tsewong's removal to the Presbyterian Hospital and had remained at the orphanage all that night. The monk had died the next morning, apparently without saying anything intelligible.

Before handing the body over to the Tibetan agent, who was to arrange for his cremation, the doctor had searched the man's pockets or, to be precise, the pouch formed by the fold of his robes, in which Tibetan men carry their personal possessions.

In the pouch, apart from the normal accompaniments of a lama – a wooden teacup (also used as a bowl from which to eat *tsampa*), the traditional metal water-bottle, normally hung from the sash, a yellow wooden rosary of one hundred and eight beads, a small *gau* or talisman-box and some medicinal herbs – the doctor found a letter written in excellent and idiomatic English, asking 'whomsoever it may concern' to provide the bearer, Tsewong Gyaltsen, with every facility, since he travelled as the personal emissary of a Tibetan religious dignitary identified only as the 'Dorje Lama'.

48

A second paper had been folded into the same packet as the letter: it contained only five lines of writing, but was in Tibetan and could not be deciphered by the doctor. He had thought it best not to give either the letter or the paper to the Tibetan Agent along with the monk's other possessions. Instead, he showed them to Frazer, who had the paper translated by his munshi. It turned out to be very simple: instructions on how to find the Mongol Trade Agent Mishig.

One thing nagged at Christopher's thoughts while he made his way to the orphanage in accordance with Lhaten's directions: if the monk Tsewong had been dying when he got to Kalimpong, and if he had in fact died the morning after his arrival at the Knox Homes, how on earth had he managed to convey Zamyatin's message to Mishig? Had someone else taken the message on his behalf? If so, who?

The orphanage, like the church beside which it was built, looked as if it had been transported bodily, like the palace in 'Aladdin', from the Scottish lowlands to the place where it now stood. Here in Kalimpong, not only did the Christian god reveal himself in open defiance of the myriad tutelary deities dwelling in the mountains above, but Scottish Presbyterianism ranged itself against the questionable mores of the unredeemed masses of India below.

Although the rest of Kalimpong luxuriated in a cold winter sunlight that seemed to have been bounced off the gleaming white slopes to the north, the Knox Homes and the pathway that led up to them were sunk in gloom, as though the very stones of the building rejected all but the greyest and most melancholy of lights. The path was lined with thick, dark green cypresses that seemed to have stepped straight out of a painting by Böcklin. Everything was steeped in shadow – not merely touched or etched by it, but steeped in it, tormented by it. The Reverend Carpenter had brought more to Kalimpong than Presbyterianism and God.

The pathway led directly to a short flight of steps that in its turn led to a heavy wooden door. There was nowhere else to go. Feeling Catholic and English and travel-stained, Christopher lifted the heavy brass knocker and announced himself loudly to the hosts of Christendom within.

49

The door was opened by an Indian girl of about fifteen, dressed in what he took to be the uniform of the Knox Homes: a dark grey dress fastened at the waist by a black leather belt. There was nothing welcoming about her face or her manner. The slight trace of a Scottish accent alerted Christopher to the possibility that she might now carry in her soul more than just a trace of Calvinist iron.

'Would you please tell the Reverend Carpenter that Mr Wylam, about whom Mr Frazer spoke to him recently, has arrived in Kalimpong and would like to see him at his earliest convenience.'

The girl looked him up and down, clearly disapproving of what she saw. In the Homes, the girls were taught of cleanliness, godliness, and chastity, and the half-shaven man on the doorstep looked very much as though he were deficient in all three. But he spoke like an English gentleman and carried himself like one.

'Yes, *sahib*. May I have your card, *sahib*?'

'I'm sorry,' he said, 'but I've just come out from England. I haven't had time to have my cards printed yet. Would you please just give the Reverend Carpenter my name and message?'

'The Reverend Carpenter is very busy today, *sahib*. Perhaps it is better you come back tomorrow. With your card.'

'I've just told you. I don't have a card, young lady. Now, please do as I ask and give my message . . .'

At that moment, the young lady was precipitately displaced in the doorway by a thin, Presbyterian-looking woman in her late thirties or early forties.

'I am Moira Carpenter,' she said in a polite Edinburgh accent that would have crushed glass. 'Do I know you?'

'I regret not, madam,' Christopher said. 'My name is Wylam, Christopher Wylam. I understand that Mr Frazer, the Trade Agent, spoke with your husband concerning me last week. Or so I was given to understand before I left Calcutta.'

'Ah, yes. Mr Wylam. How good of you to call. I was expecting . . . ah, someone different.'

When Moira Carpenter said 'different', she meant exactly that. She fitted her surroundings as though, by an act of simultaneous decree in the mind of John Knox's dour and unsociable God, they had been brought into existence in one and the same cosmic instant: dark things set down in the Indian sunlight, as though to hamper it. Like someone in perpetual mourning, she wore black – a long dress without the vice of trimmings or ornament, more a cage for the body than a fabric for the soul.

A mother – if that is not an unsuitable use of the word – to dozens of destitute Indians, she had herself given up trying to have children at the age of twenty-eight. Her womb, she had been candidly informed by doctors at the Edinburgh Royal Infirmary, was just not up to it, and the four deformed foetuses she had theretofore delivered into immediate oblivion had borne the doctors out. At the heart of her, something was broken, something that neither doctors nor prayers could fix.

As a Christian woman whose duty in life lay in the replenishment of that pool out of which the good Lord would one day choose His elect, she spoke bitterly of her loss. She sought reason for her failure in a sense of her own sinful unworthiness. But privately, she rejoiced in her barrenness, for she had never had much liking for children and none at all for the turgid conjugal act that necessarily preceded their procreation. She had never understood why the Lord had not thought of a quicker, less embarrassing, and more sanitary method.

Now, she devoted herself, *inter alia*, to the welfare of the orphans of Kalimpong, whom she had helped make world famous through the pages of a thousand parish magazines, and to the furthering of the Mission's plans to bring the Christian witness to the benighted heathens of northern Sikkim and Tibet. She was forty-four, flat-chested, nervous of temperament, and given to kidney troubles. She was going to die two years later in an accident involving two Tibetan ponies, an over-laden mule, and a two-hundred-foot drop near Kampa-Dzong. In the meantime, however, she was on one side of the doorway and Christopher on the other.

'I'm sorry if I don't match your expectations, Mrs Carpenter,' said Christopher as politely as he could. 'If it's inconvenient, I'll call again. But I am in Kalimpong on urgent business, and I would like to start my investigations as soon as possible.'

'Investigations? What have you come to investigate, Mr Wylam? I assure you, there is nothing here to investigate.'

'I think I will be the judge of that, Mrs Carpenter. If you would kindly let your husband know that I am here.'

51

The formidable presence turned and barked into the gloomy interior of the entrance hall.

'Girl! Tell the Reverend Carpenter that a person is here demanding to see him. An English person. He says his name is Wylam.'

The girl departed, but Mrs Carpenter remained, as though afraid Christopher might have designs on her brass knocker. She had brought the knocker all the way from a shop in Princes Street herself, and had no wish to see it fall into the hands of a man without a visiting card.

In less than a minute, the girl returned and, still invisible, muttered something to her mistress. The presence shifted and gestured wordlessly to Christopher to enter. As he stepped through the door, childhood tales of Protestant irregularities chattered in the back of his mind. The girl led him along a narrow, carpeted passage dimly lit by weak electric bulbs to a dark-panelled door. He knocked and a thin voice bade him enter.

8

John Carpenter's study, like his wife, his faith, and his own person, had been carried wholesale from Scotland and set down, *virgo intacta*, in the heart of heathendom. Nothing Indian, nothing dark skinned, nothing indelicately foreign had been permitted to obtrude itself into this small, unincensed sanctuary of Christian virility. On the walls, the heads and antlers of Highland stags braved the moths and biting insects of the north-east frontier, while men in kilts and bristling beards glared their defiance of the heathen and his gods.

Had Jesus Christ himself walked in – dark skinned, Jewish, and mundane – the good Reverend Carpenter would have made haste to convert him there and then and to have him baptized Angus or Duncan. The Aramaic-speaking Jewish teacher from Nazareth was nothing or worse to John and Moira Carpenter. Their Jesus was a pale Galilean, blond, blue eyed and beardless, walking miraculously above the wild flowers and heather of a Scottish hillside.

John Carpenter was standing, hands clasped behind his back, peering at Christopher through a pair of gold-rimmed half-moon spectacles. He was a man in his early fifties, spare, slightly bent, balding, with teeth that would have made a dentist turn to drink and wild women. He looked, on the whole, as though he had seen better days. Christopher thought he seemed nervous.

'Mr Wylam?' he said, in an accent to match his wife's. 'Do take a seat. We've not had the pleasure of meeting before. Is this your first visit to Kalimpong?'

That was a subject Christopher preferred to stay clear of.

'I've been here before,' he said. 'Once or twice. Just short visits. No time to socialize.'

Carpenter glanced at him sharply, as though to suggest that socializing was hardly an activity men like Christopher engaged in.

'Or go to church?' The little eyes twinkled behind thick lenses.

53

'Ah, no. I'm afraid . . . that is, I'm not a Presbyterian, Dr Carpenter.'

'Oh, too bad, too bad. Church of England, naturally.'

This was getting off to a bad start.

'Well, no, not exactly. More Roman Catholic really.'

Christopher was sure the men in kilts stiffened and drew in ghostly breaths.

'I'm sorry, Mr Wylam,' Carpenter persisted, 'but I don't quite understand. Surely you cannot be "more" or "less" Roman. The Church of Rome is not a church of compromise. *Extra ecclesiam nulla salus*, is that not so?'

'Yes, I expect it is.'

'You were brought up in your faith, I expect?'

'Yes. Ah, Dr Carpenter, I . . .'

'Of course. That is usually the way. There are few converts to the cult of saints. The Anglicans sometimes turn in that direction, to be sure. But they are half-way there already, more's the pity.'

'I'm sure. Now, if you don't mind, I . . .'

'Do you know,' Carpenter continued, utterly disregarding Christopher, 'I have often thought that your faith – meaning no disrespect – has much in common with the faiths one encounters in this dark wilderness. I think of the Hindus with their extravagant gods, their priests, and their offerings. Or the Buddhists of Tibet, with their hierarchies of saints and their candles always burning on altars of gold and silver. Of course, I have never set foot in their savage temples, but I . . .'

'Dr Carpenter,' Christopher interrupted. 'I'm sorry, but I haven't come here to discuss theology. Another time, perhaps. For the moment, I have other matters that require my attention.'

Rebuffed, the long-suffering martyr of Kalimpong smiled a gap-toothed smile and nodded.

'Yes, of course. Mr Frazer did mention to me that you were coming and that you might want to ask me some questions. He did not tell me what these might concern, but said they were of a confidential nature. I'm sure I will do my best to answer them, though I cannot imagine how your affairs could possibly concern me, Mr Wylam. I know nothing of trade or commerce. My one and only aim here is the purchase of souls from damnation, though the penny I pay is not a copper one. Nor silver nor gold, for that matter. I deal in . . .'

'I'm sorry if Mr Frazer was mysterious with you. I am here in Kalimpong on an important matter, but one that need not concern you. Nevertheless, you may be able to assist me. I require some information, information you may have. I understand you were responsible for looking after a Tibetan monk who died here some weeks ago. A man called Tsewong. Anything you know of him would be of use to me.'

The missionary gave Christopher a curious look, as though that had not been the question he had expected. It seemed to have thrown him slightly off balance. The smile left his face and was replaced by a keen, probing expression. He rubbed the tip of one finger along the edge of his nose, lifting his spectacles a fraction. He was clearly weighing his answer. When it came at last, it was cautious.

'I cannot see of what concern the monk could be to you or to Mr Frazer. He was not a trader. Just an unfortunate devil-worshipper with scarcely a penny to his name. May I ask the reason for your interest?'

Christopher shook his head.

'It's a private matter. I assure you it has nothing whatever to do with trade. I merely wished to know whether he said anything of importance while in your care, whether you recall anything that seemed significant at the time.'

The missionary looked sharply at Christopher.

'What would you deem significant? How am I to judge? I have already given an account to Mr Frazer and to Norbhu Dzasa, the Tibetan Agent here.'

'But perhaps there was something that seemed trivial to you and was not put in your report, and yet would be of interest to me. I'm trying to find out how he came to Kalimpong, where he came from, whom he had come to see. You may have some clue that would help me.'

Carpenter reached up, removed his spectacles, and folded them up carefully, one leg at a time, like a praying mantis folding an even tinier victim in delicately articulated forelegs. For a moment, the mild-mannered missionary had gone, to be replaced by another man entirely. But the substitution lasted only a second before

55

Carpenter regained control of himself and straightened the mask he had allowed to slip. As carefully as before, with the same insect-like deliberation, he unfolded his spectacles and replaced them exactly as they had been.

'The man was dying when he was brought to us,' he said. 'He died the next day. All that is in the report. Would that I could say he had gone straight to the arms of a merciful Saviour, but I cannot. He spoke deliriously of things I did not understand. I speak a little Tibetan, but only what suffices for conversations with the *dzong-pöngs* and the *shapés* when they come to visit me.'

Christopher interrupted.

'Did anyone like that visit you while the monk was here? The Tibetan Agent, perhaps. I forget what you said his name was.'

'Norbhu Dzasa. No, Mr Wylam, there were no visitors, unless you count Doctor Cormac. This man Tsewong died among strangers, I regret to say.'

'You say he spoke deliriously, that he muttered things you did not understand. Did he say anything at all about a message? Did he mention the name Zamyatin? Or my name, Wylam?'

Christopher was sure the little Scot reacted to the questions. He seemed to grow pale and then flush. Just for a second, the mask slipped again, then Carpenter was back in control.

'Absolutely not. I should have noticed something of that kind, I am sure. No, it was all gibberish about the gods and demons he had left behind him in the mountains. You know the sort of thing I mean.'

Christopher nodded. He did not believe a word of it.

'I see,' he said. 'Are any of your staff Tibetan? Or perhaps some of your orphans?'

Carpenter stood up and pushed his desk back.

'Mr Wylam,' he expostulated, 'I really would like to know just where you are driving with these questions. You are verging on the impertinent. I am willing to answer anything within reason, but questions about my staff or the children in my care pass the bounds of what I regard as proper or allowable. You are not, I take it, a policeman. Nor a government official, presumably. In which case, I would like to know what right you think you have to come here prying into my affairs and the affairs of this institution. In fact, I think it would be best all round if you were to leave at once.'

56

Christopher remained seated. He had succeeded in rattling the man.

'I'm sorry,' he said, 'I didn't mean to seem impertinent. I think it will be best if I explain. My son William was kidnapped two weeks ago. As yet, the motive for the kidnapping is not known. But I have reason to believe he was abducted on instructions contained in a message carried out of Tibet by this man Tsewong. I'm not at liberty to tell you why I think that to be the case. But I assure you my reasons are very serious.'

Carpenter sat down again slowly, as though something very sharp had punctured him. He looked more rattled than ever.

'Where exactly was your son when he was . . . ah, abducted?'

'At home, in England.'

'And you say this happened two weeks ago.'

'On the Sunday before Christmas. We had just left Mass.'

A look of sectarian distaste flickered over the missionary's face.

'You expect me to believe this?' he said. Christopher noticed that he had started playing nervously with a small ivory paper-knife on the desk. 'It is not humanly possible for anyone to have been in England two weeks ago and to be in this room talking to me today. You know that as well as I do, unless you are completely insane. Goodbye, Mr Wylam. You have wasted enough of my time.'

'Sit down. Please sit down and listen. I was in England until nine days ago, if you want me to be precise. There's no mystery about how I got here. Certain friends in England arranged for me to be flown here in a biplane. The world is changing, Mr Carpenter. Before long, everyone will fly to India.'

'And your son. The one you say was kidnapped. Where is he? Is he in India as well?'

Christopher shook his head.

'I don't know,' he answered. 'But, yes, I think he may be in India. Or, more possibly, already on his way to Tibet.'

'Mr Wylam, you may be telling the truth about how you got here. Modern science is truly miraculous: the good Lord has given us the means to spread His Gospel in the remotest regions of the globe. But the rest of your story makes no sense to me. I am truly sorry to hear about the kidnapping of your son. My wife and I shall pray for his return to you. But I do not see how I can be of any further help to you. The man who died here brought no messages. He said nothing coherent. He had no visitors. And now, forgive me, but there are urgent matters awaiting my attention.'

Carpenter stood up again and reached a hand across the desk. Christopher followed suit. The missionary's fingers felt dry and brittle.

'I'll ask Jennie to show you out.' He reached for a small brass bell and rang it vigorously. An uneasy silence followed. Christopher could see that Carpenter was eager to be rid of him. What was he hiding? And who was he frightened of? Abruptly, the missionary broke into his thoughts.

'Mr Wylam,' he said. 'You must excuse me. I have been very short with you. I am under a great deal of pressure at the moment. The Lord's work makes demands on us. And no doubt you yourself are feeling great anxiety on behalf of your son. You must be very concerned for him.

'Would it help to make amends if I were to invite you to dine with us this evening? Just my wife and myself. A simple meal, I fear: this is a house of charity, not the palace of Dives. But we have ample for a guest. And perhaps a little sympathetic company will help to ease your troubled heart.'

Ordinarily, Christopher would have declined. The thought of sitting through a meal of charitable frugality with the black-gowned Mrs Carpenter and her desiccated spouse did not fill him with eager thoughts. But the very fact of the invitation – both unnecessary and, thought Christopher, out of character – added to his conviction that Carpenter was uneasy about something.

'I'd be pleased to accept. Thank you.'

'Good. I'm glad. We dine at seven. There are no formalities. Come a little earlier and I will show you something of our work before you eat.'

There was a knock, then the Indian girl who had opened the front door to Christopher entered.

'Jennie,' Carpenter said. 'Mr Wylam is leaving now. He will be dining with us this evening. When you have shown him to the door, will you please ask Mrs Carpenter to join me in my study?'

The girl curtsied but said nothing. Christopher shook hands with Carpenter again, then followed the girl out of the study.

58

John Carpenter remained standing at his desk, his hands resting on its top as though for support. He heard the front door open and close and the sound of Jennie's footsteps going towards his wife's sitting room. The wing of the orphanage in which he and Mrs Carpenter lived was soft and silent, filled with carpets and velvet hangings, dark, papered walls and heavy chintz furniture. Sounds were muffled, light was turned to shadow, the air was thick and unnatural.

Behind him, on a low shelf, a clock ticked and ticked, forlorn and remorseless. He closed his eyes, as though to pray, but his lips remained tightly shut.

9

Kalimpong fell away from him like a dream. All the spired and domed and pillared cities of India fell away, leaving nothing but a thin ochre dust hanging in the air. He was alone, walking along a dirt road that led to the residence of the *tsong-chi*, the Tibetan Trade Agent. Above him, to the north, white mountains hung in the sky like castles of snow and ice. In the air above them, thick clouds like dragons' breaths swirled in a tattered swarm.

As he looked at the mountains he felt descend upon him a sense of unease he had first experienced eleven years earlier, not long after his marriage. He had brought Elizabeth north to Simla for the summer season, and at one point they had gone up to the Himalaya foothills. On the second day, an icy wind had come down from the north, stirring the trees in their garden. They had stood on the terrace together, drinking cold whiskey in heavy glasses and watching the clouds shift and scatter above the mountains.

'Can you feel it?' Elizabeth had asked, and Christopher had known instinctively what she meant. All the crude power, all the vast material strength of their civilization was massing about the quiet places of the earth. Christopher could feel it now as he had felt it all those years before, but redoubled in its potency. Like an octopus, its tentacles were reaching into every corner of the world, stroking at first, then squeezing, and finally draining the very life from all it touched. Ancient places, sanctuaries, the dark and the untouched realms – all were being turned into an endless battlefield where tanks roamed like black beetles and new men in new uniforms danced in a dim ballet.

He found the *tsong-chi*'s residence in a small valley about a mile from town. It was a small house built in Tibetan style, with touches of Chinese ornamentation on the roof. At the door, a tall prayer-wheel stood like a sort of guardian, reminding the visitor that religion, not trade, lay at the heart of every Tibetan.

The *tsong-chi*, Norbhu Dzasa, was at home. Christopher had originally planned on getting an introduction from Frazer, but in its absence he had produced one for himself. It wasn't much to look at, but he didn't want it to be. Here in Kalimpong, he had to act the part he had imposed on himself.

He handed the letter of introduction to the *tsong-chi*'s grave little Nepalese servant and asked him to transmit it to his master. The little man looked at Christopher as if to suggest that his very existence was an impertinence and his calling without an appointment not far from a capital offence. He took the letter, harrumphed loudly, and disappeared down a dark passage.

Christopher thought he could hear a voice murmuring in the distance: somewhere in the house, a man was praying. The sound of his voice was melancholy and remote, a single *mantra* endlessly repeated. Suddenly, he heard footsteps and a moment later the little servant reappeared out of the shadows. Without a word, he ushered Christopher inside and closed the heavy wooden door.

The room into which Christopher was shown was, in its way, as much a transplant as John Carpenter's study, even if it had travelled rather fewer miles to get to Kalimpong. It was another world entirely, a world within a world, wrapped, enfolded, miraculously set down: its colours were different colours, its shadows different shadows, its fragrances different fragrances. He stood on the threshold gingerly, for all the world like someone about to abandon one element for another, as a swimmer stands naked on the water's edge or a moth turns about the flame that will in another instant devour it without trace.

He had stumbled somehow upon a hidden and finely constructed paradise of birds' wings and dragons' eyes, meshed in a manner at once mysterious and simple with the earth in which it inhered. Like a bee drowning in honey after a season rich in blossoms, he felt himself grow heavy with sweetness.

Painted columns rose out of a bed of multi-coloured carpets to a ceiling intricate in ornamentation. Around the walls, thick curtains embroidered with red and yellow silk formed a sort of sofa. Low lacquered tables of Chinese manufacture sat among richly carved and gilded cabinets festooned with angry dragons and soft-petalled peonies. On the walls, naked gods made love, encircled by tongues of fire. At one end stood an altar of gold, studded with precious

61

stones, on which were grouped the images of Tibetan gods and saints. Incense burned in little golden stands, filling the room with dark, intoxicating fumes. In front of the altar, silver butter-lamps gave off a yellow, ethereal light.

And then, as though he had just that moment materialized in the room, Christopher caught sight of Norbhu Dzasa himself – a man masquerading as a god, a human image fashioned from silk and coral and precious stones. His dyed jet-black hair was set in tightly coiled bunches above his head, and from his left ear dangled a single long ear-ring of turquoise and gold. His upper robe was of finely woven yellow silk, delicately patterned with dragons and held at the waist by a crimson sash. He was standing motionless in a corner of the room near the altar, his hands crossed in front of him, concealed by the long sleeves of his robe.

On his way, Christopher had found a stall in the bazaar that sold *khatags*, the thin white silk scarves used throughout the region as tokens of respect at formal introductions. He held out the scarf, loosely woven from strands of the finest silk, like gossamer, and approached the *tsong-chi*. Norbhu Dzasa extended his arms and took the scarf with a slight bow, placed it on a low table, and, with his hands free of the sleeves, lifted a second scarf, which he passed to Christopher. He looked bored. The two men exchanged stiff greetings, and the little Tibetan invited Christopher to join him on cushions near the window.

A moment later, the servant who had shown Christopher in opened the door and bowed low.

'*Cha kay-sho*,' ordered Norbhu Dzasa. 'Bring us tea.'

The servant bowed, sucked in his breath, and simultaneously muttered '*la-les*'.

Abruptly, Norbhu Dzasa turned to Christopher, speaking in English.

'I'm sorry. Not ask. Take Indian tea or Tibetan tea?'

Christopher asked for Tibetan, and the *tsong-chi* spoke again to his servant.

'*Pö cha kay-sho* – ' 'bring some Tibetan tea.'

'So,' Norbhu Dzasa said when the servant had gone. 'Drink Tibetan tea. Been in Tibet?' He had learnt what English he knew here in Kalimpong, out of necessity.

Christopher was unsure how to answer. So many of his visits

there had been made illegally. With rare exceptions, Tibet was barred to foreigners – and Christopher knew from personal experience that the ban was no mere formality.

'I was in Lhasa in 1904,' he said. 'With Younghusband.'

In 1903, Lord Curzon, the Viceroy of India, had been disturbed by reports of growing Russian influence in the Tibetan capital. Determined to force the reclusive Tibetans to discuss the issue of commercial and diplomatic relations with Britain, he despatched a small force to Kampa Dzong under the command of Colonel Francis Younghusband. Ignored by the Tibetans, Younghusband obtained reinforcements – 1,000 soldiers, 1,450 coolies, 70,000 mules, 3,451 yaks, and six unhappy camels – and moved up the Chumbi valley in force.

Christopher still remembered the journey: the freezing cold, the misery of the foot-soldiers unaccustomed to the winds and the altitude, skin sticking to gun-metal in the frost, men tearing skin from their lips with frozen spoons, the sudden deaths, men and baggage plunging from narrow ledges into the abyss. Above all, he remembered the insanity of Christmas Day, when the men had been served plum pudding and turkey, and the officers had tried to drink frozen champagne.

But the real madness had begun outside Gyantse. Tibetan troops carrying muzzle-loading guns and broadswords, and wearing charms to turn aside British bullets, had advanced against men armed with modern rifles and machine guns. Christopher would never forget the massacre that followed. In four minutes, seven hundred Tibetans lay dead on the battlefield, dozens more were screaming in pain. The expedition took Gyantse and moved on unopposed to Lhasa, where it arrived in August 1904. The Dalai Lama had fled in the meantime to Urga in Mongolia to take refuge with the Living Buddha there, and the Regent was forced in his absence to sign a peace treaty with Britain on very unfavourable terms.

'Don't remember you,' Norbhu Dzasa said.

'I was much younger then,' answered Christopher, 'and of no importance. We would not have been introduced.'

Norbhu Dzasa sighed.

'Younger then, too,' he said. Their eyes met for a moment, but

63

the *tsong-chi* gave nothing away. That, as he interpreted it, was his job: to give nothing away. He was very good at it.

Tea arrived quickly. It was served in ornamental cups of jade decorated with silver. Norbhu's man had brewed it in the kitchen from semi-fermented tea bricks imported from Yunnan, mixing it in a wooden churn with boiling water, salt, wood-ash soda, and *dri*-butter. It was more a soup than tea, but Tibetans drank it in vast quantities – forty or fifty cups a day was not at all unusual. Christopher could tell at once from the way he quaffed his first cupful that Norbhu Dzasa was a record-breaker even in Tibetan terms.

Norbhu had been *tsong-chi* at Kalimpong for seven years now and was doing very nicely out of it. He could afford to drink tea in urnfuls if he wanted to. His greatest fear was to be recalled to Lhasa prematurely, that is, before he had stashed away enough rupees to ensure a comfortable future for himself and, above all, his children. He was over sixty now, though he could not be sure exactly how old he was. His mother thought he had been born in the year of the Fire Serpent in the Fourteenth Cycle, which would have made him sixty-three. But his father had been equally sure he had been born in the Wood Hare year, which would make him all of sixty-five.

'What I do for you, Wylam-la?' asked the little *tsong-chi* as he poured himself a second cup of the thick, pinkish beverage.

Christopher hesitated. He felt he had got off to a bad start with Norbhu Dzasa by referring to the Younghusband expedition. In the end, the British had gained the respect of the Tibetans – they had looted no temples, raped no women, and withdrawn their forces at the earliest possible opportunity – but the memory of the more than seven hundred dead and the profound sense of vulnerability that the expedition had created in their minds lingered even now.

The problem about the present business was that Christopher could not mention the real reason for his visit. There was ample evidence that the Mongol Agent, Mishig, had been contacted by Tsewong. But it was always possible that the Tibetan *tsong-chi* might also be involved. For all they knew, he might have been the person responsible for transmitting Zamyatin's message to the Mongol. The *tsong-chi*'s residence lay between the mountains and

64

the spot where Tsewong was supposed to have been found. The monk could very easily have paid a visit to Norbhu Dzasa before continuing his ill-fated journey.

'It's very little, really,' Christopher said. 'Perhaps you will find it sentimental of me. You'll have seen from my letter that I am a businessman. I'm here in Kalimpong to do business with Mr Frazer. I knew him years ago, back in Patna. He knows about an incident that happened back then – something that happened to my son, William. We were in Bodh Gaya, William and I, just passing through, on our way to Aurangabad. We lived in Patna then, when . . . my wife was still alive.' The combination of fact and fiction would, Christopher hoped, serve to convey a feeling of conviction to the *tsong-chi*.

'William fell ill,' he went on. 'There was no British doctor in Bodh Gaya, none anywhere near. I was desperate. The child was very sick, I thought he would die. And then one of the pilgrims visiting the sacred tree . . . It is a tree they have there, isn't it, Mr Dzasa?'

Norbhu nodded. It was a tree; he had seen it. Lord Buddha had gained enlightenment while sitting under it.

'Right,' said Christopher, warming to his tale. 'Well, one of the pilgrims heard William was ill, you see. He came to visit us and told me there was a Tibetan monk who was a sort of doctor. Anyway, I found this monk, and he came at once and looked at William and said he could treat him. He went off – it was late at night by then. I can remember it, sitting in the dark with William in a terrible fever.'

There had been a fever once, and William had almost died . . . but there had been no monk, no sacred tree, only an old doctor sent round by the DBI.

'I thought he would die, I really did, he was that bad. Anyway, he went off as I said – the monk, I mean – and then came back in about an hour with some herbs he'd got from God knows where. He made them up into a drink for the boy and got it into him somehow or other. It saved his life. He came out of the fever that night and was on his feet again two days later. I tried to find the monk afterwards, to thank him, give him something. But he'd gone.'

'Frazer knew about it. When he came here, he asked questions, but he never heard of any monk. Until a couple of weeks ago.'

Norbhu Dzasa glanced up from his steaming cup. His little eyes glistened.

'He said a Tibetan monk died here. A man with the same name as my monk. About the same age. Frazer said he carried herbs. He thought I should know: he wrote to me about it. I was coming anyway, I have business here. So I thought I'd make some enquiries at the same time. About the monk.'

'Why? You could not meet. Not thank. He is dead.'

'Yes, but he might have a family, relatives. His parents, brothers, sisters. Perhaps they need help, now he is dead.'

'What his name, this medical monk?'

'Tsewong,' Christopher answered. 'Is that a common name?'

Norbhu shrugged.

'Not common. Not not common.'

'But it was the name of the man they found here? The man who died?'

The *tsong-chi* looked at Christopher.

'Yes,' he said. 'Same name. But perhaps not same man.'

'How was he dressed?' asked Christopher. 'Perhaps it would help to identify him.'

Norbhu Dzasa saw that Wylam wanted him to lead with information rather than confirm something he already knew. It reminded him of the theological debates he had seen the monks at Ganden engage in – verbal fencing matches in which the slightest slip meant failure. What would failure mean in this case, he wondered.

'He wear dress of monk of Sak-ya-pa sect. Was monk you met Sak-ya-pa?'

'I don't know,' said Christopher. 'What would one of them look like?' But in his own mind he had already begun the process of narrowing things down. The majority of Tibetan monks belonged to the politically dominant Ge-lug-pa sect. There were far fewer Sak-ya-pas – and fewer Sak-ya-pa monasteries.

Norbhu Dzasa described for Christopher the dress of a Sak-ya-pa lama: the low, conical hat with ear-flaps, the red robes, the broad-sleeved over-mantle for travelling, the distinctive girdle.

'Yes,' said Christopher, 'he was dressed very like that.' But he wanted to move on, to narrow the field even more.

'Did you find anything,' he continued, 'that might have told you where he came from? The name of his monastery, perhaps?'

Norbhu could see what the Englishman was trying to do. Why was he playing such games with him? Did he take him for a fool?

'Where your friend come from?' he asked.

Christopher hesitated.

'He didn't say. Do you know where the dead man came from?'

The *tsong-chi* smiled.

'Not every mountain has a god,' he said. 'Not every monastery has a name.' If the Englishman expected him to play the part of the wily and enigmatic Oriental in this masquerade, he would at least put on a virtuoso performance.

Christopher recognized the shift in mood. He would have to change tack.

'Did you see this man Tsewong before he died? This house is on the road he must have taken to reach Kalimpong. Perhaps he called here. Perhaps you saw him. You or one of your staff?'

Norbhu Dzasa shook his head.

'Not see. No-one see.' There was a pause. The *tsong-chi* looked at Christopher intently. 'What you really look for, Wylam-la? What thing you look for? What person?'

Christopher hesitated again before answering. Did the little Tibetan know? Was he teasing him with this questioning?

'My son,' he said. 'I'm looking for my son.'

The *tsong-chi* sipped tea from his cup and set it down elegantly.

'Not find him here. Understanding, perhaps. Wisdom, perhaps. Or things you not wish to find. But no son. Please, Wylam-la, I advise you. Go home. Back to own country. The mountains here very treacherous. Very high. Very cold.'

The two men eyed each other closely, like fencers with raised foils. In the silence, the *mantra* sounded clearer than before.

'Tell me,' Norbhu Dzasa said abruptly. 'Is Wylam a common name?'

Christopher shook his head. *Not common. Not not common*, he wanted to say. But he didn't.

'No. There aren't many Wylams. Lots of Christophers – but not many Wylams.'

Norbhu Dzasa smiled again. There was something about his smile that unsettled Christopher. A lamp on the altar spluttered briefly and went out.

'I knew man called Wylam,' the *tsong-chi* said. 'Many years ago. In India. Look very much like you. Father perhaps?'

Had Norbhu Dzasa suspected all along? Christopher wondered.

'Perhaps,' he said. 'My father was a political agent. He died many years ago.'

Norbhu Dzasa looked hard at Christopher.

'Your tea getting cold,' he said.

Christopher lifted his cup and drank quickly. The thick, luke-warm liquid clung to his palate and his throat.

'I've taken enough of your time, Mr Dzasa,' he said. 'I'm sorry to have wasted it on a wild-goose chase.'

'No matter,' answered the little man. 'There are other geese.' He rose and clapped his hands twice. The sound of the hand-claps rang out dully in the shimmering room.

The door opened and the servant came to show Christopher out.

'Goodbye, Wylam-la,' Norbhu Dzasa said. 'I am sorry not more help.'

'I'm sorry too,' said Christopher. The heavy tea was making him feel slightly nauseous. He wanted to get out of the stuffy room.

Norbhu Dzasa bowed and Christopher left, escorted by the servant. The *tsong-chi* sighed audibly. He missed his wife and children. They had gone to Lhasa for the New Year celebrations at the end of January and the three-week Monlam Festival that would follow. It might be months before they returned. His new wife was young and pretty, and he felt almost youthful when he was with her. But here, without her, he felt age lie upon him like a covering of hard snow that will not lift. On the walls around him, gods and demons danced and copulated in solemn gradations of ecstasy and pain. So little ecstasy, he thought; and so much pain.

Curtains parted in the wall to his left. A man dressed in the robes of a monk stepped into the room. His thin, sallow face was covered with the scars of smallpox.

'Well?' asked Norbhu Dzasa. 'Did you hear?'

The monk nodded.

'Wylam,' Norbhu Dzasa went on. 'Looking for his son.'

'Yes,' said the monk. 'I heard.' He ran a thin hand over his shaven scalp. Light from the lamps flickered on his mottled skin, making small shadows, like ants crawling.

'The gods are coming out to play,' he said. 'We must be ready when the game begins.'

10

As Christopher returned to the outskirts of Kalimpong, the sun sank steeply in the west. The light was snatched away with fierce rapidity. Night invaded the world, precipitately and without resistance, save for a few pockets of illumination in the bazaar and one light burning faintly in St Andrew's church, just visible from where he stood.

He walked back through the bazaar, filled with flaring lights and the deep, intoxicating scents of herbs and spices. At one stall, an old man sold thick *dhal* in rough pots; at another, a woman in a tattered sari offered a selection of peppers, chillies, and wild pomegranate seeds. On small brass scales, in pinches and handfuls, the whole of India was being parcelled out and weighed. The old kaleidoscope had started to turn again for Christopher. But now, for the first time, he sensed behind its dazzling patterns an air of cold menace.

He found the Mission Hospital at the other side of town from the orphanage. The British cemetery lay symbolically between. Martin Cormac, the doctor who had tended the dying monk at the Knox Homes, was not available.

The nursing sister who saw Christopher was unhelpful. She said that Cormac had gone to make an urgent call at Peshok, a village between Kalimpong and Darjeeling. More than that, she said she knew nothing.

Christopher left a slip of paper bearing his name and the address of the rest-house where he had put up. The nurse took the paper between finger and thumb as if it bore embedded in its fibres all the diseases of the sub-continent and most of the plagues of Egypt. She deposited it in a small, neglected pigeon-hole half-way down the hospital's austere entrance hall and returned to the ward with a look that promised much wiping of fevered brows.

He returned to the rest-house, took a cat-nap, and fortified himself with another *chota peg* before shaving and donning some-

70

thing suitable for dinner with the Carpenters. The rest-house was quiet when he left. No-one saw him go.

He was met at the door of the Knox Homes by Carpenter himself, now dressed more formally than before, but not in evening attire. The missionary conducted him straight away to the orphanage proper, or rather, to what constituted the girls' division. There were more girls than boys in the Knox Homes: boys were economically viable offspring who might grow up to look after their aged parents: girls were burdens who would end up being married into someone else's family. Girl babies were dumped quickly on someone else's doorstep – if they were lucky.

The girls' orphanage was a scrubbed and spartan place, more a way-station than a home; its walls and floors and furniture were pervaded with the smells of carbolic, coal tar soap, and iodine, and its musty air seemed laden with the ghosts of other, less immediately recognizable smells – the thin vomit of children, boiled cabbage, and that faint but unmistakable smell that is common to all institutions where adolescent girls are gathered in one place. A sour, menstrual smell that lingers on all it touches.

In a dark-panelled hall hung with the portraits of patrons and pious mottoes edged in funereal black, Christopher was introduced to the children. Rows of silent, impassive faces stared up at him as he stood, embarrassed and awkward, on a low platform at the end of the hall. The girls were of all ages, but all wore the same drab uniform and the same dull look of incomprehension and sullen endurance on their faces. Most appeared to be Indian, but there were Nepalese, Tibetans, and Lepchas among them. Christopher noticed a few of mixed parentage, Anglo-Indians, and two girls who seemed to be of European origin. There were rather over one hundred in all.

To Christopher, the most dreadful thing about the place was the temperature: it was neither uncomfortably cold nor was it comfortably warm. Old pipes brought a certain warmth up from an ancient boiler hidden in the bowels of the place, but not so much that one could feel relaxed nor so little that one could wrap up sensibly against the chill. And the children themselves, he noticed, looked neither well fed nor thin. He guessed that they did not go hungry but probably never felt that they had eaten quite enough. It was a world of limbo, where these orphans, neither wholly

71

abandoned nor yet wholly loved, lived an in-between existence that would forever determine the tenor and the inner structure of their lives.

'Mr Wylam has come to us recently from the distant shores of England,' Carpenter began to intone in a pulpit voice. 'He came among us to seek tidings of his son, a child of tender years taken from him by dreadful circumstance. Which of us here has not prayed in the dark watches of the night for a loving father who might come searching after us, to carry us home? Which of us has not yearned for such a love as this man's, that he comes willingly and alone across the globe for the sake of his only child, to return him to the loving bosom of his family?

'How well this brings to mind the words of our Lord, in that sweet parable of the father and his sons: "For this my son was dead, and is alive again; he was lost, and is found." Perhaps in Mr Wylam's journey there may be a parable for us here. For there is a father searching for us, longing for us to return to him, contrite and full of repentance. And he will travel the lengths of the earth to reach us.'

Carpenter paused for breath. It sounded as though he was just getting into his stride. The girls looked resigned. They did not cough or fidget or shuffle their feet as English children would have done. Clearly, they had long ago decided that being preached to was as normal a part of life as eating or sleeping. Christopher had to struggle to stop himself yawning.

'Mr Wylam, our hearts go out to you in this, your hour of need, as yours, I doubt not, has in the past gone out to the widows and orphans of this godless and wasted land. These are the children of idolatry, Mr Wylam, the children of sin. Their mothers and fathers were but heathen cannibals, but through the grace of our Lord, they have been brought out of the darkness and into the light. I ask you, then, to join with us in prayer, that our spirits may be united in the presence of our all-merciful and loving Saviour. Let us pray.'

Like mechanical dolls, the uncomplaining rows closed their eyes and bowed their heads. Their necks and eyelids seemed fashioned to the task.

'Merciful Father, Who knowest our sins and our transgressions, miserable sinners that we are, look down this night, we beseech

72

Thee, upon Thy servant Christopher . . .'

And so the evening began.

The meal was a cabbagy affair with some sort of gristle-laden meat
that had long ago given up its struggle to maintain any sense either
of identity or taste. Moira Carpenter was less a hostess presiding
over her table than an undertaker directing the obsequies for
whatever poor beast lay sliced and gravied on their plates. She
kept up her end of a stilted conversation with miserable politeness.

'My husband told me of your grief, Mr Wylam,' she said, ladling
boiled cabbage on to his plate. 'I have spent most of today in
prayer, asking for your son to be restored to you. And his poor
mother at home: she must be stricken.'

'My wife is dead, Mrs Carpenter. She died a little over a year
ago.'

'I am so sorry. So very sorry.' She dropped a slab of something
off-white beside the cabbage. 'Was she carried away by illness?'

'Consumption, Mrs Carpenter. She died of consumption. She
was thirty-one.'

For the first time, Moira Carpenter's eyes seemed to light up.
Sickness enlivened her much as idolatry enlivened her spouse.

'It is a scourge, Mr Wylam, a dreadful scourge. We are blessed
to live here where the mountain air drives it away. But, of course,
we have our own afflictions to bear. You can have no conception
how these poor people are ravaged. They pay the price of a
depraved system. Syphilis, Mr Wylam, is endemic . . . please, do
eat your dinner . . . and gonorrhoea takes a terrible toll.'

It was not long before Christopher realized that his hostess was
the worst possible dinner companion anyone could have: a hypo-
chondriac who finds interest in nothing else but illness. As she
picked at her food, she regaled Christopher with tales of her own
illnesses, her husband's illnesses, the illnesses that daily afflicted
the unfortunate orphans of Kalimpong, the illnesses of the entire
sub-continent.

It was all Christopher could do to force down his sweet – a vile
yellow custard with indecipherable pieces embedded loosely in it –
while she expatiated on a recent case of cancer of the nose she had
visited in the hospital.

'This is all very well, my dear,' her husband interrupted at last.

73

'But we should not allow our guest to think that our care is chiefly for the physical ailments of these unfortunates. We leave that to those whose inclinations lie in that direction. But I assure you, Christopher – I may call you Christopher, may I not? – that, however terrible the ills that ravage the flesh of India, they are nothing to the spiritual sicknesses that torment its spirit. The Dark One is at work in this land, dragging this wretched people down to hell, generation after generation. We do what little we can, but it is an uphill struggle.'

And so he went on, detailing what were for him the principal horrors of India and its idolatrous faith. The Hindus were condemned for worshipping a multiplicity of gods, the Muslims for praying to the wrong one. Yogis were charlatans and Sufis fakes, for by definition no sort of spirituality could be found without the presence of God – and God to John Carpenter was white-skinned and Presbyterian. Christopher decided there was no point in arguing. He was little enough of a believer himself to go defending other men's faiths.

It was only towards the end of the evening that Christopher began to see that the man was playing an elaborate game with him. He was not a fool with antiquated and bizarre beliefs about religious practices on his doorstep, nor yet a simple-minded bigot rabbiting on about his personal obsessions, but a clever man playing a role.

Christopher remembered the moment earlier that day when Carpenter had removed his glasses and shown himself to him briefly. Now, as the missionary or his wife rambled on about disease or moral corruption, he caught from time to time a sneaking look on Carpenter's face – whether ironic, derisory, or merely mischievous he could not tell.

'Tell me, Christopher,' he said while they drank weak tea after the meal, 'how often have you been in Kalimpong before?'

'I came here frequently as a child. My father worked near here.'

'He was a businessman like you, was he?'

'Yes, he . . . was a tea trader.'

The missionary looked across his teacup at Christopher.

'And you? What do you trade in?'

'Most things. I've dealt in most things in my time.'

'But you seem to me like an educated man. More like the sort of man who might make a career in the Civil Service or the Political Service. Not a small trader, really. Please don't take any offence.'

'That's all right. I chose to go into business. But perhaps another career would have suited me better. Things haven't gone too well lately.'

'And you live in England now, is that correct?'

Carpenter was interrogating him, discreetly but carefully.

'Yes. My wife and son went there when war broke out. I returned last year to rejoin them, but Elizabeth died soon afterwards. I decided to stay on with William.'

'I see. What did you do during the war? You stayed in India, I take it.'

'I was a supplier to the army. Grain, fodder, rice: all the staples. I made a little money for once. But not enough.'

'And who hates you enough to steal your child? Whom do you suspect? Why did you come to India to look for him? To Kalimpong?'

Christopher sensed more than mere curiosity in Carpenter's questioning. The missionary was worried about something. He did not believe Christopher's cover-story. But there was more than that: he knew something and he wanted to know just what Christopher knew.

'I've been advised not to talk about that,' Christopher said.

'Who advised you? The police?'

'Yes. The police.'

'Did they fly you here? Forgive me for seeming inquisitive. But it puzzles me that a man like yourself should have enough influence to be flown to India. Just to look for a child, however precious he may be to you. The authorities are not normally so obliging.'

Christopher decided it was time to go.

'Dr Carpenter, I'm grateful to you and your wife for such a delightful evening. I've enjoyed your food and conversation immensely.' He turned to Carpenter's wife. 'Mrs Carpenter, please accept my thanks. You have been a most considerate hostess. But now, I fear, I must take my leave. I am still tired after my journey, and I fear I may become boring company if I stay any longer. And you must have your duties to go to.'

'Of course, of course. How thoughtless of us to keep you talking.' Moira Carpenter got to her feet. Her husband followed suit.

'If it would not tire you too much, Mr Wylam,' said the missionary, 'I would very much like to show you our boys' wing. The children are asleep now, but it would please me very much if you would step in to see them before you leave.'

The boys' section was not far away. A green baize door led to a short corridor, off which lay a long dormitory bathed in moonlight. In orderly rows, like patients in a hospital ward, the children slept in a silence that was broken only by the sound of their heavy breathing. Carpenter walked between the beds with a dark lantern, showing the sleeping boys to Christopher like a curator in a waxwork museum taking a visitor on a tour of his exhibits. On narrow beds, the boys huddled beneath thin blankets, dreaming desperately.

Christopher wondered why Carpenter had brought him here, why he had asked him to dinner at all. Had it been to reassure him, to counter that afternoon's impression of nervousness? As he watched the sleeping boys, he began to ask himself whether William had been here. Was that it? Was that what lay behind Carpenter's nervousness, behind his probing? But no sooner had the idea intruded itself than he dismissed it as ridiculous.

The Carpenters showed him to the door, still heaping sympathy on him like confetti. The rest of the orphanage was silent. Christopher imagined the girls in sleep, their dreams haunted by visions of dark gods and goddesses, black Kali dancing on the bodies of her bloody victims, Shiva with gory hands, destroying the universe. Or did they dream of cannibals in the mountains, eating the flesh of English children? And if so, what was that to them?

It was after ten when he got back to the rest-house. The common room was in semi-darkness, filled with small restless mounds: people were sleeping, planning an early start at one or two a.m. Word had come that the weather to the north was improving, and there was every likelihood the passes into the Chumbi valley would be open in a day or two.

He climbed the rickety wooden stairs to the first floor, carrying the reeking oil-lamp he had left downstairs for that purpose. The thin wooden panelling of the house kept out nothing of the freezing cold. It was stained with damp from the rains and cracked with frost. In a room along the corridor, someone was moaning in pain, but no-one came. Outside, dogs were prowling in the streets, old dogs, thin and diseased, afraid to show their faces in daylight. He could hear them howling, lonely and desperate in the night.

He did not see the man who hit him as he opened the door, nor did he feel the blow that dropped him, unconscious, to the grimy floor of his room. For a moment, he saw a bright light and faces moving in it, or a single face, blurred and shifting. Then the ground lurched and fell out from under him, and the world shimmered and reddened and was swallowed up, leaving him spinning and howling and alone in the darkness.

11

He was at sea in an open boat, tossing deliriously on blue salt waves. Then the boat vanished and the water opened up beneath him and he was sinking into the blackness again. Somehow the blackness passed and he was rising once more towards the light. There must be a storm on the surface: he was tossed again and again, a piece of flotsam on the back of giant waves. Then, as if by a miracle, the waves were stilled and he was drifting on gentle, inland waters, rocking in a soft, rhythmical motion.

There was a face, then a pair of hands pulling at him roughly, then he was no longer afloat on still waters but lying on a hard bed. The face was European and unshaven, and it kept slipping in and out of focus.

'Can you hear me, Mr Wylam? Can you hear my voice?'

The face was speaking to him in English, but with a heavy accent. His first thought was that this must be the Russian, Zamyatin; but something else told him that was ridiculous.

'Can you sit up?' the voice insisted. Christopher felt hands pushing against his armpits, raising him to a sitting position. Reluctantly, he allowed himself to be moved. Upright, his head began to spin again, and for a moment he feared the blackness would return. He felt nauseous: the mysterious meat and its lugubrious accompaniments had chosen their moment to break free: they had swollen out of all proportion in his stomach. Rapidly, they were acquiring a life of their own.

'Do you want to be sick?' the voice asked.

He managed to nod, sending flashes of green light in every direction through his reeling brain.

'There's a basin beside you. Here on your right. Just let it out. I'll hold you.'

He felt a hand guiding his head, then something exploded in his guts and travelled upwards with the violence of an express train on its home journey. Hot liquid rushed into a metal bowl.

Spitting sour vomit, he fell back exhausted against the back of the bed. Someone had taken his head off and replaced it with a spinning top. And a mad child stood over him, cracking a whip and sending the top round and round without stopping.

'Better?' the voice sounded stronger this time. He'd heard the accent before, but still could not place it. Scottish? Irish?

'If you want to be sick again, there's another wee basin here. And if you fill that, I can get another. Can you open your eyes?'

His mouth felt foul. Someone had gone for a walk in it, wearing large, muddy boots.

'Taste . . . horrible,' he managed to croak.

'Here, rinse your mouth with this. It's safe – I boiled it myself.'

The stranger held a cup to his lips. It contained water. He sipped some, rolled it in his mouth, and spat it out into the basin by his side. With an effort, he opened his eyes again.

He was in his room at the rest-house. He recognized the table and broken chair by the window. Someone had brought up a charcoal stove that was giving off a reddish-yellow glow in the middle of the room. A stinking oil-lamp was burning on the table. The man who had helped him was sitting on a second chair by the side of the bed.

'You're all right,' said the man, catching Christopher's eyes on him. 'A wee bit bruised, but you'll be none the worse for wear in a day or two. There's nothing broken. You'll have a headache for a while, and a very tender lump on your head for a few weeks, but I don't think you'll die.'

'Thanks,' said Christopher, wincing as he realized that his head did ache.

'You're probably wondering who I am,' the stranger suggested.

Christopher closed his eyes briefly, then opened them again.

'The thought had crossed my mind,' he said. His voice sounded like a cross between a camel and a hyena. It made peculiar echoes in his eardrums. His stomach had settled a little, but it gave occasional twinges as if to remind him it had not forgotten him; he guessed that some of the meat – if it had been meat – was still lying there, thinking what to do next.

'My name's Cormac, Martin Cormac. You left a wee note for me up in the Black Hole of Kalimpong. The hospital, or so they say.'

Christopher squinted to see the man properly. He didn't look like a doctor, he thought. At a guess, he would be in his mid-forties and ageing fast – grey-haired, grey-eyed, and grey-skinned. On his face was that look certain men of his age wear, of someone who has shut his eyes for a moment twenty years ago and opened them again to find himself in his present predicament. Somewhere along the way, he had lost a pound and found sixpence. At the moment, he looked dusty, as though he had been travelling. On reflection, Christopher realized he must just have arrived back from Peshok.

'You're probably wondering what the hell I'm doing here,' the doctor continued.

'That had crossed my mind as well,' answered Christopher.

'I'm sure. Well, to answer your first question – I'm not the one who hit you over the head. Not guilty. I don't know who that was, to tell you the truth. He ran off as soon as I came on the scene – I'd been waiting outside for you to come back from Cold Comfort Hall. I saw you go in here and I came behind, maybe a minute later. He was rifling your pockets, but I don't think he took anything. Your room had been given a good going over before you arrived. You can take a look later, see if anything's missing.'

Cormac paused and looked solicitously at Christopher.

'How's the head?'

Christopher stoically tried to smile, but the effort was more than his skull could bear. The smile turned into a grimace.

'Bad, eh? Well, I'll give you a wee something for it. I never come out without some of these.'

From his pocket, Cormac drew out a small brown bottle of pills. He knocked two out on to his palm, gave them to Christopher and handed him a glass of water. Christopher swallowed the pills one at a time: it felt like swallowing splinters of glass.

'A pity you've had those,' said Cormac as soon as they had been downed. 'From the way Sister Campbell talked about you, I guessed you might be in need of some refreshment after your visit to the wee darlings up the hill. So I brought along a bottle of the real stuff for us to drown our sorrows in. Assuming you had any, that was. Only, now your sorrows are such that I'll have to share the bottle with meself. Do you want me to leave, or shall I hang on?'

Christopher, who was beginning to feel nauseous again, shook his head.

'It's all right. I'd like you to stay. What's the "real stuff"?'

'Ah!' said Cormac, drawing a half-pint flask from his other pocket. 'Poteen. Irish whiskey, made from spuds. I've a friend in Newry sends me a wee bottle every now and again. I don't suppose there's another drop of this stuff anywhere between here and the Belfast ferry.'

Northern Irish – that was the accent. Probably Belfast, but Christopher couldn't be sure. He'd never heard of Newry. There were a lot of them in India: the ruled ruling the ruled. Perhaps that was what the Empire was all about, after a fashion.

'It's a funny thing,' Cormac continued, 'but, to tell you the truth, Kalimpong's not normally a place you'd expect to be set upon. There's plenty of thievery, of course, but they'll not knock a man out as a rule. In all my years here, I've never come across a case of it. A knockout in an argument, sure. But never in a robbery. When I saw him bending over you, I felt sure I'd come across a Thug about to make a sacrifice of you. Cheers! *Sláinte!*'

Cormac raised the flask and put its mouth to his lips. He swallowed hard, closed his eyes, and shivered.

'God, I needed that,' he gasped. 'Just what the doctor ordered. Mind you,' he went on, replacing the stopper, 'it's a bit rough. It'd burn your gob off, as my dear departed Da used to say. Can't be doing me any good.'

'There are no Thugs in India any longer,' muttered Christopher. 'There haven't been any for nearly a century. That's almost a hundred years.'

'Ay, I know well enough. But don't go telling that to your wee friend up on the hill. He's a firm believer in them. "The heathen in his blindness Bows down to wood and stone" – that's his favourite song, and he sings it morning, noon, and night. As, no doubt, you know by now.'

'How did you know I was at the orphanage tonight?'

'Ah,' replied Cormac, unscrewing his stopper again. 'There's not much that passes unobserved in Kalimpong. Sister Campbell made it her business to find out who you were and what you were up to. I think she was put out to discover you'd been with the Carpenters. It's not often she gets invited there herself. Mind you, it's even less often I get invited. Unless one of the wee'uns is taken poorly. And what qualifies as "poorly" up there would be next to fatal anywhere else.'

'And just what made you come here tonight to see me?' Christopher asked. As his faculties were returning, so were his instincts for suspicion.

'To tell you the truth, I'm not sure,' said Cormac. 'Maybe if you'd lived up in the Black Hole as long as I have you'd understand. I got back from Peshok earlier this evening. The first thing that confronted me here was Sister Campbell with a face like cold whey telling me about this disreputable-looking character who'd been asking after me. Then I heard a wee rumour that Lady Carpenter hadn't been all that impressed by your appearance either, but that you'd been extended the supreme honour by her good man. So, to tell you the truth, I was curious. I thought I'd come and have a look at you. Good thing I did. *Sláinte!*'

'You don't suppose I could have a drop of your "real stuff", do you?' Christopher asked.

Cormac tried to look medical and severe, but he had lost the knack.

'Ah, well, you're not supposed to have any strong drink along with those wee pills you've taken. But, then, I don't imagine a wee smidgeon will do you much harm. To tell you the truth, it'll probably do you more good than the pills. Have you a glass or anything?'

Christopher pointed mutely to one of his bags on the floor. He could see it had been disturbed and subsequently rearranged.

Cormac rummaged in the bag for a bit and finally surfaced brandishing a battered tin mug.

'This it?' he asked triumphantly.

Christopher nodded.

'Not exactly Waterford Crystal, I'm afraid,' he said.

'No,' replied Cormac as he began to pour a small libation into the cup. 'More like Rathgormuck Brass. But then you wouldn't know Rathgormuck, would you?'

Christopher smiled.

'Is there such a place?'

Cormac nodded sagely.

'Ay, of course there is. It's a wee village a few miles from

Waterford. Nothing much goes on there: they're born, they get married, they have lots of kids, they die, and the kids bury them. That's all there is to it. Much like anywhere else, I suppose.' He paused. 'I was in London once. It wasn't any different.'

He paused again and sipped a measure of poteen before continuing.

'So, what brings you to this wee excuse for a boil on the backside of the Himalayas?'

'Business, Dr Cormac, just business.'

The doctor raised one grey-flecked eyebrow.

'Oh aye? Is that with a capital "B" or a small "B"? I'm just asking. Look, mister, I've lived in this place long enough to fart in Bengali, and I knew what you were the minute I wiped your fevered brow and smelt your vomit. You're no more a box-wallah than I'm a yogi.'

Christopher sighed. First Carpenter and now this man.

'What do you think I am, then?' he asked.

Cormac shrugged.

'Couldn't say exactly. ICS, IPS . . . Heaven-born, anyway. You've got the look. You've got the manner. And you've got the voice, even if it is a wee bit on the shaky side at the moment. Do I get a prize?'

Christopher shook his head. It hurt.

'No prizes. Anyway,' he went on, trying to change the subject, 'you're no more a missionary doctor than I'm the Kaiser's mother.'

The doctor unplugged his fire-water and raised it to his lips. He made a face.

'*In poteeno veritas*, my son. You might be right . . . and then again, you might be wrong. To tell you the truth, sometimes I'm not too sure meself. I am a doctor, mind you – the real McKay. The Queen's University, Belfast, then a wee stint in Edinburgh with Daniel Cunningham, the Anatomy Professor. After that I got a post as a Junior House Surgeon in the Royal Infirmary. That's where I went wrong.' He paused and took more poteen.

'You see, there was a group of Christians in the Infirmary. You know the type: spotty faces, glandular trouble, masturbation, and daily prayer. Medics for Jesus, they called themselves. I won't tell you what other people called them.

'I'm still not sure if it was Jesus that formed the main attraction

83

or a pretty wee nurse called May Lorimer. He had the power to raise the dead, but she wasn't short of a few miracles of the same kind herself. Anyway, I put my name down, stopped drinking, started masturbating, and prayed nightly for the love of Jesus Christ and May Lorimer both.

'I was doing all right for a man with religious mania until there was a big convention out at Inverkeithing. Three days of sermons, prayers, and how's-your-father. On the last day, there was a call for medical missionaries. If we couldn't save the black man's soul, we'd save his body for resurrection and eternal torment.

'Anyway, the sublime Miss Lorimer was on the platform calling us to the Lord. I was on the floor and the flesh was calling me to Miss Lorimer. The next thing I knew, I was on the platform. And before I had time to think about what I was doing, I was on a big ship with a copy of the Bible in one hand and a bag of second-hand surgical instruments in the other. Next stop Kalimpong.' He paused. 'That was twenty years ago.'

He unscrewed the top of his flask more slowly than before and swallowed more deliberately.

'What about the divine Miss Lorimer?' asked Christopher, uncertain whether or not to make light of Cormac's morose tale.

'May Lorimer? I asked her to go with me. I offered her the possibility of serving Jesus together as man and wife. I asked her to marry me. She was very kind about it. She said she thought of me as a brother in the Lord, but not as a husband. I had Jesus, she said, what did I want with her as well? I had no answer for that then – though if the chance came my way again, I know exactly what I'd tell her now.

'A year later, I heard she'd run off with a big guardsman from Edinburgh Castle. Black Watch, I believe. Known for their sexual prowess. So I stayed on in Kalimpong without May Lorimer, without Jesus, and without much reason to go back. I took up drinking again, gave up masturbation, and became a sort of scandal. What's your story?'

For the first time, Christopher put the mug of poteen to his lips and drank. It took his breath away and made him splutter, but the fire that filled him afterwards made him feel better. He looked at the pale liquid in the tin and thought of the priest raising the chalice at mass. *Hic est enim Calix Sanguinis mei*. Wine and whiskey, blood and fire, faith and despair. He raised the mug again and drank. This time he did not cough.

'I was born near here,' he replied to Cormac's question. He thought he could afford to be honest with him. 'My father worked for the Political Service. He brought me up to love the country. I don't think he loved anything or anyone himself but India. Not my mother, not really. She died when I was twelve, and I was sent to school in England. Then, when I was fifteen, my father disappeared.'

The doctor looked at him curiously.

'What? Vanished into thin air, d'you mean? Like a fakir?' He pronounced the word as if it was 'faker'.

Christopher gave a wry smile.

'Just like a fakir,' he agreed. 'Only without a rope. No rope, no music – just himself. He was making a visit to Major Todd, our Trade Agent in Yatung back in those days. There was nobody in Gyantse then. My father left Kalimpong one day in October with a party of guides and bearers. The weather was turning bad, but they had no difficulty in making it over the Nathu-la. They were already well into Tibet when he disappeared.

'The party woke up one morning to find him gone. No note, no sign, no trail they could follow. He'd left all his belongings in the camp. They searched for him, of course – all that day and the next, but he was nowhere to be found. Then the snow got really heavy and they had to call off the search and push on to Yatung.

'He never reappeared. But nobody found a body. They sent a letter to my school; I was handed it one day in the middle of Latin class. It was very formal – no compassion in it, just the formalities. They sent me his things eventually – decorations, citations, letters patent, all the trumpery. I still keep them in a trunk at home in England. I never look at them, but they're there.'

'So you stayed in England?' Cormac interjected.

Christopher shook his head.

'Not until recently. I left as soon as I finished school and came straight out to India to join the ICS. That was in 1898. I'm not quite sure why I came back. Sometimes I think it was to look for my father, but I know that can't be right. Perhaps I just felt something had been left unfinished here, and I wanted to finish it.'

'And did you?'

Christopher stared at the wall, at a patch of damp high up, near the ceiling. There was a gecko beside it, pale and ghostly, clinging tightly to the wall.

'No,' he said, but quietly, as though speaking to himself.

'Bloody awful, isn't it?' said Cormac.

Christopher looked at him, uncomprehending.

'Life,' the doctor said. 'Bloody awful business. That,' he went on, 'is the only advantage of growing old. There's not much more of it to face.'

Christopher nodded and sipped from his mug. He felt a shiver go through him, as if it were a premonition of something. It was getting late.

'We have to talk,' he said.

12

'Fire away,' said Cormac, leaning back in his chair.

'Something's going on here,' Christopher said. 'Tonight I was attacked. Perhaps it was a thief, as you say; perhaps it was a *dacoit* who'd grown tired of ambushing people on the highways and byways; and perhaps it was someone who didn't want me in Kalimpong asking questions. I'm beginning to think that last possibility is the one with most going for it.'

'What sort of questions have you been asking, Mr Wylam?'

Christopher told him. Cormac was silent for a while, collecting his thoughts. The light of the penny candle hurt his eyes; he turned his face away from it gently.

'I don't suppose I'm allowed to ask you exactly why you've been enquiring after this monk. Or why someone would want to snatch your son in the first place, much less bring him here to Kalimpong or up to Tibet.'

'All I can say is that I used to work for the Government and that someone in a position to know thinks my son's kidnapping is related to the work I did. We know the monk brought a message out of Tibet and that the message was conveyed to a man called Mishig, the Mongol Trade Agent here.'

'Aye, I know Mishig well enough. It wouldn't surprise me to learn he was involved in something shifty. Go on.'

'The problem is finding out just how a man who was dying, who seems to have had no visitors, and who is said to have been delirious, managed to get a message to anyone. I'm beginning to think I'm wasting my time here.'

'I wouldn't be too sure about that,' said Cormac in a quiet voice.

Christopher said nothing, but he sensed that the atmosphere in the room had changed. Whether it was as a result of the poteen or the lateness of the hour or the relating of reminiscences, Cormac's mood had altered from jesting cynicism to measured seriousness. He was a man on the verge of divulging closely guarded matters.

'I think,' said the doctor, choosing his words carefully, 'the man you want is the Reverend Doctor Carpenter. He knows Mishig well enough. And, if I'm not mistaken, he knew the monk even better. But, to tell you the truth, it's just as likely that Tsewong took the message to Mishig himself. It was one or the other of them, believe me.'

A deep and seamless silence followed Cormac's words. Christopher felt himself hold his breath then release it slowly.

'Carpenter? But why? What possible motive could a man like that have to take messages round town on behalf of a man he must have considered the next best thing to a devil-worshipper?'

'A motive? With wee Johnny Carpenter? Good God man, we'd be up all night if we started talking about motives.'

'Such as?'

Cormac did not reply at once. Maybe it was his turn to feel suspicious. Christopher guessed he had set in motion a process he was beginning to regret.

'Let's begin with something else,' he said. 'Officially, this man Tsewong died of exposure. I wrote the death certificate meself. You'll find a copy with the Registrar for Births and Deaths, Kalimpong District. Man called Hughes: a Welshman from Neath. We're all Celts round here. Anyway, that isn't what Tsewong died of at all. Do you understand me?'

'How did he die?' asked Christopher. He noticed that Cormac had begun to take more of the poteen.

'He took his own life.'

The way the doctor pronounced the word, it sounded like 'tuck': 'he tuck his own life'. Christopher imagined the monk in bed, dying. 'Tuck yourself up now,' came the voice of Christopher's mother from his childhood. Tsewong had come through the cold passes into India and tucked himself up for good.

'But that's impossible.'

'Is it?' Cormac's voice was gentle, almost pathetic. He had seen the dead man, touched his face, his skin. 'You think a Buddhist monk can't kill himself? For some of them, their whole life is a slow death. There are men in Tibet who shut themselves into a wee hole in the rock and have themselves bricked up with nothing but a gap to let food in and shit out. Did you know that? That's a living death. They last for years and years sometimes. They go in young men and end up old corpses.

'Apart from that, it's a hard life anyway. There are frustrations, temptations, dark moments. A yellow robe is no guarantee against humanity.'

Neither man spoke. Wax dripped from the candle in silence. The flame flickered and straightened itself.

'How did he do it?' Christopher asked.

'Hanged himself. Carpenter says he found him in his room, just hanging there. He used the girdle, the rope from around his waist. There was a hook in the ceiling. It was an attic room, a wee room they use for storing old boxes. He hanged himself from the hook.'

Christopher shivered.

'I don't understand,' he said. 'I can't understand how someone is able to do it. To take his own life. I can understand murder, but not suicide.'

Cormac looked at Christopher. There was a sadness in his eyes that not even the whiskey could conceal.

'Lucky man,' he said. Just that, then he fell silent. In the street, the dogs were busy. Or was it a single beast padding in the stillness?

Christopher broke the silence with another question.

'Why did he kill himself? Do you know?'

Cormac shook his head.

'I couldn't tell you. I think John Carpenter knows, but you can be sure he won't tell you. I have one or two notions, though.'

'Notions?'

'I think Tsewong had problems. Maybe they were serious, maybe they just seemed that way to Tsewong: I can't tell you. But problems he undoubtedly had.' The doctor paused briefly, then proceeded.

'For one thing, I don't think he was a Buddhist. Not any longer, that is. I'd lay money on it that he was a Christian convert.'

Christopher looked at the Irishman in astonishment.

'I don't understand. He was a Tibetan. There are no Tibetan Christians. He was wearing the robes of a Buddhist monk. And he was dead. How could you tell he was a Christian?'

Cormac fortified himself with the rough whiskey before continuing.

89

'A couple of things. I had the body taken up to the hospital for examination. When I undressed him, I wanted to be sure I had all the wee bits and pieces, because I knew they'd have to be handed over to old Norbhu, along with the body. That was when I found the letter and the note, in his pouch with the prayer-book, the amulet and all the rest. But guess what he was wearing round his neck, well tucked away inside his clothes. A cross, Mr Wylam. A wee, silver cross. I've still got it hidden away in my desk at home. I'll show it to you if you like.'

'Weren't there questions about the suicide?'

'Who would ask? You don't think I'd let on to Norbhu Dzasa that one of his lamas did himself in, do you? I told you – I wrote the death certificate meself. Plenty of people die of exposure at this time of year. Quite a few of them are Tibetan monks. There were no questions.'

'What about Carpenter? You said you thought he might know why the man killed himself.'

Cormac did not answer right away. When he did, a note of caution had entered his voice.

'Did I now? Yes, I think he must know something, though I can't prove it. The thing is, the dead man was staying with Carpenter before all this happened. There was some story about a farmer finding Tsewong on the road and bringing him to the Homes the day before he died. That's probably what you heard yourself. It's what Carpenter told me, and it's what I told Frazer. But it's a load of baloney. I happen to know that Tsewong was living with Carpenter for at least a week before he killed himself. Tsewong wasn't some unfortunate wretch passing through Kalimpong who'd been taken in by the charitable Doctor Carpenter and who just happened to take his own life while on the premises. No, whatever else he came here to do, Tsewong came to Kalimpong to see Carpenter. I'd swear to it.'

'Why should he want to see Carpenter?'

'That's a good question. I wish I knew the answer to it. I've an idea Carpenter had a hand in Tsewong's conversion. For all we know, the man wasn't called Tsewong at all, but Gordon or Angus.'

Christopher smiled bleakly.

'Are you sure the man was a convert? Isn't it possible Carpenter just gave him the cross while he was with him? Perhaps Tsewong didn't realize the significance of it.'

Cormac looked at Christopher.

'I can see you weren't brought up in Belfast. I don't know whether or not Tsewong understood its significance exactly, but I'd be very surprised if John Carpenter gave it to him. Presbyterians aren't given to wearing crosses, let alone crosses with wee figures of Jesus Christ on them.'

'A crucifix, you mean?'

'The very thing. I fancy Tsewong got hold of the crucifix from another source. But I still think he and Carpenter were involved in some fashion.'

'I don't see what connection there could be.'

Cormac stood abruptly and stepped across to the window. Outside, moonlight and clouds had turned the sky to broken lace. He stood there for a while, watching the patterns of the sky break and re-form. Sometimes, he thought it would go on forever, and he felt diminished and afraid.

'What do you think you saw tonight?' he asked, his voice low yet carrying. 'A man of God, maybe? A man at any rate. But John Carpenter isn't a man. He's a mask – a series of masks, one inside the other, deeper and deeper until you think you'll go crazy trying to get to the face underneath. And if you ever did get to the face, you'd be sorry you'd done so. Take my word for it – I know.

'For one thing, he's ambitious. Not like an ordinary man – he's sick with it. He's turned fifty, and what's he got to show for himself? Here in Kalimpong, he's a big man, but that's like saying he's made a name for himself collecting stamps or that he's the Lord Mayor of Limavady. One thing's for sure – he doesn't want to live out his days in this hole with all these wee heathen shites. No more does Mrs Carpenter – who is, by the way, made of cast iron and twice as frigid.

'Carpenter knows there's more, and he knows where he can get it. It's eating him up inside. It's been eating him up for twenty-five years and more. If he wants to become the Indian Livingstone, he'll have to pull off something big, something that'll get him noticed. And round here that means just one thing.'

He paused and lifted the flask to his lips. The whiskey was working, dreaming in his veins.

91

'What's that?' asked Christopher.

'Tibet,' answered Cormac. 'Open up Tibet. A mission there would crown anyone's career. It would even help the Pope make a name for himself. It's never been done, at least not since some Jesuits tried in the seventeenth and eighteenth centuries. A Presbyterian church in the Forbidden City, overlooking the Potala maybe. Convert the Dalai Lama, tear down the idols, proclaim the land for Christ. Jesus, he could go home in triumph. There'd be a statue to him on the Mound in front of New College. They'd tear down the Scott Monument and put the Carpenter Memorial in its place. Ladies in tweed skirts and sensible underwear would queue up to write the story of his life. A few of them would doubtless lift their skirts and let him tell his own story.'

'Could it be done?'

'I don't see why not, if you could find your way through the underwear.'

'I didn't mean that. Could Carpenter actually open a mission?'

Cormac grunted.

'Are you mad? But that won't stop the wee bastard trying. He has his contacts, or so he lets on. Before long, there'll be a British Ambassador in Lhasa. Don't look so surprised – I know a bit about what goes on round here. And the Ambassador will need a chaplain. That would be a start. He's got it all worked out, believe me.'

'And you think Tsewong was part of this plan?'

'It wouldn't surprise me.'

Christopher nodded. It sounded plausible. Plausible but harmless. And he was convinced that whatever was going on here was far from harmless.

'Perhaps you're right,' he said. 'But it sounds innocuous enough to me. Where do I come into this? And my son. He wasn't kidnapped because of some ecclesiastical plot to open a mission in Lhasa.'

Cormac shrugged.

'I wouldn't know. I'm not in that business meself. Something tells me that would be more in your line. But you can be sure of one thing: if Carpenter's laying the foundations for a Tibetan mission, it's costing him plenty. There's people to buy, influence to attract, men in high places to win over. That sort of thing doesn't come cheap. And there are other prices too. Concessions. Quid pro quos. Favours. As you know, Bibles and trade often go hand in hand. And not too far behind trade come the guns. Johnny Carpenter's in deep, whatever he's mixed up in.'

The penny I pay is not a copper one. Nor silver nor gold, for that matter . . .

'Where does he find the money? If you're right, he must need a lot of money. I've been at the Homes – there's no wealth there.'

Cormac gave Christopher a look so intense it made him flinch. It was like hatred.

'Isn't there?' he snapped. Then, abruptly as he had spoken, he took hold of himself.

'I've had too much to drink,' he said. 'You'll have to excuse me. We're on dangerous ground, mister. We'd better not go any further until I'm sober and you've had a rest. Perhaps we'd best go no further at all.' He took a deep breath before continuing. 'But maybe you've a right to know more. Come and see me in the morning. I'm not on duty until tomorrow afternoon. I'll be in my bungalow – they'll tell you how to find it at the hospital. I've some things in my desk I'd like you to see.'

The doctor fell silent and glanced out through the window again. Someone had lit a fire on the hills. He could just make it out, a tiny, lonely speck in the darkness.

'Jesus,' he said, his voice low, as though he were speaking to himself. 'Sometimes I wonder why we ever came here, why we stay. It's no place for the likes of you and me: it swallows us up alive and spits us out again. Have you never felt that? As though you were being eaten. As though a tiger had your flesh between his teeth and was chewing you. A carnivore that had developed a taste for human meat.'

He shuddered at his own imagery. He had treated men attacked by tigers. What was left of them.

'What about the letter?' Christopher asked. 'The English letter that was found on Tsewong. Could Carpenter have written it?'

The doctor shook his head.

'He could have, but he didn't. It wasn't in his handwriting. It wasn't in any handwriting I recognized. But I know one thing: whoever wrote it had been brought up speaking English. Speaking it and writing it.'

93

'The letter said Tsewong was an emissary.'

'That's right.'

'For someone called the Dorje Lama. I've never heard of such a person. Have you?'

Cormac did not answer straight away. He watched the fire on the hillside. Someone was out there in the snow, feeding the flames, watching.

'Yes,' he answered, in a voice so quiet Christopher was not sure he had spoken. 'They don't talk about him often. And never to foreigners. But one of my patients told me a little – oh, it was years ago. He's a sort of legend. There's a monastery up there somewhere, a secret place. People are frightened of it. And the Dorje Lama is the abbot. There's been a Dorje Lama for hundreds of years, so they say.'

The doctor turned and faced Christopher. The effects of the whiskey had vanished, to be replaced by a haunted look.

'And Tsewong was his emissary?' Christopher said.

'So the letter said.'

'Do you believe it?'

Cormac hesitated.

'I think,' he said, 'you'd better see what I have to show you. Come in the morning. We'll talk about it then. I'll tell you everything I know.'

13

Christopher woke the next morning with the worst headache he had ever known. He took more of the tablets Cormac had left, but they did little good. Outside the rest-home, the girl had resumed her singing. She sang the same song, as though she knew no other; but this morning her voice tore like a rusty blade through Christopher's head, and he cursed her as he dressed.

He shaved, cutting himself twice, and combed his hair, but he still felt untidy: there was a section of his head he could not bear to touch with the comb. Downstairs, he paused just long enough to drink a cup of black tea and eat some buttered chapatis. The boy, Lhaten, looked at him oddly, but said nothing. The house was almost empty – the caravaneers had gone off that morning early as planned, but Christopher had fallen into a disturbed sleep by then and had not heard them leave. The place seemed dull without them.

As Christopher was leaving, Lhaten approached him nervously.

'Are you all right, *sahib*? The doctor-*sahib* said you had an accident last night. He said you fell on the stairs.'

Christopher nodded.

'Yes,' he said, 'that's right. I fell on the stairs. I'll be more careful tonight.'

A look of concern passed across Lhaten's face.

'Yes, *sahib*. You must be careful. Call me when you come tonight. I'll be awake.'

Christopher sensed that the boy either guessed or knew more than he said.

'Thank you, Lhaten, I'll remember that.'

Lhaten flashed a smile and vanished towards the kitchen. Christopher heard the shrill voice of the Lepcha woman.

Outside, the sun was shining and the air smelt fresh and clear. Perhaps the world was clean after all, Christopher thought; perhaps he carried the dirt around inside himself.

95

To his left, he heard the voice of the mysterious girl singing her *bhajan*. He turned and saw her, sitting on the ground with her back towards him. Long black hair fell gracefully down her back. Her head moved gently from side to side in time with her singing. He could just see that she was working with something on the ground in front of her.

> *Aro ekdin shamero ai bangshi*
> *bejechilo kanone.*
> *One day that flute of the dark lord's*
> *Played again in the forest.*

Something pulled him towards her. He wanted to see her face, to watch her mouth as she sang, to watch her fingers move at her work. Softly, so as not to frighten her, he walked past her, then, several paces away, turned.

She did not see him looking at her. All her attention was focused on the object in front of her. She went on singing, like an angel whom nothing can distract from song. But her face was appalling in its ugliness, and misshapen legs stretched out in front of her like bent sticks. One eye was stitched tightly closed, and long scars disfigured her left cheek. Her skin was sore and blistered – on face and arms and legs equally. But none of this horrified Christopher quite so much as the sight of what she was doing with her hands.

He thought it had been a dog, but he could not be sure. The knife she was using was blunt and rusted, and the work of butchery was painfully slow. The passers-by averted their gaze, shunning the girl and the meat she was preparing; but Christopher stood as though transfixed, unable to tear his eyes away from her. She sang gently as she worked, and Christopher realized that she was crooning to the dead animal in her lap. Her fingers were covered in blood, and the cuffs of her long sleeves were smeared with it. Turning away, Christopher set off down the narrow, crowded street. Behind him, the mad girl's voice rose and fell in an unending supplication of the beast. He remembered the dogs he had heard in the night, remembered their voices tearing the darkness.

He walked to the hospital through streets crowded with men and animals. The blind beggar was there on his spot in the bazaar again, muttering prayers beneath his breath. Christopher hurried past, ignoring his cries. Out of an opening on his right, a small group of singing men came into the main street. They were Bauls, members of a wandering cult that sought God outside the rituals and ceremonies of organized religion. They carried simple musical instruments in their hands and played and sang as they walked. As they approached him, Christopher recognized suddenly the song they were singing – it was the same song the girl had been singing a few minutes earlier.

> *Bondhur bangshi baje bujhi bipine*
> *Shamer bangshi baje bujhi bipine*

He felt hemmed in, like someone in a nightmare, and ran on, the voices of the men ringing in his ears, and beneath them the girl's voice, unforgettable and cold.

The hospital stood next door to the Government Dispensary, to which it was connected. It was a small place with only twenty-eight beds, but it was smart and well kept. The small, white-painted entrance hall was empty when Christopher stepped inside. On the wall, a varnished wooden plaque commemorated the opening of the hospital and dedicated it to the glory of the Christian God. Beside it stood a two-tier dressing trolley holding several kidney dishes, a saline irrigator, and a pair of Cheatle's forceps in a glass jar. In a white enamel basin, a blood-stained bandage intruded on the surrounding sterility. Above the trolley, a blonde-haired Jesus, smug as a new pin, smiled down, surrounded by hordes of bright-faced, laughing children, none of whom looked remotely Indian.

'*Koi hai*,' Christopher called, his voice echoing in the stillness. A smell of ether drifted towards him. Somewhere, someone called for assistance and fell silent again. Someone else began to cough with a dry, racking sound that ended in vomiting. Metal banged against metal.

A *peon* appeared from nowhere. He was dressed in a starched white uniform with a tightly wound *pugaree* that bore the badge of the hospital.

'Did you call, *sahib*?'

'Yes,' said Christopher. 'I'd like to see Dr Cormac; he's expect-

97

ing me. He said I would find him in his bungalow. Can you show me the way?'

'When you go out the main entrance, *sahib*, turn left. You will come to a row of deodars. There is a gate. Follow the path to the third bungalow. I would be happy to take you, *sahib*.'

What he meant, of course, was that he would be happy to keep an eye on Christopher.

'No, thanks. I'll find the way myself.'

Without waiting to see if the man would follow him, Christopher went back into the sunlight. A *dome* was sweeping the gravel path in front of the building; back and forwards, back and forwards the long brush swept as he moved down the path, as though he had been walking there all his life. He looked up as Christopher came out, then away again, averting his gaze in case the *sahib* might find it unclean.

There was a stretch of neatly trimmed *doob*-grass beside the hospital, then the deodars, their broad branches sweeping low towards the lawn. The gate bore a small sign, painted in stark black letters on a white board: 'Out of bounds to Native Staff.' Christopher raised the latch and passed through.

There were six bungalows in all, nestling together beneath another row of deodars. The path up to Cormac's was flanked on both sides by rows of potted chrysanthemums, mainly red and pink. There were still traces of water at the bases of the pots: the hospital *mali* was probably nearby – Christopher doubted that Cormac would have his own men to do the work of gardening.

He knocked on the door three times and waited. There was no reply. Perhaps the whiskey had been a bit much for Cormac after all. Christopher knocked again, more loudly this time. No-one came. That was odd. He had formed the impression that Cormac was not the sort of man to keep much of a household, but surely he would need one or two servants.

The door was unlocked. Christopher stepped inside and closed it behind him. He found himself in a small cream-painted entrance vestibule. From floor to ceiling, the walls were hung with glass cases containing hundreds upon hundreds of brightly coloured butterflies. Nearby Sikkim was famous for them, a paradise heavy with their drugged and painted wings. Here, in the little hall of Cormac's house, they lay silent and still, as though fresh from the

98

miracle of chloroform. Bright scarlet trails traversed their wings like wounds on purple flesh.

He called Cormac's name, but his voice echoed flatly in the empty hallway and was swallowed up by the silence.

He opened a second door. Beyond it lay the main room of the bungalow. Pale light filled it, dappled and watery on the sparse furniture. A few cane chairs and a small table, a battered desk — rented furniture from a go-down in Darjeeling, worth a few rupees a year. A faded linen table-cloth from Belfast, photographs of school and university groups on the walls, an oar bearing the names of some forgotten eight, a black and gold tasselled rugby cap gathering dust, some medical textbooks on clumsily built shelves.

Like the butterflies in the entrance hall, the fragments of Martin Cormac's past hung on his walls as though they too had just been lifted by thin and ragged wings from the killing-bottle. Or perhaps this was the killing-bottle: this room, this bungalow, the hospital, Kalimpong. A transparent bottle of concentric rings through which a dying man could look out and watch the stars.

He was not sure when the buzzing first became audible. It had been there from the moment he entered the room, of course, but so low his ears had not at first picked it up. He stood for a moment, listening. It was a deep, angry sound, like the wings of huge insects hovering in the heat of summer, like the buzzing of large flies above a slaughterhouse, drawn by the smell of blood in the last days. But it was winter: there should not be flies.

The noise came from behind a door at the far end of the room. The door was partly open, but from where he stood, Christopher could not see into the room beyond it. He called out again, almost frightened by the sound of his own voice.

'Cormac, are you there? Is anyone there?'

But there was only the buzzing. The buzzing and a smell that seemed familiar, but so faint it was impossible to place.

He approached the door cautiously. Narrow shafts of light fell through a slatted blind. In the thin golden strips, specks of finely scattered dust spun freely. Christopher's heart tightened within his chest. He felt blood leap in his veins, felt it pound in his already aching head. The room was full of flies. Hot, buzzing flies in a dense swarm that shook and shimmered in the shifting golden

99

light. Wave upon wave of them, black, violent, moving in dark battalions, circling, droning, their wings alight. He felt nausea rise in him, he recognized the smell. He wanted to run, but his feet moved towards the door instead. It was winter: there should not be flies.

He entered the room, shielding his face with his hands, half-blinded by the moving forms that circled through the light and the darkness. In one corner, white curtains hung, huge and diaphanous, across the edge of the blinds, lifting and falling in a fine breeze, speckled with the coarse black bodies of blowflies. Above his head, the insects had gathered like a thick carpet on the *punkah* hanging from the ceiling. On the floor, his feet crushed the bodies of dead flies, staining the floorboards with purple.

The bed was a seething mass of flies, as though something living was moving there, straining to take on form in the half-light. Keeping himself away from the bed, Christopher moved to the window and pulled the cords that operated the blinds. He raised them a little, not too far, but far enough to allow more light into the room. He had to force himself to turn and look at the bed.

It was Cormac all right. The flies had congregated mainly on the body, where the blood was. He could make out enough of the face to recognize the man. His throat had been sliced through from side to side as he slept. On the pillow, Christopher saw the scalpel that the killer had used, bright and shining and stained with blood. The body had not moved much in its last agony. One arm had twisted back, the hand reaching for the torn throat, the fingers pale and bent, drained of blood. Cormac had died early that morning, possibly within an hour or two of falling asleep. The blood had congealed and dried, the limbs had begun to stiffen.

Christopher turned away from the bed and the seething carapace of flies and blood that moved on it. He opened the window and breathed in lungfuls of fresh, clean air. Behind him, the droning of the flies echoed in the small, fetid room. He wanted to be sick, to rid himself of the clinging, sweet smell.

Abruptly, he turned and left the room, without another glance at the thing on the bed. As he came into the main room, he saw something that had escaped him on his way in: Cormac's desk had been tampered with. He went up to it. Drawers had been pulled out and small cupboards opened. Papers were heaped on the writing surface in total confusion: letters, bills, reports, all thrown together at random. Some lay on the floor, crumpled where someone had stepped on them. He picked up a large blue file and set it on the desk. It bore a title in large black letters: 'Kalimpong Houseflies: A Statistical Survey of Breeding Rates in Captivity'. That explained the flies: Cormac had been running an experiment, and his killer must have broken his breeding cases and let the insects loose. The sound of their buzzing still hammered out mindlessly from the bedroom. They were dying, cold and blind and gorged with blood.

He glanced through the papers carefully, but found nothing of interest. Whoever had killed Cormac had taken what he had come for. The silver cross that the doctor had said he found on Tsewong was not there either. Had the killer taken that as well? Then Christopher remembered what Cormac had said: 'I've still got it hidden away in my desk.' Was there a hidden drawer somewhere?

It did not take Christopher long to find it. A simple lever at the back of one of the recesses operated a spring mechanism that released a drawer near the top of the desk. He reached in and drew out a packet of thick brown paper. Inside were several photographs, perhaps about two dozen in all. For the most part, they were in pairs, held together with plain pins. Most of them were pictures of girls from the orphanage – first, a photograph of each girl in the grey Knox Homes uniform that Christopher remembered from the evening before, then a second showing the same girl, usually in a sari, wearing jewellery and make-up. All of the first photographs seemed to have been taken by the same camera and against the same background, but in each case the second photograph differed in size, in quality, and in setting.

There were also a few unpaired photographs of boys in what appeared to be the male equivalent of the girls' uniform. At the bottom was another set of photographs, again of a girl. The top photograph showed her, like the others, in the grey uniform of orphanhood. But when his eyes fell on the second photograph, Christopher felt himself gasp for breath and grow dizzy. The buzzing of the flies as they feasted blurred and mingled with the roar of blood rushing in his head. He put out a hand to steady himself.

The second photograph was of the girl in the street, the girl

101

whose bloody fingers Christopher had watched at work less than an hour before. She was looking straight at the camera like someone staring at something a long way away. It was the same girl as the one in the first of the two photographs. The same girl and not the same girl. In the first photograph, she seemed perfectly normal, even pretty. She had not been disfigured when she lived at the Knox Homes.

On the back of each second photograph, someone, probably Cormac, had pencilled a few words: a personal name, a place name, and, in several cases, a date. 'Jill, Jaipurhat, 10.2.15'; 'Hilary, Sahibganj, 9.5.13'. But on the back of all the photographs of boys, the place name never varied and was always followed by a question-mark: 'Simon, Dorje-la?, 1916'; 'Matthew, Dorje-la?, 1918'; 'Gordon, Dorje-la?, 1919'. *Dorje-la:* was that the name of the monastery presided over by Tsewong's mysterious Dorje Lama?

Christopher wrapped up the photographs in the paper and stuffed them into a pocket of his jacket. His heart was still beating. It was like a nightmare in which he was haunted first by the voice and now by the face of the mad girl from the street. Had these photographs something to do with whatever it was Cormac had been talking about the night before? Had it been them that the doctor had intended to show him? One thing seemed clear: whoever had killed the doctor had not even guessed there might be something in the desk.

He put his hand into the drawer again, to the very back. His fingers came in contact with something cold and hard. There was a fine chain attached to something. It was the silver cross. Christopher lifted it out carefully. The flies were buzzing more loudly, and he was growing afraid.

It was a plain cross bearing the nailed figure of Christ. Both wood and flesh had been transformed to silver. Something about the cross made the hair on the back of Christopher's neck rise. It was so improbable that he did not see it at first. He recognized the cross. It was not strange that he did: he had seen it many times before. As a child, he had held it in his hands often. He turned it over and saw on the back, cut into the silver beside the hallmark, the letters 'R. V. W.' – his father's initials. Robert Vincent Wylam. It was his father's cross, the one heirloom that had not been sent to England with the medals and the cuff-links. From the feet and

hands of the tiny Christ-figure, the heads of minute nails pro-
truded. When he was little, Christopher had touched them in
wonder. Now, his hand clenched tightly about the cross until its
sharp edges began to cut into his flesh; a thin, red trickle of blood
ran out between his fingers.

He heard the voices of the flies, mumbling feverishly in the
darkened room, and the voices of the dogs prowling along dark,
stinking lanes in search of offal, and the voice of the girl singing to
him out of the gloom. His bleeding fingers clutched the cross and
he stood in the centre of the room, crying bitterly, adrift, abandoned, not knowing where he was or why.

14

Christopher lost all sense of time passing. He remained in the room, clutching the crucifix, oblivious of his surroundings. He had entered the presence of Beelzebub, the Lord of Flies, there in that tiny room, amid the clamour of wings. His head was filled with images of his father dying in a blizzard, of the disfigured girl singing outside his window, of men he had killed or watched die.

And yet a part of his brain was icily calm and thinking hard about what had happened. Someone had overheard his conversation with Cormac the night before – of that he was convinced. And that had led to a hurried and bungled attempt to suppress the doctor's knowledge and its imminent revelation. Carpenter or someone close to Carpenter was responsible for the killing. Christopher no longer doubted that the missionary was mixed up deeply in whatever was going on. And that meant he was somehow involved with William's kidnapping. Beyond that, he hardly dared think; but in a corner of his mind his father's voice was whispering from the past, whispering words Christopher could not quite hear.

He stood up at last and put the crucifix carefully into the inside pocket of his jacket. He spent a little while going through the contents of Cormac's desk, but could find nothing else connected to Carpenter, Tibet, or the photographs.

It was time to go. He knew exactly where he was headed. This time John Carpenter would tell him all he knew, even if Christopher had to drag every word out of him by brute force. He got up from the desk.

There was a heavy knock at the front door. Christopher froze. Suddenly, footsteps sounded in the entrance hall.

'Doctor Cormac! Are you all right?' It was the orderly who had given him directions at the hospital.

A second later, the door of the living room burst open and three men stepped inside: a British police captain and two Indian constables. The orderly hung back in the corridor outside.

Without speaking, the captain motioned to one of his constables to search the other rooms. The man made straight for the bedroom. Christopher could still hear the sound of flies buzzing loudly. Moments later, the constable returned looking distinctly sick. He stepped up to the captain, muttered a few words to him, and then went with him to the bedroom.

When the captain came out of the room, he had turned pale. He was young, probably just out of police academy, and this might have been his first murder. What rotten luck, thought Christopher.

'What is your name?' the captain demanded.

'Wylam. Major Christopher Wylam.'

The word 'Major' threw the policeman a little. But he quickly pulled himself up to his full height and addressed Christopher in the prescribed manner, as laid down in regulations.

'Major Christopher Wylam, it is my duty to place you under arrest for the murder of Doctor Martin Cormac. I have to advise you that you will now be taken into my custody, to be delivered in due course to the Chief Magistrate of Kalimpong District for examination with a view to being referred to trial. I must also caution you that anything you now say may be recorded and used later in evidence against you.'

He nodded at the constable who had found the body. The man unhooked a set of handcuffs from his belt and stepped towards Christopher. Now that routine had taken over, the policeman seemed more at ease.

'Please hold your hands in front of you,' he said.

Christopher did as instructed. The man came closer and made to clip the first cuff over Christopher's right wrist. As he did so, Christopher swung round, grabbed the policeman's arm, and spun him in a circle, grabbing him across the neck with his free hand. It took only a moment to find and retrieve the man's gun. Christopher raised it and held it tight against the policeman's head.

'You!' he shouted at the orderly, cringing in the passage. 'Get in here! *Juldi!*'

A European would have made for the door and raised the alarm. But Indian hospital orderlies suffered a double dose of authoritarianism: a medical hierarchy headed by representatives of the master race. The *peon* stepped into the living-room.

'Put your guns on the floor, then place your hands on your

105

heads,' Christopher instructed the two remaining policemen. 'Slowly, now!'

They did as he told them. He spoke to the orderly again.

'Go to the bedroom. Find something to tie these men up: neckties, strips of bedding, anything. But hurry up!'

The orderly nodded and did as instructed. Christopher heard him retching when he got inside the room. A minute later he re-emerged with a sheet.

'Tear it into strips,' Christopher ordered. 'Then tie them up.'

The orderly's hands were shaking and he looked as though he might be on the verge of fainting. But he managed somehow to make his fumbling fingers do what was demanded of them. The policemen were told to sit in straight-backed chairs while they were trussed up. All the time, the English captain fixed his eyes on Christopher, as though committing his face to memory.

'Now this one,' Christopher ordered. The orderly tied the third man to another chair.

'Please, *sahib*,' he pleaded when he had finished. 'You don't have to tie me up. I am staying here as long as you want. I am keeping quiet. Not interfering.'

Christopher ignored his pleas and tied him to the desk chair. He turned to the captain.

'I'm sorry,' he said.

'You'll be a good deal sorrier when you're pulled in. You won't get away, you know. Better to give yourself up now. Save yourself a lot of trouble. Save yourself getting hurt.'

'Yes,' said Christopher. 'I'd like to do that. But I didn't kill Martin Cormac and I don't have time to waste proving it. This isn't a police matter. Tell your people to keep their noses out of it. Speak to somebody at DBI. Ask to talk to Winterpole. He'll explain. He'll explain everything.'

He turned and made for the door. Behind him, the flies had started moving into the living-room.

15

Two large cars were parked outside the Knox Homes. Christopher recognized them as Rolls-Royce Silver Ghosts: they were popular cars with some of the local potentates. Evidently, Carpenter had visitors. Important visitors.

He saw the confusion on the girl's face as soon as she opened the door: she simply did not know what to do with him. Christopher was no longer *persona non grata* – he had taken dinner with the Carpenters the night before and been introduced to the assembled orphans as a man of sorrows. But something held her back from granting him immediate admission. He resolved her dilemma by pushing past into the hallway. Ignoring her cries of protest, he made his way directly to Carpenter's study and flung open the door. It was empty. The vacant eyes of dead animals stared at him from the walls. He closed the door on them and headed for the Carpenters' drawing-room. He did not bother to knock.

Moira Carpenter was receiving visitors: a wealthy Indian lady dressed in the indoor garb of a Muslim nobleman's wife and a spinsterish European woman in serviceable clothes, who sat and held her teacup with the bored self-deprecation of a governess in the throes of middle age. When the door opened and Christopher burst in, the governess spilled tea into her ample lap and Moira Carpenter almost scalded the cat. Only the begum held her ground, as though rude interruptions were part of the daily round for her.

Christopher was the first to speak.

'Where's your husband, Mrs Carpenter?' he snapped. His nerves were on edge.

'Mr Wylam, I . . .' Moira Carpenter began, carefully replacing her blue and white china teapot on the doily-topped table by her elbow.

'I want to speak with him. Where is he?'

'Really, this is most improper.' Mrs Carpenter was recovering

107

quickly from her shock. 'Just what do you mean bursting in here like this? You . . .'

'Martin Cormac is dead. Murdered. I think your husband knows something about it. Where is he?'

Moira Carpenter had been half-way to her feet when Christopher broke the news. Her legs seemed to give way under her and she sank back into the chair. The colour that had started to rise in her face deserted it instantly and was replaced by a ghastly pallor. Christopher thought for a moment that she would faint, but within seconds her true nature had reasserted itself. Cormac had been right: beneath the skin, she was cast iron – cast iron of the highest quality.

'Explain,' she said. Her lips were taut and pale. 'Martin Cormac dead – explain.'

'I found him at his bungalow less than half an hour ago. In bed. Someone had cut his throat. That's all I know.'

'And you think my husband knows something you do not. Explain.'

'I'll explain that to your husband, Mrs Carpenter, if you'll kindly tell me where he is.'

All this time neither of the other two women had spoken. The pale governess was plainly distressed and kept rubbing mindlessly with a small lace handkerchief at the tea stains on her lap. The begum watched unperturbed, as though the cutting of throats, like rude interruptions, was a commonplace of her unruffled existence.

'You will explain it to me, Mr Wylam, or not at all,' Moira Carpenter riposted. She was still pale, but the blood that had fled her face was doing its work elsewhere.

'Martin Cormac knew something about your husband, something the Reverend Carpenter may have wanted to remain hidden. I went to Cormac's place this morning to find out what it was. I found him dead and his desk broken into. That is your explanation. Now, will you tell me where your husband is?'

'The Reverend Carpenter is with my husband.' It was the begum's voice. She was a plumpish woman in her forties, clearly a senior wife whose power in the harem owed less to personal beauty than political acumen. Christopher thought she would, in truth, be no stranger to sudden and unexplained death.

'I regret,' she continued, 'that they cannot be disturbed under

108

any circumstances. Perhaps Mrs Carpenter will arrange an appointment for this afternoon. In the meantime, you will be good enough to show yourself out.'

'And who exactly is your husband, madam?' Christopher demanded. He was not in a mood to be cowed by a woman who took her governess for morning tea in a Silver Ghost.

'The Nawab of Hasanabad,' Moira Carpenter explained, as if in deference to some obscure point of Muslim etiquette that did not allow the begum to utter her husband's name. 'And what the Begum says is correct – they are not to be disturbed. Go home, Mr Wylam. Collect yourself. Think about what you have been saying. And if you still feel you should speak to my husband, return later this afternoon as the Begum suggests and he will be pleased to entertain you. Would you like me to send a boy to notify the police of your gruesome discovery?'

With an effort, she was casting a veil of normality over the scene. The governess had begun to breathe more easily. The tea stains would wash out.

'His throat was cut from side to side,' Christopher barked at her. 'With a scalpel. Would you like me to show you? Why don't you all drive up to the hospital with me in one of those shiny cars outside and see for yourselves? We could bring tea and sandwiches. You'll just have to be careful about the flies – there are rather a lot of them just now.' He sensed that he was on the verge of snapping, but it didn't seem to matter.

The two European women blanched visibly at Christopher's tirade, but the begum remained unmoved. Unlike the others, she had seen men with their throats cut from side to side. The talk of flies made her think the stranger was insane.

'Please leave at once,' she said, 'or I shall have to call for my husband's men to throw you out. They won't be gentle, and I won't be upset if they break your neck.'

Christopher swore and stormed out of the room. He had wasted enough time already.

The transition from the Carpenters' quarters to the orphanage was effected by a double doorway. He felt the chill as he went through – the Carpenters kept their own heating high. The evening before, he had formed only a hazy impression of the place's layout. The

109

ground floor, which he had briefly toured, consisted of the assembly hall, classrooms, dining-room, and kitchens. On the first floor to his right were the girls' dormitories and bathrooms. To his left lay the boys' section, which he had visited the evening before.

He headed there first. Going through a plain door, he found himself in a long, empty corridor. On either side were wooden doors set with panes of glass in their top register. Glancing through the first, he saw a teacher at a blackboard and the first two rows of desks. The voices of the boys came to him through the glass, singing in a monotone:

'Nine times seven is sixty-three; nine times eight is seventy-two; nine times nine is eighty-one; nine times . . .'

The voices faded as he moved on. The corridor led directly into a tiled hall, where his feet echoed. Away from the classrooms, where only the dreary chanting of parrot phrases gave any hint of life, the building was heavy with a peculiar, cloying silence. It was a silence grown from misery and boredom as weeds are grown from their particular seeds, dense, desolate, and forbidding. He felt himself slow down and move on the balls of his feet, falling instinctively into harmony with the atmosphere of the place. A broad staircase lay to his left, connecting with the floor above. He moved toward it, drawn without any reason to the upper floors.

The staircase led on to a narrow corridor, redolent with the smells of unperfumed soap and starched bed-linen. The walls were white and stark, without concession to mortality or pain. Here, sleep was a chore like any other, with fixed times and set rules. Only the dreams escaped regimentation. The dreams and the nightmares.

Christopher opened the door of the dormitory. It was a long, bed-lined room, like the one he had slept in at Winchester, but colder and more cheerless. Someone had left a window open. A cold wind moved restlessly through the room, its appetite undiminished after its long journey from the mountains.

He felt a sense of inquietude grow in him. Pale sheets were moving in the gusts from the open window. The small beds with their iron frames, the white walls, the rows of foot-lockers without colour or personality – all reminded him once more of the ward of a hospital . . . or an asylum. What nightmares *did* the children of the Knox Homes have when they lay dreaming in their narrow

110

beds on a winter's night? he wondered. Dark gods . . . or the Reverend and Mrs Carpenter smiling their slow smiles and reading comforting words from the Bible?

Next door, there was a cold bathroom. Water dripped from a washerless tap on to white enamel. Damp towels hung limply on wooden rails. Lattices of pale light lay on the tiles like bars.

At the end of the corridor was a small wooden door marked 'Sick-bay'. Christopher knocked softly, but there was no answer. He tried the handle. The door was unlocked. Inside was a low bed covered in tightly folded sheets, and beside it an enamel washstand with a hand-towel draped over the bowl. Even here there were no concessions. He remembered how Moira Carpenter had tried to explain to him that sickness was a token of sin, that the sick should be cared for but not coddled. To comfort sickness was to comfort sin.

He was about to leave when something caught his attention. Along the wall opposite the bed stood a small linen-chest. It seemed to have been shifted recently, about two feet further from the door, leaving a noticeable patch of lighter paint on the wall where it had stood. Christopher could not understand why it had been moved: its new position was awkward, much too close to the washstand to allow the drawers to be opened fully.

He opened the lid and looked inside. Just a pile of sheets, all neatly folded and stacked evenly. There were two drawers at the bottom of the chest. He opened each of these in turn, but found only towels and a few basic medical items. Perhaps there was something wrong with the wall behind the chest. He squeezed between the chest and the washstand and pushed. The chest was heavy, but it moved across the uncarpeted floor without much difficulty.

He had to step away from the wall in order to allow the light from the window to shine on it. It was so unobtrusive that he might not have noticed it but for the business of the chest. Someone had cut two letters in the wood, using a nail or possibly a pocket-knife. He had seen the letters before, he did not have to ask what they meant or who had written them: WW : William Wylam. He had devised the simple monogram about two months ago for his son's use. There was no longer any doubt. William had been here.

16

He ran all the way back to the entrance hall. At the foot of the stairs leading to the girls' dormitories, two exquisitely dressed figures were standing, evidently the Nawab's personal bodyguards. As he approached, one of them stepped towards him and held a hand palm forwards in his direction.

'Very sorry, *sahib*, but I have been given instructions not to let you go any further. You have been asked to leave. I will take you to the door.'

Christopher was in no mood to argue. He reached for his belt and raised the revolver he had taken from the policeman at Cormac's house. He pointed it straight at the bodyguard's forehead.

'We're going nowhere near the door,' he said. 'Over there,' he ordered, waving the gun in the direction of the living-room. 'Your friend as well. Tell him to move or I'll blow your head off.'

The man knew better than to argue. With his colleague, he made for the living-room door.

'Open it and go inside.'

They did as ordered. Inside the room, the trio of women were still sipping morning tea and nibbling at caraway cake. This time the governess dropped her cup and saucer on to the floor. The begum looked up from her plate, saw what was happening, and gave Christopher a look that was probably the nearest thing to a death sentence in Hasanabad. Moira Carpenter looked like the antithesis of Christian charity reluctantly made flesh. No-one said a word.

Christopher stepped inside only long enough to remove the key from the lock. He closed the door again and locked it, putting the key into his trouser pocket. He wondered if they had had time to warn Carpenter.

Upstairs, he visited each of the rooms in turn. All were cold and empty. Somewhere, a door slammed. There was a brief flutter of voices in the distance, then silence again. At the end of the corridor, a flight of narrow stairs led up to an attic storey. Christopher remembered it had been in the attic that Tsewong had hanged himself.

The stairs led directly to a plain wooden door. Christopher climbed slowly, waiting on each step, his feet patient, his ears straining for a sound. His heart was beating rapidly. He thought he could hear voices beyond the door, but the sound faded and he could not be sure he had heard anything at all. And yet he imagined that, beneath the silence, there was something else.

There was nothing behind the door but a narrow, wood-panelled passageway, a dark tunnel lit by a single bulb. At the end of the passageway was a second door, identical to the first. He advanced cautiously, feeling cramped by the dark walls on either side. A floorboard cracked and he stood still for what seemed an age.

A sound of scraping came from behind the door, a steady, rhythmic sound, muffled and indefinable. *Scrape-scrape*. Then a brief pause. *Scrape-scrape*. Another pause. *Scrape-scrape*. A pause. And so it went on.

Christopher hesitated, listening, trying to work out what the sound could be.

Scrape-scrape. Pause. *Scrape-scrape*.

Set into the door at eye height was a small shutter with a knob, about six inches long by three high. It reminded Christopher of the shutters on prison doors. He thought perhaps the room must be the girls' sick bay, a place where fevers could be isolated or heartaches given room to heal. The monk Tsewong would have been kept here.

Scrape-scrape. The noise came more loudly now.

Christopher put his hand to the knob and drew back the shutter. Through a small glass pane, part of the room came into view. The walls and floor were powdered with light and dust. Through a skylight of marbled glass, sunlight filtered, effortless and slow, into the tiny room. Christopher stepped closer to the glass and put his eye to the aperture.

Immediately opposite, his back turned to Christopher, John Carpenter sat hunched over a low fire. In one hand, he held a long poker which he was dragging mechanically across the top of the grate. It was this that was making the scraping noise. The fire seemed old, a thing of cinders mostly, its few coals grey and smouldering. Here and there, flashes of red struggled for life in the ashes, but the weight of all that greyness about them was too great, and they fell deeper and deeper into oblivion. Carpenter moved the poker in and out of the ashes listlessly, raising from time to time a solitary spark that rose briefly above the cinders and was gone.

But it was not Carpenter that drew Christopher's eyes. Carpenter was peripheral, a side-show to what was happening in the centre of the room. Two people stood there, a man and a girl, a living tableau caught in the angry sunlight. The man was an Indian, but he wore a Savile Row suit and leaned on a silver-headed cane. He was a man of perhaps fifty, small and round and soft. He looked as though someone had taken him off and polished him – like an old spoon in an antique shop, all gleaming and mellow and filled with curious reflections. His eyes were on the girl, watching her with a wild intensity that held him captive.

The girl was naked. A white shift lay on the floor where she had discarded it. Long black hair fell across her shoulders and gently touched the edges of small, shadowed breasts. She was perhaps fifteen or sixteen. Her eyes were shut, as though she were trying to dream the room away, but Carpenter's little nightmare was all about her, sweet and tight and inescapable.

The man reached out a hand to touch her lightly, running soft fingers along her skin, sweeping them against the soft hairs of her forearms. Then he made her turn. Round and round he made her turn, like a dancer, like a tiny mechanical dancer spinning on top of a music-box, to the sound of an old melody. He made her raise her arms above her head and lower them again, watched her breasts rise and fall, admired the smooth line of her throat as she held her head back. There was no sound but the scraping of the poker in the grate. Finally, that too stopped and there was silence. The naked girl turned to music she alone could hear, lost in gardens of amazing symmetry, from which there was no escape. She was the dancer at the edge of the dance, alone and silently turning in a dream.

Christopher opened the door. No-one noticed him enter. Carpenter was lost in contemplation of the embers in the fireplace, the Nawab's attention was all on the girl, and the girl was in a trance.

114

He stood for a long time watching them, waiting for their ritual to end. It was the Nawab who noticed him first, out of the corner of his eye. The little man turned, a look of incredible fury on his face.

'I say! What do you mean bursting in here like this? Who the hell do you think you are? By Jove, I'll have you flogged if you don't leave at once!'

The Nawab had been to Eton and Oxford, where he had studied how to be an Oriental gentleman. Eton had taught him English manners and Oxford how to row. He had taught himself how to treat anyone who was not a Nawab or a Viceroy.

'I would like to speak to the Reverend Carpenter,' said Christopher. 'The matter doesn't concern you, so you can just get out. Before I throw you out.'

'Do you know who you are speaking to? I can have you horse-whipped for this insolence!'

'You aren't in a position to argue,' Christopher snapped. He pointed the revolver at the Nawab. 'And I don't have time. I'll shoot you if I have to. It's entirely up to you.'

The man spluttered and lifted his cane as if to strike Christopher, but he was not fool enough to do it. Still expostulating to himself, he made for the door. As he was leaving, he turned.

'My chaps downstairs will put you in your place. You'll be sorry you were ever born when they're through with you. By God, I'll see you're sorry!'

Christopher slammed the door in his face. He glanced at Carpenter, who had remained seated in front of the fire, then picked the girl's shift from the floor. She was standing absolutely still, her eyes watching him, wondering what was going to happen next.

'Put this on,' he said, holding it out to her.

She took it from him, but remained holding it, as though uncertain what to do.

'Put it on,' he repeated.

She remained unmoving, so he took the shift and pulled it over her head, helping her slip her arms through the sleeves.

'You have to leave,' he said. 'Get away from here. You mustn't stay here, do you understand?'

She looked at him, uncomprehending. He had to make her understand.

'You'll only come to harm here,' he insisted. 'You must go away.'

As though he had not spoken, she began to turn, just as she had turned before, raising and lowering her arms. Christopher snatched at her and slapped her face, trying to bring her to her senses. She looked at him as though nothing had happened.

'Don't you understand?' he shouted. 'This is no place for you. You must leave!'

'Leave?' she said. Her voice quavered. 'Where can I go?' she asked. 'This is my home. There is nowhere else to go. Nowhere.'

'It doesn't matter where you go,' he said. 'Just as long as you get away from this place.'

She looked at him with blank eyes.

'It matters,' she said almost inaudibly.

'Leave her, Wylam. She understands it all better than you ever will.' Carpenter had got up from his seat in front of the fire. He came across to the girl and put an arm round her shoulders. They walked together to the door, the missionary and his charge, while he talked to her in a low voice, inaudible to Christopher.

Carpenter opened the door, said something further to the girl, and let her out. He watched her walk away down the narrow passage, then closed the door and turned to face Christopher.

'Tell me, Mr Wylam,' he said. 'Do you believe in God?'

The question seemed bizarre and out of place to Christopher.

'I don't see what God has got to do with this,' he said. 'I told you before, I haven't come here to discuss theology.'

'Oh, but Mr Wylam, don't you see? It all goes back to theology in the end. It all goes back to God. How could it be otherwise? But if you are not yourself a believer, you may find it hard to understand.'

'I'm not here to understand. I'm here to find my son. He was here in this orphanage. For all I know, he may still be here.'

Carpenter went over to his seat by the fire and sat down. He looked tired and unhappy.

'What makes you think he was here?' he asked.

'I found his initials carved into the wall behind a chest in the sick bay. So let's stop playing games. Martin Cormac was killed sometime this morning because he had information about you and your activities. Until something happens to convince me otherwise, I'm holding you responsible.'

116

The look of shock on the missionary's face seemed genuine enough.

'Cormac? Dead? What do you mean? I know nothing about any killing.'

Christopher explained. As he did so, the blood drained from Carpenter's face. The look of horror grew more pronounced.

'I swear I know nothing whatever about this,' he stammered. 'I swear it to you. I know about your son, yes. I know about the monk, Tsewong, yes. But this other thing, I swear I had no hand in it. You must believe me.'

'Tell me about my son. Where is he?'

Carpenter looked away.

'He's not here. You are right: he was. But he left a week ago.'

'Who is he with? Where have they taken him?'

'Mishig took him, the Mongol Agent. They left for Tibet. I think he planned to travel over the Sebu-la.'

'Where are they headed?'

Carpenter shook his head. He looked directly at Christopher.

'I don't know,' he answered. 'They're going to Tibet: that's all I know.'

'Are they going to Dorje-la? Is that their destination?'

The missionary seemed agitated. He shook his head vigorously.

'I don't know where you mean. I've never heard of a place called Dorje-la.'

'You sent some of your children there. Never girls, just boys. The monk Tsewong came from there, didn't he? He was sent here by the Dorje Lama.'

Carpenter took a deep breath. He was shaking.

'You know a great deal, Mr Wylam. Who are you? What do you want? What's so important about your son?'

'I thought you might tell me that.'

'I only kept him here until they were ready for the journey. Mishig told me nothing. Tsewong told me nothing. You must believe me!'

'Where is Dorje-la?'

'I don't know!'

'Who is the Dorje Lama?'

'The abbot of Dorje-la! That's all I know, I swear.'

Christopher paused. Just what did Carpenter know? What was

117

he prepared to do, who was he prepared to sell, for a little influence, a little funding?

'And you know nothing about Martin Cormac's death?'

'Nothing! I swear.'

'Did they pay you?'

'Pay me?'

'To keep William here. To hand him over to Mishig.'

The missionary shook his head.

'Not money. Promises. Promises of help. Listen, you must try to take the broader view. I have important work to do, the Lord's work. There are souls to be saved. Do you understand that? They are going to hell, all these millions, with no Saviour to redeem them. I can rescue them, I can give them Paradise. Don't you see? The Lord is using us: you, me, my orphans, your son. We're all his tools. It's mysterious, the way He works is mysterious. Unless you understand that, you will understand nothing. I do what I do for His sake, for the sake of His work.'

Christopher reached out and grabbed hold of the man. He pulled him out of his chair to his feet.

'You sell little girls for God? You sell boys to convert the heathen?'

'You don't understand . . . !'

Christopher threw him back into the chair.

'Have they harmed him? I pray God they haven't harmed him. For your sake.'

The Scotsman shook his head violently, protesting.

'No! He's safe, he's well. I swear it! They haven't harmed him. They won't harm him. They want him for something. They want him safe. He's important to them. Believe me, he's safe.'

Christopher could not bear to touch the man again. There was nothing he could say to him, nothing that would bring back Martin Cormac or draw William an inch nearer to him.

'When you have your mission in Lhasa,' Christopher said, 'remember what it cost. Think about it every day. Every time you hear the trumpets in the temples drowning your prayers. And ask yourself if it was worth it. Ask yourself if God is worth that much.'

He opened the door and went out slowly. It closed behind him with a dull click.

Carpenter looked at the remains of the fire: no phoenix, no

bright feathers, no flurry of sudden wings – just ashes crumbling into dust. He glanced up and caught sight of the hook in the ceiling. The sunlight lay on it like gold leaf. He still had the girdle that the monk had used: he had not given it to Cormac. It was in a drawer in the corner. The chair was just high enough to allow him to reach the hook.

17

There was a policeman at the rest-house door. He looked as though he had always been there, a fixture, a solidity in the flux of the busy street. He wore the regulation blue uniform with a dark *pugaree* bearing his divisional badge. Huge moustaches sagged over and round a humourless mouth. He stood rigidly, like a tin soldier on parade. Christopher knew he was waiting for him. Waiting and planning a promotion based on his arrest. He carried a thick riot stick and looked as though he knew how to use it.

Smoothly, Christopher slipped into the shadows on the side of the street. A buffalo cart screened him further from the eyes of the policeman. He became invisible. Until now, he thought, he had been stumbling about like a beginner. It was time he grew up again. Breathing deeply, he scanned the street rapidly in both directions. He had to leave Kalimpong now. But he had left his equipment and money in the rest-house, the latter well hidden beneath a floorboard.

There was a back entrance. Slipping through a maze of stinking alleyways, he made his way unobserved to the small, rubbish-choked courtyard at the rear of the house. As he expected, the police had forgotten to post anyone there. Cautiously, he tried the rickety door. It was unlocked. He slipped inside and found himself in a gloomy passage at the end of which a dusty shaft of sunlight beckoned. He closed the door gently; the stagnant air of the rest-house began to fill his lungs. The smell of rancid butter permeated the place.

The house was quiet, and he succeeded in making his way unchallenged to his room. The room itself was unguarded. He let himself in with the simple iron key.

The man in the chair showed neither surprise nor welcome as Christopher entered. Christopher closed the door gently and put the key back in his pocket. He saw that the room had been given a

120

thorough going-over again, but he did not think his visitor had been responsible. The man was dressed in the robes of a Tibetan monk, but he was clearly no ordinary *trapa*. His clothes, his bearing, his eyes, his lips all gave token of a man of some standing. His face was badly scarred by smallpox. He stared at Christopher without blinking.

'Who are you?' Christopher asked. 'What do you want?'

The monk regarded Christopher with an intense scrutiny that went far beyond the merely curious. His gaze tore away skin and scar tissue, exploring living flesh.

'I want nothing,' he said in a soft voice. His English was clear but stilted. 'But you,' he went on, 'are in quest of something. I wonder what it is you want.'

'If you want nothing, what are you doing here?' asked Christopher. The monk's gaze unnerved him. Being in the same room with him unnerved him.

'To warn you,' said the monk, very quietly.

'Warn me?'

The gecko on the wall shifted in its search for shadows and concealment.

'You have been asking questions. Indelicate questions. Improper questions. Questions that have no answers you can understand. You are holy, I cannot touch you. But already one man has died. I will carry his blood on my hands. Do you understand? Into the next world and beyond. You are holy for me, but others can harm you. I know you do not understand. It is better for you that you do not. But this is my advice: leave all thought of the *lama* who died here. Leave all thought of your son. Leave all thought of revenge. Go home. All other ways are closed. The gods are only playing now. Leave before they grow tired of games.'

What did he mean, 'you are holy for me?' Christopher remembered the thin man in Hexham. 'I am ordered not to harm you,' he had said.

'Are you telling me you killed Martin Cormac?' Christopher took a step towards the monk. The man did not move.

'You do not understand,' the monk whispered. Christopher thought he could hear flies buzzing in the room. He could see sunlight spilling on to white, disordered sheets. He felt suffocated.

'I understand,' he shouted above the buzzing.

The monk shook his head.

'You understand nothing,' he whispered.

Christopher stepped nearer, but something held him back from actually attacking the man.

'Please,' said the monk. 'Do not try to harm me. If you do, I will be forced to prevent you. And I do not want that on my conscience. I have put blood on my *karma* today. But you are holy: do not make me touch you.'

Inarticulate anger grew in Christopher, but the very placidity of the monk made it hard for him to strike him. The man stood up, his robes falling elegantly into place around him.

'I have given my warning,' he said. 'Leave Kalimpong. Go back to England. If you seek to go further, I cannot be responsible for what will happen to you.'

He passed Christopher on his way to the door, brushing him with the edge of his outer robe.

Christopher never knew what happened next. He felt the touch of the monk's robe against his hand. He remembered the touch of Cormac's mosquito-net against his bare skin and felt a surge of anger rise in him. The monk's placidity was nothing: he wanted to strike him, to drag him down to some sort of justice. He reached out, intending to haul the man round, at the very least to confront him. Perhaps he had intended to strike him, he could not be sure.

All he felt was the monk's hand on his neck, a gentle touch without violence or pain. Then the world dissolved and he felt himself falling, falling endlessly into a lightless, colourless abyss out of which nothing ever returned.

He dreamed he was in silence and that the silence clung to him softly, like wax. The wax melted and he was walking through empty corridors. On either side, vast classrooms stood empty and silent; chalk-dust hung like bruised white pollen in long beams of sunlight. He was climbing stairs that stretched above him towards infinity. Then he was on a landing that took him into another corridor. From somewhere, he could hear the sound of buzzing. He passed through the first door he came to and found himself in a long white dormitory drenched in silence. Two rows of rusted hooks had been screwed into the ceiling over the central aisle.

From each hook a rope was suspended, and at the end of each rope the body of a young girl was hanging. They all wore white

122

shifts and their backs were turned to him, and their hair was long and black and silken. He watched in horror as the ropes twisted and the bodies turned. The sound of buzzing filled the room, but there were no flies. A door slammed suddenly, sending echoes throughout the building.

'Wake up, *sahib*! Wake up!'

He struggled to open his eyes, but they were glued together.

'You can't lie here, *sahib*! Please get up!'

He made a final effort and his eyes opened painlessly.

The monk had gone. The boy Lhaten was bending over him, a look of concern on his face. He was lying on the floor of his room, flat on his back.

'The monk told me I would find you here, *sahib*. What happened?'

Christopher shook his head to clear it. It felt full of cotton wool. Cotton wool mixed with iron filings.

'I don't know,' he said. 'How long have I been here?'

'Not long, *sahib*. At least, I don't think so.'

'Lhaten, are there still police outside?'

'One man. They say they are looking for you. Have you done something, *sahib*?'

He shook his head again. The cotton wool was feeling a little more like cement.

'No, Lhaten. But it won't be easy to explain. Can you help me up?'

'Of course.'

The boy put an arm under Christopher's neck and raised him to a sitting position.

With the boy's help, Christopher made his way to the chair. He felt more winded than anything, as though all the air had been forced out of him suddenly. Whatever the monk had done, it had rendered him unconscious briefly but left him otherwise unharmed. He had often heard of such techniques, but until now had never witnessed them used.

'Do the police know I'm here, Lhaten?'

The boy shook his head. He was sixteen, seventeen perhaps. By his accent, Christopher guessed he was Nepalese.

'I need to get out without being seen,' Christopher confided in the boy. 'Can you help me?'

'No problem, *sahib*. There's no-one watching the back. But where will you go? They say there are police everywhere, looking for you. You must have done something very wicked.' The boy seemed pleased by that possibility.

Christopher tried to shake his head, but his neck refused to join in.

'I've done nothing, Lhaten,' he said. 'But a man has been killed. I found him.'

'And the police think you killed him?' Lhaten raised his eyebrows and whistled. Christopher remembered that William used precisely the same gestures to express amazement.

'Yes. But I didn't. Do you believe me?'

Lhaten shrugged.

'Does it matter? No doubt he was a very bad man.'

Christopher frowned.

'No, Lhaten – he wasn't. And it does matter. It was Dr Cormac. He was with me last night. Do you remember?'

This seemed to sober Lhaten up. He knew Cormac. The doctor had treated him on several occasions. He had liked him.

'Don't worry, *sahib*. I'll get you out. But you must have somewhere to go.'

Christopher hesitated. He wasn't sure if he could trust the boy. But already he was on his own. Nobody in London would vouch for him. Nobody in Delhi would want to interfere. He needed the boy's help badly.

'Lhaten,' he began, knowing he was taking a risk. 'I want to leave Kalimpong. I have to get out of India.'

'Of course. You should not stay in India. Where do you want to go?'

Christopher hesitated again. If the police questioned the boy . . .

'You can trust me, *sahib*.'

What did the boy want? Money?

'If it's money you . . .'

'Please!' A look of genuine pain crossed the boy's face. 'I don't want money. I want to help you, that's all. Where do you want to go?'

Christopher realized he was wasting time. The police could return to his room at any moment to make a further check on his

124

belongings – he guessed it was they who had given the room its second going-over.

'I want to cross the Sebu-la,' he said in a low voice. 'Into Tibet. I want to leave tonight if possible.'

Lhaten looked at him in disbelief. It was as if he had expressed a wish to visit the moon.

'Surely you mean the Nathu-la, *sahib*. The Sebu-la is closed. It will remain closed all winter. Even the Nathu-la and the passes beyond it may be closed again if the weather changes.'

'No, I mean the Sebu-la. Along the Tista valley past Lachen, then through the passes. I need a guide. Someone who knows that route.'

'Perhaps you're not feeling well, *sahib*. That blow last night. And today . . .'

'Damn it, I know what I'm doing!' Christopher snapped.

'Yes. I'm sorry, *sahib*.'

'That's all right. I'm sorry I shouted, Lhaten. I must sound a bit doolaly, eh?'

The boy grinned.

'Thought so. Well, do you know anyone who'd be fool enough to take me at least that far? I wouldn't want him to come across with me. Just to take me to the Sebu-la. I'll pay well.'

'Yes. I know someone.'

'Excellent. Do you think you can get me to him without being seen?'

Lhaten grinned again.

'Very easy.'

Christopher stood up. His head spun.

'Let's go, then.'

'No need, *sahib*, your guide is here already. I can take you to the Sebu-la. Maybe I'm a little doolaly as well.'

Christopher sat down again. He felt irritated by the boy, though he knew he ought not to be.

'Bloody right you are. I'm not going on a picnic. I'm trying to get into Tibet without an alarm going off half-way across the Himalayas. The main purpose of the exercise is to get there in one piece. I need a proper guide, not a rest-house pot-boy.'

Lhaten's face fell. It was almost as though Christopher had slapped him.

'I'm sorry if . . .' Christopher began, but Lhaten interrupted him.

'I am not a pot-boy. I am eighteen. And I am a proper guide. My family are Sherpas. We know the mountains the way farmers know their fields. I have crossed the Sebu-la with my father many times.'

'In winter?'

The boy hung his head.

'No,' he said. 'Not in winter. No-one crosses the Sebu-la in winter. No-one.'

'I am going to cross the Sebu-la in winter, Lhaten.'

'Without my help, *sahib*, you will not even make it to the first pass.'

Lhaten was right. In this weather, Christopher would need more than just luck and his own limited experience to find and cross the Sebu-la. At this point, he wasn't even thinking about what he would do when he got there. One thing was certain: he could not attempt the journey by way of the Chumbi valley and the more popular route to the east. There were sentries everywhere. All the caravans and isolated travellers were stopped and examined closely. If he was fortunate, he would merely be turned back. More probably, his visitor of half an hour ago and his chums, whoever they might be, would be waiting for him – and the monk had made it clear that his friends would have no compunction about harming him.

'Why do you want to risk your skin on a journey like this, Lhaten?' Christopher asked.

The boy shrugged.

'This is my third winter in this place, *sahib*. How many winters could you spend here?'

Christopher looked at the room, at the shabby furniture, at the gecko sleeping on the wall.

'Aren't you frightened to make such a journey in this weather?'

Lhaten grinned, then looked more serious than ever.

'Very frightened.'

That decided Christopher. He would take the boy. The last thing he needed on this journey was someone who didn't know the meaning of fear.

18

They were lost. For two days now, they had been battling against the snow and the wind, but there were no signs of the *chörten* that Tobchen said would mark the entrance to the valley of Gharoling. They had lost the pony. It had fallen into a deep crevasse the day before, taking with it most of their remaining provisions. He could not forget the sound of the dying animal, trapped beyond reach, screaming in pain: the sound had carried in the stillness and followed them for miles.

The old man was growing visibly weaker. Not only physically, but in his mind. His will-power was slackening, and the boy knew he was near the point of surrender. Several times he had had to rouse Tobchen from a reverie or a sleep out of which he did not want to be wakened. Sometimes they climbed up into banks of freezing cloud, where everything was blotted out in the all-consuming whiteness. He felt that the old man wanted to walk on into the cloud and disappear, so he held his hand tightly and willed him to go on. Without him, he would be lost forever.

'Will the Lady Chindamani come to Gharoling, Tobchen?' he asked.

The old man sighed.

'I do not think so, my lord. Pemá Chindamani must remain at Dorje-la. That is her place.'

'But she said we would meet again.'

'If she said it, it will happen.'

'But not at Gharoling?'

'I do not know, lord.'

And the old man continued to plod on into the blizzard, muttering the words of the *mantra, om mani padme hum,* like an old woman ploughing in her field. Yes, that was it. He was just like an old woman ploughing.

*

He lost the old man on the seventh day, early, between waking and first halt. There was no warning. Tobchen had gone in front as usual, into a bank of cloud, telling the boy to follow slowly. At first all had seemed normal, then the cloud had lifted and the way ahead was empty. On his left, a sheer precipice plunged away from the path, its lower depths hidden in cloud. He called the old man's name loudly, pleadingly, for over an hour, but only dull echoes answered him. A ray of sunlight bounced off the peak of the tall mountain opposite. Suddenly Samdup felt terribly alone.

He was ten years old. Tobchen said he was many centuries old, but here, trapped in snow and mist, he felt no more than a child. Without the old man, he knew he was finished. He had no idea which way to turn: ahead or back, it was all the same to him. The mountains seemed to mock him. Even if he was centuries old, what was that to them? Only the gods were older than they.

He carried enough food in his bag to last him for about two days, if he was frugal. If only he could see the *chörten* or a prayer-flag or hear the sound of a temple-horn in the distance. But all he saw were pinnacles of ice and all he heard was the wind rising.

He spent the night in the dark crying, because he was cold and alone and frightened. He wished he had never left Dorje-la Gompa, that he was there now with Pemá Chindamani and his other friends. No-one had asked him if he wanted to be a *trulku*. They had just come to his parents' house seven years ago and put him through some tests and told him who he was. He had liked living with his parents. True, it was nothing near so grand as life in his *labrang* at Dorje-la, but nobody had made him study or expected him to sit through long ceremonials, dressed in silk and fidgeting.

When the night ended, the world was shrouded in mist. He stayed where he was, feeling the damp seep into his bones, afraid to move in case there was another precipice. He knew he was going to die, and in his childish way he resented it. Death was no stranger to him, of course. He had seen the old bodies of the abbots in their golden *chörtens* on the top floor of the *gompa*, where no-one could stand above them. One of his first acts at Dorje-la had been to preside over the funeral of one of the old monks, a Lob-pon named Lobsang Geshe. And everywhere, on the walls and ceilings of the monastery, the dead danced like children. From the age of three, they had been his playmates. But he was still afraid.

128

Time had no meaning in the mist, and he had no idea what part of the day it was when he first heard the footsteps. He listened, petrified. There were demons in the passes. Demons and *ro-lang*, the standing corpses of men struck by lightning, who walked the mountains with eyes closed, unable to die and be reborn. In the long nights of the *labrang*, Pemá Chindamani had entranced him with spooky tales, and he had listened pop-eyed in the candlelight. But here, in the mist, her stories returned to freeze his blood.

A figure appeared, tall, shadowy, swathed in black. The boy pressed himself back against the rock, praying that Lord Chenrezi or the Lady Tara would come to his protection. He muttered the mantras Tobchen had taught him. *Om Ara Pa Tsa Na Dhi*, he recited, using the *mantra* of Manjushri he had recently learned.

'Rinpoche, is that you?' came a muffled voice. The boy closed his eyes tightly and recited the *mantra* faster than ever.

'Dorje Samdup Rinpoche? This is Thondrup Chophel. I have come from Dorje-la in search of you.'

He felt a hand on his arm and almost bit his tongue in fear.

'Please, Rinpoche, don't be afraid. Open your eyes. It's me, Thondrup Chophel. I've come to take you back.'

At last the boy conquered his fear and allowed himself to look.

It was not Thondrup Chophel. It was not anyone he knew. It was a demon in black, with a fearsome, painted face that scowled at him. He leapt up, thinking to run. A hand gripped him by the arm and held him fast. He looked round at the demon, panicking. The creature lifted a hand to its face and removed a mask. It was a leather mask, like one of those the travellers had worn three days earlier. Underneath was the familiar face of Thondrup Chophel.

'I'm sorry I frightened you, lord,' the man said. He paused. 'Where is Geshe Tobchen?'

The little Rinpoche explained.

'Then let us be grateful to Lord Chenrezi that he guided me to you. Look, even the mist is lifting. When we have eaten, it will be time to leave.'

They ate in silence at first, plain tea and *tsampa* as always. Thondrup Chophel had never been a talkative man. The boy had never liked him: he was the Geku of his college in the monastery, the official responsible for disciplining the monks. Samdup remembered him in his heavy robe with padded shoulders, striding between the rows of shaven heads at services in the great temple-hall of Dorje-la. He never disciplined Samdup personally – that had been the task of Geshe Tobchen, the boy's *jegten gegen*, his chief guardian and teacher. But Thondrup Chophel had often given him fierce looks and was never backward about reporting him to Tobchen.

'Have you come to take me to Gharoling?' the boy asked.

'Gharoling? Why should we go to Gharoling, lord? I have come to take you back to Dorje-la Gompa.'

'But Geshe Tobchen was taking me to Gharoling, to study with Geshe Tsering Rinpoche. He said I was not to return to Dorje-la. Not under any circumstances.'

The monk shook his head.

'Please do not argue, lord. I have been instructed to bring you back. The abbot is concerned for you. Geshe Tobchen did not have his permission to take you away, let alone bring you to Gharoling of all places. You are too young to understand. But you must return with me. You have no choice.'

'But Geshe Tobchen warned me . . .'

'Yes? What did he warn you of?'

'Of . . . danger.'

'Where? At Dorje-la?'

The boy nodded. He felt unhappy, unable to defend his teacher's wishes.

'You must be mistaken, lord. There is no danger at Dorje-la. You will be safe there.'

'And if I choose to go to Gharoling myself?'

He saw the anger rise in the Geku. He was a powerful man with a short temper. Samdup had often seen him mete out punishment.

'You would die before you reached Gharoling. This is not the path. Gharoling is far from here. I have come to take you back to Dorje-la. There will be no argument. You have no choice.'

The boy looked into the mist. The world was indeed a terrible place. Animals and men fell into its empty places and did not return. If he stayed here, he too would fall and be swallowed up. Geshe Tobchen would have known what to do. He had always known. But Geshe Tobchen was gone into the mist. There was no choice: he would have to return to Dorje-la.

PART TWO
Incarnation

'I remained to dream the nightmare out to the end.'

Joseph Conrad, *Heart of Darkness*

Dorje-La

19

They left Kalimpong late at night, when it was fully dark and not even a glimmer of moonlight could betray them. Only the barking of stray dogs marked their passage. On a balcony somewhere, hidden from them, a woman was sobbing into the darkness. In the Knox Homes, behind the church, bed-time prayers were over; a little girl lay sleepless in her bed, listening to the dismal cry of a screech-owl.

Christopher had spent the rest of the day in a disused outhouse while Lhaten bought supplies – a few here, a few there, so as not to arouse suspicion. He had purchased a little food, mostly *tsampa* or roasted barley flour, some butter, some tea, some strips of dried beef, and salt. Christopher had also given him a list of items whose purpose Lhaten could not guess: a bottle of dark hair-dye, iodine, walnut juice, some lemons, and a jar of glue. He also changed a little money, giving *rupees* for Tibetan *trangkas* at the rate of one for five. At his own discretion, Lhaten had further changed some of the *trangkas* for smaller copper coins: only a very wealthy man or a *pee-ling* would carry that many silver *trangkas*, and he didn't think his new friend would want to be identified as either.

At the Post Office in Prince Albert Street, Lhaten sent a telegram to Winterpole: 'News of Uncle William. Complications here make it impossible stay Auntie's. Friends suggest camping in hills. May be out of touch for next month.' He also left a more detailed sealed message at the British Trade Agency, for Frazer to transmit to London by a more secure route. It was to let the folks at home know how young Christopher was getting on in distant India, and it asked Winterpole to get Delhi CID moving on an investigation of Carpenter and the Knox Homes.

Before leaving, Christopher transformed himself. Shivering, he stripped to the skin and daubed himself liberally with a mixture made from the walnut juice and iodine. When the dark stain had dried, he dressed again, putting on heavy clothes suitable for the conditions ahead. Over these, he draped an ensemble of evil-smelling rags and much-patched cast-offs that Lhaten had dredged up from somewhere unspeakable. Christopher had not asked where – he preferred not to know. The hair-dye worked well enough for something labelled: 'Phatak's World-Renouned Hare-die and Restore, Effektive against Greyness of Hed, Baldiness, and Skalp Itchingness.' There was enough left in the bottle for a touch-up every week or so – provided Christopher's hair hadn't all fallen out by then. The last touch was the most difficult: he squeezed a few drops of lemon directly into his eyes. It stung like hell, but when he was able to look in the mirror again, he could tell that his eyes had lost most of their blueness and were now dark enough to match his skin and hair.

They travelled as far as they could that night, to be well away from Kalimpong by morning. Their first destination was Namchi, about seven miles to the north-west. In the darkness, without sign or token, they passed over the border between British India and Sikkim. Christopher knew that more than a physical frontier had been crossed. The mountains that lay ahead were in the mind as much as in nature.

They passed Namchi soon after midnight. It was a collection of bamboo houses, silent, unguarded, sleeping. Christopher could not tell how Lhaten found his way in the darkness. The path went upwards, sometimes steeply, across damp meadows and once through a patch of forest. The forest would grow thicker later on, before they left the treeline and entered the pass country.

On Lhaten's advice, they made camp about three miles from Namchi. Christopher felt wide awake and wanted to go on, but Lhaten insisted they rest.

'You will be tired tomorrow, and we still have a long way to go before we leave the villages behind. Even if you can't sleep, you should rest. I'm going to sleep. I've had a tiring day . . . and I know what's ahead.'

It was as if Lhaten had shed a false skin since leaving Kalimpong. There, he had been obsequious, almost servile, constantly calling Christopher 'sahib' and behaving in all respects as a member of a subject race should behave towards his master. The further they moved away from the town, however, the more some innate

136

sense of independence asserted itself in him. He used the word *sahib* far less frequently and with increasing irony coupled, perhaps, with a little affection. Christopher still wondered why the boy had volunteered to act as guide to a murder suspect. But it was evident from the start that he had not been boasting when he said he had done this sort of thing before.

Christopher made an effort to sleep, but he managed nothing more than a fitful doze, out of which he would start from time to time to hear Lhaten breathing evenly beside him. The ground was hard and the air bitterly cold. It would soon warm up during the day, but that was no comfort now. For Christopher, the images of the day before were still too close and fresh to shut out from his thoughts.

The sky turned hazily purple, then scarlet and gold, as the sun returned above the hills of Bhutan. Lhaten woke with the light. He wanted to make good progress today, to get as far away as possible from the beaten track. At a distance, the *pee-ling* might pass as a Nepali traveller, but he did not want the disguise put to the test close up. Apart from anything, Christopher's height would draw unwelcome attention. And there was nothing they could do about that.

At Damtung, the road forked. On their left, a path led to the Buddhist monastery of Pemayangtse, and on the right a broader road began to descend toward the River Tista. This was the main road to Gantok, the Sikkimese capital.

'We've got to take the Gantok road, *sahib*. No choice. If you're seen, leave the talking to me. I'll say you're dumb.'

The descent was steep. At the bottom, the Tista ran high, still swollen from recent rains. It was a large river, but it had the tight violence of a mountain stream churning through steep gorges. They bypassed the villages of Temi and Tarko, like men in a hurry, eager to get to Gantok by market day. The heat became unbearable. By noon, they were walking stripped to the waist. The cold of the night was like a dream or a distant memory.

All around them, the dark, humid jungle closed in with suffocating intimacy. It touched them as they passed, with fingers of damp green leaves and tendrils that hung from moss-covered boughs, snake-like and slimy to the touch. Giant ferns struggled for space with bamboos and palms. Vines and creepers twisted themselves

137

round everything in sight. Orchids grew in profusion, white grave-flowers heavy with a drugged and sickly scent. In the shadows, bright-patterned snakes glided through tangled and rotten under-growth. The air was moist and heavy and full of corruption. They breathed it reluctantly, like men in a place they know to be full of contagion.

Here in the forest, life and death were inextricable: things died and rotted and provided food for the profusion of new life that sprang up everywhere. Life seethed around them, hot and green and restless. There was a fever upon everything: insects, flowers, birds, snakes, animals – all were burning with it.

Once, Christopher saw a horde of butterflies quivering in a sunbeam close to the ground. Their wings caught fire: reds and blues and yellows spun like fragments of stained glass in a dark cathedral. But when he approached more closely, he saw that they had battened on the decaying body of a small animal, on which they seemed to be feeding in some fashion. On another occasion, Lhaten showed him an isolated flower of great beauty, a scarlet jewel hanging from a long branch: and above it, secreted in darkness, spun about the flower's stem, was a thick spider's web in which dying insects, attracted by the red petals, struggled helplessly.

From the beginning, they were plagued by leeches. Like short, thin earthworms, the little creatures dropped on them at every available opportunity, insinuating themselves through the narrow-est of apertures until they reached the naked flesh they so coveted. Once there, they would suck blood until sated. It was useless to pull them off – if they snapped, the mouth would remain intact, if torn away, they would leave a suppurating wound. Every few miles, Lhaten and Christopher would stop and apply small bags of salt dipped in water and the leeches would shrivel and fall away.

For much of the time, they walked in silence. The heat and the stifling air made speech a luxury. There were bright-plumaged birds to speak for them, and frogs and monkeys and all the chattering denizens of their greenhouse world. The jungle itself wove a spell over them, sucking words from their tongues as the leeches sucked blood from their veins.

But at night when they stopped to sleep, they would whisper in

138

the darkness while beasts of prey stalked their victims and the ripe flowers gave up their perfumes to the night.

'Did you fight in the war, *sahib*? In the Great War? Did you see tanks and aeroplanes?'

'No, Lhaten. I saw none of those things. I was here in India. There were spies, German spies. They wanted to bring the war here, to take India away from us.'

'From you. They wanted to take India from you.'

'Yes, of course. But not to give back to the Indians. They wanted it for themselves. There would have been a German Raj.'

'Would that have made a difference?'

Christopher pondered. For the British, yes; of course. But for the Indians? Or Nepalese like Lhaten? He would have liked to say 'Yes' to that as well, but he felt no conviction and could not say it.

'Did you catch Germans in India?'

'Yes.'

'Did you kill them?'

'Some of them. The rest were put in prison.'

'Because they wanted to conquer India?'

'Yes.'

'Like the British?'

'Yes.'

In the darkness, something moved. An inarticulate cry was followed by the fluttering of wings. Predators and victims came and went in an intricate night-time game.

On the third day, they stumbled across the ruins of a temple in a weed-choked clearing. Ivy worshipped the fallen images of Shiva and Vishnu after its own fashion, with slow and intimate fingers. Eveywhere, stone lay upon fallen stone, cracked and twisted by rain and heat and the green creeping flesh of the jungle.

Christopher stepped inside the clearing, drawn by morbid curiosity. But Lhaten hung back, unwilling to set foot within a place so long abandoned. He watched Christopher walk from moss-covered stone to moss-covered stone, his fingers tracing ancient carvings and forgotten inscriptions. He glanced fearfully at the strange gods, leaning at crazy angles in the grass. He watched a black snake glide through the fingers of Shiva like a living rod in the god's hand.

'You should not go there, *sahib*,' he called from the trees, his

139

obsequiousness returning through fear. 'There are bad spirits in this place. You should apologize and go, *sahib*.'

High up, in the treetops, a bird screeched once and was silent. Here, in the vicinity of the ruins, the jungle seemed quieter, as though this was the heart of some ancient silence. Christopher turned and saw Lhaten beckoning to him from the side of the clearing, fear visible on his face.

'It's all right, Lhaten,' he shouted, but his voice sounded flat and coarse and out of place. On a low wall to his left, he could make out the figures of men and women making love, their limbs softened by the remorseless green moss. Nothing stirred. There was no breeze, no freshening wind to move the leaves. At his feet, the broken hand of a statue clutched at the moist air. Christopher felt the walls of the jungle close in on him. He wanted to get on suddenly, to break away from this place and breathe the air of the mountains. Wordlessly, he rejoined Lhaten. They skirted the clearing and pushed on through the undergrowth, heading north.

That night in the darkness, Lhaten returned to his questioning.

'There are no Germans now, are there, *sahib*?'

'In India, you mean?'

'Yes.'

'I don't think so.'

'The British and the Germans are good friends now. Is that right?'

Christopher shrugged.

'I don't know about "good", but we have made peace with one another.'

'So you are not looking for Germans.'

'No, Lhaten. I'm not looking for Germans.'

'Who are you looking for?'

Christopher wished they could light a fire. How many more nights of this darkness would there be?

'I have a son,' he said. 'A boy of ten called William. Someone kidnapped him. He was brought to Kalimpong. But they've taken him further now – into Tibet, across the Sebu-la.'

Lhaten was silent for a while.

'You have spoken about this to the Reverend Carpenter Sahib?' he asked at last.

'Why should I talk to him?'

140

'Because he knows about such things. About boys who disappear. Girls who are never seen again. He is a very religious man. A very Christian man – don't you think, *sahib*?'

'What do you know about the Knox Homes, Lhaten?' Christopher remembered the boy's original reaction to his enquiry about the place.

'It is a place where they keep children. And sometimes the children leave and go elsewhere. A very Christian place.'

'Do many people know about this, Lhaten? That the Reverend Carpenter sells boys and girls to rich customers?'

Lhaten nodded. 'Some people know, yes. But the Reverend Carpenter is a very holy man, a very good man. We are all very grateful for his Christian charity. If I had told you when you first came that children disappeared, would you have believed me? If your own son had not been one, would you have gone to look for them?'

Christopher shivered. The boy was right. Hypocrisy had more allies than any other vice.

'Where are they taking your son?' asked Lhaten.

Christopher knew the answer, or at least he was reasonably sure he did.

'Have you ever heard of a place called Dorje-la?' he asked.

Only the jungle answered.

'Lhaten, I asked if you had heard of somewhere called Dorje-la.'

The thin piping of a bat echoed nearby.

'I think it is time for sleep, *sahib*,' Lhaten said at last. He did not answer Christopher's question.

20

They crossed the river on a shaky bridge at Shamdong – three
bamboo poles across the icy torrent. The jungle gave way abruptly
to more open country. By the sixth day, they had reached seven
thousand feet and the climate had started to change. It was no
longer warm. On the mountain-tops, now visible from time to
time, snow fell in broken patterns. Shadows shifted on the distant
peaks, as though shelves of ice were cracking and breaking away.
Grey and white clouds gathered and dispersed above them,
bringing a chill, drizzling rain that fell in cold spasms. They took
their mountain clothing out of the rolls on their backs and put it
on.

Christopher's heart felt heavy. Not even Lhaten's banter and
laughter could dispel the gloom that had fallen over him. He
looked up at the mountains, watching the shadows move behind
the snow, and he shivered as though he were already there, in that
dark solitude.

They passed deserted bamboo houses, abandoned for the winter.
Sometimes they would shelter in one. Sometimes there was nothing
but rain for miles. They saw almost no-one, for they gave a wide
berth to any villages or clusters of huts that fell across their path.
Those few travellers they did meet they ignored, walking on
huddled and unresponsive into the driving rain.

After Tsöntang, the river branched, becoming the Lachung on
the right and the Lachen on the left. A soft dank mist filled the
narrow Lachen valley. Without speaking, Lhaten led the way into
it, picking his path nervously between stones and clumps of *duk-
shing*, a poisonous weed that seemed ubiquitous. On the following
day, the mist lifted and by evening they saw the first real signs that
they were close to the passes: patches of ice and unmelted snow lay
in pockets across the valley floor.

The next morning, flakes of icy snow began to fall from a leaden
sky. They trudged on in silence, each thinking his own thoughts.

Lhaten looked worried, but he said nothing to Christopher. The journey was proving harder than he had expected, and he knew that the going would get much worse up ahead. And if the weather deteriorated any more, every further step they took would bring them nearer to the point of no return. Calculating when they reached that point was the single most important thing he had to do.

Not only that, but they were getting close to the critical altitude of twelve thousand feet, beyond which further ascent could prove dangerous or even fatal. Christopher had assured him he had been well above that height more than once. But a man changes: even the heart of a fit man might not stand the strain.

Night descended and they were lost in a huddle of cold and blackness. They could feel the snowflakes descending, slow and soft and deadly, cold presences from another world. They were twelve miles above Lachen village, at the extremity of things. Beyond them remained only Tangu, the last village before they entered the passes. If the weather and the gods allowed them entry.

The steep climb from Lachen had brought them to the critical height. They would camp here and see how Christopher fared before deciding to proceed or not. If the strain of altitude proved too great, they would have to move back down as quickly as possible. Even a day's delay could prove fatal.

They pitched their tiny yak-hair tent in a sheltered position near the valley wall. In the night, Lhaten tossed and turned, unable to sleep. The boy was worried. He had not been certain at first, but for the past twenty-four hours he had been sure: they were being followed. They had been followed from at least as far as Nampak, soon after the jungle ended. In all probability, their pursuers – he was sure there were at least two – had been with them in the forest as well, but he had not been aware of them then.

Christopher slept uneasily while the snow fell in uninterrupted torrents, like white petals in a dark and noiseless spring. Inside, the tent was hot, sealed tight against the freezing cold outside. The elements were turning against them. In the mountains, soft winds were moving slowly across sheets of naked ice.

*

143

In the morning, they argued. Lhaten wanted to wait where they were for several more days, until Christopher had had time to acclimatize. Technically, the boy was right, though he could not have explained why. At twelve thousand feet, the alveolar oxygen pressure drops to about 50mm; when this happens, ventilation increases and the carbon dioxide pressure in the lungs begins to fall. The result is hypoxia, a lack of oxygen which can have serious and even fatal consequences if the body fails to acclimatize. During the present journey, they would have to climb to about eighteen thousand feet. If Christopher had done it before, he should be able to acclimatize quickly. But on his own admission, he had never been through the passes in weather like this before.

'I don't need to acclimatize. I'm feeling perfectly fine,' he insisted.

'Please, *sahib*, don't argue. It's been easy going up to here. But now things get hard. Give your body time to adjust.'

'Damn it, I've done it before, Lhaten. I didn't bring you with me to give advice. Just show me how to get to the passes, that's all. You can turn back now and welcome.'

Lhaten said nothing. Irritability was often the first sign of altitude sickness.

'I said I'd come with you to the passes,' the boy said finally. 'If you like I'll take you through them. You won't get far on your own.'

'I'll be all right. Don't mother me.'

'Won't you wait at least one day, *sahib*? Until the weather clears.'

It had stopped snowing earlier that morning, but there were deep drifts everywhere, both ahead of them and behind.

'No. We've got to leave now. If it snows again, we may not get through at all. Or perhaps you'd like that. Is that what you pray for – enough snow to block the passes?'

'No, *sahib*. I'm asking the Lady Tara for protection. And for good weather.'

But even as he spoke, he glanced at the dark clouds building behind the mountains. Left to himself, he would have turned back two days ago. Any one of his family or friends would have done the same. But Christopher, like all *pee-lings*, was stubborn. He lacked a nose for danger. Whatever happened, he would try to push on, even if it meant taking stupid risks. And that meant

144

someone would have to be there to get him out when the time came. Lhaten sighed. There wasn't any choice about who that someone would be.

They moved on just after 10 a.m., Christopher going ahead, sullen, irked by the snow-drifts that hindered his progress. Using his body as a plough, he forced a path through the packed snow that lay at times four feet high. Lhaten followed him, carrying far more than his share of the baggage. On either side of the narrow valley, steep hillsides restricted the view. There was no way through them. The only path lay ahead and up.

All that day and the next they pushed on until they came to a flat region almost free of snow. The weather held, but it was growing colder the higher they climbed. In the more open country before the passes, they were exposed to sharp winds that rushed on them like vampires, sucking away their breath and chilling their blood. Lhaten kept an anxious eye on Christopher, watching for further signs of altitude sickness. Sometime about the middle of the second night, a gale-force wind lifted their fragile tent and hurled it off into the darkness. To the dangers of altitude was now added the threat of exposure in the freezing nights ahead.

'If we go further,' whispered Lhaten in the darkness, 'it means going deeper into this. The winds will get stronger, strong enough to tear our flesh. And it may snow again. Not a little, like before, but a great deal. There may be a blizzard. Nothing can survive in that, *sahib*. Nothing.'

But Christopher did not listen. He felt driven now, and in love with the ice and snow. He could feel his heart beating more rapidly as the air grew thinner and his blood tried to regain lost oxygen. Lhaten could hear his rapid breathing in the darkness, but he said nothing. He would let the altitude stop him, then lead him back the way they had come, like a lamb.

They reached the Chumiomo Glacier the next day. From there, a narrow side-passage would take them to the first pass. The ascent was steep, and Christopher was forced to stop more than once to rest. When he walked, he leaned heavily on his climbing stick. His breathing was becoming more laboured, and Lhaten wondered how long it would be before exhaustion forced him to surrender and turn back.

145

They had just reached a point about half-way along the defile when the avalanche came. There was a low rumbling that grew in volume rapidly, like an express train bearing down on them out of a black tunnel. Lhaten knew the sound at once. He looked round, terrified, knowing they were trapped in the canyon. He saw it at once – a mass of snow and rock and fine white spume tumbling at breakneck speed down the face of the steep slope to their left. The whole world seemed to shake and their ears were filled with crashing and pounding as ton after ton of dislodged matter thundered towards them.

Frozen to the spot, they watched it come: crystals of snow leapt shimmering into the air, catching the light, dancing in space, cavorting as they fell. It was a thing of beauty, not heavy at all, but free of mass: rare, white and mysterious, fashioned from air and water, as fine as cloud or mist . . . and as destructive as sheets of beaten steel.

Lhaten broke from the spell and snatched at Christopher's arm.

'Run!' he shouted, but his voice was drowned in the roar from above.

Christopher was like a man in a trance. His feet felt like lead and his legs had no strength left to move them.

'We have to run, *sahib*,' shouted the boy again, but the thunder snatched his words away like feathers. He pulled at Christopher.

Like a man in a dream who drags himself through a clinging swamp, Christopher followed Lhaten. The first clumps of flying snow started to land in the canyon, striking them with uninterrupted force, snowballs in a deadly game. Fear gripped Christopher and he felt power surge back into his legs. He began to run, following Lhaten up the narrow path. It felt as though he were trying to run at full speed up the side of a mountain.

A stone struck him on the arm, then a larger one chipped his leg. Ahead of him, the world was turning white. Lhaten disappeared in a cloud of whirling snow.

Christopher ran on, his lungs tearing inside him, desperately struggling for air. He thought his heart would stop beating, it hammered so thickly in his chest. He felt himself stumble, then regain his feet and stagger on. The world was nothing but roaring in his ears and redness in front of his eyes. Two steps, three steps, each one an individual agony. The world vanished and he was wrapped in snow and the roaring of snow. All light, all other sounds were blocked out. His body became heavy, then his feet would not move, and he felt himself pitch forward.

The roaring died away and the last snow settled on top of the debris. Silence returned to the valley. The mountains watched, unmoved, uncaring, smug in their white and unsoiled remoteness. They had seen it all before and they would see it all again.

21

In the silence, he could hear his heart thumping like a drum at a funeral, slow and melancholy, but alive. He opened his eyes, but there was nothing, only blackness. For a moment, he panicked, thinking he had gone blind. Then he realized he had been buried in the avalanche. He could feel the weight of the snow on top of him, pressing him down. Heavy, but not too heavy. He was sure he could push his way out.

They had been caught at the end of the slide, where the fallen snow came to only a few feet in depth. It did not take Christopher long to struggle free. Finding Lhaten took him rather longer. The boy had been in front when the avalanche struck, so Christopher looked for him there, scrabbling with his bare hands at every likely looking mound. As he searched, he kept glancing up anxiously at the slopes above him: the crash of the avalanche might well have dislodged more snow higher up or on the opposite slope.

He found Lhaten curled up beneath about three feet of snow, several yards from where he himself had been. Christopher thought he was dead at first, he was so still. But a quick check showed that the boy was still breathing. There was blood on his left temple and a large stone nearby, and Christopher assumed he had been knocked unconscious. It was only when he dragged him clear of the snow that he noticed the leg.

Lhaten's left leg lay at an awkward angle. There was blood on his trousers below the knee, and when Christopher ran his fingers over the leg, he encountered something hard beneath the cloth. The boy's shin had been fractured in his fall, and the broken bone had cut through the thin layer of skin.

Christopher reset the bone while the boy was still unconscious and prepared strips of bandage from his own undershirt. Using thicker pieces cut from his *chuba*, the sheepskin coat Lhaten had obtained for him in Kalimpong, he made pads to place between

148

the boy's legs and then tied them together firmly, having first bandaged the actual wound.

When he had finished, he collapsed beside the boy and fell into a deep sleep. If another avalanche began, that would be too bad: Christopher could not move another step, even to save his life.

When he finally woke, it was dark. A wind had sprung up, a black wind from nowhere, an old wind full of sadness and unreasoning anger. It was lonely and hungry and malevolent. The whole world was filled with it: sky, mountains, passes, glaciers – all the high places, all the footpaths of the damned. It moved through the gully in which they lay, raging with all the fraught intensity of a lost soul.

Because of the wind, Christopher was not at first aware that the boy was groaning. Then he heard him, moaning into the darkness like a dog cast out into the storm. Christopher shifted towards him.

'Lhaten,' he called, trying to make himself heard above the din. 'It's me, Christopher! Are you all right?'

There was no answer, so he bent down closer, bringing his mouth near the boy's ear. This time Lhaten responded.

'I'm cold, *sahib*. And my leg hurts. Someone has tied them together – my legs. But my fingers are too cold. I can't untie them. And there's a terrible pain in my left leg.'

Christopher explained what had happened and the boy grew calmer. Then he pulled Christopher close and said,

'We've got to find shelter, *sahib*. If we stay in this, we'll die.'

The boy was right. In their weakened condition, exposure would kill both of them, if not tonight, then tomorrow or the day after. In a matter of hours, Christopher might be too frozen to stir, and once that happened they were both doomed. Fortunately, the enforced rest had done him some good. It was the longest stop he had made in a while, and it had given his body a chance to make some progress with acclimatization. His previous experience at high altitudes had rendered his system better able to cope with the abrupt changes of the past few days, and after his crisis he was beginning to return to normal. Now, the real danger was not height, it was the wind and the rapidity with which it could strip the human body of heat.

Christopher found the large canvas bag that had been slung round Lhaten's neck and which had still been with him when he

149

was found. His own smaller bag had been lost in the slide. Inside Lhaten's, he found the tiny trenching tool he had insisted they bring with them. It was small, but sturdy. With luck, it would save their lives.

The wind was still rising as Christopher made his way back to the site of the avalanche, crouching low to prevent himself being picked up and spun over by the gale. There was just enough light to find his way by. Once in the snow, he began to cut out blocks, each about two and a half feet long by a foot wide. When he had cleared a six-foot area in this way, he started to stack the blocks edgeways, forming a wall. It took him an hour to build a crude, rectangular igloo, roofed by slightly thicker, longer blocks.

When he got back to Lhaten, the boy was shivering uncontrollably and showing signs of severe heat-loss. He was moaning again and muttering to himself. When Christopher tried to talk to him, he showed no sign of hearing him. His pulse was sluggish and his breathing slow and shallow. It would be impossible for him to walk to the shelter, even with Christopher's assistance. If nothing else, the wind would just tilt them over like skittles.

Christopher dragged him. It was only a matter of about ten yards, but the wind and Christopher's desire not to dislocate the boy's leg again made it seem like a hundred. After the exertion of building the snow-shelter, his lungs were making it clear they would not stand much more of this treatment. He closed his eyes and hauled. Not now, he prayed, not now.

The words of prayer came easily to him. They came unbidden but necessary to his lips, the child in him praying for the man, the believer for the unbeliever. In the howling wind, like Lhaten with his *mantras*, in another tongue, in another season of faith, he prayed to the Virgin. He prayed for love, for life, for strength to pull the boy another foot across the wind-torn floor of the valley.

Holy Mary, Mother of God, pray for us sinners, now and at the hour of our death. Holy Mary, Mother of God, pray for us sinners, now and at the hour of our death. Holy Mary, Mother of God . . .

The words were torn from him by the wind. He rested briefly, then pulled again. The boy felt heavy, though he should have been light to Christopher. It seemed an age before they made it to the shelter.

Christopher settled the boy in the back of the dug-out, on a

150

blanket taken from his bag. That done, he sealed the entrance with more blocks cut for the purpose, trimming and squaring them as best he could to ensure a close fit. As the last block slotted into place, the noise of the wind was abruptly cut off, leaving Christopher and the boy in the midst of silence, as though they had found the eye of the storm and entered it. Christopher filled the gaps in the makeshift construction with loose snow and curled himself up at the boy's feet. Within minutes, he was asleep again. He dreamed of harvest and abundance in autumn, of golden sheaves and ripening apples on the bough.

That was the night the weather changed. It was the twelfth of January. The night two caravans were trapped on the Nathu-la and a hurricane tore the roof from the temple at Mindroling. The night a meteor was seen in the sky above Tashi Lhumpo.

That was the night the gods stopped playing and came to walk in places they had never walked before.

By morning, the temperature inside the shelter had risen to a comfortable level. Lhaten had recovered consciousness and said he felt all right, except for the pain in his leg, about which Christopher could do nothing. Christopher found some dried yak-dung left by a summer caravan further up the defile and used it to light a fire. In Tibet, where there were so few trees, it was almost the only fuel.

He had to light the fire inside the shelter, making a hole to let out the smoke. Outside, the wind still raged. At one point, thick, stinging hail hurled itself into the canyon. In a black sky, rolling clouds collided angrily with one another.

He made hot tea and added it to some *tsampa* in a bowl. There was a little butter in Lhaten's bag, and Christopher added this to the *tsampa* mixture. The boy ate it greedily, then drank some lightly buttered tea. In spite of his pain, he was beginning to look more himself. But Christopher knew it was only a matter of time before he began to weaken again. He would have to have proper attention as soon as possible.

'We'll have to head back as soon as you're able to walk,' he told the boy.

'I'll need a splint,' Lhaten said.

'I've thought of that. I'm going out now to find my bag and my climbing stick. They'll be near the spot where I was hit by the

151

avalanche. It should be no trouble to dig them out. The stick can be cut to fit your leg. It won't be easy, but if you lean on me, we should be able to get down.'

'What about the avalanche? The snow. The canyon must be blocked. I won't be able to get through. Leave me here. You can get help at Tsöntang. If you hurry, you can be back here in a few days.'

But the boy was lying. He knew what way the weather was going. And there was something else, something he kept to himself as well. Just before the avalanche started, he had heard a sharp crack, high up, like a gunshot. Someone had started the snow-slide deliberately. Perhaps Christopher too had heard the crack. But he had not known they were being followed.

'I thought there might be a way round. Even if we have to go up a little to join it. Surely you know of a way.'

Lhaten shook his head.

'I'm sorry, *sahib*. There's only one way – that's back the way we came. Every inch of the way. You must start soon if you're to clear the snow before nightfall.'

Christopher did not answer. There could be no question of his going back without the boy. And he was not sure that he himself could make it through the avalanche. There was only one alternative: they would have to go on into Tibet and make for the nearest village. It would probably mean Christopher's capture, but at the moment the boy's life seemed more important to him even than finding his son.

They set off just before noon that day. Christopher walked bent over so that the boy could use him as a crutch. Even with the splint, Lhaten's leg would not bear the slightest weight. When, by accident, he leaned on it, it gave, causing them both to stumble.

In the afternoon, the wind rose. An hour later, snow began to fall. Except that it did not fall, but became part of the wind. It was as if the wind had been a spirit that craved a body and now found it in the snow. The higher they climbed, the fiercer the wind grew. It was like walking against razors. Every breath had to be snatched before the wind could tear it away. They took hours to cover as much ground as they would previously have walked in an hour.

152

That night, they were too tired even to build a proper shelter. Christopher dug a deep trench in the snow and they sheltered in that, huddling beneath Lhaten's *namda*, a large felt blanket like a rug.

In the morning, Lhaten complained that his left foot hurt more than on the previous day. Christopher undid the boy's boot and removed the sock underneath. The foot was hard and white and freezing to the touch, like stone. The cold had combined with the interrupted blood-flow to cause severe frost-bite. Saying nothing, Christopher replaced the sock and boot.

'What is it, *sahib*? Is it frost-bite?'

Christopher nodded.

'Yes.'

There was no point in trying to thaw the foot – it would only freeze again, worse than ever. Christopher was worried that the boy's other foot might go the same way. His boots were made of cheap leather and his socks were too thin. Christopher sacrificed two strips from the *namda* to provide extra insulation, but he feared it would not be enough.

That day the blizzard set in in earnest. It was as if the fabric of the world was being torn apart. Wind and snow hurtled down from the passes in fits of insanity. Visibility was reduced to almost zero. When they could no longer walk, they crawled, Lhaten dragging his leg. He made no sound, but Christopher knew he must be in unbearable pain.

By midday they had covered very little distance, but Lhaten could go no further. The gale had not lessened in the slightest, and they still had not reached the pass. Christopher was beginning to think he would have to leave the boy after all, to go for help. But would he be able to persuade anyone to return with him in these conditions?

He built another shelter from the snow. They huddled inside, shivering. From time to time, Christopher made Lhaten eat dry *tsampa* and wash it down with a handful of snow. In his mind, Christopher was back at Carfax, in front of the roaring fire of logs in the library, reading a tale of Arthur Mee's to William.

In the night, Lhaten grew feverish and talked in a delirium of frightened words and inarticulate cries.

'Take it away,' he shouted loudly, loud enough to cover the screams of the wind outside.

'Take what away?' asked Christopher. 'What do you see?'

But the boy never answered clearly, and Christopher could only talk to him, offering reassurance that he knew was meaningless. The night was long. When dawn came, it brought only the faintest of lights.

Lhaten slept at last, like a baby worn out by crying. When he woke, his head was clear, but he complained of feeling weak. He could not keep down the *tsampa* Christopher offered him. His other foot was frost-bitten now.

Christopher made him walk. It was that or leave him to die. Like children in a nightmare, holding on to one another as anchors, they clawed their way through the madness of the storm.

They reached the first pass, Sebu-la, that afternoon. Its surface was broad and flat, and they could see a little more clearly through the blizzard there.

'*Lha-gyal-lo. De tamche pham,*' Lhaten whispered, thanking his gods for giving them this victory. 'The gods have triumphed,' he said. 'The demons have been defeated.' It was this formula all travellers used when they reached the top of a pass in safety. But on the boy's frozen lips, the words were charged with an intense and cruel irony.

'*Lha-gyal-lo,*' Christopher repeated, cursing all gods in his heart. He thought they were still playing games. But the games were over.

Lhaten wanted to stay at the top of the pass, but Christopher forced him to move on when they had rested. It was too exposed there. The path went down now for a bit before rising again to the second and final pass. Every foot nearer was a triumph to Christopher.

They spent that night between the passes. In the early hours of the morning, the wind began to drop, and by dawn the blizzard had stopped. When Christopher looked out, it was as though the world had been restored to him. Out of a grey sky, a grim light filtered down on everything.

That day they made it to the top of the pass, but Christopher knew they were almost at their end. He had to carry the boy on his back much of the way, leaving behind several pieces of baggage to make it possible.

They made their camp just below the pass, in a large cleft in the rock. Lhaten said he could not go any further, and this time Christopher did not argue. He would leave in the morning and head towards the Kampa basin. If the weather held off, someone would return with him. If not, he would buy wood and make a trestle on which to bring Lhaten back.

In the end, it was unnecessary. The next morning, Christopher helped Lhaten out of the cleft into the valley and set about building a snow-shelter for him. It would be warmer than the cleft and easier to find again.

While he was working, cutting and stacking blocks, he heard a voice. It was a man's voice, calling from lower down the valley. He stopped work and waited as three men approached. They were dressed in heavy travelling clothes, and their faces were muffled behind thick scarves. One was taller than the others and walked ahead as though he were in charge of their party. The men were monks – Christopher could see the edges of their orange robes protruding from beneath their *chubas*. They approached slowly, with the caution all travellers show when meeting strangers in the open.

The taller man came up to Christopher and greeted him in Tibetan.

'*Tashi delay.*'

'*Tashi delay.*' Christopher answered.

'Have you been travelling in the storm?' the stranger asked.

Christopher nodded.

'Yes. We were cut off before the Sebu-la. My friend is hurt. I was going to leave for help today. You've come just in time.'

'What's wrong with him?'

Christopher explained. The man did not pull his scarf down, but scrutinized Christopher over the top of it with dark, piercing eyes. Christopher imagined for a moment that he saw a look of recognition in the stranger's eyes, as though they had met before.

'When did this happen?'

'Five days ago.'

'I see. You say you were in the canyon before the Sebu-la.'

'Yes.'

155

'Were you alone? You saw no-one else?'

'No. We saw no-one.'

'Let me look at the boy.'

The man went across to Lhaten and bent down to examine him. The two monks stood near Christopher, watching. Carefully, the stranger looked at Lhaten's feet and leg, then examined his general condition. The boy was bad again. He had lost consciousness about an hour earlier.

Christopher did not see what happened next until it was too late to do anything about it. The man stood up and drew something from his pocket. He bent towards Lhaten and put his hand to the boy's temple. There was a loud report, and Christopher realized with horror that the stranger had just shot the boy. The man straightened up and put his revolver back into his pocket.

For what seemed an age, Christopher stood rooted to the spot. The gunshot echoed in his head, as if the bullet were crashing again and again into Lhaten's skull. He looked down and saw a trickle of bright red blood stream from the boy's temple on to the white, innocent snow.

He cried out in pain and rage, and threw himself at the boy's killer, but the monks had already seized him by the arms and held him at a distance.

'Why?' shouted Christopher. 'Why did you kill him?'

'He would have died anyway,' the stranger said in an unruffled voice. 'We are still too far here from help. It was better like this. Better for him. Better for us all.'

'We could have saved him! There's a village a few miles from here.'

'We aren't going to the village. He would have delayed us. Delayed us badly. The weather may deteriorate again. A cripple would have been a threat to all of us.'

Christopher struggled, but it was useless. He wanted to hit the man, to tear his scarf away, to see his face. But the monks held him firmly.

The man cast a glance at the limp body on the ground behind him.

'You were warned, Mr Wylam. You were warned not to enter Tibet. There has already been a tragedy as a result of your disobedience. There must be no more.'

He paused. A gust of wind lifted the corner of his scarf and dropped it again. His eyes looked keenly at Christopher again, as though searching for something.

'Who are you?' Christopher asked. But he already knew.

The stranger lifted his hand and pulled down the scarf from his face. Christopher recognized the heavily pitted skin.

'I didn't think you would make it this far, Mr Wylam,' said the monk. 'But now that you have done, perhaps you had best accompany us the rest of the way.'

'The rest of the way? Where are you planning to take me?'

'You wanted to find your son,' the monk said. 'I can take you to him.' He glanced up at the sky, at banks of grey cloud. 'It's time we left. We have a long journey ahead of us.'

22

By the second day, they were deep into the mountains. At the bottom of the descent from the passes, near the point where the track entered the Kampa plain, preparatory to turning toward Kampa Dzong, they had veered west, skirting the mountains along their northern edge, then re-entering along a valley whose opening it was impossible to detect with the naked eye.

Christopher could never work out how they traced their path, but the monks appeared to know the way unerringly. They climbed high, sometimes taking what seemed like impossible passages past steep drops or by the edges of dark crevasses. They made their way in silence through the heart of a white, sleeping world, their tiny figures dwarfed by walls of rock and frozen snow. Sometimes fresh snow fell, not violently as before, but in soft showers that covered them quietly in mantles of white. They passed ice-falls that resembled vast abandoned cities encased in glass. In the mornings, out of banks of white mist, pinnacles of rock jutted into view, carved over centuries by remorseless layers of frost. In the evenings, the rays of the setting sun would fall on decaying towers of ice and frozen curtains woven from long, thin icicles.

They walked for days, stopping only briefly to eat and rest. Christopher, exhausted by his exertions over the past week, felt driven almost beyond endurance. He moved in a dream, urged on by the monks, who shoved and pulled him over the hardest parts. Sometimes, there was real climbing to be done, and he was afraid he would slip and fall to his death. But luck and dogged perseverance kept him going.

He persevered because he wanted to kill the lama, but no opportunity presented itself. At night, they tied his arms and legs tightly with rope and made him sleep at a distance, trussed up and aching in the bitter cold. He lay awake for hours, thinking of Lhaten and the callousness of his death, of Cormac bloody beneath the buzzing of flies.

158

The lama's name was Tsarong Rinpoche. He spoke little to Christopher after the first day. He had brief conversations with the two monks from time to time, but otherwise he journeyed in silence.

The monks were even more silent. When they rested, they prayed. When the going was easy, they brought small silver *mani-khors* out of their robes and spun them, filling the air with a whirring sound. The prayer-wheels were finely decorated drums set on polished wooden handles, about whose axis they turned, driven round by the action of a counterweight attached to a small chain. Inside, block-printed sheets bore the formula of the *mani* prayer repeated thousands of times. At each revolution, the prayers were 'recited' by the mere act of turning. In a single day, the monks sent up millions of invocations. And while they did so, their lips muttered other prayers, muffled behind their scarves.

Christopher could not reconcile their apparent piety with their indifference to Lhaten's murder or their harshness with him on the journey. Or was it simply a kind of piety he could not hope to understand?

Sometimes they woke in the middle of the night and filled the brutal silences of Christopher's insomnia with the reading of *sutras* that seemed to have no meaning. Out of a sky washed clean of cloud, bands of frozen moonlight glided across their still figures. On several occasions, Christopher saw the lama rise in the middle of the night and walk in and out of the shadows, like someone who cannot bear immobility. He slept little, yet in the mornings never seemed tired or irritated.

Once, he came across to where Christopher was lying, bound in the darkness.

'I'm sorry you have to be tied,' he said. 'But I have no choice. I know you want to kill me. You must take revenge for the boy and the doctor. Since you do not understand and will not easily be made to understand, you must be prevented. I am sorry.'

'Would it have meant much delay to have saved the boy's life? A day, two days perhaps.'

'We were in a hurry. We still are in a hurry.'

'If I fall behind, will you kill me as well?'

'You will not be allowed to fall behind.'

His voice made strange verbal patterns in the darkness. Words

159

like 'choice', 'understand', 'prevented', and 'allowed' were the links in a subtle chain that was fastening hard round Christopher.

'But if I fall and injure myself, what then?'

'They will carry you. You will not be permitted to come to any harm. They have been given their instructions.'

Christopher remembered his words in Kalimpong: *You are holy: do not make me touch you.*

'What about you?' he asked.

'I am here to see they carry them out.'

'When shall I see William?'

The monk shook his head. 'That is not for me to decide,' he said.

'At least tell me if he's safe!'

'Yes, he is safe. Or he was safe when I last saw him. If Lord Chenrezi wills, he is still safe.'

'Where is he?' Christopher asked abruptly. 'Where are you taking me? Are we going to Dorje-la?'

The lama reached out a naked hand and touched Christopher's cheek.

'You are like a child,' he said. 'A child who cannot sleep.'

'You haven't answered my question.'

'Haven't I?' replied the stranger and stood up. He walked away into the darkness, silent and tense, waiting for the dawn to come.

They travelled for six days. Christopher tried to work out where they were, but it was useless. There were landmarks – the peaks of Kachenjunga, Chombu, Kachenjhau, Panhunri, and Chomolhari lay in the distance, now visible, now hidden from sight by lower but nearer masses of rock or ice. As they progressed, however, it became increasingly difficult to distinguish even the more distinctive peaks. Christopher had never set eyes on them from this angle, and most of the time he was guessing their identity on the basis of comparative height and position.

To make matters worse, the mountains themselves seemed determined to play a madcap game of disguises. First one would put on a crown of clouds, then another would wreath itself in mist while a third drew down on itself a heavy fall of snow that quickly distorted its shape. Light and shadows danced at intervals on every crag and gully they could reach. What seemed a valley one moment might in the next be transformed into a glacier; a flat buttress would suddenly become a razor-edged ridge; a bright snow-field would in the blink of an eye be replaced by a swathe of the deepest shadow. Nothing was constant, and Christopher despaired of ever making sense of the path he followed or of being able to find his way back again. Once or twice, even the monks stopped and consulted before deciding which of two possible routes to follow.

Late on the sixth day, Christopher saw that they were approaching a broad pass. The air felt incredibly thin and he had difficulty breathing. Even the monks, he noticed, were labouring. They stopped just short of the pass to rest.

'Our journey will be over soon,' the lama whispered to Christopher. 'That is our destination.'

He pointed upwards in the direction of the pass. Fading sunlight beaded the edges of a curved ridge. A lammergeyer swooped effortlessly down through the opening, then rose again, catching the sunlight momentarily on its wings. Beyond the light, at the head of the pass, a bank of mist moved lazily.

'I see nothing,' Christopher said.

'Look more closely,' the lama told him. 'Up there, just to the left of the mist.' He pointed again.

Christopher saw something fluttering. It took him a few moments to make out what it was – a *tarcho*, the traditional pole bearing down its length a cotton flag printed with prayers and the emblem of the wind-horse. Somewhere nearby, there would be a habitation – a small village or a hermit's cell.

Suddenly, as though Christopher's discovery of the *tarcho* had been a signal, the valley reverberated with sound. From high above came the deep notes of a Temple prayer-horn. It was no ordinary trumpet but a giant *dung-chen*. Low and deep-throated, the voice of the great horn penetrated every corner of the pass and the valley below. In that dreadful silence, in that vast solitude, its bellow filled Christopher with something akin to terror. He felt his flesh creep as the sound echoed and re-echoed over everything.

And then, as suddenly as it had come, the sound ceased. The last echoes died away and silence flooded back.

They began to climb towards the pass. The ascent was steep and treacherous. Wide patches of ice forced the men to crawl part of the way. Although the head of the pass had seemed near from

161

below, now it appeared to tease them, receding and receding ever further into the distance as they climbed. It was some sort of optical illusion, caused by a curious combination of shadow and the light of the setting sun.

Finally, they reached the top and rounded the corner of the pass. The monks shouted '*Lha-gyal-lo! Lha-gyal-lo!*' loudly. It was the first sign of anything approaching exuberance Christopher had ever observed in them.

Tsarong Rinpoche came up close beside Christopher and grasped his arm. There was a look of intense excitement in his eyes. The rest of his face was hidden by his scarf.

'Look up,' he said in a sharp whisper that sounded exaggeratedly loud in the crisp air.

Christopher looked. At first, he could see nothing out of the ordinary: just a rock face that rose up and up into a curtain of swirling mist. The mist seemed to fill the region ahead of them, rising like a wall into a bank of freezing cloud. On either side of them, ice and mist formed a cradle in which they were gently rocked.

'There's nothing,' Christopher murmured. 'Stones and mist. That's all.'

Suddenly, the trumpet sounded as before, but nearer this time. Much nearer. Its deep, throbbing notes travelled through the mist like the blasts of a foghorn at sea. But wherever he looked, Christopher could see nothing but rocks covered in ice, rolling mist, and low cloud.

'Wait,' whispered Tsarong Rinpoche. 'You will see.'

The other monks were busy whirling their prayer wheels, adding the tinny whirring sound to the reverberations of the unseen trumpet that blared out from behind the mist.

And then, quite remarkably, as though the trumpet had wrought a miracle in the heavens, a portion of mist parted, revealing a golden roof and a terrace below it on which an orange-clad figure stood motionless against the dying light. The man blew into a large trumpet resting on wooden blocks. Obliquely, the sun's rays caught the bowl of the instrument, turning it to fire. Then, it fell abruptly silent once more, and across the silence, like the murmur of waves falling on a pebbled shore far away, the sound of chanting

162

voices came faintly to their ears. The figure on the terrace bowed and vanished into the mist.

As Christopher watched, the mist parted further, revealing bit by bit the clustered buildings of a vast monastery complex. The great edifice seemed as though suspended between earth and sky, floating impossibly on a cushion of mist, its topmost pinnacles lost among clouds.

At the centre stood a vast central building, painted red, to which a variety of lesser buildings clung like chicks about a mother hen. The main edifice was several storeys tall, with brightly gilded roofs and pinnacles that burned in the light of the setting sun. Its windows were already shuttered against the evening wind. Icicles hung from eaves and lintels everywhere, like decorations on a giant cake.

Christopher was awed by the sight after so many days of unrelieved whiteness and desolation. The colours of the place dazzled him. He had forgotten how much life there could be in colour. Like a hungry man, he feasted on the golden vision in front of him until the sunlight turned violet and began to fade, taking the warm colours with it. His vision turned to darkness and he wondered if it had really been there at all.

'What is this place?' he whispered, to no-one in particular.

'Our destination,' said Tsarong Rinpoche. 'The pass we have just climbed is Dorje-la. The monastery in front of you is Dorje-la Gompa. But its proper name is Sanga Chelling: the Place of Secret Spells.'

Christopher looked up again. In a window high up near the roof, someone had lit a lamp. Someone was watching them. Someone was waiting for them.

23

Dorje-la Gompa, southern Tibet, January 1921

They entered the monastery the following morning after dawn. The sound of the temple-horn had awakened them, braying high up on the wide terrace, calling in the darkness for the light to return. And it did return, lingering briefly on the broad peaks of the Eastern Himalaya before sliding reluctantly down into the dark valley below Dorje-la.

The ascent to the building was made on a long wooden ladder that threatened to give way at any moment and send them spinning back on to the rocks below. Christopher climbed without emotions of any kind; dread, anticipation, even triumph at having reached this place – all had deserted him.

The first morning assembly had finished by the time they entered the building. They came in through a small red gate, but the monks were still in the Lha-khang taking tea before resuming their devotions. The travellers were met by a fat little monk dressed in the robes of a steward. The two trapas mumbled greetings and at once scuttled off down a dimly lit corridor, like rabbits returning to their warren. The lama entered a doorway on the left and closed the door behind him without a word. Christopher was led in a different direction, along a passage lit by rancid butter-lamps that gave off a jaundiced, almost sulphurous glow. The all-pervasive smells of ancient *dri*-butter and human sweat were doubly noxious to Christopher after so long in the fresh and rarefied air of the mountains outside.

The steward showed Christopher to a small room on the first floor and asked if he wanted food.

'No, thank you,' he said. 'I'd like to sleep. I'm very tired.'

The monk nodded and backed out, closing the door behind him. Against one wall was set a low pallet bed. Without pausing to inspect the rest of the room, Christopher threw himself on to the bed. The last thing he thought of before sleep overpowered him was Lhaten's reaction when he had asked the boy if he had ever heard of Dorje-la.

164

'I think it is time for sleep, *sahib*.'

And it was.

When Christopher awoke, he could not tell how much time had passed. The butter-lamp left by the steward still burned steadily on a little table near the door, but it had been full to begin with. The comfort of the bed and the profundity of his sleep had only served to accentuate the depth of Christopher's tiredness and the aching he felt in every joint and muscle. He could have lain there forever, he thought, neither sleeping nor waking, but in a state between.

From somewhere far away came the sound of voices, many voices, rising and falling in a dirge-like chant, whether of celebration or lament he could not tell. The chanting was punctuated by the sounds of a variety of musical instruments. A large drum was being struck in slow, steady beats; a conch-shell wove in and out of the deeper notes raised by a shawm; from time to time, small cymbals clashed with a tinny sound. Christopher recognized the tight, nervous sound of a *damaru*, a small drum fashioned from a human skull and used in the lower Tantric ceremonies.

Slowly, as he lay in the darkness listening to the sound of the monks at prayer, the reality of his situation was borne in upon Christopher. It still made little sense: though all the separate parts seemed to connect, there was a lack of logic to their connection that made him despair. But of one thing he was absolutely certain now – his son William was here, within these walls. Whatever madness lay behind his being here, that was all that mattered.

The music and chanting stopped abruptly, and the monastery was returned to silence. Nothing stirred.

Christopher glanced around the room. A draught from the window teased the flame of his lamp and sent speculative little shadows here and there. Above the bed hung a large *thangka* depicting the Buddha surrounded by eight Indian saints. Opposite, an old lacquer chest had been transformed into a private altar, adorned with paintings of lotuses and various sacred emblems. On the wall over the altar hung a wooden cabinet with glass doors: inside were painted images of Tsongkhapa and his two disciples. Near the window stood a small table and a chair, and on the wall above them a narrow wooden shelf holding bound copies of scriptural texts.

He stood up and went to the window. Tibetan monasteries did not as a rule have glass in their windows, so the heavy wooden shutters were kept permanently closed throughout the long winter months. He found the latch and pushed one half of the shutter open. Outside, it was night again. A sharp wind had whipped the clouds away, and in the black expanse just visible above three distant peaks, the sky groaned with the weight of innumerable stars. From somewhere outside Christopher's range of vision, moonlight fell like icing on the crystal landscape of the pass below.

He closed the shutter, shivering, and sat down on the chair. He was feeling hungry now and wondered how he could get hold of someone to bring him food. Perhaps they were waiting for him to give some indication that he was awake. He stepped across to the door and pulled on the handle. It was locked. His monastic cell was to serve as a prison cell as well.

24

In the morning, he found food waiting for him on a low table: some lukewarm tsampa, a few barley-cakes, and hot tea in a covered cup. It was plain enough fare, but after days of nothing but cold tsampa, its warmth alone was delicious. After he had eaten, he opened the shutters and looked out of the window. Sunlight had grown out of nothing overnight, spreading itself across the valley below. He could just make out the path he and his companions had followed the day before. Patches of grey mist still clung to the rocks at the foot of the monastery, like small pools of colourless water left on the seashore by the departing tide. If he craned his neck upwards, he could just make out the shapes of distant mountains through gaps in the cliffs surrounding the small valley.

There was a light tap on the door. Christopher closed the shutters and called.

'Who's there?'

There was the sound of a key turning in the lock, then the door opened and the steward of the day before entered. He held a tall staff in one hand, less for support than as a token of his office. In the other, he carried a flickering butter-lamp.

'You're to come with me,' he said.

'Why am I being kept locked in this room?'

The steward ignored his question.

'You have been summoned. Please follow me.'

'Who is summoning me? Where am I being taken?'

'Please,' the steward said, fixing his abrasive eyes on Christopher. 'Don't ask questions. There is no time. You have to come with me now.'

Christopher sighed. He was in no position to argue. And anything was better than being cooped up in this tiny room indefinitely.

*

The steward led the way in silence along a different route to the one along which he had led Christopher the previous morning, along deserted and unpainted corridors. It grew cold. No-one passed them. After a while, they entered regions that seemed to predate the main monastic foundation. No-one lived here any longer. Christopher could feel the touch of the wind as it forced its way through untended cracks in the fabric of the building. At last they reached a heavy door covered with painted eyes. The paint had long ago faded, but the eyes still seemed to possess the power of sight.

The steward opened the door and motioned Christopher through. For a moment, he thought they had abruptly left the monastery and gone outside. He stood on the threshold, bewildered, trying to make sense of the sight that met his gaze.

Snow fell in patches, bright and translucent, fine white flakes like the forms of tiny angels descending, wing upon white wing, in heavy, dreaming multitudes. Someone had lit thousands of butter-lamps and placed them all around the room: they lay thick on the snow-covered ground, a shifting carpet of fireflies catching breath. The tiny flames trembled and cast pale patterns on walls of naked ice.

Everywhere, a caul of snow and ice lay silent upon the sleeping room, veil upon white veil, glaze upon frosted glaze, year upon frozen year. It was a room of ice and ivory, its broken ceiling open to the sky and its mirrored walls exposed to the endless breath of the mountains. Shafts of sunlight lay everywhere like slanting rods of glass: the snow fell through them, flickering as it dropped earthwards. On plinths throughout the room, statues of gods and goddesses stood unrecognizable beneath thick garments of tattered frost. Their hair was white and stiff with icicles; from their frozen hands, long strands of ice trailed to the floor.

At the far end of the long chamber, hidden away among shadows, in an area out of reach of the shafts of sunlight, Christopher made out a grey figure seated cross-legged on a throne of cushions. Slowly, feeling his heart trip repeatedly in his breast, he made his way towards the shadows. The figure did not move, did not call out. He sat immobile, hands resting on his knees, back straight. His eyes were fixed on Christopher.

The figure was dressed in the simple robes of a monk. On his head, he wore a pointed cap with long ear-flaps that hung down to

168

below his shoulders. His face was partly hidden in shadows. It seemed lined and full of sadness. The eyes, above all, ached with sadness. Christopher stood in front of him, not knowing what to do or say. He realized that he had not brought a *khata* scarf with him, that he could not perform the ritual of greeting. Some time passed, then the stranger raised his right hand gently and motioned to Christopher.

'Please,' he said, 'be seated. You do not have to stand. I have had a chair brought for you.'

For the first time, Christopher noticed a low chair just on his left. He sat down, feeling self-conscious. He could sense the old man's eyes on him, scrutinizing him with a fierce intensity mixed with terrible sadness.

'My name is Dorje Losang Rinpoche. I am the Dorje Lama, the abbot of this monastery. They tell me your name is Christopher, Christopher Wylam.'

'Yes,' said Christopher. 'That's correct.'

'You have come a long way,' said the Dorje Lama.

'Yes,' said Christopher, his voice feeling cracked and awkward. 'From India. From Kalimpong.'

'Further than that,' the abbot contradicted him.

'Yes,' Christopher said. 'Further than that.'

'Why have you come? Please be truthful with me. No-one comes here for a trivial reason. There must be matters of life and death to bring a man to us. What has brought you here?'

Christopher hesitated. He feared and distrusted the abbot. This man had played a major rôle in what had happened. For all he knew, Zamyatin was himself a pawn in a greater game.

'I was brought here,' he replied. 'By three of your monks: Tsarong Rinpoche and two *trapas*. Tsarong Rinpoche killed my guide, a Nepalese boy named Lhaten. He killed him merely because Lhaten was injured. Before I answer any of your questions, I demand justice for the boy.'

'You are making a serious charge.' The abbot bent forward, as though trying to see the truth in Christopher's face.

'It is not my only charge. I met Tsarong Rinpoche before that in Kalimpong. He admitted killing someone else there: an Irish doctor called Cormac. Did you know of that? Was he acting under your orders?'

The abbot sighed and straightened himself again. His face was that of an old man, but extremely pale. The eyes were still pools of sadness, but Christopher sensed another emotion in that look. Compassion? Love? Pity?

'No,' he said. 'He was not acting under orders from me. I had no reason to want either the doctor or your guide dead. Please believe me. I have no wish to cause the death of any sentient being. My purpose on earth is to diminish suffering in any way I can. If Tsarong Rinpoche has acted wrongly, he will be punished.'

The abbot paused and blew his nose gently on a small handkerchief which he took from inside his long sleeve. The ordinariness of the man's action was more reassuring to Christopher than his words.

'Tsarong Rinpoche tells me,' the abbot continued, 'that when he met you, you were on the borders of Tibet, just beyond the Sebula. Is this true?'

Christopher nodded.

'Yes.'

'He also tells me that he warned you not to leave India, not to attempt to enter Tibet. Is that also true?'

'Yes. That is true as well.'

'You had been warned of possible danger. Danger to yourself and anyone who travelled with you. You chose a route that you must have known to be almost impassable. Tsarong Rinpoche tells me he thinks you were already seeking for this place, for Dorje-la. Is that true too?'

Christopher did not say anything.

'You do not deny it is true? Very well, then I must conclude that something of great importance drove you here. Or perhaps I should say "drew you here". What would that thing be, Wylamla? Can you tell me?'

Christopher remained silent at first, his gaze fixed on the old man. On the abbot's chest, a silver *gau* caught particles of light from the lamps and transformed them into shadows.

'Not a thing,' Christopher said at last. 'A person. My son. His name is William. I believe he is here, in this monastery. I have come here to take him home.'

The abbot stared at Christopher with a look of intense sadness.

170

All around, snow kept falling. It lay sprinkled on the old man's hair and covered the cushions on which he sat.

'Why do you think your son is here, Mr Wylam? What possible reason could there be for his presence in this place?'

'I don't know the reason. All I know is that a man called Zamyatin ordered my son's kidnap. Zamyatin's instructions were carried out of Tibet by a monk named Tsewong. Tsewong is dead, but a letter was found on him that identified him as your representative. Carpenter, the Scottish missionary in Kalimpong, has told me that my son was taken to Tibet by a Mongolian called Mishig. Mishig is Zamyatin's agent.'

The Dorje Lama listened to all of this with his head bent, as though Christopher's words weighed him down. There was a lengthy silence.

'You know a great deal, Wylam-la,' he said finally. 'A very great deal. And yet you know very little.'

'But I'm right. My son is here. Isn't he?'

The abbot folded his hands.

'Yes,' he said. 'You are right. Your son is here. He is alive and well. He is being looked after with the greatest possible attention. There is nothing for you to worry about.'

'I want to see him. Take me to him at once.' Christopher stood up. He felt faint and angry.

'I'm sorry,' the abbot said. 'That will not be possible. There is so much you do not understand. But he is no longer your son. That much you must try to understand. For your own sake. Please try to grasp what I am saying.'

'What do you want with him?' Christopher was shouting now. He could hear his voice echoing in the empty, snow-filled chamber. 'Why did you bring him here?'

'He was brought here at my request. I wanted him brought to Dorje-la. As yet even he does not understand. But in time he will. Please do not make it difficult for him. Please do not ask to see him.'

The abbot reached down and picked up a small silver bell from a low table. He rang it gently, filling the room suddenly with a loose, fluttering music, like fine crystal being struck. There was a smell of old incense, like crushed flowers in a tomb.

'You will have to leave now,' he said. 'But we shall meet again.'

Footsteps sounded behind Christopher. He turned to see the

steward waiting for him. As he walked away from the abbot, the old man's voice came to him out of the shadows.

'Mr Wylam. Please try to be wise. Do not attempt to find your son. We do not wish any harm to befall you: but you must take care. You ignored Tsarong Rinpoche's warning. Do not ignore mine.'

25

Christopher was taken back to the room in which he had been confined before. He sat for hours in the silence of his own thoughts, trying to come to terms with his situation. The revelation that William was alive and being kept here in Dorje-la had shaken him. He needed time to think, time to decide what to do next.

Several times he went to the window and looked down at the pass below. Once, he saw a party of monks moving along a narrow path away from the monastery. He watched until they vanished from sight. Later, he saw someone running to the monastery from a point just above the pass. From time to time, he heard the sound of chanting, punctuated by the steady beats of a drum. On a terrace below him and to his left, an old monk sat for hours turning a large prayer-wheel. At sunset, the trumpet on the roof brayed into the coming darkness; it was quite near him and very loud.

A monk came and left him some food, lit his lamp, and left again without saying a word in reply to his questions. There was soup and tsampa and a small pot of tea. He ate slowly and automatically, chewing and swallowing the balls of roasted barley without enjoyment. When he had finished eating, he lifted the cover from the teacup. As he raised the pot to pour, his eye caught sight of something white pressed into the cup.

It was a sheet of paper, folded several times and pushed firmly down. Christopher took it out and unfolded it. It was covered in Tibetan writing, in an elegant Umay hand. At the bottom was a small diagram, a series of intersecting lines that lacked any obvious pattern.

He took the sheet across to the table by the bed, where the lamp was burning. His knowledge of written Tibetan was limited, but with a little effort he was able to decipher most of the text:

I am told you speak our language. But I do not know if you can read it also. I can only write and hope that you will be able to read this. If you cannot read it, I will have to find a way to send someone to you; but that may be difficult. The trapa who brings your food does not know that I had this message placed in your cup: do not speak of it to him.

I am told you are the father of the child who was brought here from the land of the pee-lings. I am told other things, but I do not know whether to believe them.

You are in danger in Dorje-la. Be careful at all times. I want to help you, but I too must be careful. I cannot come to you, so you must come to me. Tonight, your door will be unlocked. When you find it open, follow the map I have drawn below. It will lead you to the gön-kang. I shall be waiting for you there. But take care that no-one sees you leave.

There was no signature. He re-read the letter several times, making sure he had understood it. Now that he knew the diagram was meant to be a map, he thought he could make some sense of it, even though he could not relate the rooms and corridors it showed to places he had actually seen.

He stood up and went to the door. It was still locked. He sighed and went back to the bed, feeling restless now that a possibility for action had at last presented itself. Who had sent him the message? He knew no-one in Dorje-la. And why should one of the monks want to help him, a stranger?

Several times over the next few hours he went to the door and tried it. It was always locked, and he began to think that the mysterious letter-writer had been unable to carry out his plan. The last service of the day was sung, the monks returned to their cells for the night, and a profound silence settled on Dorje-la at last. About an hour later, he heard a low fumbling sound at his door. He got up and advanced cautiously to it. Silence. He reached out a hand and tried the handle. It turned without resistance.

Quickly, he found his lamp and stepped outside. He was in a long corridor: at the far end, a single butter-lamp burned. There was no-one in sight. All around him, he could feel the monastery sleeping. It was freezing in the corridor.

Consulting the map, he set off slowly to his right, down to where the corridor joined another. The second corridor stretched away into shadow. There were lamps at intervals, faint offerings to the surrounding gloom. In the dim light from his own lamp, the painted walls seemed half alive, seething with a dark, tormented

174

movement. Everywhere, red predominated. Faces appeared for a moment out of the darkness, then vanished again. Hands moved. Bared teeth grinned. Skeletons danced.

Imperceptibly, a sense of deep antiquity began to impress itself on Christopher as he padded deeper into the sleeping monastery. He could see, if only imperfectly, how the character of the regions through which he passed was undergoing a gradual change. Like geological strata, the individual sections of the *gompa* showed clearly how they had been built up, a little at a time. The further he penetrated, the more a primitive quality revealed itself to him in the paintings and carvings. Chinese influence gave way to Indian and Indian to what Christopher recognized as early Tibetan. He could feel growing in him a sense of trepidation. This was like no monastery in which he had ever set foot before.

The final corridor ended in a low door on either side of which the images of guardian deities had been painted. Two torches burned in brackets half-way up the wall. This was an ancient part of the monastery, perhaps a thousand years old.

He stood at the entrance to the *gön-kang*, the darkest and most forbidden place in any *gompa*. Christopher had only ever heard descriptions of such places from Tibetan friends, but he had at no time been allowed to set foot in one. They were dark places, narrow crypt-chapels where the masks for the sacred dances were kept. This was the ritual abode of the *yi-dam*, the tutelary deities, whose black statues watched over the monastery and its inhabitants. It was the seat of the sacred horror at the heart of Tibetan religion.

Christopher hesitated at the door, oddly frightened at the prospect of entering. He had no reason to be frightened: there was only darkness inside, darkness and strange gods in whom he did not believe. But something made him hesitate before finally putting his hand to the door and pushing.

It was unlocked. Immediately behind lay a second door bearing the brightly painted face of a *yi-dam*. Red, staring eyes confronted him like living coals. The light of his lamp flickered and shone on old paint and flecks of gold leaf. He pushed open the second door.

Darkness visible, darkness like velvet pressing against his eyes, darkness palpable and entranced. Here, night was permanent. It had never been truly broken, it would go on forever. A strong smell of old butter filled the stale, lightless air. It was like entering a tomb.

Christopher held up his lamp. From the ceiling near the entrance hung the stuffed carcases of several animals: a bear, a yak, a wild dog. These ancient, rotting things were an integral part of every *gön-kang*, as much an element in the place's dark mystery as the figures of the gods on the altar. Christopher felt his skin crawl with disgust as he passed underneath, crouching low to avoid contact with the mouldering fur hanging loosely from the poorly preserved cadavers. They had been hanging there for God only knew how long, and would go on hanging in the same places until they finally decomposed and fell apart. Generations of spiders had added a thick outer carapace of their own to the mildewed fur. Dusty cobwebs brushed Christopher's cheeks as he went through.

It was old. He knew as soon as he was inside that the *gön-kang* was an ancient place, older than the monastery, half as old as the mountains themselves. It was a cave, low and dark and dedicated from the beginning of time to the most hidden mysteries. The dance-masks hung by thick ropes from the ceiling to Christopher's right, images of death and madness, painted long ago and set here in the darkness with the grim guardians of the monastery. Once or twice a year, they would be taken out and worn in the ritual dances. They would turn and turn to the sound of drums and flutes, like the naked girl Christopher had seen in the orphanage, her face a mask hiding the dull terror beneath. The faces of the masks were grotesque and larger than life – the malign features of gods and demi-gods and demons, faces that would transform a dancing monk to an immortal being and a man to a god for a day.

Near the masks, set against the wall, were piles of old armour – spears and swords and breastplates, hauberks and crested helmets, Chinese lances and pointed Tartar hats. It was ancient armour, rusted and useless for the most part, kept there as a symbol of sudden death, weapons for the old gods to wield in their battle against the forces of evil.

Standing before the rear wall were the statues of the *yi-dam* deities, their many arms and heads swathed in old strips of cloth placed there as offerings. Yamantaka, horned and bull-headed and festooned with a coronet of human skulls, leered out of the darkness. In the flickering shadows, the black figures seemed to

176

move, as though they too were dancing in their eternal night. Filled with a foreboding he could neither understand nor master, Christopher went closer.

Something moved that was not a shadow. Christopher shrank back, holding his lamp out in front of him. Before the altar at the back of the room, facing the *yi-dam*, sat a dark figure. As Christopher watched, the figure moved again, prostrating briefly in front of the gods before resuming a seated position. It was a monk, wrapped up against the bitter cold, engaged in meditation. He did not appear to have noticed the light from Christopher's lamp or heard him enter.

Christopher was uncertain what to do next. He guessed this must be the monk who had written the letter, but now he was about to confront him, he felt suddenly wary. Was this perhaps nothing more than an elaborate trap, set by Zamyatin or Tsarong Rinpoche? He had, after all, just violated the monastery's innermost sanctum. Had that been the intention all along – to provide someone with an adequate justification for his death?

The figure moved, not abruptly like someone startled, but gently, like a man woken from sleep and still half in the world of his dream. He stood up and turned. A shadow fell across his face as he did so, veiling him.

'You have come,' he said. The voice was soft, like a girl's. Christopher guessed the monk was a *ge-tsul*, a novice. But what would a novice want with him?

'Was it you who wrote the letter?' Christopher asked, stepping towards the figure.

'Please! Don't come any closer,' the monk said, stepping back further into shadow.

Christopher froze. He sensed that the *ge-tsul* was nervous, in some way frightened by Christopher's presence.

'Why did you ask me to come? What do you want?'

'You are the father of the *pee-ling* child?'

'Yes.'

'And you have travelled from far away to find him?'

'Yes. Do you know where he is? Can you take me to him?'

The monk made a hushing sound.

'Do not speak so loudly. The walls of Dorje-la have ears.' He paused. 'Yes,' he continued, 'I know where your son is being kept. And I can take you there.'

'When?'

'Not now. Perhaps not for several days.'

'Is he in any danger?'

The novice hesitated.

'No,' he said. 'I don't think so. But something is happening in Dorje-la, something I do not understand. I think we may all be in danger very soon.'

'I want to take William away from here. I want to take him back through the passes to India. Can you help me?'

There was silence. Shadows gathered about the small figure by the altar.

'I can help you take him from Dorje-la,' he said at last. 'But the way to India is too hazardous. If you want your son to leave here alive, you must trust me. Will you do that?'

Christopher had no choice. However mysterious, this was his only ally in a world he did not understand.

'Yes,' he replied. 'I will trust you.'

'With your life?'

'Yes.'

'With your son's life?'

He hesitated. But William's life was already in jeopardy.

'Yes.'

'Go back to your room. I will send another message to you there. Be sure that you destroy any letters I write to you. And speak of this to no-one. No-one, do you understand? Even if they appear to be a friend. Do you promise?'

'Yes,' Christopher whispered. 'I promise.'

'Very well. Now you must leave.'

'Who are you?' Christopher asked.

'Please, you must not ask. Later, when we are safe, I will tell you. But not now. There is too much danger.'

'But what if something happens? If I need to find you?'

'You are not to look for me. I will find you when it is time. Please leave now.'

'At least let me see your face.'

'No, you must not!'

But Christopher raised his lamp and stepped forward, letting

178

the light fall directly on the shadows before him. The mysterious stranger was not a novice, not a monk. Long strands of jet-black hair framed small, delicate features. An embroidered tunic shaped itself about a slender body. The stranger was a woman. In the shadowed light, her green eyes sparkled and the tiny yellow flame cast drops of liquid gold over her cheeks. Her hair was filled with golden ashes.

She stared at Christopher, her eyes startled. One hand sprang to her face, covering her from his gaze. He took another step, but she recoiled, stumbling back into the shadows once more. He heard her feet run softly across the stone floor. Holding the lamp high, he followed, but the light fell on nothing but figures of stone and gold. On the walls, paint crumbled and fell slowly to dust. Time stood still. The bright patterns of a dozen heavens and a dozen hells shuddered like tinsel in the darkness. The girl had vanished utterly into the shadows out of which she had come.

26

He returned to his room, passing through the sleeping monastery like a phantom. As far as he was aware, no-one had seen him leave or re-enter the room. About half an hour after his return, he heard the sound of fumbling at his door again, and when he tried the handle he found it had been locked once more.

He lay in bed, trying to get warm, his thoughts in turmoil. There were so many unanswered questions. Who was the woman who had brought him to the *gön-kang*? What did she really want with him? And could she really help him get William out of this place? He tossed and turned in the darkness, tiring himself without coming any closer to satisfactory answers. In the end, his restless thoughts became restless dreams. But even in sleep there were no answers.

He was woken abruptly by a sound. His light had gone out and the room was in pitch darkness. He could hear his own breathing but nothing else. What had wakened him? Breathing evenly, he lay in the darkness listening. It came again, a soft, fumbling sound. Someone or something was outside his door, trying to get in. This was not like the sound he had heard before, when his door had been unlocked and locked again. This was furtive, secretive, not intended to be heard.

A key turned in the lock. Whoever was outside was taking great care not to waken him. He cast back his blankets and swung his legs over the edge of the bed. Working by instinct, he found his boots and slipped them on. The key turned gently, with an almost inaudible grating sound. He stood up, careful not to make the bed creak. The door began to open, an inch at a time. He got up and crept to the other side of the room, next to the shrine.

The intruder did not carry a light. Christopher could see nothing, hear nothing. He pressed himself against the wall. As his eyes grew accustomed to the darkness, he realized that a small amount of illumination came through the shutter, which he had closed imperfectly. A slight creak drew his attention back to the door. A shadow was easing itself through the opening. Christopher held his breath.

The shadow moved to the bed on silent feet. There was an abrupt movement as it bent down, then Christopher saw it fumble with the blankets in confusion. There was a glint of something metallic in the darkness: a knife-blade. Christopher waited for the figure to straighten up, then dashed forward, his right arm extended, and grabbed for the neck.

The intruder grunted as Christopher pulled back with his forearm against his throat. He heard the knife clatter to the floor. Then there was a quick movement and Christopher felt himself being twisted. A sudden blow took him in the small of his back, near his kidneys. As he jerked away from the blow, the man turned again and freed himself from the armlock. A second blow took Christopher in the pit of his stomach and sent him reeling back against the shrine. Bowls crashed to the ground, spilling water everywhere and clanging like bells in the stillness. The stranger did not speak.

Suddenly he lunged, and Christopher felt something tighten round his neck. It was a thin cord and the man was pulling hard on it. His head spun as the cord tightened and air and blood were cut off. He had seconds before he began to weaken. Throwing himself forward, he crashed into his assailant, causing him to stumble and fall back against the bed. The cord slackened and Christopher grabbed hold of it, ripping it from the man's hands. He tossed it aside.

Christopher realized that his one advantage was his weight. The man beneath him was much smaller than he, but clever with his hands. Without warning, Christopher's attacker uncoiled himself and directed a blow to his throat. His chin took most of the blow's force, but he felt a searing pain run through his jaw. He remembered the way the monk in Kalimpong had disabled him so effortlessly. Springing back, he hit the chair and knocked it over. Without thinking, he picked it up.

'Who are you?' he hissed, but his assailant said nothing in reply. He saw the shadow move towards him, lifted the chair, and struck out. He felt the chair connect with his attacker, lifted it again, and struck a second time. There was a dull cry, then the sound of feet

181

stumbling as Christopher's assailant tried to find his balance. He saw the man stagger, then straighten up and make for the door.

Christopher made a dash after the man, groping for him in the semi-darkness, but one foot caught on an altar-bowl and he tripped. When he got to his feet, his attacker had gone. Christopher went to the open door and looked in both directions along the corridor. There was no sign of anyone. He took the key from the lock and closed the door, locked it and put the key inside his boot.

Further sleep would have been madness. He remained awake until dawn, then tidied the room, replacing the bowls on the altar as accurately as possible. He found his assailant's knife, a thin weapon with an eight-inch blade, and tucked it into his other boot. He was beginning to feel that the attack had turned in his favour.

Breakfast came long after dawn and the first morning service. There was no message in the cup this time. When the monk returned later that morning to take the crockery away, Christopher told him that he wanted to see the abbot. At first the man denied that this was possible, but Christopher implied there would be trouble if his message were not passed on. The monk said nothing when he left, but later that afternoon the steward returned and told Christopher to come with him.

They did not follow the same route they had taken the day before. Instead, they climbed dark stairs that led to the top floor of the building. Christopher guessed that he was being taken to the abbot's private quarters. As befitted an incarnation, he would live in the highest storey, so that no-one would be able to stand or sit above his head.

They seemed to be leaving behind more than just the lower monastery. Up here, it was another world. At the top of the stairs, a large window looked out across the pass; it was glazed, not with the wax paper often used in Tibet, but with panes of real glass that must have been carried all the way from India. Christopher paused for breath and looked out: in the distance, sunlight was resting on the peaks of dazzled mountains, dappled and quiet among the white snow. He felt closed in, a prisoner in this murky place, shut away from the air and the sunshine.

The steward led him through a doorway with huge bronze rings round which coloured ribbons had been tied. Above the door, a

Chinese inscription proclaimed a message incomprehensible to Christopher. An imperial name, a paean, a warning?

The door closed behind them and they were in a square chamber filled with painted cages within which birds of all sizes fluttered and hopped. The air was thick with birdsong, a greedy twittering that bounced off the walls and ceiling in strange, bewildered echoes. There were blue pigeons and redstarts, grey and red accentors, snow pigeons cloaked in white, thrushes, finches, and canaries from China, bright-plumaged parakeets from India, and two birds of paradise with feathers like the edges of rainbows. Coloured plumage coruscated in the light of the lamps, awakening silent echoes on the unpainted walls. But for all that, the room was a prison, a cell where shadows and wood and wire conspired to dim all brightness. As Christopher passed through, heavy wings flapped against bars on every side; there was a deep, deep fluttering, like cloth in a nightmare. The steward opened a second door and ushered Christopher into another room.

Great bottles stood everywhere, each the height of a tall man and correspondingly broad – terraria filled with living plants brought up from the jungle regions below. Each was a universe forever sealed in a cycle of growth and decay. Among the plants, huge butterflies soared and swooped, beating cramped wings silently against the glass sides of the bottles, or moving from flower to flower restlessly. More prisons, more cells. Light fell on the bottles through glass shafts set in the ceiling, and the plants fought and strained to suck what life they could from the thin blades of tired sunshine that entered.

They went through several more rooms, each as bizarre as the one before. In one, great spiders scuttled in glass cases and wove savage webs like clouds of silk. In another, fish swam in giant tanks, endlessly prowling back and forth in the dark, quiet waters, turning and turning nervously, never still, never at rest, like sharks that will die if they stop moving. And finally there came a small room filled with bright flames. Everywhere, lamps burned, throwing tongues of fire into the shadow-encrusted air. Earth and air, water and fire – all the elements and creatures from each one. The world in miniature.

At the end of the fire-room was a door different to the others they had passed through. It was painted with mandalas – circular

183

patterns in which the worlds of air and land and sea were depicted. From reality to shadow, from the shell to the kernel. The steward opened the door and stood aside to let Christopher pass.

Beyond the mandala door lay a great chamber that seemed to stretch across most of the upper storey. Shafts of dust-laden light drifted lazily through apertures in the ceiling, but they were insufficient to dispel the abundant shadows lurking everywhere. The tiny flames of butter-lamps wavered in the distance like fireflies above a dark lake. Christopher heard a sound behind him. He turned to see the door close. The steward had gone.

As his eyes grew accustomed once more to the gloom, Christopher saw what sort of room it was he had entered. He had heard of such places before, but had never expected to see one. This was the *chörten* hall, where the tombs of all the past abbots of the monastery were ranged along one wall: great boxes, vaster than the deaths they contained, untarnished, polished, dusted – gleaming receptacles for decaying flesh and mouldering bones. The lights flickered and picked out the façades of the great tombs, built from bronze and gold and silver, encrusted with jewels and precious ornaments.

Each *chörten* stood on a large pedestal and rose almost to the ceiling. In an impermanent world, they were tokens of permanence, like crystal in ice or gold in sunlight, never melting, never shifting through the dark, uncertain boundaries of change and chance. Inside each one, the mummified remains of an abbot had been placed. From time to time, salt was added to keep the mummies in a state of semi-preservation. Through grilles set in the front of the *chörtens*, the gilded faces of their inhabitants gazed out forlornly on a world of grey shadows.

Slowly, Christopher walked along the row of golden tombs. Outside, he could hear the whistling of the afternoon wind. It was cold up here, cold and alone and, somehow, futile. There were twelve *chörtens* in all. Some of the abbots would have died as old men, some as children – but if the monks were to be believed, they were one and all incarnations of the same spirit, the same being in a multitude of bodies. Each living abbot would dwell up here all his life, side by side with his old bodies, as a man will dwell with his memories or his cast-off clothes, waiting for his own body to join the others, waiting to take on a new form – but never a new identity.

The abbot was waiting for him just like the day before, in a niche at the far end of the long hall, seated on cushions among gilded shadows and gods like fire. He seemed more diminished here, dwarfed by the huge *chörtens*, a pale figure lost among his own past lives. It was as if he had been sitting there, on that same throne, on that same spot, down long centuries, watching the *chörtens* being built and occupied, waiting for someone to come and say it was finished, that it was time to leave at last. Christopher bowed low and was told to seat himself on a padded seat facing the abbot.

'You asked to see me,' said the old man.

'Yes.'

'An important matter.'

'Yes,' said Christopher.

'Go on.'

'Someone came to my room last night. While I was sleeping. Do you understand? He entered my room while I was sleeping. He tried to kill me. I want to know why. I want you to tell me why.'

The abbot did not answer straight away. He appeared shaken by Christopher's revelation.

'How do you know he wanted to kill you?' he asked at last.

'Because he had a knife. Because he carried a garrotting cord and tried to use it on me.'

'I see. And you think I know something about this, that I am perhaps responsible for it.'

Christopher said nothing.

'Yes. You think I tried to have you killed.' There was a long pause. The abbot sighed audibly. When he spoke again, his voice had altered. It was weaker, older, sadder than before.

'I would not have you harmed. That you must believe, even if you doubt everything else you see or hear in this place. That alone is true. Do you understand me? Do you believe me?'

You are holy to me. I cannot touch you. The words came unbidden into his mind, like birds that had been caged and suddenly set free. They fluttered grey wings at him and were gone. *But I can harm you,* he thought. He could feel the cold blade of the knife nestling against his calf.

'How can I believe you?' he said. 'You've taken my son by force and killed a man while doing so. One of your monks has killed a boy whose only crime was to have been injured. And a man comes

185

to my room in the dark, carrying a knife. Why should I believe a word you say?'

He saw the abbot's eyes watching him intently.

'Because I am telling you the truth.' There was a pause. 'When you met me first, you mentioned someone called Zamyatin. Tell me now what you know of him.'

Christopher hesitated. He knew so little of Zamyatin himself, and so much of what he did know depended on information that would be meaningless to the abbot of a remote Tibetan monastery that he scarcely knew where to start. It seemed easiest to begin with the basic facts that Winterpole had supplied him with.

When he had finished, the abbot said nothing. He sat motionless on his throne, carefully sifting everything Christopher had told him. After what seemed an age, he spoke again.

'Zamyatin is here, in Dorje-la. Did you know that?'

'Yes. I guessed he must be.'

'He has been here for several months. He came as a pilgrim. At first. Tell me, do you think he was behind the attempt on your life?'

Christopher nodded. It was highly likely.

'You are enemies, you and this Russian?'

'Our countries are . . . not at war, exactly. But in a state of rivalry. Tension.'

'Not your countries,' said the abbot. 'Not your people. Your philosophies. Not long ago, your countries were allies in the great war against the Germans. Is that not so?'

Whoever this abbot was, thought Christopher, he had under-estimated his knowledge of the world outside his monastery.

'Yes, we were allies . . . But then the Russians had a revolution. They killed their king and his family – his wife and children. A party called Bolsheviks came to power. They killed anyone who stood in their way – tens of thousands, guilty, innocent: it made no difference.'

'Perhaps they had a reason for killing their king. Was he a just king?'

Not just and yet not a tyrant, thought Christopher. Just weak-willed and inept, the figurehead of an autocratic system he could not change.

186

'I think he wanted to be just. To be loved by his people,' he said.

'That is not enough,' the abbot answered. 'A man may want to enter Nirvana, but first he must act. There are eight things necessary for liberation from pain: the most important is right action. When a just man takes no action, the unjust will act instead.'

'That is true but Zamyatin must be stopped,' Christopher said. 'The Bolsheviks are planning to take control of Asia. They will reach out and take each country on their borders. And then they will go further. No-one will be safe. Not even you, not even this place. Zamyatin has come to Tibet to further those ends. If you value your freedom, help me stop him.'

The old man sighed audibly and leaned forward again. The trace of a smile crossed his lips.

'And you,' he said, 'what will you do when you have stopped him?'

Christopher was unsure. It depended on what Zamyatin was up to. Would he have to stay . . . and turn Zamyatin's work to the advantage of Britain? Or would stopping Zamyatin be enough? .

'I'll return home with my son,' he said, acutely conscious of the half-truth. Winterpole had offered him William – at a price.

'And what will your people do? Will they leave us alone once the Bolsheviks are defeated?'

'We have no desire to be your masters,' Christopher said. 'We helped the Dalai Lama when he fled the Chinese. When the Chinese were defeated, he was free to go back to Lhasa. We didn't interfere.'

'But in 1904 you invaded Tibet yourselves. Your armies entered Lhasa. You showed your fist. You interfered directly, more than the Russians have ever interfered in this country. And you rule India. If you can enslave one country, you can enslave another.'

'The Indians are not our slaves,' Christopher protested.

'But they are not free,' said the abbot quietly.

'We do not oppress them.'

'Last year, you massacred hundreds in the Jalianwala Bagh in Amritsar. If they rise against you one day, as they did before, as the Russians did against their king, will it be because you wanted to be just and did not act . . . or because you were unjust and

187

acted? I want to know.' There was a sharpness in the abbot's voice now. Christopher wished to see him clearly, but the shadows clung to him tenaciously.

'I don't know the answer to that,' Christopher said. In his own mind, old doubts came soaring in like moths to a flame. 'I think we are sincere. I think we act justly most of the time. Amritsar was a mistake, an error of judgement on the part of the officer commanding the troops that day. It was an aberration.'

'An aberration!' The abbot spoke angrily. His composure had slipped and his voice grown rough. 'Amritsar was inevitable in a country where one race rules a subject race. It was no aberration, no mistake – it was a result of years of petty injustices, of arrogance, discrimination, blindness. Amritsar was a symbol of all that is rotten in your Empire. And you come to me with tales of Bolsheviks, you try to frighten me because a single Russian has set foot in these mountains, you tell me your people have no intentions towards Tibet. Do you take me for a fool?'

The old man fell silent. There was a pause, a long pause. As quickly as the anger had come, it went again. Christopher felt the old man's eyes on him, sharp and probing, yet still sad. When the abbot spoke again, it was in a changed voice.

'You should know better, Wylam-la. You should not be a prey to such foolishness. Were you not brought up to be one with the Indians – to eat their food, to breathe their air, to lose your identity in their identity? Weren't you taught to see the world through their eyes, to listen with their ears, to taste with their tongue? And you talk to me of errors of judgement, you talk to me of aberrations, you talk to me of dead kings? How can you have forgotten what I taught you? How can you have strayed so far from what you once were?'

Christopher felt a deep chill take hold of him. He was afraid. He was dreadfully afraid. His whole body shook with the beginnings of this fear. The shadows shifted about the abbot and his throne, ancient shadows, thin things that moved like hungry ghosts. Lights flickered. The room seemed full of voices whispering to him – voices from his past, voices from long ago, voices of the dead. He remembered the crucifix he had found in Cormac's desk, its sharp edges digging into his flesh.

'Who are you?' Christopher asked in a voice made dry by fear.

The old man came forward into the light. Slowly, the shadows gave up their hold on him. He had dwelt so long in them and they so long in him, but now, for a brief moment, they parted and returned him living to the light. He stood up, a frail old man in saffron robes, and stepped down from the dais on which his throne was set. Slowly, he came towards Christopher, taller than he had appeared seated on the cushions. He came right up to Christopher and knelt down in front of him, his face only inches away from his.

'Who are you?' whispered Christopher again. The fear was a living thing that struggled in him, threshing about in his chest like a caged animal or a bird or a butterfly.

'Don't you know me, Christopher?' The abbot's voice was low and gentle. It did not strike Christopher at first that these last words were spoken not in Tibetan but in English.

The world shattered.

'Do you not . . .'

The fragments crumbled to dust and were scattered.

'. . . remember me . . .'

A wind howled in Christopher's head. The world was a void filled with the dust of the world that had been. He heard his mother's voice, calling him:

'. . . Christopher.'

And his sister's voice, in the long days of summer, running after him on a sunlit lawn:

'. . . Christopher.'

And Elizabeth, her arms stretched out in pain, her eyes distended, dying:

'. . . Christopher.'

And at the end, his father's voice, in the centre of the void, reassembling the dust, refashioning the world:

'. . . Christopher? Don't you remember me, Christopher?'

27

They stood by the last of the *chörtens* together. Christopher's father had opened shutters in the wall so that they could see out across the pass. For a long time, neither man spoke. The sun had moved, and from its new position it carved patterns of light and darkness on dim white peaks and snow-filled gullies. Apart from shadows, nothing moved. The whole world was still and silent.

'That's Everest,' said the old man suddenly, pointing south and west, as a father will point something out to his child. 'The Tibetans call it Chomolungma, the Goddess Mother of the Earth.' He paused while Christopher located the peak to which he had pointed. Fragments of cloud covered all but the last extremity of the great mountain, dwarfed by distance.

'And that's Makalu,' he answered, pointing a little further south. 'Chamlang, Lhotse – you can see them all from here if the air is clear. Sometimes I stand in this spot for hours watching them. I never grow tired of this view. Never. I can still remember the first time I saw it.' He fell silent again, thinking of the past.

Christopher shivered.

'Are you cold?' his father asked.

He nodded and the old man closed the shutter, confining them inside the *chörten* hall once more.

'This was my last body,' Christopher's father said, brushing his hand against the burnished metal of the tomb.

'I don't understand,' said Christopher. Would even two and two make four again, or black and white combine to make grey?

'Surely you understand this much,' his father protested. 'That we put on bodies and take them off again. I have had many bodies. Soon I shall be getting rid of this one as well. And then it will be time to find another.'

'But you're my father!' Christopher protested in his turn. 'You died years ago. This isn't possible.'

'What is possible, Christopher? What is impossible? Can you tell me? Can you put your hand to your heart and say you know?'

'I know that if you are my father, if you are the man I knew as a child, you can't be ... the reincarnation of some Tibetan holy man. You were born in England, at Grantchester. You married my mother. You had a son. A daughter. None of this makes sense.'

The old man took Christopher's right hand and held it firmly in his own.

'Christopher,' he said, 'if only I could explain. We're strangers now, you and I; but believe me that I've never forgotten you. It was never my wish to leave you. Do you believe that?'

'I don't know what you wished. I only know what happened. What they told me happened.'

'What did they tell you?'

'That you disappeared. That you left camp one night and could not be found in the morning. After some time had passed, it was assumed you were dead. Is that true? Is that what happened?'

The old man let go of Christopher's hand and turned away from him a little.

'After a fashion,' he said in a quiet voice. He was a small man, dwarfed by the tombs of his predecessors. His lined and wrinkled face showed signs of great weariness.

'It is true, but only after a fashion – like most things in this world. The deeper truth, the truth they could not guess, much less tell you, was that Arthur Wylam had been dead long before he walked out of his tent that night. I was a shell, I was empty, there was absolutely no substance to me, none at all. I acted, I performed my duties, such as they were, I passed for a man. But inwardly, I was already dead. I was like one of the *ro-langs* people believe they have seen in these mountains.

'When I left the camp that morning, I didn't know what I was doing, where I was going. I remember very little, to be honest. All I know is that there was nothing more for me in that life. I'd exhausted everything it had to offer and found it rotten at the core. All I wanted to do was walk. And that is exactly what I did. I walked and climbed and stumbled for days, deeper and deeper into the mountains. I had no food, I had no idea how to find any, I was lost, and my mind was in total confusion.'

191

He paused, remembering, tasting again the emptiness and the horror of those days.

'They found me at a place called Sepo – two monks from Dorje-la. I was in a state of collapse, close to death. Nothing extraordinary, really – a dying man, cold, hungry, with his mind in tatters. But in Tibet, nothing is quite ordinary either. They find signs in everything – in a meteor, a monstrous birth, a bird circling a hill. It is often the tiny things that draw their attention – the shape of a child's ears, the way the thatch lies on a farmer's roof, the path smoke takes as it rises from a chimney. Things you and I would not even notice. We have grown out of touch.

'The place they found me at was a junction where two glaciers met. There was a sharp peak to the east and a steep precipice to the west. On the day they found me, two vultures had been seen nearby, just hovering. I rather think they were waiting for a meal once I was finished. All simple things those – but they took them as signs. They said there was a prophecy, that the new abbot of Dorje-la would be found in a place of that description. To this day, I don't know if that was true or not, if there was a prophecy or not. But they believed it. And afterwards . . . I came to believe it too.'

Christopher broke in, still not comprehending.

'But you weren't a child,' he said. 'You were a man of forty, an adult. They always choose children as new incarnations, at the age of three or four.'

His father sighed and placed a hand on Christopher's shoulder.

'This isn't an ordinary monastery, Christopher. This is Dorje-la. Things happen differently here.' He paused and sighed again. 'I am the thirteenth abbot of Dorje-la. My predecessor died in the same year I was born and left instructions not to seek for his successor until forty years had passed. He said the new incarnation would come from the south, from India. And that he would be a *pee-ling*.'

He fell silent. Christopher said nothing. If the old man believed this nonsense, what right had he to object? And perhaps it was not nonsense after all. Perhaps there was some substance to it that Christopher's western mind could not appreciate.

'Shall we go to another room?' the old man asked.

Christopher nodded.

'I'm in your hands,' he said.

His father looked at him, still trying to find in the man the child he had left so many years before. Was there anything left, anything at all?

'No,' he said, 'you're in your own hands.'

They left the *chörten* hall and passed through heavy curtains into a small room. It was a circular chamber, about twelve feet in diameter, empty of the usual cushions and hangings, devoid of ornamentation. At the end of the world, Arthur Wylam had found austerity. A plain carpet covered the floor and a long bolster ran along a section of wall. In niches books were ranged in small piles. Several lamps hung from a shallowly domed ceiling.

They sat down together, leaning against the bolster, father and son.

'It's very simple, I'm afraid,' the old man said. 'No birds, no butterflies, no fish.'

'Why do you have them?' Christopher asked, meaning the animals and plants in the rooms he had passed through earlier.

'My predecessor began the rooms. He was curious about things. He wanted to have examples of the world about him. I preserve them, replenish them when necessary.'

'They represent the elements? Is that their significance?'

The abbot nodded.

'The elements, yes. That and more. They show us decay. And birth. And the levels of existence. And much else besides.'

'I see.' Christopher hesitated. He wanted to talk about other things. 'After they brought you here,' he said, 'why didn't you try to get in touch with someone, explain what had happened? You never even wrote to me. I thought you were dead.'

'I wanted you to think that. What else could I have done? Told you I was alive, but that I was never coming back? You would have tried to find me. At first, I didn't understand this place or what it stood for. I didn't even know who I was, who they expected me to be. So how could I have coped with your coming here, seeking me out, reminding me of who I had been? And later . . . later I began to understand. And when I understood . . . there was no going back.'

'What about love?' asked Christopher. 'What about trust?'

The old man sighed. He had not heard those words in any language for a very long time.

'Don't you see I was beyond all that?' he replied. 'Beyond love, beyond trust. I had no more of either in me – not a shred, nothing. I pray you never reach that state. Not, at least, in the way I came to it. In the end, you will have to abandon all such things – love and trust and desire. Especially the last, especially desire. Otherwise they will devour you. Believe me, they are greedy. Desire is insatiable, it knows no beginning and no end. There are no boundaries to it. But they are the cords that bind you to suffering. They will bind you for the rest of your life if you do not prevent them. And for all your future lives.'

'Why did you steal my son?' Christopher asked abruptly.

The abbot did not answer. His face was troubled. He looked away from Christopher at shadows.

'He's important to you for some reason, isn't he?' Christopher persisted. 'Because he's your grandson. That's the reason, isn't it? You want him to be some sort of incarnation as well, don't you?'

His father bent his head.

'Yes.' he said.

Christopher stood up angrily.

'Well, you're wrong. William is my son. My wife's son. You have no part in him. It was your choice to die. Very well, stay dead: the dead have no claims on the living. William is my son and he belongs with me. I'm taking him home with me.'

The old man looked up.

'Sit down,' he whispered.

Christopher remained standing.

'I am old now,' his father said. 'I don't have much longer to live. But when I die, Dorje-la will be without an abbot. Please try to understand what that means. These monks are like children, they need someone to be a father to them. Now especially, when the world outside is changing so rapidly. They may not be able to remain secluded here much longer. When the world comes knocking on the gates of Dorje-la, there must be someone in charge who can meet it on its own terms. An outsider, a *pee-ling* like ourselves.'

'But why William, why my son?'

The old man sighed.

'There is a prophecy,' he said. 'It doesn't matter whether you

194

believe in prophecies or not. The monks here believe in them, and in this prophecy in particular.'

'And what does it say, this prophecy?'

'The first part refers to myself. So they believe. "When Dorje-la is ruled by a *pee-ling*, the world shall be ruled from Dorje-la." The second part refers to "the son of a *pee-ling*'s son". He will be the last abbot of Dorje-la. And then the Buddha of the last age will appear: the Maidari.'

'And you think William is this "son of a *pee-ling*'s son"?'

'They believe all Europeans marry and that the child must be the grandson of the *pee-ling* abbot. I did not believe that at first. Even if you had a son, I could see no way of ever bringing him here. I had no means.'

'What made you change your mind?'

The abbot paused. Whatever was troubling him had returned with renewed force. Christopher thought he was frightened by something.

'Zamyatin changed my mind,' he said finally. 'When he came here, he already knew of the prophecy. He knew of me: who I was, where I had come from. He told me that, if I had a grandson, he could arrange to have him brought here. At first I argued, but in the end he persuaded me. I needed the boy, you see. I needed someone to carry on the line.'

'Couldn't you have tried to find a new incarnation in the normal way? Here, in Tibet. A Buddhist child, one whose parents would have been happy for him to be chosen.'

The old man shook his head.

'No,' he said. 'There was the prophecy. During the years after my predecessor died, before I came here, there was a vice-regency. A man called Tensing Rinpoche ruled in the abbot's place. When they brought me here at first, he opposed my selection as the new abbot. He died two years later, but a section of the monks has always thought of him as the true incarnation.'

'When he was a young man, he belonged to another sect, one that does not require its monks to be celibate. He had a son. That son is now an important man in his own right here. His name is Tsarong Rinpoche. If I leave Dorje-la without an abbot most of the monks can accept, Tsarong Rinpoche will have his opportunity.

There are enough who will follow him. And I need not tell you what it will mean if he proclaims himself abbot.'

'Why don't you get rid of him?'

'I cannot. He is the son of Tensing Rinpoche. Believe me, I cannot send him away.'

'Why did Zamyatin offer to help you? What was in it for him?'

The abbot hesitated. Behind him, a candle stirred in the chill air.

'He came to Tibet in search of something. What he sought was here, in Dorje-la. He made a deal with me: my grandson in exchange for what he wanted. At first I refused, but in the end I saw I had no choice. I accepted his offer.'

'What was it he came here to find?'

'Please, Christopher, I can't explain. Not yet. Later, when you have been here a little longer.'

'And William – will I be allowed to see him?'

'Please be patient, Christopher. Eventually, when it is time. But you must understand that you cannot be allowed to take him away. You must reconcile yourself to that. I know it will be hard, but I can teach you how. You may stay in Dorje-la indefinitely. I would like it if you stayed. But you can never leave with your son. He belongs to us now.'

Christopher said nothing. He went to the curtains and pulled them aside. Outside, the sun had set and darkness had taken hold of the *chörtens*. He could feel the knife in his boot, the hard metal against his skin. It would be so easy to hold the blade against his father's throat, force him to give William up to him. No-one would dare to stop him while he held their abbot hostage. He wondered why he was unable to act.

'I want to be taken back to my room,' he said.

His father stood and came to the doorway.

'You can't go back there. Zamyatin has tried to have you killed once: he won't make a mistake the next time. I'll give instructions for you to be housed on this floor, near me.' He looked out at the darkened chamber beyond. 'It's already dark. I have my devotions to attend to. Wait here: I'll send someone to show you to your new room.'

The abbot turned and went back into the little room. Christopher watched him go, his hair white, his body bent. His father had come back from the dead. It was like a miracle. But if it meant he could take William out of this place, he would gladly wipe out the miracle and send his father back to the grave.

28

The room to which Christopher was shown was larger than the
cell in which he had first been confined. It was square and finely
furnished, with high walls that were finished with brightly glazed
tiles that had come all the way from Persia. Peacocks strutted and
sloe-eyed maidens cast alluring glances over brimming bowls of
wine. On a blue sky, the silhouettes of nightingales and hoopoes
formed patterns elaborate as birdsong. It was a place of riches,
hardly a monastic room at all; but for all that, it was as much a
prison as the tiny chamber below had been.

He lay awake afterwards in a tight darkness that smelled to him
of childhood. His butter-lamp had extinguished itself, leaving him
to relive his past in the sudden knowledge that his father had been
alive all along. While Christopher had mourned, his father had
been here in Dorje-la, perhaps in this very room, assuming the
contours of a new identity. Did it make any difference at all? he
wondered. Nothing could change what had been. He fell asleep
uneasily, just as he had gone to sleep that first night long ago, on
the day news of his father's death had reached him during a
passage of the *Aeneid*.

He was awakened by a small sound, and at once saw a light
flickering in the room. Someone was standing near his bed,
watching him silently. At first he thought it was his father, come
to watch over him while he slept; but then he saw that the figure
with the light was smaller and unstooped.

'Who's there?' he called out; but he knew.

'Shshsh,' the intruder hissed. In the same moment, the small
light was lifted higher and he saw her, captured for him in its glow.
How long had she been standing in the half-darkness, watching
him?

She came over to his bedside, without a sound.

'I'm sorry if I startled you,' she whispered. Close by, he could at
last make out her features perfectly. He had not imagined it: she

198

was extraordinarily beautiful. Her face bent out of the darkness towards him with a look of concern.

'I came to see if you were awake,' she continued, still in a whisper.

He sat up. Even though he was fully dressed, the room felt cold.

'It's all right,' he said. 'I don't think I've been asleep long. To tell the truth, I'd rather stay awake.'

She put her lamp down on a low table and moved back into the shadows. He sensed that she was frightened of him.

'Why did they move you to this room?' she asked.

He explained. She was very subdued when he finished.

'How did you know I was here?' he asked.

She hesitated.

'My old nurse Sönam knows everything that goes on in Dorje-la,' she said. 'She told me you had been moved here.'

'I see. How did you get here? The monk who showed me to this room said the door would be watched all night.'

He thought she smiled to herself.

'Dorje-la was built to hold secrets,' she whispered.

'And you?' he asked.

'I don't understand.'

'Are you one of its secrets?'

She looked down at her feet. When she looked up again, her eyes seemed darker, but full of stars.

'Perhaps,' she answered in a small voice.

Christopher looked at her. Her eyes were like pools, deep pools in which a man could drown if he were careless enough.

'How do you come to be here?' he asked.

'I have always been here,' she said simply.

He looked at her again. It seemed impossible that such grace could belong in a place like this.

'There has always been a Lady at Dorje-la,' she went on.

'A Lady?' he said, not understanding.

'Someone to represent the Lady Tara,' she answered. 'The goddess Drölma, Avalokita's consort. She has always dwelt here in Dorje-la, in the body of a woman.'

He gazed at her in horror.

'You mean you're a goddess? That they worship you?'

She smiled and shook her head.

199

'No,' she said. 'Tara is the goddess. Or Drölma, if you prefer – she has many names. I am a woman. She incarnates herself in me, but I am not she; I am not the goddess. Do you understand?'

He shook his head.

'It's simple,' she said. 'We are all aspects of the eternal Buddha. My aspect is Tara. She can be seen in me and through me. But I am not Tara. I am Chindamani. I am just a vehicle for Tara, here in Dorje-la. She has other bodies in other places.'

Christopher shook his head again.

'None of this makes sense to me. I could believe you are a goddess, that's not hard. You're lovelier than any statue I've ever seen.'

She blushed and looked away.

'I am only a woman,' she murmured. 'I have known nothing but this life, this body. Only Tara knows my other bodies. When I am reborn, Tara will have yet another body. But Chindamani will be no more.'

Outside a gust of wind clattered briefly and was still.

'I'm sorry this is hard for you,' she said.

'I'm sorry too.'

She looked at him again and smiled.

'You should not be so sad.'

But he was sad. Nothing would turn him from that now.

'Tell me,' he said, 'what does the name Chindamani mean? You said Tara had many names. Is that one of them?'

She shook her head.

'No, it's a Sanskrit word. It means "the wish-fulfilling jewel". The jewel is part of an old legend: whoever found it could ask for all his wishes to be fulfilled. Do you have stories like that where you come from?'

'Yes,' said Christopher. But to himself he thought that they all ended in tragedy.

'You have not told me your name,' she said.

'Christopher,' he replied. 'My name is Christopher.'

'Ka-ris To-feh. What does it mean?'

'It's difficult to explain,' he said. 'One of the names of the god my people worship is "Christ". "Christopher" was the name of a man who carried him on his shoulders when he was a child. It means "the one who carried Christ".'

200

He though she looked at him oddly, as though his words had struck a chord in her. She was silent for a while, lost in thought. He studied her face, wishing it were daylight so he might see her better.

'Chindamani,' he said, changing the subject, 'I know who the Dorje Lama is. I know why he brought my son here, why he wants to keep him here. You said you could help me take William away. Are you still willing to do that?'

She nodded.

'Why?' he asked. 'Why do you want to help?'

She frowned.

'I need your help in return,' she said. 'I can find a way out of Dorje-la for you and your son. But once we are outside I am helpless. I was brought to this place as a little girl: the world is just like a dream to me. I need you to help me find my way in it.'

'But why should you want to leave at all? Help me to get William out and I will take him the rest of the way.'

She shook her head.

'I told you there was danger here,' she said. 'I have to leave.'

'You mean you're in danger?'

She shook her head again.

'No. No-one would dare harm me. But others are in danger. One in particular: his life is in great danger. I have to help him escape. I want you to help me.'

'I don't understand. Who is this person? Why is his life in danger?'

She hesitated.

'It isn't easy to explain.'

'Try.'

She shook her head.

'No,' she said. 'It will be better if you see for yourself. Come with me. But be quiet. If we are discovered, I won't be able to help you. He will have you killed.'

'Who? Who will have me killed?'

'A Mongol. They say he comes from a distant place called Russia. His name is Zamyatin.'

Christopher nodded.

'Yes,' he said. 'I know about him. Is he the source of the danger here?'

201

'Yes. Zamyatin and those who support him. He has followers in the monastery. The man who brought you here, Tsarong Rinpoche, is one of them.'

It was still unclear, but Christopher could see the beginnings of a pattern.

'Where are we going?' he said.

She looked at him directly for the first time.

'To see your son,' she said. 'I promised I would take you to him.'

29

They left Christopher's room through a hidden door in the wall, behind a heavy hanging. There was a long, musty passage that led them to a second door, through which they entered a public corridor. Chindamani knew her way impeccably. He watched her glide ahead of him, a mere shadow blending with other shadows. They remained on the upper storey, passing along curiously shaped corridors and through dark, freezing rooms. Finally, they came to a spindly wooden ladder that led up to a hatch set in the roof of the passage. On hooks near the ladder several heavy sheepskin coats were hanging.

'Put one of these on,' ordered Chindamani, passing a *chuba* to Christopher.

'We're going outside?'

She nodded.

'Yes. Outside. You'll see.'

She slipped into a *chuba* that was several sizes too big for her, drew its hood over her head, and without another word turned and scrambled dexterously up the ladder. At the top, she used one hand to raise the hatch. It was like opening a door into a maelstrom. A freezing wind came down like a breath from a northern hell. Chindamani's lamp was snuffed out instantly, leaving them in total darkness. Christopher climbed up after her.

'Stay close to me!' she shouted.

The wind drove into her face with a brutal force that almost toppled her from the ladder. She crawled out on to the flat roof, bending low in order to avoid being caught by the wind and tossed aside. The darkness was not darkness, but a mass of indecipherable sounds: the howls and whimpers of lost souls in a wilderness of pain.

Christopher clambered out beside her and replaced the hatch with difficulty. He reached out and found her in the darkness. She took his hand, gripping it tightly with cold and frightened fingers.

203

As his eyes grew accustomed to the darkness, Christopher could make out vague shapes around them: the golden cupolas and finials, prayer-wheels and gilded statues that he had seen from a distance on the day of his arrival at Dorje-la. Chindamani knew her way across the roof from long experience. Together, they moved through the gale until they came to the very edge. Chindamani pulled Christopher close and put her lips to his ear.

'This is the hard part,' she said.

He wondered where the easy part had been.

'What do we have to do?' he asked.

'There's a bridge,' she shouted. 'It goes from the roof to another shelf of the mountain. It isn't far.'

Christopher looked into the darkness beyond the roof.

'I can't see anything!' he yelled. His lips brushed her ear; he wanted to kiss her. Now, in the darkness, in the storm.

'It's there,' she called back. 'Believe me. But in this wind we have to go on our hands and knees. There are no rails. Nothing to hold on to.'

'How wide is it?' This did not sound like a very good idea.

'As wide as you want it to be,' she said. 'Ten miles wide. As wide as Tibet. As wide as the hand of Lord Chenrezi. You will not fall off.'

He looked into the darkness again. He wished he had her confidence.

'Don't be so sure,' he said.

She let go of his hand and dropped down on all fours. He could just make her out, a small dark figure ahead of him, crawling into the night.

He followed suit. The *chuba* made him feel huge and awkward, an easy target for the wind to snatch and bowl over. He felt acutely anxious for Chindamani, fearful that her tiny figure would be no match for the fierce gusts, that she would be taken like a leaf and thrown into the void.

The darkness swallowed her up, and he crawled forward to the spot where he had last seen her. He could just make out the first few feet of a stone bridge jutting out from the roof. He had asked how wide it was, but not how long. As near as he could judge, it was less than three feet wide, and its surface seemed as smooth as glass. He preferred not to think about what lay beneath it.

His heart beating uncomfortably, he held his breath and moved out on to the bridge, gripping the sides with his hands, keeping his knees close together, praying that the wind would not gust suddenly and tear him off. In spite of the freezing air, he felt hot beads of sweat form on his forehead and cheeks. The *chuba* kept getting in the way, threatening to entangle itself with his legs and trip him. He could not see Chindamani in front. There was only wind and darkness – darkness that had no end, wind that kept on coming, blind and inexhaustible.

He moved a limb at a time: left hand, right hand, left knee, right knee, progressing in a shuffling motion, certain his balance would go and the bridge slip from his grasp in a single, irretrievable instant. Twice an updraught took him from below and started to lift him, using the *chuba* as a sail, but each time he hunkered down, flattening himself against the surface of the bridge until the gust had moved on. His fingers were freezing, so much so that he could scarcely feel to grip the bridge. He could not see or hear or feel: his whole passage over the bridge was an act of will and nothing more.

It seemed to him as though the crossing took several lifetimes. Time stood still while he crawled endlessly through space. His former life was nothing but a dream: this and this alone was reality, moving in darkness, waiting for the wind to take him into its arms and play with him before finally breaking him like a doll on twisted rocks.

'What took you so long?' It was Chindamani's voice coming to him out of the darkness. He was on the opposite ledge, still crawling as though the bridge would never come to an end.

'We can stand up here,' she said. 'It's more sheltered than the roof.'

He noticed that the wind was quieter here and that it fell less heavily on his face when he turned into it. She was standing beside him again, small and absurdly bulky-looking in her outsize *chuba*. Without thinking, driven only by a desperation born in him while he crossed the bridge, he stepped towards her and held her to him. She said nothing, did nothing to repel him, but let him hold her, the thick *chubas* holding their bodies apart as much as the darkness or her dozen lifetimes. She allowed him to hold her, even though she knew it was wrong, that no man should ever hold her. A great fear began to grow in her. She could not give it a name, but she

205

knew it was centred somehow in this strange man whose destiny had so cruelly been joined to hers.

'It's time,' she said finally. He had not kissed her or touched her skin with his skin, but she had to make him let her go before the fear became too great. She had never understood before that fear and desire could lie so close together, like a god and his consort, entwined in stone forever.

He let go of her gently, releasing her into the night. She had smelt of cinnamon. His nostrils were inflamed by the smell of her. Not even the wind could take her perfume away.

She led him across an expanse of bare rock pocked with slivers and pools of ice. Above them, the mountain rose up into the darkness, huge and invisible, its mass more felt than seen. In spite of the shelter, it seemed almost colder here on the rock, against the grim flank of the mountain.

'They call it Ketsuperi,' she said.

Christopher said he did not understand.

'The mountain,' she explained. 'It means "the mountain that reaches heaven".'

Suddenly, they were standing right against the mountain wall. Chindamani put her hand to the rock face and pushed. Something moved, and Christopher realized that it had not been rock at all but a door set in the side of the mountain. Light streamed out from lamps hanging behind the doorway. Chindamani pushed again and the door swung all the way open.

In front of them, a narrow passageway stretched out for perhaps seventy or eighty feet. It had been cut down through the solid rock, but the walls had been smoothed and plastered over. Ornate lamps hung on fine gold chains from the ceiling, flickering gently in the draught from the open doorway.

Chindamani closed the door and threw back her hood. The air in the passage was much warmer than that outside.

'What is this place?' asked Christopher.

'A *labrang*,' she said. 'This is the residence of the incarnations of Dorje-la. This is where they live when they are first brought to the monastery from their families. The present abbot – your father – never used it. He lived from the beginning on the upper floor of the main building. To my knowledge, he has never set foot here.' She paused.

206

'When you held me then, outside,' she said hesitantly, 'what did you feel? What did you think of?'

The questions frightened her, coming as they did from a part of her consciousness that had been dormant until now. Before this, she had never needed to ask what anyone thought of her. She was Tara, not in the flesh, but in the spirit, and that took care of that. Her own flesh was unimportant, a vehicle, nothing more. She had never even thought of having an identity of her own.

'I thought of the cold,' he said. 'Of the darkness. Of the years I had spent on the bridge, thinking you were gone forever. And I though how it would be if there was warmth. If there was light. If you were just a woman and not some sort of goddess.'

'But I told you, I am a woman. There is no mystery.'

He looked at her, finding her eyes and holding them with his.

'Yes,' he said, 'there is mystery. I understand almost nothing. In your world I'm blind and deaf, crawling in darkness, waiting to fall into nothingness.'

'There is only nothingness,' she said.

'I can't believe that,' he protested.

'I'm sorry.' She turned her face away, reddening. But what she had said was true: there was only nothingness. The world was a dragonfly shimmering in silence over dark waters.

He stepped towards her, aware that he had hurt her. It had not been his intention.

'Come with me,' she said. 'Your son is waiting. He will be sleeping. But please, whatever you do, do not try to waken him or speak to him. Promise me that.'

'But . . .'

'You must promise. If they know you have seen him, they will make it impossible for us to get to him again. Promise.'

He nodded.

'I promise,' he said.

At the end of the passage, a door opened to the left. It led into a temple-room filled with statues and painted figures. From here, three more doors led into further rooms.

Chindamani motioned to Christopher that he should be silent, and opened the door on the right.

He saw at once that it was a bedroom. Only a dim light gave it any illumination, but he could see the small bed covered in rich brocades and the figure in it, etched by shadows.

Chindamani bowed low, then straightened and, putting a finger to her lips, slipped inside. Christopher followed her.

It was as though Dorje-la and all the vast wilderness of snow and ice that circled it had been swept away. Christopher imagined he was in Carfax again, looking down at his son sleeping in a quiet bedroom filled with toys and books. The only nightmare was in Christopher's head. He, not the child, was the dreamer who could not awaken, however hard he tried.

Cautiously, he went up close to William. The boy's hair had fallen over one eye. Gently, Christopher straightened it, touching his son's forehead. The boy stirred and mumbled something in his sleep. Chindamani took his arm, afraid he might waken the child. Christopher felt his eyes grow hot with tears. He wanted to pick William up and hold him, tell him that all was well, that he would take him away from this place. But Chindamani drew him away and out of the room.

It was a long time before Christopher could speak. Chindamani waited patiently, watching him. She was destined never to have children of her own, but she could understand some of the emotions he was feeling.

'I'm sorry,' he said at last.

'There's no need,' she told him. 'When the moment comes, you may speak to him. But it's best he doesn't know you are here just yet.'

'You said you were going to show me something else. You said there was someone in danger from Zamyatin.'

'Yes. We are going to see him now.'

'Zamyatin came here in search of something. When I was with . . .' – Christopher hesitated – 'my father, he said he had done a deal with Zamyatin: my son in exchange for what Zamyatin wanted. Has this other person something to do with all this?'

Chindamani nodded.

'Yes,' she said. 'Zamyatin came here to find him. I want you to help me get him away from him.'

She led the way to one of the other doors. Another dimly lit chamber, another bed covered in gorgeous fabrics. A child was sleeping in the bed, hair tousled, eyes shut against the darkness, one hand loosely curled on the pillow as though about to clutch or relinquish a dream.

'Here,' she whispered. 'This is what Zamyatin was looking for. This is what brought you here.'

A boy? A child wrapped in shadows? Was this really all?

'Who is he?' Christopher asked.

'Who would you like him to be?' asked Chindamani in reply. 'A king? The next Emperor of China, perhaps? The surviving son of the murdered Tzar? You see, I'm not entirely uninformed about your world.'

'I don't know,' he said. 'He could be anyone. I didn't expect something like this.' But what *had* he expected? Had he expected anything?

'He's just a little boy,' said Chindamani quietly, but with feeling. 'That's all he is. That's all he wants to be.' She paused. 'But he has no say in the matter. He cannot be whatever he wants to be because other people want him to be someone else. Do you understand?'

'Who do they say he is?'

Chindamani looked at the sleeping child, then back at Christopher.

'The Maidari Buddha,' she said. 'The ninth Buddha of Urga. And the last.'

'I don't understand.'

She shook her head softly, sadly.

'No,' she said, 'you do not understand.' She paused and glanced at the boy again. 'He is the rightful ruler of Mongolia,' she whispered. 'He is the key to a continent. Do you understand me now?'

Christopher looked down at the boy. So that was it. Zamyatin had been looking for a key to unlock the treasure house of Asia. A living god to make him the most powerful man in the East.

'Yes,' he said slowly. 'Yes, I think I am beginning to understand.'

She looked back at him.

'No,' she said. 'You understand nothing. Nothing whatever.'

30

They left the children sleeping and went out into the night again, returning to the main buildings by way of the bridge. The monastery was still fast asleep, but Chindamani insisted they move quietly until they reached Christopher's room.

She stayed with him that night until just before dawn. He was withdrawn at first in spite of her presence, for seeing William had flattened his spirits greatly. She made tea on a small stove in the corner of Christopher's room. It was Chinese tea, pale *wu lung* in which white jasmine flowers floated tranquilly, like lilies on a perfumed lake. When it was ready, she poured it carefully into two small porcelain cups set side by side on a low table. The cups were paper thin and soft blue in colour, like eggshells. Through the fine glaze, Christopher could see the tea, gleaming golden in the soft light.

'The Chinese call them *t'o t'ai*,' Chindamani said, touching the edge of one cup with her finger-tip. 'They are very special, very rare. These two were part of a present to one of the abbots of Dorje-la from the K'ang-hsi Emperor. They are over two hundred years old.'

She held the cup towards the light, watching the flames struggle in the amber liquid. For the first time, Christopher had an opportunity to see her properly. Her skin resembled the porcelain of the cup in her hand, in its smoothness and delicacy. She was tiny, less than five feet tall, and each part of her echoed that diminutiveness in a subtly modulated harmony of form. When she moved – to pour tea or lift the fragile cup to her lips or just to brush a strand of stray hair from her eyes – it was done with an infinitely exquisite grace that he had never seen in a woman before.

It was not a studied or a mannered gracefulness, but a natural ease of movement that had its origin in a total harmony that existed between her body and the world she inhabited. He felt that she might walk on water or cross a meadow without bruising a single blade of spring grass. And he felt sad, because such perfection seemed so far beyond his clumsy reach.

They drank the tea, saying nothing at first, watching the shadows melt and re-form on the walls. He was lost in thought, miles away, like a man drifting on a raft across an open sea, unable to tell where the shore might be or if there was a shore at all. She did not face him, did not try to break into his silence or tempt him from his pain. But when he looked up from time to time, she was there, her face half-hidden among shadows.

Finally, he began to talk, in small, clustered fragments of speech interspersed with long and painful silences. The tea grew cold and the jasmines shrivelled and drowned, and the wind sang in the mountains like a lost soul. There was neither order nor system in anything he said: thoughts simply poured out of him at random, to be followed by yet more silence. Now he spoke of his childhood in India, now of Aunt Tabitha and the long summers at Carfax, summers that had once seemed without end. Or he would tell her about men he had killed, men he had betrayed, a woman he had once betrayed long ago on a cold afternoon in the dead of winter. He told her of Cormac's death and how it preyed on him, the mindless droning of the flies constant in his thoughts; of the girl in the orphanage, naked and betrayed; of Lhaten slaughtered like a calf on a high field of driven snow.

She listened in silence like a priest hearing his confession, without absolution, without blame. And he sought for neither, finding sufficient blessing in her presence and grace enough in her silence. At the end, he told her about his father, about the mysterious and terrible rebirth that had taken place among the tombs that afternoon. A long silence followed. At one point, he realized that her hand was in his, small and fragile, like a shell or a piece of porcelain: a fragment of something he had known long ago and lost.

'How did the boy come to be here?' Christopher asked. 'The one Zamyatin came here to find.'

'His name is Dorje Samdup Rinpoche,' she said. 'He was born in a village far to the west of here, near the sacred lake Manosarowar. That was over ten years ago. When he was still very small, some monks came to Manosarowar from Mongolia. They found signs that he was the new incarnation of the Maidari Buddha.'

211

That would have been about 1912, thought Christopher. Now he knew what it was Maisky and Skrypnik had found at Manosarowar, what Zamyatin had set out to rediscover.

'At first the monks wanted to take Samdup back to Mongolia, to the holy city of Urga. But others advised against it. There is still a Khutukhtu on the throne of Urga: if he had learned of the boy's existence, he would have tried to have him killed rather than let himself be replaced by him.'

'A Khutukhtu?' Christopher had never heard the term before.

'It's what the Mongols call their incarnations. Samdup is the true Khutukhtu of Urga. The Jebtsun Damba Khutukhtu. The true ruler of Mongolia.'

'I don't understand. How can there be two Khutukhtus at the same time? How could one replace another while they are both alive?'

'There are not two Khutukhtus,' she replied. 'They are one and the same. They dwell in different bodies, that is all. But the eighth body has ceased to be a suitable vehicle. The Maidari Buddha has chosen to incarnate himself in another body before the eighth has been destroyed. It's very simple.'

'Yes, but what I don't understand is why Zamyatin should want to waste so much time coming here to look for the child. Why doesn't he just go to Mongolia and try to influence the present Khutukhtu?'

Chindamani shook her head.

'The Khutukhtu in Urga has no power. I do not understand such things, but I have heard the abbot and others talking. They say that, about the time Samdup was born, the Emperor of China was defeated in a great rebellion. Is that true?'

Christopher nodded. In 1911, the Manchu dynasty had been overthrown and a Republic established in China.

'When that happened,' Chindamani continued, 'the Khutukhtu at Urga rebelled against the Chinese, who had ruled over Mongolia for centuries. He was proclaimed ruler and the Chinese left the country. At first, another country, far to the north, gave him protection. They say it was one of the lands of the *pee-lings*, but I do not understand that.'

'Russia,' Christopher said. 'Their king wanted to have influence in the East. Go on.'

'The Khutukhtu ruled with their help for several years. And then the king of the *pee-lings* was overthrown just like the Emperor of China. Is that true?'

'Yes,' he said. 'It is true.'

'When that happened, the Chinese returned to Mongolia. They forced the Khutukhtu to sign papers on which he renounced all power for himself. They imprisoned him in his palace. He is an old man now and blind. And his people no longer believe in him. Zamyatin wants to take Lord Samdup to Urga and put him on the throne in his place.'

'You said the present Khutukhtu was no longer a suitable vehicle. That his people no longer believe in him. What did you mean?'

She seemed embarrassed to talk of such matters with him.

'I only know what Sönam has told me,' she said. 'The present Khutukhtu was born fifty years ago in a village just next to Lhasa. From an early age he showed signs of unsuitability: there was a . . . tension between the man and the spirit he incarnated. It sometimes happens. It's as though something goes wrong at the moment of incarnation.'

She paused, then plunged on.

'The Khutukhtu began to drink. He married, not once, but twice. His second wife is a slut: she invites men to her tent – young men, *trapas*, men who should know better. But he is worse. He sleeps with both men and women.'

'Some lamas complained about him a few years ago. They said he was bringing the faith into disrepute, that he was demeaning the office of Khutukhtu. He had them executed. Now no-one dares speak out against him.'

She looked at Christopher, uncertain what he would make of this.

'Do I shock you?' she asked. 'Do you think such a thing impossible?'

He shook his head.

'I don't know what's possible in your world,' he replied. 'I see nothing strange in a man wanting to drink or have a woman. A man is just a man, whatever resides in him.'

She sensed the unvoiced implication of what he said – that a woman too was just a woman, whatever men said resided in her.

'Such things happen sometimes,' she said. 'It was the case with the sixth Dalai Lama,' she said. 'The Great Fifth died while they were still building his palace in Lhasa, the Potala. For ten years, his Regent concealed his death from the people, saying he was in seclusion, meditating. When the sixth was finally discovered, he was a boy of about thirteen. He had lived in the world. He had smelt flowers. He had experienced desire.'

'They brought him to Lhasa and shut him up in the Potala. It was dark and gloomy, and he hated it. He wanted to live in the sunshine, among ordinary people – and they made him dwell in the dark with only gods and priests for company.'

He could hear the sympathy in her voice. She was expressing her own longings, speaking her own thoughts.

'Later, when he was old enough to have some control over his own affairs, he began to go into the town at night, disguised as an ordinary man. He went to taverns and found women to sleep with. And when the night was over, he slipped back to the darkness at the top of the Potala. He lived like that for years. And then the Chinese came. They took control of eastern Tibet. They garrisoned the road to Lhasa. And they killed the Dalai Lama.'

She fell silent.

'Didn't the people have doubts about whether he was truly an incarnation?'

She shook her head.

'No,' she answered. 'They never doubted him. He was gentle. Not like the Khutukhtu in Urga. Men said that he had two bodies – a real body and a phantom body. They said the real body stayed in the Potala while the phantom went round the taverns, testing their faith. He wrote poetry. Love songs. But his poetry was sad. Like perfume on a dying man.'

She began to recite lines from one of his poems:

High in the Potala, I dwell alone within dark chambers,
I am a god walking, I am an unearthly thing;
But when the narrow streets enfold me
and I walk in shadows among other men,
I am a thing of earth, a king of dancers,
I am the world itself learning to sing.

214

In the silence that followed, she understood for the first time just how alone she had been. Not even the Lady Tara could substitute for the presence of flesh and blood. She tried to remember her mother's face bending over her when she was tiny, but she could see nothing but shadows.

'I'm sorry for him,' said Christopher. 'He must have been very sad.'

She was looking down; not at him, not at anything.

'Yes,' she whispered. 'But perhaps no more sad than other Dalai Lamas, other incarnations. We all live lives like his. We're all disfigured in the same way. Our bodies are pale, Christopher. Our flesh is like ice. Our lives are endless rituals.'

She looked up quickly, as though afraid he might have disappeared.

'In my whole life,' she said, 'I have never smelt a flower. Only incense. Only butter-lamps. There are no flowers here.'

No flowers anywhere in this world, thought Christopher. Only snow. Only ice. Only frost.

Chindamani got up and went across to the window. Like other windows on the top floor, it was glazed. She looked out into the darkness beyond, past her own reflection, past the reflection of the lamp, gazing out of a world of shadows into a world of shadows. It was not yet dawn, but the sky held the first signs of light. She stared into the darkness, at the still edge of the night.

'We come from darkness,' she said, 'and we go back into darkness.'

The *pee-ling* confused her. He had turned everything upside-down. All her life she had known no other place than Dorje-la. For twenty years, she had watched the sun rise on the same mountains, prayed to the same gods, wandered the same corridors.

Silently, she returned to her seat.

'Ka-ris To-feh,' she said in a quiet voice, 'do you love your son very much?'

'Of course.'

'What if you found a destiny?' she asked. 'Here, in these mountains. In Dorje-la perhaps. Would you turn aside from it in order to go home with your son?'

'Are you offering me a destiny?' he asked in return. 'Is that what this is about?'

215

'I don't know,' she said simply, and he saw that her eyes were still troubled.

'What is it you want me to do?'

She fell silent and gazed into the little cup she held between her hands. If the cup broke, it could not be reborn. It would be gone forever. Not all things were permanent. Transience lay at the heart of everything.

'Take us away from Dorje-la,' she said. 'Samdup and myself. Take us northwards. There is a monastery far to the north where Samdup will be safe. Your son will be safe there too – until it is time for you to take him home. Will you help us?'

He hesitated. It would mean lengthening his journey and William's considerably. And such a diversion would not be free from danger. Common sense said he should answer 'no'. But he knew already he could not do that.

'How will we find the way?' he asked.

'I have a map. Sönam found it for me in the abbot's library.'

He looked at her face, at her eyes. He could not look away.

'Very well,' he said. 'I'll come with you. We'll find your sanctuary.'

She smiled and stood.

'Thank you,' she whispered. Her heart felt as though a great weight had been lifted from it. Why, then, did she still feel so frightened?

There was a sound of a trumpet blaring outside.

'It's time for me to go,' she said. 'I'll come back later today. You need to sleep now. We don't have much time. I think Zamyatin plans to leave here very soon.'

He stepped up close to her.

'Take care,' he said.

She smiled.

'Sleep well.'

He bent and kissed her gently on the forehead. She shivered and turned her face away.

'Goodbye, Ka-ris To-feh,' she said, then turned and went out by the secret entrance through which she had come in.

Christopher went to the window and gazed out. If he looked hard, he could just make out the shape of mountains emerging from the darkness.

216

31

He was dreaming of Carfax, and in the dream William came out to the gate to meet him. He saw him in the distance, waving, his tiny white hand making patterns against the sky. It had been so long, he thought, and Tibet had been so cold. How William must have grown, and how warm the fire in the library must have become. With every step he took, the boy grew bigger, and now here he was directly in front of him, not a boy at all but a man. William's hair had grown white at the temples, just like his own, and his face bore heavy lines, whether of grief or simple age he could not be sure. From nowhere in particular, a child's voice recited in Christopher's ear:

> 'You are old, little William,' his father said,
> 'And your hair has become very white.
> 'And yet you incessantly wear it to bed –
> 'Do you sleep at your age every night?'

'You've been gone a long time, father,' William said. 'We thought you were dead. We thought you'd disappeared like grandfather.'

'I was dead,' answered Christopher. 'But now I'm alive again.'

'Are you?' asked William, smiling a little smile.

He waited for Chindamani all that day, but she did not come. No-one came, except for a young monk who brought him food on two occasions and left without saying a word. Once, in the late afternoon, he thought he heard the sound of voices raised in anger, but after a while they died away and left him once more in silence. At sunset, the trumpet was not sounded. When the boy came to clear away his dishes, he seemed frightened, but he would not answer Christopher's questions and left in a hurry.

He went to bed early, uneasy. For a long time he could not

sleep. He strained for sounds in the night, but there was only the wind as always. He lay in the dark, wishing sleep would come. Or Chindamani, to banish it. And it came quietly, when he was not expecting it.

The next thing he was aware of was a figure bending over him in the dark. It was Chindamani, and her hand was clapped hard over his mouth. She put her lips to his ear and whispered fiercely.

'For all our sakes, Ka-ris To-feh, don't make a sound. Get out of bed as quietly as you can, then follow me. Please don't ask any questions, there's no time.'

He sensed the urgency and the fear in her voice. Without hesitation, he slipped out of bed and stood up. On the table by the bed was the knife he had taken from his assailant of two nights ago. Bending down, he fumbled for his boots, but she pushed them into his hand. He snatched up the knife and thrust it into his boot.

Outside the door of his room, the corridor had been plunged into pitch darkness. Chindamani held his hand as before. She used her other hand to follow the wall. Somewhere, loud voices called; there was a crashing sound, as though a large object had fallen. He thought he could hear feet running and then grow still. He thought he heard someone cry out and fall silent again.

Chindamani fumbled in the darkness. Then there was a door and they went through it. He heard the sound of a match being struck, then a sudden flame stabbed the darkness. Chindamani lit a small butter-lamp and set it back on a low cabinet. Her hand was trembling.

The girl was terrified. A long cut on her forehead was bleeding quite badly. Christopher stretched out his hand to wipe away the blood. She winced and drew away from him.

'What's happening?' he asked in a low whisper.

'I don't know,' she answered. 'I heard noises and went to investigate. There was someone in the corridor, one of the monks – I don't know his name. He . . . he told me to go back to my room, to stay there. He spoke to me as though he didn't know who I was. Or didn't care. I grew angry; I told him to mind his manners and explain what he was doing there. No-one is allowed on this floor without permission. He was carrying a stick. When I challenged him he just lifted it and struck me. I fell down. I think

218

he was going to hit me again, I don't know. Just at that moment someone called him from nearby and he left me.

'I went straight to your father's chambers to look for help, but there was no-one there. At least . . .' She hesitated. He saw the lamplight twist about her face in a ragged, jittery sort of dance. Her eyes looked frightened and blood ran over one eyebrow, matting its fine black hairs.

'There are several monks whose job is to serve the abbot,' she continued, collecting herself. 'They were all there. They . . .' She paused, leaning against the edge of the cabinet. Her hand touched the coiled tail of a sea-serpent. She had gone pale.

'They were dead,' she said in a hoarse voice. She shuddered, remembering. Christopher moved as though to take her in his arms and comfort her, but she flinched and held herself away from him. It was too soon for comfort. Perhaps it would never be the right time for it. The blood had not yet dried on her forehead.

'There was . . . blood everywhere,' she stammered. 'The room was red with it, bright, bright patches of blood in every corner. It had run across carpets, cushions, everything. Pools of it had collected in hollows, little red pools. Their . . . their throats had been cut. Not gently, not cleanly, but with something large and heavy, a sword or a billhook, without hesitation. They were butchered like animals.'

'My father . . . Was he . . .?'

She shook her head, biting her lower lip fiercely with small white teeth.

'No,' she whispered. 'He wasn't among them. I was afraid. But I stayed to look for him. I looked in all his rooms, but there was no sign of him. Perhaps he has hidden somewhere. There are secret chambers, places he could take refuge. But I was frightened, I didn't want to call out. It had sickened me, all that blood. I can't tell you . . .' She shivered again, the memory taking her like an ague, filling her flesh with a dark, unexpungeable chill.

'Then I thought of Samdup and your son,' she said. 'I thought of them alone, not knowing what was happening. I ran up to the roof and got across to the *labrang*, but they were already gone. Someone has taken them, Christopher. Perhaps they have already killed them. I'm frightened. I don't know what to do.'

He gestured as if to comfort her again, but still she recoiled from his touch, not out of fear of him, but more from a simple dread of his humanity. The world had suddenly been brought close to her, and at this moment he was its nearest representative.

Christopher thought he knew what was happening. Zamyatin must have decided to act. To take control of Dorje-la alone would be a matter of little consequence to him. But to have both children and a base from which to manipulate them – that would transform this little operation into something that could swing the political balance of Asia. But what had prompted his sudden action?

'Did you tell anyone of your plans to take Samdup away?' he asked.

She hesitated, then nodded slowly.

'Yes,' she whispered. 'I told the abbot this morning. I wanted his permission to go.' She paused. 'He refused. He said he knew a little of Zamyatin and his plans, but that he was in control of the situation. He thought he could make use of Zamyatin.'

'Make use of him?'

She blinked and nodded again.

'Your father had his own plans, his own ... dreams. Samdup was part of them, I think. And Zamyatin. And ... I think, your son.'

'What sort of plans?'

She shook her head.

'I don't know exactly. Dreams of power. Not for himself, but for the *dharma*, the doctrine of the Lord Buddha. Dreams of a barrier against all foreign interference, against Britain, against Russia, against China. There is a prophecy that when Dorje-la is ruled by a *pee-ling*, the world will be ruled from Dorje-la. Not literally, but in some sense. He believed that. He believed he had a destiny.'

'He talked of this to you?'

'A little,' she said. 'The rest I guessed. But I think it's too late now. If you are right, if Zamyatin has taken control.'

'This morning,' Christopher continued, 'were you overheard? Or would my father have told anyone else?'

She hesitated, then a look of dismay came over her face.

'At one point Losang Khyongla was in the room. He's the abbot's secretary. He ... I've just realized that he wasn't among the dead men I found in your father's quarters. You don't think he ...?'

220

Christopher nodded.

'Quite possibly. Anyway, that isn't important now. We have to find out what's going on. Do you have any idea where they might have taken my father and the boys?'

She thought briefly.

'The most likely place is Thondrup Chophel's room. It's a large room near the Lha-khang. Monks are often sent there to be punished. Thondrup and his assistants would take care of anything like that!'

'Who is Thondrup Chophel?' Christopher asked.

'He's the Geku, of course. He keeps discipline in the monastery. It's normal for a Geku to be frightening. Some of the monks get out of hand. But I don't like Thondrup. He's . . .' She paused.

'Yes?'

'He can be brutal,' she said. 'The abbot has had to reprimand him several times for his severity. Once he broke a man's arms, just because he made a mistake while reciting the Tangyur.'

'Why hasn't he been replaced?'

She smiled wanly at him.

'This is Dorje-la,' she said. 'The Geku is never dismissed. Discipline must come first. Broken bones can be mended.'

He looked back at her, his eyes full of concern.

'What about broken hearts?'

She sighed.

'Hearts are like cups of porcelain,' she whispered. 'Once they are broken, they can never be mended.' The smile left her face and she grew serious.

'Very well,' he said. 'We'll visit Thondrup Chophel's room. Can you get me there without being seen?'

She nodded.

'I think so.'

She lifted her hand nervously to her forehead. The blood had dried a little and the wound was beginning to sting.

They travelled by dark or partly-lit passages, creeping like mice in and out of shadows, listening for voices or footsteps. Occasionally there were sounds in the distance, and twice they had to take cover in darkened rooms until little bands of monks went past. They acted on the assumption that, if anyone was moving, he was unfriendly. On the lower floors, Zamyatin's handiwork was in evidence. The bodies of his victims lay in untidy bundles everywhere. Some had had their throats cut, others had broken necks, and a few had died from injuries to the skull. It had been silent work, mute and bloody.

Chindamani explained in whispers that a limited number of monks received training in Chinese martial arts from Tsarong Rinpoche. These men had been foremost among those attracted to Zamyatin. She thought he exercised some sort of control over them through Tsarong Rinpoche.

As they neared the Lha-khang, a low droning sound came to their ears.

'Listen,' whispered Chindamani. 'They're chanting hymns to Yama.'

'Who is Yama?' asked Christopher.

She looked at him oddly, a distant lamp catching fire in the black pupils of her eyes.

'He is the Lord of Death,' she answered simply, turning her face away.

They left the Lha-khang behind, but the sound of chanting followed them on heavy feet. At the far end of the corridor, they came to a red-painted door in the right-hand wall.

'Is this the only entrance?' asked Christopher.

She nodded.

They put their ears to the door, but no sounds could be heard from behind it. Christopher felt naked, with only the small knife to defend himself with.

'This is no good,' he said. 'We need weapons. These people mean business – we can't keep them off with our bare hands.'

She thought for a while, then nodded.

'All right,' she said. 'Wait in here.'

There was a small room nearby, where robes and other items were kept for use in the Lha-khang. Chindamani left Christopher there and hurried off down the corridor. Her feet made no sound on the cold stones; she might have been a shadow. He waited in the darkness for her, anxious and nervous, knowing that matters were reaching a climax.

She returned within five minutes carrying a short sword. It had come from the *gön-kang*, she explained. Most of the other weapons had already been taken.

They went back to the door of the Geku's room and listened again. It was still silent. But from the Lha-khang the hymn to Yama continued. Christopher put his hand to the door and pushed.

Afterwards, Christopher often wondered why he had not cried out at that moment. Had the horror been too great for his mind to take in all at once? Or had he passed in a single instant beyond all ordinary horror, into another realm where silence was the only speech?

He felt Chindamani clutch his arm, but it was as if his flesh and her flesh both belonged in a world he had just left behind. Someone had lit lamps and hung them at intervals from the walls, so that eveything in the room stood out clearly.

Ropes had been tied to rafters in the ceiling, dozens of them, like creepers in a forest, hanging down from low branches into a bright clearing, bearing obscene and over-ripened fruit. The ropes were taut, and they twisted slowly in the shadows. Something heavy hung at the end of each one, a man's body, turning ponderously in the gloom. The bodies hung like dummies in a tailor's warehouse, anonymous, waiting to be displayed in a shop window in a distant town; or like rag dolls waiting for giant children to cut them down and play with them.

Christopher felt a terrible cold pass through him. All his body was filled with it, his veins flowed with ice. He remembered his dream of the girls hanging in the orphanage, the staring eyes turned to him, the red lips parted. But this was no dream.

He stepped into the room, walking slowly among the bodies, looking for one body among the rest. To one side he saw the stool on which the victims had been made to stand while they were despatched. He imagined a practised foot kicking the stool out from underneath each time, the body dropping, the face in agony as the rope bit into the neck. All the men's hands had been tied behind their backs. Death had been slow and painful.

Suddenly, he heard Chindamani call out behind him, a cry of pain or horror. He whirled round, ready to run to help her. But it was too late. Tsarong Rinpoche held her firmly, one arm round her throat. In his free hand he held a pistol pointed at her head. Behind him, in the doorway, stood a group of monks, all armed.

'Drop your weapon to the floor, Wylam-la,' the Rinpoche said. 'If you do not, the Lady Tara will have to look for a new body.'

223

32

'You were warned not to enter Tibet,' Tsarong Rinpoche said, addressing Christopher. His voice was sad, as though he found his position distasteful but unavoidable. 'You decided to ignore that warning. A boy died. Now your own life hangs in the balance. I would have saved you from all this. Remember that.'

But inwardly the Rinpoche was very pleased with himself. The gods had smiled at his efforts. The Russian was pleased – and his masters in Moscow would send the assistance they had promised. There would be no more fumbling now that he was in control. The gods would repay him abundantly. He turned to Chindamani.

'I'm sorry, my lady,' he said, 'but I have instructions to bring you with me. If you behave yourself, no harm will befall you.' He removed his arm from her neck and let her move away from him. She stepped back towards Christopher and took his hand tightly in her own.

'Were you responsible for . . . this?' She gestured towards the room behind her.

'The executions were necessary,' the Rinpoche said, 'if there was to be no attempt to undo my work. Zam-ya-ting supervised them. He has carried out such tasks before.'

'What about my father?' Christopher asked. 'Has he been harmed?'

Tsarong Rinpoche shrugged.

'He was the abbot,' he said. 'I could not leave him alive and hope to rule in his place. He was a *trulku*. It was time for him to be reborn.'

For the second time in his life, Christopher received news of his father's death in silence. The old man had come back to him out of darkness and returned to it again, unrecognized, unforgiven, almost unremembered. Christopher was an heir to darkness now. In the shadows behind him, the heavy bodies moved as a single

224

body: this was his inheritance and he knew it would soon be time for him to claim it.

'Was the Russian responsible for his death as well?'

The Rinpoche shook his head.

'No. I took care of it myself.' He paused. 'There is no time to talk. Zam-ya-ting would like to see you. You have been much on his mind since your arrival here.'

They set off at once, Tsarong Rinpoche leading the way, followed by Christopher and Chindamani, each with a monk at either arm. As they walked, Christopher pondered on what had happened. The work of clearing the monastery had been finished and Zamyatin was in complete control – of that there could be little doubt. Nominal leadership of the monastery had passed to Tsarong Rinpoche – Christopher had already guessed that. But the controlling force, the hand on all the strings, would be Zamyatin's. And beyond Zamyatin the new regime in Moscow.

They climbed towards the upper storey, passing bodies that had fallen on the stairs

'What will you do with the men you have killed?' Christopher asked. 'How will you get rid of so many bodies?'

At first he thought the Rinpoche was not going to anwer. Then he spoke, his voice remote and unconcerned, as though he had been a schoolmaster, one of whose pupils had asked a question about the Great Plague: 'How did they bury them all, sir?'

'There will be a great sky burial,' the Rinpoche said. 'The air will be black with vultures. It will take several days at least, but they are greedy birds and monks are thin meat.'

Christopher understood what he meant by a 'sky burial'. In a country where there was little soil and less timber, corpses were seldom buried or burned. Instead, the bodies of the dead were taken out to high places and expertly dissected by men using butchers' knives. The meat was given to the vultures and the bones pounded to fine powder before being mixed with the brain and offered as a final titbit. Christopher had once watched a vulture after such a feast, too heavy to lift itself from the ground, its great wings flapping obscenely in the silence of the hills.

Their path led inexorably to the top of the monastery, and at last to the long *chörten* hall, where the tombs stood silent in the

225

half-light. Copper and gold and silver gave off a dull glow, like death. Waiting for them at the far end, bathed in candlelight, was a figure dressed all in black.

Zamyatin was dressed in the plainest of costumes: a cotton Chinese jacket and trousers. His hair was cropped short, not shaven like that of the monks. He sat cross-legged on a throne of cushions, for all the world like an incarnation of a deity from the underworld. Christopher remembered something Winterpole had said to him before he left, about how the Bolsheviks all but worshipped History, how they had made it into a divinity that ordered all things in their universe. Looking down the long hall at Zamyatin, he thought he saw History enthroned at last, the word made flesh again in a man.

Beside Zamyatin sat the two children, William and Samdup. They were both clearly frightened, but were making a sustained effort to master their fear. William was wearing Tibetan clothes in which he was manifestly uncomfortable. Samdup wore an expensive brocade robe, and on his head he sported a blue pointed cap. Both boys were staring sullenly at their feet.

Christopher could feel his heart pounding. With every step, he expected William to look up and recognize him. He raised a finger to his lips to tell his son not to make a sound, but he had to make an effort not to dash forward himself and embrace him.

Now they were within feet of the throne. Zamyatin did not take his eyes off them once. He watched them like a bird of prey that has seen its next victims and is waiting for the moment to swoop. Christopher noticed that he had long, thin hands like claws. They lay on his lap without moving, like the hands of a waxwork figure in a museum.

Suddenly, Samdup glanced up and saw Chindamani. He cried out to her and rose to run in her direction, but Zamyatin reached out a long arm and pinned the boy by the wrist.

'Time enough, lambkin,' he said, 'time enough.'

At that moment, William too looked up. He looked straight at Christopher without recognizing him immediately. Then Christopher smiled and the boy's face altered in an instant.

'Father!' he cried.

Christopher stopped in his tracks, frightened to say or do anything. He knew he should run forward, but now the moment had come, something inward held him back. Was it an instinct that he should show no emotion in front of this man?

William cried out again and tried to rise. Zamyatin took his wrist too and held him tight by his side. He looked straight at Christopher. As he did so, a shadow passed over his eyes and was gone. It had only been there for a moment, but Christopher had felt the animosity like a physical blow.

They were only feet away now. Christopher stopped and fixed his eyes on Zamyatin. The Russian's skin was pale, but his eyes were dark and quite alien to the rest of his face: they were restless, Oriental eyes, torrid, yet without real warmth. But it was the mouth rather than the eyes that betrayed the man. The lips were by nature soft, almost sensual; but he had trained them to a hardness that thinned and mutilated them. Whatever in him was given to softness, whatever inclined him to luxury, had been starved and beaten until it cringed like a whipped dog in the darkest corners of his personality.

'What is my son doing here?' demanded Christopher. 'I insist you free him at once.'

'You may speak only when I speak to you, Mr Wylam,' said Zamyatin in a weary voice. 'If you do not understand, I will help you understand.'

'For God's sake, the boy has been through enough! Will *you* try to understand? You've got what you came here for. Let him go!'

Zamyatin said nothing. He simply raised one finger of his right hand and gestured with it to someone standing behind Christopher. Tsarong Rinpoche stepped forward, lifted a hand to Christopher's neck, and pressed gently. The pain was excruciating. Christopher cried out and clasped his neck: the skin was unbroken, but the nerves still throbbed with agony.

'I assure you, Mr Wylam,' Zamyatin said, 'that the new abbot of Dorje-la is not in the least like his predecessor. But you may have guessed that already.'

'What are you doing with Lord Samdup?' burst out Chindamani. 'Why have you taken him from his *labrang*?'

Zamyatin reached out a thin hand and caressed the boy, running sharp fingers along his cheeks, as if he were a pet. The expression on his face mocked her.

227

'Samdup and I are learning to be friends. Aren't we?' he replied. But Samdup shifted uneasily, pulling away from his hand.

'The boy is tired and frightened,' Chindamani said. 'He should not be here. You have no right to be here, and no right to be with the boy.'

Zamyatin gave her a look that was like a slap across the face. She reddened visibly as he snapped his answer.

'Don't talk to me of rights, miss. All the privileges are gone. The people have taken this monastery. I am their representative. Tsarong Rinpoche is Dorje Lama now. He will decide what rights and duties you have.'

Suddenly, Samdup leaned away from Zamyatin and appealed to Chindamani.

'Please, Chindamani,' he said. 'I don't want to stay here. I don't understand what's happening. Where is the Dorje Lama? Who is this man?'

'I'm your friend,' Zamyatin said, raising his hand to stroke the boy again.

'You're not my friend,' Samdup retorted. 'Chindamani is my friend. Please, Chindamani, take me with you. I don't want to stay here.'

'He doesn't want to be with you,' Chindamani snapped. She was not going to let herself be cowed by Zamyatin and his bullying. 'Let me take him with me. And the other child too. They both need to sleep. There are rooms on this floor we can go to. You needn't worry – we won't escape. There's nowhere to go.'

Zamyatin seemed to think it over.

'Very well, take them out of my sight for a while. Read them bedtime stories – I hear you're very good at it.'

He paused and turned to Tsarong Rinpoche.

'Take her and the boys. See they're given comfortable quarters for tonight. And make sure they're well watched. I'll hold you responsible if you let them give you the slip. Now, all of you get out. I want to speak with Mr Wylam alone.'

As William passed, Christopher smiled at him and reached out a hand to touch his cheek. The boy was crying, all elation at his father's appearance dashed to nothing by the realization that Christopher was as helpless here as himself.

'Don't worry, William,' Christopher called to him. 'We're not

228

done for yet. Keep your spirits up.' But his words sounded trite and hollow. Things could scarcely be worse.

The Rinpoche and his men went out silently, taking Chindamani and the boys with them. At the door, she turned to look at Christopher. Their eyes met for a moment, then someone pulled her by the arm and she was gone.

33

'I see you like the girl,' Zamyatin said.

He spoke in English now, relaxed, urbane, mocking. The disinherited nobleman had picked up a veneer of sophistication somewhere along the way. Or had his urbanity come with the blood and the Slavic lips?

'She's very nice, I don't blame you. I toyed with the idea myself at one point. But women are a distraction – you should know that.'

'A distraction from what? From murder?'

'From real life, of course. From the things that matter. Here, come and sit near me. It's time we talked.'

Christopher took a cushion and sat facing Zamyatin, but he kept his distance: he wanted no intimacy with this man.

The Russian looked directly into his eyes.

'Your loyalty has impressed me, Major Wylam,' he said. 'I am not given to sentiment, but I will admit that this has taken me by surprise. Clearly, it does not pay to discount the baser emotions. You have my congratulations. And my sympathy. Though perhaps you rather think yourself in need of neither.'

Christopher said nothing.

'Believe me,' Zamyatin continued, 'your son was not taken from you gratuitously. It may have seemed that way to you, of course. But I assure you, higher issues were at stake than you can possibly comprehend. I would not expect you to support the ends for which your boy was kidnapped. But I do expect you to acknowledge that what was done was done for the highest reasons. Not for profit or sensual gratification, but for the very highest of motives. You may condemn the action, but you must understand the justification.'

Christopher was growing angrier every moment.

'I'm the boy's father!' he exploded. 'How the hell do you expect me to tolerate what you've done? Nothing gives you the right to kidnap a child and drag him off half-way across the world. Nothing.'

'I'm sorry to hear you say that, Major. I had expected at least some acknowledgement of sympathy for my position. We are both professional men, you and I. You work for a country, I work for a cause. If I were an enemy soldier, surely I would be entitled to your respect. But I am fighting for a cause that stands above all petty particularities of race or nation – the very prejudices that led to the world war. And yet you refuse to accord me the honour you would accord an enemy soldier.'

'Soldiers risk their lives in battle. You plot the snatching of a child from a safe distance. You send other men to do your dirty work for you.'

The Russian's cheeks flushed. He stared hard at Christopher.

'And you Major Wylam – when did you last go into battle? How many men have you killed or had killed in the course of your intelligence operations? How many agents have you instructed to kill on your behalf? For the common good. For the sake of the Empire. Don't talk to me about morality. If your superiors told you to kidnap a Russian child tomorrow in the belief that it would help overthrow our revolutionary government, I don't believe you would hesitate for a moment.'

Christopher said nothing. The horror was that Zamyatin was right. Higher necessity had dogged Christopher's footsteps for every inch of his career in intelligence. In their gilded tombs, the sleeping dead listened. Light played on gold and bronze. Christopher felt the blade of the knife against his leg, pressing into his skin.

'Come to the point,' said Christopher. 'You haven't asked me to stay for a cosy chat. What do you want from me?' He eased himself into a position from which he could more easily reach the handle of the knife.

Zamyatin moved his hands for the first time, lifting them from his lap and placing them together, palm to palm in front of him in an almost religious gesture. Oddly enough, it did not seem out of place for him to do so, even if he himself was a living contradiction of his surroundings.

'All I ask from you is a little help, a little information,' he said. 'You were an important man. Not so very long ago, you occupied a leading position with British intelligence in India. You have been

231

deeply involved with your country's plans for the region north of the Himalayas. You are a mine of information.

'Frankly, Major Wylam, I regard your presence here as an enormous bonus. When I first had investigations made into you and your son, I had no idea who you might be. Imagine my surprise and delight when I found such a central figure in an area of intelligence so close to my own heart. Perhaps there are gods after all. Perhaps they are smiling on me.'

'I no longer work for British intelligence.' He scratched his knee, letting the fingers of his right hand move down towards the knife handle.

'I disagree. How did you get to India so quickly? Who told you where to go, what to look for?'

Christopher was nervous. A year was not very long. He still possessed information that could prove invaluable to Zamyatin and to the communist cells in India.

'Why should I tell you anything?' he said.

Zamyatin smiled.

'Please don't insult my intelligence, Major. The cards are stacked against you: I beg you to bear that in mind. Your son has served his function. Admittedly, there are other uses to which I may be able to put him. But I have been weighing those up against the information I know you must possess. Your son may be more valuable to me dead than alive. Think about that, please.'

'If he dies, you can expect nothing from me.' Hidden by a thin shadow, Christopher's fingers had found the top of the knife and were easing it upwards gently.

'Of course. I'm not a fool. But remember that death can be very slow. And remember that there is an alternative. Your father made a deal with me. I am willing to make one with you. At the price of a little information – hard information – you may buy your son's life.'

'He's only a child, for God's sake!'

'We are all children. You, me, your son. Men are still infants, silly and immature. The world grows up very slowly, very slowly indeed. We will only reach adulthood when a new society is created on earth. That is why I must be so hard now. "Spare the rod and spoil the child" – isn't that what you say? "I must be cruel to be

232

kind." "You can bend a sapling, but not a tree." You English have so many ways of expressing the idea.'

'And what happened tonight,' Christopher retorted warmly, 'was that bending saplings?'

'Listen to me,' Zamyatin said. 'Your world is gone. The old order is being rolled up. A new one is being spread out in its place. When a building has been declared unsafe, you don't waste time papering over the cracks and putting nails in the plasterboard. You knock it down. And you use the rubbish as a foundation for a new building. Don't you see? – it doesn't matter if blood is spilt or sons lose their fathers or mothers lose their daughters. They will all become rubble for the foundations.'

He looked at Christopher with a look almost of entreaty.

'You can choose which you want to be,' he said, 'part of the rubble or part of the new edifice.'

'What if I want to be neither?' Christopher asked. The handle of the knife was out of his boot. He began to ease the blade out, a fraction at a time.

'You do not have that choice. You must be one or the other. That has been decided for you by the dialectic of history. None of us has any say in the matter. We can only choose which side to throw in our fortunes with.'

'Did any of the monks you killed tonight have a choice? Were they asked whether they wanted to join your revolution?'

Zamyatin shook his head slowly. He was like a man who carried a heavy weight on his shoulders. He saw himself as a man of sorrows.

'This is not the revolution, Major Wylam. This is not even the first stirrings of the revolution. There is no urban proletariat here, no capitalist system to be overthrown. Only gods and demons and priests.'

He sighed, as though he had spent his life bowing and scraping at dark altars, lighting candles at the feet of old gods.

'They need new leaders,' he went on, 'men who will lead them away from their superstitions. You want to give them schools and law courts and cricket pitches. But they already have books and laws and games. What they need is freedom. Freedom from oppression. Freedom from injustice. Freedom from want.'

'And you will give them that?'

'We will make it possible. They will grant freedom to themselves.'

'What about the freedom to choose?'

Zamyatin's eyes flashed.

'They will have that along with the rest. But first they have to be weaned from their feudalism. That will be a painful process. Many will die before it is finished. But every death will bring the masses a step closer to liberation. It is inevitable. The forces of history are on our side.'

Like a true believer with his rosary or prayer-wheel, Zamyatin muttered the formulae of his own liturgy, invoking History in his days of gracelessness. Christopher remembered now what Winterpole had said to him: *The Bolsheviks speak of historical inevitability in the way your Jesuits talk of perfect obedience. History has no feelings: no pity, no love, no hate, no elation, no bitterness. It moves on an appointed course. And God help those who get in its way.*

Christopher felt trapped, morally and emotionally. He had come so far to save his son, but to do so he would have to betray innocent men and women elsewhere. Zamyatin would not be content to be fobbed off with a few crumbs of insignificant information. He would find ways of checking whatever Christopher told him, he would have questions to which he would expect reasonable answers. And when Christopher had completed his betrayals, what guarantee did he have that the Russian would honour his word? People were pawns to him, and Christopher did not imagine for a moment that Zamyatin would want to waste time ensuring his safety or that of his son.

'I need time to think,' he said. He had the knife now. He held it by the tips of his fingers, ready to leap on the Russian.

Zamyatin pursed his lips. The candles were burning low. Beyond the windows, night was in control.

'I can't give you time,' he said. 'I have none to give. You will have to make your mind up tonight. Tomorrow I leave for Mongolia. The Tibetan boy is about to be made a god. Your son comes with me, though whether he survives the journey or not depends on you. I hope you understand me, Major Wylam.'

'I understand.' Christopher stood up.

'I will see you are taken to your room. If there is anything you need, the steward will see it is brought to you.'

'Tell me,' Christopher said, 'why did you kill so many people? You had made an arrangement. You had what you wanted. Was it necessary to massacre them?'

Zamyatin stood up and took a step towards Christopher.

'Your father went back on his agreement,' he said. 'He told me to leave, ordered his monks to throw me out. I rather feared something of the sort might happen when I heard Tsarong Rinpoche had brought you here. Your father allowed emotions to creep in. Half a lifetime subduing his passions and then a moment's inadvertence. He was as much a child as any of us. I had no time to argue. Do not make the same mistake he did.'

Christopher decided he would not. He took firm hold of the knife, lifted it, and sprang for Zamyatin. The blade slashed through the Russian's sleeve, tearing the cloth away from his arm, as he spun himself sideways. Christopher fell flat on the cushions, righting himself as he toppled, holding the knife away from himself, aiming it at Zamyatin.

The Russian had landed on his side awkwardly. Cushions impeded his movements, getting in his way as he struggled to wriggle away from Christopher. Christopher made a second lunge.

Zamyatin caught his arm in his left hand, gasping as he forced the point of the knife back from his chest. It was less than an inch away. Christopher fought to drive it home, bearing down heavily on his opponent. He felt rage explode in him like a sudden storm, giving him strength, but weakening his judgement. He swore as Zamyatin brought a knee up, thudding into his stomach and throwing him backwards. He toppled into a row of candles, knocking them over on to the cushions. A piece of fine cloth caught fire, flaring up and setting light to the cushion beside it.

Christopher grunted as the Russian rolled over on top of him. He still held the knife, but his arm was pinned down by Zamyatin's knee. In spite of appearances, the Russian was a trained fighter. Christopher brought his left arm up to his opponent's throat, pushing him up and back. But Zamyatin's own hands were free. He struck Christopher hard against the side of his neck, causing him to stiffen and drop the knife from nerveless fingers.

Zamyatin picked up the knife and brought it down slowly until it touched Christopher's neck. It pricked the skin, drawing blood. Behind them, the fire was taking hold of the cushions. An acrid smoke had begun to billow round them, making them both splutter.

The Russian intended to kill him. Christopher could see it in his eyes. He was breathing heavily, the simple fury of pain giving way to a deeper rage. It was suddenly clear to Christopher that Zamyatin hated him. He remembered the look in Zamyatin's eyes when he had entered, the animosity that filled them. And he realized the reason for it. The Russian, abandoned by his own father, hated him because of his love for William. History be damned, he thought, the bastard's just trying to get back at his father.

Suddenly, there was a sound of running footsteps. Someone had seen the flames. A group of monks ran up. One of them had had the presence of mind to rip down a heavy hanging, which he tossed on to the flames. The others stamped at isolated pockets of flame or threw untouched cushions aside, out of the path of the fire. Within less than a minute, the blaze had been brought under control.

With so many candles extinguished and without the fire, it was dark in the *chörten* hall. Zamyatin remained kneeling on Christopher, the knife hard against his throat. A thin trickle of blood ran down Christopher's neck to the floor.

The monks fell silent and gathered in a tight circle about the two men. Christopher sensed the struggle in Zamyatin's mind. He wanted to kill Christopher; but he knew the value of the information he could obtain from him. Gradually, his breathing grew lighter and his grip slackened on the handle of the knife. Abruptly, he took the knife away and stood.

'Get up!' he snapped.

Christopher rose painfully to his feet.

Zamyatin looked at him.

'You have a few hours, Wylam. What you decide to do is up to you. But rest assured that your son will suffer if you refuse to co-operate. I want names, addresses, codes, and methods of operation. I require full details of all intelligence your people have gathered on the Indian communists. I'd like to know about what your man Bell is up to in Tibet. You can fill in the rest yourself. Give me as much or as little as you want: your boy will be treated accordingly. So much as one little trick, so much as a single false lead, and I'll slit the little bastard's throat with your own knife.'

He turned and spoke rapidly to one of the monks.

'Take him to his apartment. Lock the doors and put guards on them. If there's a secret entrance, find it and block it up. If he escapes, I'll hold you personally responsible – and, by God, you'll pay for it. Bring him back first thing in the morning.'

His voice echoed among the tombs and died away. It would be morning in another seven hours.

34

William was frightened. The sensation was, of course, nothing new to the boy. He had been frightened ever since that moment when the men had come for him after church. Time had ceased to have any meaning since then, and he could not have said how long had passed. All he knew was that what had started as a bad dream had become an unending nightmare out of which he desperately longed to awaken.

He remembered every incident of the past weeks with a vividness beyond his years: the murder of Father Middleton, the men bundling him into the car, the mad drive through snow and fog to a port somewhere. Then they had transferred to a boat, the three men still bad-tempered and uncommunicative. He had been particularly frightened of the third man, the thin one who gave the orders. They had sailed into a storm, almost foundering among waves the height of houses. He had no idea where they had landed.

Only the thin man had accompanied him the rest of the way. An aeroplane had been waiting for them at a field not far from the beach where they had come ashore. They had flown north at first – he knew how to work out directions from the sun and the pole star – and then due east. From what he knew of geography, he thought they were flying over Russia. They landed often to refuel and several times to carry out repairs on the aircraft. After a while, they began to go south.

He had been exhausted on their arrival in India, but he had hated the orphanage they took him to, even though it meant he could sleep in a bed. He could never think of the Reverend Carpenter without a shudder. The journey afterwards had been terrible. Mishig, the man in charge of the small caravan, was a brute, and he had made William's life a misery.

In the monastery, nothing seemed real to him. Everywhere, there were frightening pictures and statues, everywhere thin men with shaven heads who stared at him as though he were something

238

in a circus. The old man who spoke English and said he was William's grandfather had told him not to be afraid, but he could not help it: he was alone and bewildered and lost. Not even the other boy, who spoke to him in a language he could not understand, or the lady, who had spoken to him with the help of his grandfather, had been able to calm his fears.

But tonight had been the worst time of all. They had come for him and the other boy, Samdup, in the middle of the night, dragging them over that terrible bridge. He had seen men being killed, dozens of them. Then he had seen his father brought in, and that had destroyed his last hope. If his father was in the hands of these people too, then who was going to come for him, to rescue him?

Chindamani had persuaded Tsarong Rinpoche to let her take the children to her room. Two guards had been posted at the door, neither of whom was known to her. The Rinpoche had left with a warning that he would be back early in the morning.

Her old nurse Sönam was there. Chindamani had found her hiding beneath the bed where she had left her. The old ama-la had been Chindamani's constant companion since the day the little girl had been brought to Dorje-la from the village in Tsang province where she had been born. That had been sixteen years ago.

Sönam had been an old woman even then; now she was positively ancient. She had served two incarnations of the Lady Tara, bathing and feeding them as infants, passing on her love to them as children, sorting out the problems of puberty, and listening to their troubles as women. Twenty years ago she had embalmed Chindamani's predecessor and clothed her in her finest garments before placing her in the small *chörten* long reserved for her in the Tara temple. Four years later they had brought Chindamani to her, a tiny girl pathetically clutching a wooden doll and pleading to be sent back to her mother. The doll was still there, well worn and unlovely now. So was the little girl.

'What can we do, ama-la?' Chindamani asked the old woman. Her own initiative seemed to have evaporated since the moment she stood in Thondrup Chophel's room watching the hanging bodies bob in the shadows. She had told Sönam almost nothing of what she had seen: enough to satisfy the old woman's curiosity but not enough to frighten her.

'Do? What can we do?' splutterd the old crone. Little black eyes darted about like fish in a face as dry as parchment. She still wore her hair in the traditional one hundred and eight plaits, but over the years the plaits had become thinner and thinner, not to say greasier and greasier. Her mouth had long been untenanted, but she never grumbled: she had lived on tea and tsampa all her life and had never tasted let alone craved for either flesh or fish. Between her hands she held a prayer-wheel, which she was nervously turning with her gnarled fingers.

'You say Tsarong Rinpoche has deposed the *pee-ling trulku*,' she went on. 'Pah! That won't last long. The *pee-ling*'s more than a match for him. I knew that Tsarong when he came here as a boy. He was always a nasty bit of work. He used to pull the wings off flies, then the legs, then the heads. A methodical little bastard he was. When he was beaten for it, he'd say he'd done the flies a favour – perhaps they'd be reincarnated as something better: dragonflies or butterflies or bats. He's vicious, but he isn't popular. They won't stand for him. The Dorje Lama will soon be back in charge.'

Chindamani sighed heavily. She hadn't wanted to cause the old woman pain. But she had to know something of the truth.

'The Dorje-Lama is dead, ama-la,' she whispered.

'Dead? How?'

Chindamani explained what Tsarong Rinpoche had told her. It was not easy, and when she came to an end she found she was crying. Samdup watched her, the sense of horror and outrage growing in him.

'Murdered?' Sönam repeated. 'Oé! This will cost Tsarong Rinpoche a hundred lifetimes! He'll come back a wingless fly, wait and see. And if he does, I'll stamp on him.' But the anger and the raillery were a façade. Deep down, the old woman's world was being smashed. She had taken time to get used to the *pee-ling trulku*, but in the end she had grown fond of him.

'We're all in danger, ama-la. There's a man here from the north, a Buriat. He wants to take Lord Samdup and the *pee-ling trulku*'s grandson away.'

'And you, my jewel – what do they want with you?' The old

nurse stretched out a leathery hand and stroked Chindamani's hair gently.

'I think Tsarong Rinpoche will have me killed as well,' answered Chindamani as calmly as she could. 'He knows that, if I chose, I could still rally the monks round me, that I could put an end to his games. But he won't allow that. Nor will the Buriat.' She paused, taking Sönam's hand in hers and clasping it hard.

'They won't touch you!' exclaimed Samdup, rising and crossing to Chindamani. 'I won't let them. They need me. I won't do what they say if they hurt you.'

Chindamani took the boy's hand.

'Thank you Samdup. I know you would do everything you could. But you wouldn't be able to stop them. Tsarong Rinpoche is frightened of me. I have power he does not possess: I'm an incarnation, he is not.'

'But I'm a incarnation! I can . . .'

'Yes, Samdup, love; but you're also a child. The Dorje Lama was an incarnation, but they killed him. Others would not have killed the Dorje Lama. Remember how they brought you back when you tried to escape with Tobchen Geshe.'

Samdup frowned and sat down again, remembering his helplessness on that occasion, how easily Thondrup Chophel had escorted him back to Dorje-la.

Chindamani turned to face Sönam again.

'Listen, ama-la,' she said. 'Listen carefully and don't fidget. I have to escape. And I have to take the children with me.'

'Alone? You and the boys? You'd never make it out of the pass.'

'Not alone,' said Chindamani. 'They haven't killed the Dorje Lama's son. At least . . .' She paused. 'They hadn't killed him when we were sent away. If I can get to him . . . I have clothes and provisions already hidden for a journey.'

'And how will you get out of Dorje-la?' the old woman croaked. She knew all about Christopher. For two days now, Chindamani had talked about little else.

'No-one will be asleep tonight. You know it's impossible to climb down even with ropes. You haven't got wings, you aren't birds. Is this Ka-ris To-feh a magician? Can he fly like Padma-Sambhava? Or perhaps he's a *lung-pa* who can run hundreds of miles in a day and be away from this place before they know he's gone?'

'No,' said Chindamani, shaking her head. 'He's none of those things.'

'Neither am I,' muttered the nurse. 'Neither are you, for that matter. Just because the Lady Tara . . .'

'Leave the Lady Tara out of this, Sönam,' Chindamani retorted. 'I never mentioned magic and I'm not mentioning it now.'

'Well you'll need magic if you're to get out of this place without being seen. And more magic to get away before that Tsarong Rinpoche comes chasing after you. Rinpoche indeed! He's no more a Rinpoche than I'm a yak's backside.' The old dame chuckled; she wouldn't be put down by her ward, even if she was an incarnation of the Lady Tara.

'Ama-la, this is serious. We can't afford to wait. Surely you must know some way out, some way even I don't know. A secret passage through the rock, perhaps. Didn't you mention . . .?'

'Mention? What did I mention? I mentioned nothing.' Sönam had become serious suddenly. Her little eyes would not hold still for a moment. She could not look Chindamani in the face. She knew what the girl was going to ask.

'Please think, Sönam dear,' Chindamani exhorted her. 'Years ago, when I was a little girl, you told me of a passage that had been constructed when they built Dorje-la, a secret tunnel connecting the monastery to the pass. It went down through the mountain, you said. Is it true? Is there a passage?'

The old woman seemed to shiver.

'No,' she said. 'There's no such passage. I was telling fibs, stories for a little girl. You shouldn't listen to everything your old ama-la tells you.'

But Chindamani knew her nurse too well to be fooled for an instant.

'Ama-la, please – you're lying now. What you told me was the truth, I can tell it in your voice. Please don't lie to me. There isn't time. Where is the passage? How can I get to it?'

Sönam took Chindamani's hand in hers and began to knead it with her fingers. She was visibly frightened.

'I swore I'd never tell anyone,' she said. 'Your last body told me. I don't know who told her.'

The little woman took a deep breath. Her pulse was racing and she was sweating.

'There's a passage beneath the gön-kang,' she whispered. Chindamani had to lean close to hear her. Samdup came across and sat next to her. William watched from his seat next to the wall. He wished he knew what they were talking about. He could sense the fear and excitement in their voices, but he could not understand a word of what they said.

'It runs for about one hundred yards. Then there's a flight of stairs cut through the rock, into the mountain. They're known as the stairs of Yama, I don't know why. They lead down to a spot below the pass, out of sight of the monastery. They were built in the days of the old kings, thousands of years ago.'

Chindamani guessed that the 'old king' had been Lang Darma and that the stairs had been constructed as an escape route from the gompa so that the abbot could get to safety in the event of an attack by the royal forces. That had been hundreds of years ago, when the Buddhist faith was in danger of being stamped out all over the country.

Samdup clapped his hands excitedly.

'But that's perfect,' he exclaimed. 'Chindamani knows lots of secret ways to the gön-kang. All we have to do is to get there and we're safe. They'll never know which way we've gone.'

But the old woman shook her head furiously. She shook it so hard it looked as though her neck would snap and send it spinning off into Chindamani's lap.

'No, my Lord, no!' she cried. 'You mustn't go that way. I haven't told you everything.' She paused again, as if gathering courage to say more.

'Hundreds of years ago,' she began, 'when the first Chöje came here, he brought a great treasure from Lhasa – gold and silver and precious jewels, to be made into his trance garments. You've seen him wear them in the Lha-kang when he enters the holy state and is ridden by the gods.'

The Chöje was the Oracle of Dorje-la. In a state of mystic trance, he could enter into communication with the spirits or the gods themselves and pass on messages to other men. The ceremonies at which he appeared took place only a few times every year, but they were by far the most exciting events in the monastery's calendar.

His regalia was indeed impressive: the great hat, so heavy that it needed two men to support it until the Chöje rose in his trance, was a mass of rubies, emeralds, and amethysts; the Oracle throne on which he sat was studded with gems of every description, and its frame was encased in solid gold. The great mirror of divination that he wore on his chest was made of solid silver and encircled with precious stones of the finest quality. 'Have you never wondered,' the ama-la continued, 'where those precious things are left when they are not in use? Have you never wanted to look more directly at them?'

Chindamani shook her head. The Oracle's performances in the incense laden gloom of the Lha-khang had always filled her with a state of dread, and she had never sought closer contact with the darkly numinous world he represented.

'Only a few people know that particular secret,' the old woman whispered. 'The Chöje himself, his assistants, and the abbot. And myself, of course – though none of them has ever known that I know.'

Chindamani interrupted.

'I always assumed they were left in the Chöje's own room. Or perhaps in the old temple hall where he goes to meditate.'

Sönam shook her head.

'That's what most people think. But they've been somewhere else all the time. In a small chamber just below the gön-kang.'

She looked up into Chindamani's eyes. The girl could see the fear in the old woman's glance, quite unmistakable now, steadying its grip on her. She felt it herself now, naked, tangible, calling her to itself.

'To get to the tunnel that leads to the stairs,' the ama-la said, 'you have to pass through the chamber in which the Oracle treasures are kept. Do you understand? You have to go through the Chöje's chamber.'

'Ama-la, I don't understand,' pleaded Chindamani. 'What's wrong with going through the chamber? I won't touch the Chöje's jewels. We'll leave them exactly as they are. We won't even look at them closely. The gods won't be offended. What danger could there be in our just passing through the chamber?'

The old woman shuddered. Chindamani felt her own flesh creep. What was the ama-la frightened of?

244

'Don't you see?' Sönam pleaded. Her voice had become whining, trembling with fear. 'They put a guardian down there. Long ago, when they put the treasures there, they set a guardian over them. It's been there for more than five hundred years. It's still there.'

35

'What sort of guardian?' Chindamani asked, struggling to fight down the sensation of nausea in her stomach.

'I don't know,' Sönam protested. The old woman had frightened herself more than she had expected. 'Does it matter? It's down there, whatever it is.'

'How does the Chöje get his regalia? He has to go down there three times a year, doesn't he? Why doesn't this guardian harm him or his assistants?'

'I don't know. He must have some power over it. He has magical powers. More than you, my Lady. And more than that Tsarong Rinpoche.'

'I don't have magical powers, ama-la. I have told you that often enough.' Nor did she believe that anyone else possessed them; but that was an opinion she kept firmly to herself.

'Tell me, Sönam,' she went on, 'does anyone know what this guardian looks like?'

The old woman snorted.

'Of course. The Chöje knows. The abbot knows. At least . . .' she halted, remembering the news Chindamani had just brought. 'At least he did know. And the Chöje's assistants know. That's all. I'm sure that's all.'

Chindamani sighed. She had no wish to distress the old woman further; but she had already seen the bodies of the Chöje and his three assistants among those hanging from the ceiling in Thondrup Chophel's room.

She made her mind up.

'We'll have to risk it,' she said. 'If the Chöje and his assistants could go in there without coming to harm, so can we.'

The old woman put her face in her hands and began to moan, rocking backwards and forwards.

'Please, ama-la,' pleaded Chindamani. 'There isn't time for this. Trust me. The Lady Tara won't let me come to harm.'

But the old woman paid no attention. Her moaning was becoming more intense as the reality of their situation mingled in her mind with a lifetime's fantasies about the supernatural horrors of the universe she inhabited.

Chindamani turned to Samdup.

'Samdup,' she said, 'please look after the *pee-ling* boy. Try to tell him not to be frightened. And look after Sönam as well. Tell her there's nothing to worry about. Ask her to help you get our clothes and equipment ready. I've put everything in that large chest. Take it all out and sort it into piles. There won't be time to waste later. I can't help you: I have to go to find Ka-ris To-feh.'

But the boy just sat rigid on his seat, staring at her.

'What's wrong, Samdup?' she replied.

'I'm frightened,' the boy said. 'I don't want to go to the gön-kang tonight. And I don't want to go through any tunnels.'

Chindamani went across and sat down beside him.

'I'm frightened too, Samdup,' she whispered. 'But we both have to be brave. It's very important for you to be brave tonight. Like you were when you tried to get to Ghaloring with Tobchen Geshe.'

'But I wasn't brave then, Chindamani. When Tobchen Geshe was lost, I got very frightened and cried.'

'I know,' she said, putting a hand on the boy's head. 'But you had reason to be afraid. You were alone and in very real danger. If Thondrup Chophel had not arrived when he did, you might have died.'

'But Thondrup Chophel frightened me more than anything!'

'Only at first. After that, you were just unhappy. But you weren't in danger. Now, tonight you are in danger. No-one's going to try to kill you, you're worth too much to them. But a time may come when they decide it would be in their interests to get rid of you. That's why we both have to get away tonight. Do you understand?'

'Yes. I see, but . . .'

'There's nothing to be frightened of in the gön-kang.' She leaned across and whispered quickly in his ear, 'And I wouldn't worry about old Sönam's story. It's just an old tale; there's nothing down there.'

But privately, she was worried. It might not be the sort of horror

247

the old nurse imagined, but someone could have prepared a nasty surprise for them.

She squeezed Samdup's hand tightly and smiled. The boy smiled back hesitantly. She went over to William, wishing she could say even a few words in his language to reassure him. All she could say was his father's name, Ka-ris To-feh, but she could not be sure that he understood what she meant. She smiled and kissed him lightly on the forehead. He tried a small smile in return, but he was still frightened.

She crossed the room to a large lacquer chest. Inside, she kept the things she had put away for their journey: clothes for the four of them, a tent, food and a bag of fuel stolen from the kitchens, and money. She had never used money in her life, but she understood its purpose and knew it would be safer to carry than gold or jewels, the only other form of portable wealth she possessed. The money had been obtained through Sönam, who had ways of laying her hands on just about anything.

Chindamani put on a heavy man's robe that still allowed her some freedom of movement, unlike a chuba. She said a few more reassuring words to her old nurse, smiled at the boys again, and went to the window.

Once, long ago, when she was a little girl, she had discovered that a narrow ledge ran along the side of the upper storey, just below the windows. She had tried walking along it to a room nearby, where one of her teachers lived, but had been discovered and severely punished by Sönam. Now she prayed for enough balance to make it as far as Christopher's room, which was on the same side of the gompa as her own.

The cold bit into her face and hands like slivers of ice burrowing beneath the skin. Slowly, she lowered herself down to the ledge and found it nearer than she had expected: she had forgotten to make allowances for the couple of feet she had grown since her last venture outside. But if the ledge felt nearer, it also felt narrower – much narrower than the bridge to the labrang and hard up against the wall.

The wind was worse than the cold. It blew across the face of the monastery, as it hurtled through the pass out of nowhere and into nowhere. The dark and cold and wind conspired against her, to blind and numb and snatch her away into the void. Within seconds, the light and warmth of the room had become a distant memory, and one that she had to drive from her mind by an effort of will. All her energies, all her thoughts were concentrated now on one thing: how to survive the next few minutes.

She moved inches at a time, never allowing her feet to leave the ledge, sliding across to the left, hands flat against the wall. The stone was uneven: plaster had fallen away in places, making it difficult to judge the surface. The wall and the ledge and the black void at her back had become the entire world for her. There was no other world, neither in memory nor in prospect. She edged her way along the ledge for no other reason than that she was there: all other reasons, all other motivations had vanished.

Suddenly, her left foot slipped and she started to topple sideways. For long moments she hung poised, all her weight on the right foot, desperately fighting against the awful pull of gravity that was trying to bear her down and give her to the wind. Her frozen fingers clutched at bare stone, blindly searching for the tiniest crack to hold on to.

Part of the ledge had given way. Perhaps it had always been that way – she could not remember how far she had got the last time. The problem was: just how wide was the gap? Six inches? A foot? Ten? She was carrying nothing with which to test the distance. In the pitch dark, she could see nothing. If she tired and misjudged, she would lose her balance and fall to her death on the rocks below. If she returned for something to measure the gap, she knew she would lose her nerve and be unable to climb back out again.

Gingerly, holding her weight on her right leg, pressing hard against the wall for maximum balance, she edged her left foot out again, feeling for the resumption of the ledge. The wind whistled in her ears, distracting her. It tugged at her body, trying to tear her away from the wall. Her heart shuddered inside her chest.

Her weight was already beginning to shift, and she still had not found the next stretch of ledge. She wanted to bend her right knee, to bring her torso lower, but that would only push her out further from the wall. Sweat poured out of her. On her face and the palms of her hands, it turned almost instantly to ice. She shivered and felt herself teeter on the edge of balance. Still nothing. She could not be sure just where to put her left foot down. The muscles of her right leg were pulling badly. A vicious pain shot up her thigh; the leg felt as though about to go into cramp. Still nothing. She wanted to scream, to break the tension somehow, to relax her muscles.

She moved her left arm just a fraction, then her right. She stretched another inch leftwards with her foot. Still nothing. Inside her brain, an insidious voice was repeating: 'Let go, let go, let go!' She wanted to drop, to let the void solve all her problems. Why not? The Lady would find another body. Still nothing.

In another fraction of an inch she would have reached her limit. And already she was frightened that, without realizing it, she had passed a point of no return, where no effort on her part would rectify her state of imbalance and return to her starting position. Her right leg was screaming in agony, it could not possibly support the strain of moving back. She moved the final fraction. Still nothing. She moved again.

She felt her balance go. One second she was static, just holding on; the next she was out of control, moving, lurching into the darkness.

Her toe caught the corner of the ledge and held. Just. She hung there, between life and nothingness, mentally letting go, forcing herself to strain every muscle until she had balance again. Her heart pounded as if about to burst. The darkness seemed to vanish, and she was alone in a world of light. Then the light faded and she was back again on the cold ledge, shuddering and on the verge of panic.

She fought down the rising terror and edged her left foot up on to the ledge, praying it would hold. Somewhere in her mind, the Tara mantra was being recited, but she had lost all sight of the goddess within herself. Her senses were the only things binding her to reality now. The feel of her foot on the hard ledge was bliss beyond any bliss that prayers or offerings could bring.

Gradually, her heartbeat and her breathing slowed and life began to come back into her right leg. She moved her left foot along just far enough to leave room for the right, shifted her balance towards the left, and crossed the gap. That was it. She knew she could never face that a second time. If she could not find a way back into the monastery from here, she would either freeze to death or fall out of the world forever.

By her calculation, Ka-ris To-feh's room should be the fifth along, but it was difficult to make out anything clearly in the dark and she was terrified that she would make a mistake and go past unwittingly. She prayed his shutters had not been closed since the morning before: she could not remember how they had been earlier that night when she had gone to his room to waken him.

She was grimly conscious that time was passing quickly. Fear urged her to panic and hurry, but she forced herself to move slowly, inch by inch, willing time itself to slow down and keep pace with her.

Her fingers had become a problem. If she remained outside much longer without caring for them, she could contract serious frost-bite. Already, feeling had gone from them and she was able to use them only by an effort of will.

She felt that hours had passed by the time she reached the fifth window. To her joy, she could make out the glow of a dim light coming from inside the room. Once she was positioned right underneath, she reached up and peered through the window, using the heels of her hands, then her elbows.

She looked inside. Christopher was not there.

36

Tsarong Rinpoche was growing more worried by the minute. With the help of the Buriat Zam-ya-ting, he had taken control of Dorje-la at last. Zam-ya-ting thought he was in charge, but he would soon show him who had the final say in things here. He was more worried by the woman, Chindamani. She represented the goddess Tara, and Tara was extremely popular among the monks, just as she was with the people. Given time, the bitch could undermine all his efforts by a direct appeal to the loyalty of the *trapas* couched in suitably emotive language. She would have to be eliminated – and that would take some subtle arranging if it were not to backfire.

The Englishman Wy-lam had served his purpose. By bringing him to the monastery, he had helped implicate the *pee-ling* abbot in the machinations of the British. Zam-ya-ting had known a lot about Wy-lam and had been able to persuade the monks that both he and his father were involved in some sort of plot together. Perhaps they had been. But it didn't seem to matter now.

What did matter was that Wy-lam could prove more of a threat than even the woman. The office of abbot was not hereditary. The Englishman could not claim to be a *trulku*, nor did Tsarong Rinpoche fear he would. But everyone at Dorje-la knew the words of the prophecy found in an old *terma* book: 'When Dorje-la is ruled by a *pee-ling*, the world shall be ruled from Dorje-la'. And they knew the sentence that followed it in the book: 'In the year that the son of a *pee-ling*'s son comes to the Land of Snows, in that year shall Maidari appear. He shall be the last abbot of Dorje-la, and the greatest.'

The Englishman would not know any of that, of course; but he was sure the girl would make him aware of it and use it to help them rally support within the monastery. All it needed was for Wy-lam to persuade his son to co-operate by playing whatever role the girl suggested for him. The Rinpoche could not be sure of most

252

of the monks yet. A little push might send them running in another direction.

That would have to be prevented at all costs. He did not know what plans the Buriat had for Wy-lam or the woman. But his own were unambiguous: the girl and the Englishman must be killed tonight.

The catch on the window gave without much pressure. It had not been designed to keep anyone out – from the pass, it was impossible to climb anywhere within one hundred feet of it. Chindamani dropped down into the room. It felt warm. Christopher had been here since she last saw him. His outdoor clothes – the ones in which he had come to Dorje-la – were gone. He must have been brought back here, dressed in them, then left again. Just what was going on?

She stepped cautiously to the door. Her heart was still beating hard from her nerve-racking passage of the ledge outside, and her hands hurt as the circulation tried to return to normal. More than anything, she longed to throw herself on the bed and sleep. To escape all this in dreams seemed to her the most desirable of all things at this moment.

The door was partly open. Holding her breath, she opened it further. A man was lying on the ground about a yard away, not moving. A long halberd from the gön-kang had fallen from his hand and lay near him. Chindamani walked to the man and bent down. He was dead. As far as she could tell, someone had broken his neck. Was the fighting still going on? Or had Ka-ris To-feh done this in his determination to escape?

If it had been Ka-ris To-feh, he would be trying to find a way out of the monastery. And the quickest way he knew was over the roof – the way they had gone together when she had taken him to see the boys in the labrang. But if he hoped to escape that way he was making a stupid mistake: the roof led nowhere. And the bridge only led to the labrang.

She set off rapidly in the direction of the hatch through which she and Christopher had got on to the roof. The monastery had fallen silent again, but tonight it was a threatening silence, not the meditative quiet to which Chindamani was accustomed. Before, she had moved quietly when she went abroad at night out of respect for the sleep or the prayers of the monks in their cells. Tonight, she did so out of fear for her life.

When she got to the hatch it was closed. But the ladder had gone, and she guessed Ka-ris To-feh had pulled it up after him in order to delay any possible pursuit. Without it, there was no way she could get out through the hatch. The only other possibility was a second hatch nearby, a private hatch used by the abbot whenever he wanted to go to the labrang or just spend time on the roof watching the clouds pass.

The ladder to the second hatch was in place. It was a matter of moments for Chindamani to get out on to the roof. She prayed no-one would come and find the ladder and the open hatch, but there was no time to waste covering her tracks.

The cold seized her with vicious fingers, jealous of the time she had just spent out of its clutches. On the rooftop, the wind blew unimpeded by any obstacles. Pieces of dry snow whipped across her face out of the unrelieved darkness. The roaring of the wind combined with the pounding in her chest to blot out any other sounds. Like a swimmer swimming in green depths amid a terrible silence, she opened her mouth and called his name but heard nothing. The sound of her voice was swallowed up in the general din, thin and futile. Again and again she strained to be heard, shouting his name aloud in steady measures, a repeated mantra unheard and unheeded. He was here somewhere, there was nowhere else for him to go.

She wandered through the blackness calling him. It was a secret wonder to her, invoking his name like this, a man's name, a name she could scarcely pronounce. It disturbed her that just to call his name in the darkness gave her such pleasure, even while the thought that he might have gone out here to his death disquieted her deeply.

She found him sitting on the plinth of an old bronze dragon set to guard the chörtens, staring into the blackness, a dim shape in the night, scarcely distinguishable from his surroundings.

'Ka-ris To-feh,' she said, sitting beside him. 'We have to go. We have to get out of Dorje-la.'

'I've tried,' he said. 'But there's no way out. And even if there was a way out, there's nowhere to go. It's all like this – cold and bleak and meaningless. What does it matter if you're alive or dead up here? There isn't even anyone to care.'

'I care,' she said.

'You?' he exclaimed. A dry sound like a laugh leapt from his lips and was carried away on the wind. 'You care about nothing but your gods and your Buddhas and your child incarnations. You don't know what the real world's like. You don't know what damage they can do, these gods of yours. What wounds they can inflict.'

'I care for you,' she said, drawing close lest the wind would snatch her words away. 'I love you.'

As soon as she spoke the words, she knew she had sealed her fate. Whether he heard or understood or remembered, it would not matter. If they succeeded in escaping Dorje-la, those few words bound her to him more intimately than any of her childhood vows had ever bound her to the Lady Tara or the dharma or the Buddha. She belonged to him now as she had never belonged to anyone, least of all herself.

They made it back to the hatchway, battling against a head-on wind. Inside, with the hatch closed and the ladder stored away, they stood together in the silence.

'We have to get to my room,' she said. 'There's a passage near here that will take us there without being seen.'

'And then?' he asked.

She hesitated.

'I'll . . . explain that when we get there,' she said.

If Tsarong Rinpoche had been worried before, he was now quite beside himself. The *pee-ling* had killed his guard and managed to get out into the monastery. He could be anywhere. If he succeeded in making his way to the woman's room, she might find some way of hiding them both until the right moment came.

At least he might be able to do something to prevent that. The gun that Zam-ya-ting had given him was still in his pocket. He fingered it gently, sensing its mute perfection against his fingers. It was a message from another world, speaking to him of the possibilities inherent in earthly power. There was a mastery in it that he had sensed in nothing else. He remembered pulling the trigger when he killed the Nepalese boy on the pass: the thrill of

255

that moment still lived with him, urging him to repeat the experience. Not even tonight's hangings had brought him such a rush of raw excitement.

But, for all that, the presence of the gun in his pocket filled him with apprehension. He had broken every vow he had ever made. If there were other lives beyond this, he would pay a terrible price for the things he had done. He hoped Zam-ya-ting was right and that this life was the only one a man had. He had staked everything on that. Otherwise, what he was about to do would bring such suffering on his head that five hundred lifetimes would not suffice to bring him peace again.

He loosed the safety catch and set off in the direction of Chindamani's room.

They wasted no time. Chindamani's secret passage ran from a small chapel dedicated to Tara directly to her room. Only she and Sönam and Christopher's father had known of its existence: it had been built centuries ago to allow the Tara incarnation to pass between her own quarters and her private chapel without being seen by anyone else. For Chindamani – as, no doubt, for many of her predecessors – it had played more than just an ancillary role to her devotions, providing as it did easy access to other parts of the monastery. From the Tara chapel, other passages connected with different floors: one to the main Lha-khang, where there was a curtained chamber from which the Tara incarnation could watch the services; one to the old temple-hall, now rimed with ice and frost, where Christopher had first met his father; and one to the gön-kang, in case the Tara *trulku* ever wanted to commune with the dark yet benign protector deities.

The passage led to a door concealed behind hangings on the wall of Chindamani's bedroom. When she and Christopher emerged, they found Sönam and the two boys exactly as Chindamani had left them. William was sitting on the couch. Samdup was seated by the old woman, trying to comfort her while she wept.

'Ama-la,' said Chindamani, 'I'm back – I've brought Ka-ris To-feh, the Dorje Lama's son.'

At the sound of the younger woman's voice, Sönam glanced up. Her old eyes were red and filled with tears. In the act of weeping, her distress had deepened and become potent, like a drug in her ancient veins.

'Little daughter,' she cried, 'they've killed the Dorje Lama. What are we to do?'

'I know, ama-la,' Chindamani whispered. 'I know.' Now that the moment to leave had come, she felt sick and guilty. How could she leave Sönam here with Tsarong Rinpoche and his followers? The old woman had been like a mother to her.

She sat down beside the old woman and put one arm around her. Then she turned to look at Christopher, but he had already gone to his son, hugging him tightly, whispering words of reassurance and comfort. As she looked at them, she felt a sudden, unexpected pang of jealousy, an emotion she had never experienced before. It unsettled her to discover how she resented the child's claim over his father.

Suddenly, there was a sound of footsteps in the corridor outside. Christopher leaped to his feet. He looked round desperately for somewhere William might hide: having found him at last, he would die before he gave his son up again.

The door opened without a knock and Tsarong Rinpoche entered, closely followed by the monk who had been standing guard outside. The Rinpoche could not believe his luck. It occurred to him in a flash of inspiration that, with the man and the woman eliminated and the English boy in his hands, he really had no need for Zam-ya-ting at all.

'Sit down!' he ordered, addressing Christopher.

Christopher stepped towards him, but the Rinpoche took a gun from his pocket and jerked it menacingly in his direction.

'You've seen this gun before, Wylam-la,' he said. 'You know what it can do. Please sit down on that chest and keep quiet.'

The monk closed the door firmly. The draught caught one of the butter-lamps and set it flickering, sending oddly-shaped shadows across the faces of the two men.

Christopher was in no mood to sit. Since coming down from the roof, he had felt a sense of purpose returning. Chindamani had given him something like hope to hold on to, and William had made the hope seem real and tangible. He had started to believe it might be possible to get at least as far as the pass beyond the walls of the monastery.

257

'How many will this be?' he asked the Rinpoche. 'Enough to keep you crawling about in mud for the rest of eternity, I should think.'

'I told you to keep quiet,' the Rinpoche snapped. He could feel his confidence evaporating already. This would not be easy. Killing one of them alone would not have been difficult. But the two of them together, in the presence of the boys and the old woman . . .

Suddenly, everyone froze. In an uncannily high-pitched voice, old Sönam had begun to mutter the words of what sounded to Christopher like an incantation of some sort. He saw Tsarong Rinpoche turn pale and grip the gun as if to crush the metal in his bare hand. The old woman's voice continued to rise and fall, quavering yet quite inflexible, filling the little room with curious echoes.

'Shut up!' Tsarong Rinpoche yelled at Sönam. Christopher noticed that the guard had blanched as well and was stepping back towards the door.

'Ama-la, please!' Chindamani urged, pressing the old woman's shoulders in her hands. 'Stop reciting.' But the little nurse paid no attention. Eyes fixed on the Rinpoche, she went on with her incantation, pouring the words out implacably into the shadows that hung about him.

'Be quiet!' the Rinpoche shouted again, stepping towards the old woman and waving his gun loosely in the air. His eyes were wild and staring. Christopher could see that he had been gripped by some kind of superstitious dread, although he did not understand a word of the rhyming lines that the old nurse was reciting. He guessed that it must be a curse of some sort and that Tsarong Rinpoche took it very seriously.

'Please, Sönam, don't,' Chindamani was pleading. The boy Samdup sat frozen to the spot, his eyes fixed on the ancient figure, watching in horrified fascination as her wrinkled form rocked backwards and forwards in a steady rhythm, echoing the stanzas that rolled from her lips.

'Stop her!' the Rinpoche shouted. 'Or I'll kill her. I swear I'll kill her if she doesn't stop!'

'Stop it, ama-la,' Chindamani pleaded. She had recognized the pain in Tsarong Rinpoche's voice and knew he would indeed pull the trigger if Sönam went on much further. She knew why he was frightened.

But nothing would shut the old lady up. She was into her stride now, spitting the dark words of her curse out as though they were poison and could kill. Perhaps she thought they could.

Tsarong Rinpoche fired his revolver. A single shot, then the gun hung limply from his fingers. The bullet hit the ama-la in the throat. There was a terrible choking sound. She did not fall back, but went on sitting as though unhurt. But the bullet had entered through the front of the throat and exited again by the back of her neck, severing the top of the spinal column. A plume of blood sprayed out from the wound. There was a choking sound. Bright red blood foamed on her lips. Her old eyes glazed over and a moment later her body went limp and she fell back into Chindamani's arms.

Nobody said anything. The room was filled with a dreadful silence that stretched into more than a minute. Outside, a gust of wind fell heavily against the window and rushed away again. It was as if it had come to take another soul from Dorje-la and carry it to the mysterious realm of Bardö.

The first person to move was Chindamani. There was a cold rage in her eyes that had never been in them before. She let go of Sönam's body, lowering it to the bed, then stood up slowly, her gaze fixed on Tsarong Rinpoche. The lama's face was twitching. A nerve was working in his right cheek. The hand that held the gun shook uncontrollably.

Chindamani began to recite the curse from where Sönam had left off. She spoke in a voice that was almost a whisper, but it carried clearly to the man at whom it was directed. She raised a finger and pointed at him and her voice trembled with anger.

As though mesmerized, Tsarong Rinpoche stood frozen for a moment, then his hand began to move. He raised the gun slowly and pointed it at Chindamani. It shook terribly and he set his teeth together, forcing his nerves to grow still. Then, just as slowly and just as deliberately, he turned the gun until it was pointing at his own face. The weapon was heavy, his fingers weak, drained of strength. He opened his mouth, then rested the edge of the gun-barrel on his lower teeth. His whole body was shivering now. Chindamani's voice filled the world. He wanted to cry out, to scream against the incantation, but his limbs were paralysed. Only his finger moved, tightening against the cold metal of the trigger.

Christopher watched in horror, unable to understand what was happening. The lama was terrified beyond measure. But surely the power of superstition alone could not be responsible for his unreasoning fear of the incantation. Tsarong Rinpoche had committed every sacrilege there was. And yet a few words from an old woman had been enough to undermine him completely.

Christopher held William's face tight against his stomach. The boy had seen enough horrors already. Chindamani's voice sounded in his ears, hard and relentless as a scalpel cutting through skin.

Tsarong Rinpoche closed his eyes.

37

The explosion blew most of Tsarong Rinpoche's skull apart. Blood marked the walls of Chindamani's apartment with bright, angry drops. A great shudder went through all the limbs of the Rinpoche's body, then he toppled and fell backwards. Chindamani faltered and closed her eyes but remained standing. Samdup cried out in horror and threw his hands over his eyes. William, who had heard but not seen the explosion, clung to his father tightly. The monk who had entered the room with Tsarong Rinpoche was drenched with blood. Without a word, he dropped his weapon and ran through the door.

Christopher shuddered. For what seemed an age, he stood there holding William, looking at Tsarong Rinpoche's bloodied corpse, at the blood streaming across the naked wall. Slowly, he became aware that Chindamani's voice had faded away. He turned his head and saw her, still standing in the same spot, her arm outstretched, her finger pointing at the empty space where the Rinpoche had been standing.

He set William down on the couch and stepped towards her. Tentatively, he took her in his arms. The shock of what had happened was rapidly leaving him, and he realized that it would not be long before someone came to investigate the gunshots.

'Chindamani,' he whispered. 'We've got to go. Zamyatin will send someone to see what's going on. The monk who was here will tell others. We have to leave now or we'll never make it.'

She was still staring ahead, her eyes unfocused, her body rigid. He took her by the shoulders and began to shake her. She did not respond.

Suddenly, he noticed Samdup by his side. The boy had made a tremendous effort to shut out the horrors he had seen.

'Chindamani,' he said. 'Please answer me. The *pee-ling* is right — we have to escape. Please hurry or they'll find us here.'

As if the boy's voice worked some sort of magic on her, the girl blinked and began to relax. Her arms dropped to her side and she looked down at Samdup.

'I feel cold,' she said in a scarcely audible whisper.

Samdup looked up at Christopher.

'There are things for the journey in that chest,' he said. 'I was supposed to get them ready, but I had to look after Sönam and forgot.'

'William,' said Christopher. 'Come and help us get ready to leave. Help Samdup take things out of the chest.'

While the boys hurried to sort out clothes, tents, and bags of food, Christopher helped Chindamani to a seat. He put his arm round her, remembering how, not so very long before, their roles had been reversed.

'Where are we going, Ka-ris To-feh?' she asked.

'Away from here,' he answered. 'Far away.'

She smiled wanly and reached down to pick up some bags from the floor.

'Don't waste time tying those on,' said Christopher. 'We can do that later. The main thing at the moment is to get out of this room.'

Chindamani turned and took a last look at Sönam. The old woman lay back on the bed where she had fallen, a startled look in her eyes. Chindamani bent down and straightened her arms and legs. With one hand she closed her eyes, then kissed her softly on the lips.

A sound of running feet came from the passage outside.

'Quickly!' Christopher hissed. 'Let's go!'

While Christopher held back the hanging, Chindamani slid the door aside and stepped in after Samdup and William. Christopher followed, closing the door behind him with a click. Even if someone drew the hanging aside, the entrance would remain invisible to the casual eye.

A lamp was burning on a bracket nearby. Chindamani took it and led the way along the passage. Behind them they could hear muffled voices coming from the apartment they had left.

'What happened, Chindamani?' Christopher asked, as soon as they had put some distance between themselves and the entrance. 'What did you do to him? Why did he kill himself?'

She did not answer at first. Christopher could not see her face as

262

she walked on ahead of him, holding the lamp. The walls of the passage were rough and unfinished; but at one point someone – one of Chindamani's predecessors, no doubt – had painted a domestic scene, a mother and her children standing outside their farm, surrounded by sheep and yaks. The light played on the painting for a moment, then passed on into darkness.

'It was a curse,' she said at last, to no-one in particular.

'A curse? Surely you don't believe . . .?'

'Sönam didn't know what it meant.' Chindamani continued, as though she had not heard him. 'It was a Tantric curse, a very powerful one. She should not have known it – that was what frightened him. Only the most advanced adepts know it. But Sönam used to come down this passage to the Lha-khang when they were undergoing instruction. It fascinated her, and she learned all sorts of things. She understood nothing, of course; but she memorized whole rituals, whole spells . . . whole curses!' She stopped and turned around to face Christopher.

'I think Tsarong Rinpoche was almost mad with guilt already. When he heard that curse spoken by someone who had no knowledge of such matters – as he thought – he must have imagined that the gods were speaking, condemning him.'

'And you. How did you know how to continue?'

'Oh, Sönam taught me all the things she heard down in the Lha-khang. Sometimes we'd go together and watch the rituals for hours. But . . .' She hesitated. 'There was something else, something that made me do what I did. The feeling's gone now. But when he shot Sönam, I felt as though something took me over.'

'Anger?'

'No, more than that. Something quite different. I can't explain.'

'There's no need. Come on, we've got to get moving. You still have to explain to me how we're supposed to get out of Dorje-la.'

From the Tara chapel, a series of wooden steps and short passages led them down to the gön-kang. The small crypt-chapel was empty, save for the stuffed animals and gods that kept watch over it. A few lamps were lit, filling parts of the room with a creamy, yellow glow.

Chindamani explained to Christopher the details of the escape route described by Sönam. He listened to her grimly, unable to guess how much of the old woman's story might be true and how much mere legend.

They tightened their travelling clothes and tied on the items of equipment Chindamani had prepared. Christopher found a short rusty sword among the small clutter of weapons left in the gön-kang and slipped it into his belt.

'William,' he said. The boy was close by his side, determined not to let his father out of his sight again. Christopher reached into a fold of his *chuba* and drew out something soft. It was a small and very battered teddy-bear.

'I've brought old Samuel from Carfax,' said Christopher, holding the ragged toy out to the boy. 'I thought you might like to have him with you. To remind you of home.'

The boy took the bear and hugged it to his chest. It had always been his favourite toy, his inseparable bedtime companion, repaired, restuffed, restitched half a dozen times. He looked up at his father and, for the first time, smiled. With Samuel, he could face any number of dangers.

Samdup watched, bewildered. Stuffed animals were nothing new to him, but he had never seen one like this before. And why did the strange *pee-ling* boy want to carry one round with him? Was it some sort of god?

William put Samuel into his bag.

'We'll soon be back in Carfax, Samuel,' he said. Christopher smiled. How he wished he could believe that.

They rolled back several rugs in front of the main altar. Underneath, they could make out the shape of a narrow hatchway set flush with the floor and provided with a brass ring.

Christopher turned to Chindamani. Her cheeks were flushed and her eyes gleamed in the sickly light. He scarcely dared look directly at her.

'You don't have to come,' he said. 'You or Samdup. You'll be quite safe, I'm sure of it. Tsarong Rinpoche is dead. You were a threat only to him. Zamyatin will find it better to let you live. He'll use you as a symbol, but you will be alive. And the boy – he's more use to Zamyatin alive than dead. You don't know what there is down there. Or what could be waiting on the journey.'

'I was responsible for the Rinpoche's death,' Chindamani said.

'Or at least that is what the monk who was with him will say. His followers won't stand for that. And Samdup wouldn't be safe with Zam-ya-ting. You know that. You know why.'

There was nothing he could say to that. She was right: he knew why.

'Very well,' he replied. 'We'll go together. We can't afford to wait here any longer – they'll already be looking for us everywhere. I don't know what's down beneath this hatch. It may be nothing; it may be something more dangerous than anything Zamyatin and his men have to offer. But we've no choice. If we're going out, this is the only way left open to us.'

He turned to Samdup and spoke to him directly for the first time.

'What about you, Samdup? Do you feel up to this?'

The boy did not answer at once. He looked back at Christopher with an unsettling seriousness in his eyes. Since his discovery as a trulku and his installation here at Dorje-la, he had never really been treated as a child. He had clearly recovered his composure quickly since the scene in Chindamani's room.

'You should not call me "Samdup",' he said finally. 'My proper name is Dorje Samdup Rinpoche. You may call me Samdup Rinpoche or, if you prefer, Lord Samdup. Only those who are very close to me may call me by my given name alone. And you must use the proper verbal forms at all times when addressing me.'

There was that in the boy's look and tone of voice that endowed his words with an adult seriousness few British children of his age could possibly have emulated. Christopher felt thoroughly rebuked.

'I'm sorry . . . my Lord,' he said. 'There are many things I have to learn.'

'Don't worry,' the boy said. 'I will teach you. As for leaving here – I don't think we have much time to waste.'

Christopher said nothing. The die was cast. They were going into the passages beneath the gön-kang. He bent down and lifted the ring of the hatch in his right hand.

The hatch was heavy. It came up slowly, without a sound.

38

There was nothing below but darkness, black, clammy, and cold. A stale smell rose out of the pit, or perhaps it was a mixture of smells, not quite identifiable in themselves, not quite reducible to ordinary odours. It was an evil stench and it clung to the nostrils with grim tenacity. Chindamani turned her face away and made a brief gagging sound. Christopher pulled his heavy scarf up over his mouth and nose. The others followed suit.

'I'll go first,' whispered Christopher. 'Then William, then Lord Samdup. Then Chindamani. We'll all carry lamps, and if anyone's goes out they're to say so immediately and get a fresh light from someone else. Make as little noise as possible. And close the hatch behind us.'

Peering into the hole with the help of his lamp – a large one that Chindamani had found on a side altar – Christopher made out the first few rungs of a wooden ladder.

They went down slowly. The ladder took them about ten feet below the floor of the gön-kang. When Christopher, William and Samdup reached the bottom, Chindamani tossed the more bulky baggage down to them before closing the hatchway and climbing down herself.

The darkness was absolute, a thing in itself, an object and not a mere absence of light. It seemed to breathe and live and grow stronger every moment. The light of their lamps was swallowed up in it and rendered flat and insubstantial. It clung to them like a dim halo, scarred and denatured by the all-encompassing blackness.

They were in a small stagnant chamber about fifteen feet by ten. Against one wall, Christopher made out the shapes of lacquered chests and boxes. Beside them stood a huge, jewel-encrusted throne. He stepped across to a tall box ornamented with bright red peonies and lifted the lid. For a moment, it seemed as though the light thrown by his lamp had been shattered into a thousand fragments. Everywhere, tiny specks of coloured light danced in the

266

darkness. Rubies, emeralds, diamonds and amethysts lay packed in the chest like pebbles on Brighton beach.

Christopher picked up a handful and let them trickle back through his fingers. They felt cold to the touch and curiously light, as though all their substance lay in colour and luminosity. The colours shifted and flew about, like the quick wings of humming-birds in a forest glade, shimmering in a sudden ray of sunlight.

He picked up a second handful. They would need money for their journey. And after that, money to look after Chindamani and the boy. Out there, in what Christopher regarded as the real world, to be a representative of a goddess or an incarnation of the Maidari Buddha counted for nothing.

'Are you hungry?' It was Samdup's voice, close beside him. Christopher looked down and shook his head.

'No, my Lord,' he said.

'Are you thirsty?'

'No.'

'Then you have no need of them. There is food in our bags: we will not starve. There is snow: we will not go thirsty. If you take them, they will become a heavier burden than the whole of Dorje-la.'

Christopher opened his fingers and the jewels dropped one by one back into the box. This time, for no real reason that he could see, they seemed trivial to him, like pieces of coloured paste or red and green candies for a greedy child. He closed the lid and raised his lamp again.

The walls were alive with paintings: among the usual gods and demons were vividly coloured mandalas and charms in the shape of lotus-flowers covered in fine writing. Little square flags printed with the image of a winged horse bearing a mystic jewel on its back had been hung at intervals; they were faded and tattered and covered in dust. Thick cobwebs hung everywhere, some ancient and tattered like prayer-flags, others clearly fresh.

They listened for the sound of something living, but the room was occupied only by inanimate objects. Christopher began to think that talk of a guardian was little more than a ploy to deter would-be thieves. But in that case, why had the story been kept so quiet?

In the wall opposite the spot where they had entered the room

267

was the entrance to a broad tunnel. It had obviously not been used in some time: a thick, dusty spider's web covered most of it.

'At least,' Christopher whispered, 'we don't have to make up our minds which way to go.'

Using the short sword, he swept away the web: it tumbled down, leaving the gaping opening free for them to pass through.

Christopher went ahead, holding his lamp out in front of him in his left hand while hefting the sword in his right, ready to strike out at the first signs of life. His heart pounded heavily in his chest: he thought he could hear it echo off the walls of the tunnel. The stench was more pronounced here and seemed to be growing stronger all the time.

The passage was not quite high enough for Christopher to walk in unstooped, but it was sufficiently wide to allow him to pass through without difficulty. He felt certain that they were already passing out of the monastery. The chill that pervaded the tunnel was unlike that in any of the passages they had come through on their way from Chindamani's apartment. That had been icy, but tinged with a residual warmth that seemed to have seeped through the walls from the inhabited areas through which the tunnels passed. This was a fetid, uneasy chill, raw and bitter, as though nothing human had breathed the air down here for centuries.

Christopher's foot touched something. Something hard and slightly brittle. He lowered the lamp slowly, trying to hold it at an angle in order to shed light on the ground in front of him.

He could not make it out at first. It seemed to be a bundle of some kind, about five feet long, angular in places, dirty and grey. Then he held the light closer and all at once it became clear to him what it was . . . or what it had been.

The small body had shrunk beyond all reason, as if something had sucked it dry over a long period. Nothing was left but dry skin stretched over old bones. Thin hands like talons clutched at the throat. The head was pulled back acutely, away from the body, as if death had been an agony. From head to foot, the corpse was covered in dust-laden strands of something like rotten fabric, similar to the cobwebs they had seen earlier. The whole thing resembled a cocoon, neatly packaged and left to dehydrate here in the tunnel. It had been down here a long time. Perhaps as long as five centuries. Christopher shuddered and lifted his lamp.

'What is it, Christopher?' Chindamani whispered. 'Why have you stopped?'

'It's nothing. Just . . . an obstruction in the tunnel. Keep to the right and you'll be able to get by.'

He walked on, hesitant now, on the alert for whatever might be waiting further along the tunnel. Sönam's guardian was slipping out of the mists of legend and growing into a thing of substance. Behind him, he heard the others gasp as they caught sight of the obstruction.

The next body was a few yards further along. It had died in a seated position, propped against one wall. Its arms were thrust out in front of it, as thought fending off something coming out of the darkness. Like the other corpse, it was shrivelled and shrunken. Pieces of leathery flesh, dark brown in colour, could be glimpsed beneath layers of the dusty fabric. It seemed to Christopher as though something had trussed it up and sucked it slowly dry.

'Who are they, Christopher?' Chindamani's voice came from close behind him. She was standing, one arm around Samdup, looking down at the little corpse. The boy seemed disturbed, but not frightened. Christopher remembered that he had been brought up in a culture that had little fear of the paraphernalia of death. Instead of Bo Peep and Humpty Dumpty, the walls of Samdup's nursery would have been painted with dead flesh and mouldering bones. Instead of a teddy-bear, he would have been given a statue of Yama to place by his bedside.

'I think this one was a child,' he said. But it was only a guess, based on the corpse's apparent height. 'It seems . . . more recent than the other. Less dusty.' He paused. 'There may be more. Do you want to go on?'

'Of course. We have no choice – you said so yourself.'

About five yards after that, Christopher encountered a heavy web that all but blocked the tunnel. He swept it aside only to meet another and then another. Vast, heavy strands of cobwebs filled the air. The miasmatic odour was growing in intensity. Christopher was beginning to have a good idea what had trussed up the bodies they had found. But surely no ordinary spider could have sucked them dry as well.

All at once the tunnel ended and opened out into an area of undefined proportions. The light from Christopher's lamp shed illumination over a limited radius, but as the children and Chindamani added their lights to his, the nature of their surroundings became gradually clear.

It was a chamber thick with spiders' webs, huge structures of ancient manufacture that looped a fantastic tracery from floor to ceiling and from wall to wall. The lamplight played complicated shadow-games among the interlacing cords and filaments. Some hung like hammocks, others billowed from the wall like grey lace curtains. No matter where they looked, the room was thick with them.

And no matter where they cast their eyes, they could make out the bundled, mummified remains of human beings. The webs were full of them; they hung like flies, light and grey and bloodless. The room was a subterranean larder of God knows what antiquity. In places, body had been piled upon body, the mouldering remains sewn together in huge packages. In one corner, what seemed to be a relatively recent addition to their meat supply was being drained of its remaining fluids by a small army of spiders that moved across their prey with quick, quivering motions. To his horror, Christopher estimated the size of the spiders: the largest had a leg-span longer than a man's forearm, from fingertips to elbow.

Everywhere black shapes were walking in the shadows. The webs were alive with them, trembling as they crawled from thread to thread on huge, misshapen legs.

'For God's sake, get back into the tunnel!' Christopher cried. He had seen stings on the ends of the bulbous bodies – and he guessed that the spiders had not overpowered their prey by brute force.

Woodenly, they stumbled back, past the webs at the entrance to the food-chamber, as far as the first body. William was shaking with fright and loathing – nothing in his worst nightmares had prepared him for such a sight. Samdup too was rigid with fear.

'The horror of it! The horror of it!' Chindamani kept repeating. She was brushing and brushing her arms and body, desperately trying to rid herself of anything that might be clinging to her. She could feel their soft bodies and cold legs against her flesh. To be poisoned and pinned down and sucked dry by such creatures . . .

Christopher checked for spiders. None seemed to have dropped on them or followed them – so far. These, then, were the guardians set over the Oracle's treasure. A species of spider, mutated by the

270

thin air and the darkness, discovered or placed down here to sting and kill intruders. But why had there been none in the treasure-chamber? And where did their victims come from?

'Chindamani, Samdup,' Christopher ordered. 'Get out any extra items of clothing you have in your bags. Wrap your hands and faces tightly. Leave no gaps, just a space for your eyes. Help each other. And hurry. We've disturbed them – it won't be long before they start investigating.' He bent down and quickly repeated what he had said to William. The boy had taken Samuel out of his bag and was clutching it to him nervously.

'Put Samuel away,' Christopher said softly. 'You'll need your hands free.' William complied reluctantly.

Feverishly, Chindamani and Samdup wrapped each other up, using spare scarves and leggings they had packed. When they were ready, Chindamani helped William bind himself, then Christopher.

'We can still go back,' he said.

She shook her head.

'No,' she said. 'Zam-ya-ting is waiting for us there. It's death whichever way we go. But perhaps we have a chance down here. That place is their lair. The stairs of Yama must be beyond it. If we can make it that far, we'll be all right.'

Christopher prayed she was right.

When they were ready, he led the way down to the exit from the tunnel. He could hear the rustling of their legs in the darkness, stiff wire bristles on paper – a host of spiders coming to investigate the disturbance.

If only he could make out an opening somewhere – that would enable them to make a straight run for it. There was a risk that, if they became entangled in the vast network of spiders' webs and confused by fighting off their hideous inhabitants, they would lose their lamps and be plunged into absolute darkness. And that would almost certainly be fatal.

A large spider, its legs moving jerkily, like a badly oiled machine, came scuttling towards him at shoulder height along a swathe of tattered web. He swept at it with the sword and sent it tumbling back into the shadows. Another ran at his feet with a queer sideways motion. He kicked down hard and felt it give way beneath the heel of his boot.

'Which way do we go, Christopher?' Chindamani asked, pressing against him from behind.

'I don't know,' he said. 'If there are stairs, they could be anywhere.'

'There have to be stairs. Sönam was right about everything else.'

'Perhaps.' He paused. 'There's one way to find out. The most likely place is right opposite. I'll make a dash for it. Watch me closely. If I get through and there are stairs, I'll call. Don't waste any time – come running.'

'Be careful, Christopher,' she said. He could only see her eyes peering out above her scarf. With one hand, he reached out and touched her. She lifted a hand and put it over his. In a world of spiders, among dark threads and silken fabrics of most intricate and passionless death, they touched for a moment in silence. Skin did not touch skin, lips could not meet, there was a deathly chill upon their hampered breath.

A huge spider landed on Christopher's back. William cried out and Christopher spun, dashing the monster to the ground and crushing it.

'Run!' cried Chindamani.

He ran, cutting a path through meshes of doubled and redoubled web, pulling, tearing, scything as he staggered through the room. The floor was littered with small wizened corpses, pathetic bundles no longer recognizable as human. At every step, more spiders dropped on to him, clinging to his back and arms and legs, stinging again and again into the thick layers of cloth and fur.

How he made it to the other side he did not know. He swept the last web curtains aside. There was nothing but rock. Frantically, he thrashed about, severing webs like cheesecloth, ripping them apart. There was nothing but bare rock. Something struck his lamp and sent it skittering from his hand. The world was plunged into darkness. He dropped the sword with a clatter.

A large spider dropped on to his head, then another on to his shoulders. One of the corpses caught his foot and he fell helplessly to his knees. He reached out desperately and his fingers caught nothing but a tangled mass of spider's web.

39

'Christopher!'

Her voice echoed in the narrow confines of the tunnel. There was no answer, and she called again, more desperately this time.

'Christopher, where are you? What's happening? Answer me!'

But after the echoes, there was only silence. She had seen Christopher's lamp go out. Now he did not answer. The spiders were everywhere now, malign, implacable, without pity. She shuddered and called again.

'Christopher!'

There was something – a muffled sound from the far side of the room.

'He must have fallen,' Samdup said. 'We've got to get to him!'

Chindamani clenched her teeth and prayed to Chenrezi for the strength to do what had to be done now.

She took the boy by the shoulders and made him face her. William looked on, his eyes filled with terror.

'Samdup,' she said. 'I've got to help Ka-ris To-feh. Wait as long as you dare. If I don't come back, leave the way we came. Go back to the gön-kang. Take the boy with you. You'll both be safe; they won't harm you. Do you understand?'

But even as she spoke, William suddenly broke away from them, running into the room of webs, his lamp bobbing as he ran, calling after his father. Chindamani reached out a hand frantically, but he had already eluded her grasp and her fingers found nothing but cobwebs, old and dirty.

Without a moment's thought, she hurried after him, threshing her way through the hanging threads, flailing her arms to knock away the quivering bodies with which she came in contact.

A last grey curtain parted and she saw them – Christopher on his back, fighting to throw off the dozens of spiders that crawled over him, his son using Christopher's sword to sweep them aside. But the black shapes kept on coming and coming.

She grabbed Christopher's hand and helped him stagger to his feet. Had he been poisoned? If so, how long did he have before the venom began to work?

'There's no way out!' he cried. 'We've got to get back to the tunnel.'

A spider moved on to Chindamani's left leg, then another, then a third. She kicked them away, but others came. One brute landed on William's neck and clung there. Christopher grabbed it with his bare hands, dragging it off. He thought it had stung the boy, but there was no time to check.

Suddenly, William shouted: 'Look!'

He was pointing at a spot in the rear wall. There was a door – heavily encrusted with spider's webs but just distinguishable.

Chindamani shouted frantically to Samdup.

'Hurry!' she cried. 'This way! This way!'

They could see his lamp weaving through the darkness. He stumbled and Chindamani dashed back for him. There were spiders everywhere now, angry and murderous. Chindamani found Samdup and helped him over the last few yards.

'It's over here!' Christopher shouted, pointing to the door. They ran, scything through layer after layer of soft web. And the dried bodies everywhere, like pods that had spawned the spider brood.

The door was jammed. Christopher pulled on the ring handle, but it would not give. William and Samdup did what they could to keep the spiders at bay. Chindamani joined Christopher at the door, pulling with him, tearing her muscles in desperation. How long since the door had last been opened? A century? Ten centuries? They redoubled their efforts, knowing they would never make it back to the tunnel now. It was the door or nothing.

It gave an inch then stuck again, harder than before. Christopher thought his fingers were breaking, but he kept pulling, using the pain to spur him.

There was a snapping sound and the door moved. Not much, but just enough for them to get past. Christopher grabbed William and pushed him through, then Samdup, then Chindamani. He picked up the lamp Chindamani had left on the ground. She took it from him and he pulled the door closed. They had made it. So far.

Several spiders had made it with them. William struck at them with the sword, hewing them again and again with a sustained and vicious anger that had grown too immense for his child's body to contain. It was the first adult anger he had known, a rage less against the spiders that had provoked his immediate fear and revulsion, more against Tsarong Rinpoche and the Russian, against all those that had torn the fabric of his world to shreds. It was rage and sadness and doubt combined: rage at betrayal, sadness at the loss of all he had known, doubt of the fixed certainties that had framed his world until then.

There were stairs as Sönam had said: stark and steep and very beautiful in the light from their single lamp. They sat forever on the small landing at the top, no-one speaking, willing the horror to leave their minds, willing the last descent to the open air and freedom. The thought that no-one voiced was whether the stairs held any hidden surprises for them.

Christopher held William tightly. Once, he looked at the boy's neck. There was an angry red mark where the spider must have stung him. But William said it scarcely hurt. He had had a lucky escape.

'It will soon be dawn,' Chindamani said. 'We should be away from here before then.'

Christopher nodded. She was right. He wanted to put as much distance between them and Dorje-la before Zamyatin realized they had escaped from the monastery.

In single file, with Christopher in the lead as before, they started down the stairs. The steps had been cut roughly in the rock, without precision or refinement. They were cold and dark, and they plunged down perilously, as though eager to be finished. They had not been made to linger on.

The cold air took away the awful stench. They uncovered their mouths and breathed in deeply, filling their lungs. With every step they took, a weight lifted from their shoulders. Death had never seemed so real or so close or so unwholesome. Not even a belief in endless reincarnation could mitigate the horror of death when it became so unnatural and so intimate.

They reached the bottom of the stairs. The rock wall had been cunningly cut in order to render the opening invisible from outside, and to make the deceit perfect, a curtain of ice hung over the front.

Outside, the wind had cleared the clouds away. A pale moon thin as silver-leaf was just setting behind a dim peak to the west. Across a purple sky, broad swathes of stars trembled with cold and their own brightness. High above where they stood, the dark shape of Dorje-la Gompa loomed over the pass, vast and sinister, harbouring its secrets in silence.

Christopher looked up, peering into the darkness. A single light could be seen, in an unshuttered window on the top floor. Chindamani stepped close beside him and took his hands in hers.

'Look,' he whispered.

Her eyes followed his to the lighted window.

'He's watching for us,' he said.

'Who?' she asked.

'Zamyatin. I can sense it.' He paused. 'He won't let us go this easily. Samdup belongs to him. In a way, I belong to him too. He'll come after us – be sure of it.'

She said nothing for a while, but stood with Christopher's hand in hers, staring up at the lighted window, wondering.

'It's time to go,' she said.

But Christopher did not move. Like a moth held by the yellow light, he stood lost in thought.

'Ka-ris To-feh,' she said, tugging gently at his arm.

He looked round. In the moonlight, her face was pale and ghostly. He felt remote, impermanent, displaced. He could hold nothing, like a sieve from which water runs out.

'Do you understand what will happen if you come with me?' he said. 'I have to go to India, then back to England. It's William's home, I have to take him there. Once we reach India, I will no longer be able to help you. There are others there, men like Zamyatin who will want Samdup for their own purposes. Once they learn who he is – and they will learn, believe me – he will become their pawn. You don't know what the world is like, what it does to people. Do you understand what I'm trying to say?'

She shook her head. One culture shaking its head at another, a world denying another world.

'We seem to have no understanding of each other, Ka-ris To-feh. Is it so much to be human? Not to understand?'

'Don't you see?' he said. 'Your Maidari Buddha has become a commodity, a coin. He's worth so much to Zamyatin. He would

276

be worth so much more or less to my own masters. What Zamyatin does not or cannot control, they would have me manipulate for their own ends. I don't want to play that game. I'll finish the one I began, but that's as far as I go. I'll take you to Lhasa, but I'll leave you there. Do you understand?'

Desire for her was like a fever inside him. Denying his will in her, his love and his lust for her, was an even greater hurt, a stinging that filled his flesh and his mind equally, making him whole and tearing him apart at once.

She did not reply. Instead, she stood and picked up her bag. With Samdup's hand in hers, she set off in the direction of the pass. Christopher felt his heart contract. He stood up and helped William to his feet. They followed Chindamani and Samdup at a short distance.

As they picked their way down the slope, William raised his face to Christopher.

'What about grandfather?' he said.

'I don't understand,' said Christopher. His father must have told the boy who he was, he realized.

'Aren't we going to take him with us?'

Christopher shook his head.

'I'm sorry,' he said. 'Your grandfather is dead. Really dead this time.'

'How do you know?'

'Tsarong Rinpoche told us. Just before we were brought into the room where you and Samdup were sitting with Zamyatin. He said he had killed him himself.'

William stopped, forcing his father to do the same.

'But that can't be true,' the boy said.

'Why not?'

'Because I was with grandfather just before you came.'

'How long before?' Christopher felt his heart grow cold with apprehension.

'Not long. A few minutes. Some men came and said I had to leave. Grandfather told me they were going to lock him in his rooms. The Rinpoche man was never there.'

'Are you sure, William? Maybe they killed him after you left?'

'No, because we went past his rooms on our way to the lady's room. I knocked on his door and called. He answered me. He wished me goodnight.'

40

Christopher called to Chindamani to halt. He ran up to her with William and explained what his son had just told him.

'Zamyatin said nothing about the abbot being killed,' he said, 'only that he had been replaced. Tsarong Rinpoche was lying. He wanted to make us believe my father was dead, because the old man could still be a threat to him. But even he must have drawn the line at actually putting an incarnation to death.'

Christopher remembered the Rinpoche's words to him: 'You are holy to me, I cannot touch you.' He had been holy because he was the son of an incarnation. Brutal as he was, it was clear that the Rinpoche had still been deeply superstitious. Some crimes were beyond the pale.

But Zamyatin would not feel constrained by superstitious awe. He was more than capable of having Tsarong Rinpoche's boast translated into stark reality.

'I have to go back,' said Christopher. 'Even if it's only a hope, I can't leave without trying to save him. He is my father. Whatever he's done, I can't just abandon him.'

Chindamani reached out a hand. She wanted so much to hold him to her until all this had passed away.

'Take me with you,' she said.

Christopher shook his head.

'I can't,' he said. 'You know I can't. We've been through so much to escape, we can't just throw it all away by going back up there. You must stay here with William and Samdup. If I don't return by noon tomorrow, you'll know I'm not coming back. Take the boys and leave. Try to find your way to Lhasa: you're an incarnation; Samdup's an incarnation – they'll find a place for you there. Take William to a man called Bell – he's the British representative in Tibet. He'll see to it that the boy is taken home safely.'

'I'm frightened for you, Ka-ris To-feh!'

278

'I know. And I for you. But I have no choice. I intend to return with my father. Wait for me here.'

He turned to William and explained to him as well as he could that he had to go back for his father.

'Chindamani will look after you until I return,' he said. 'Do what she tells you, even if you don't understand a word she says. Will you be all right?

William nodded. He hated to see his father go again, but he understood.

'How's your neck? Does it hurt?'

William shook his head.

'It itches a little, that's all.'

Christopher smiled, kissed the boy on the cheek, and began the ascent to the monastery. Chindamani watched him go. As he disappeared into the darkness, she saw shadows creep across the stars. She could feel the world going out of her, far, far away, like a cloud dissolving in a storm.

It took him an hour to reach the foot of the main building. The ladder was in place. He looked up, but from where he stood he could not see Zamyatin's window. He put a foot on the first rung and began to climb.

Two men had been put on the door. They opened it to Christopher's pounding, their faces surly, unfriendly – and, Christopher thought, more than a little frightened. They guessed that he might be the dangerous *pee-ling* they had been given orders to capture. But they had expected to find him inside the monastery, not coming from the outside.

Christopher had taken Tsarong Rinpoche's gun before leaving Chindamani's room. Now he fingered it in his pocket, a dull weight reminding him of another existence.

'I've come to speak with Zamyatin,' he said.

The monks eyed him cautiously, unable to understand where he had sprung from. His clothes were soiled and matted with cobwebs and his eyes were troubled by something beyond their guessing. They were armed with Chinese halberds, heavy, long-bladed tools of war that could inflict serious injury even when blunt. But neither man felt comfort in the feel of the heavy weapon in his hands. They

279

had heard – in a much embellished form – of Tsarong Rinpoche's fate. Zamyatin had ordered them to watch the door, but superstition travelled more easily in their veins than the stranger's commands.

'No-one is allowed to disturb Zam-ya-ting,' said one of the men, braver or more stupid than his companion.

'I intend to disturb him,' Christopher replied in a matter-of-fact tone. It rattled the monk even more to find the *pee-ling* implacable rather than angry or blustering. They were in any case already feeling the first pangs of conscience about what had happened. From an orgy of death, they – and most of their colleagues – had passed to a hangover of uncertainty. Without the Rinpoche to hector them, they were like children whom a party game has led into unintended naughtiness.

Christopher sensed their hesitation and walked past. One of the men called out to him to stop, but he went on regardless and the shouting subsided.

The monastery was silent. Although dawn was near, no-one had ventured out to sound the summons to morning prayers. Dorje-la would sleep late to-day – if it slept at all.

He climbed to the top storey, tired, sad, defeated. He passed quickly through the rooms of the five elements and reached the hall of the chörtens. No-one stopped him. He heard no voices, saw no sign that anyone had been there.

The long hall was empty. Only the bodies of the dead watched him enter. The first pale light of dawn crept through the unshuttered window, near which a lamp still burned. Christopher's weariness changed slowly to a profound sense of unease. Where was the Russian?

'Zamyatin!' he called. His voice sounded unnaturally loud in the echoing room. There was no answer.

'Zamyatin! Are you there?' he called again, but no-one replied.

He walked down the room, past the window that overlooked the pass, past memories all the more poignant for their freshness, past his father coming to life again among the shadows, past himself staring astonished at the old man. Too many ghosts. Too many shadows.

He headed for the abbot's bedroom. The door was locked, but without someone to guard it, it was a flimsy enough affair. The lock was more ornamental than practical, and Christopher was able to kick it open without difficulty.

The old man was seated cross-legged in front of a small altar, his back to Christopher, his bent figure haloed by the light of a dozen butter lamps. He showed no sign that he had heard Christopher knock down the door. He did not turn his head or speak, other than to continue with his devotions.

Christopher stood by the door, feeling suddenly embarrassed and awkward, an intruder on his father's privacy. The old man murmured inaudibly, oblivious of his surroundings. Christopher might have been Tsarong Rinpoche returned to kill him after all, but the abbot paid no attention.

Christopher stepped a few paces into the room. He stopped, listening to his father's prayer, hesitant to disturb him. Then, with a shock of recognition, he understood the words the old man was reciting:

Nunc dimittis servum tuum Domine . . .
   'Now Thou dost dismiss Thy servant, O Lord, according to Thy word in peace. Because mine eyes have seen Thy salvation, Which Thou hast prepared before the face of all people . . .'

It was the Canticle of Simeon, the old man who besought God to let him depart the world in peace, having set eyes on the Christ child. Christopher stood still, listening to the familiar words, wondering if anything more than a dream separated him from that fateful evening after mass.

At last the abbot came to an end. Christopher stepped forward and laid a hand on his shoulder.

'Father,' he said. It was the first time he had used the name when speaking to the old man. 'It's time for us to go.'

The abbot looked up, like someone who has long been expecting a summons.

'Christopher,' he said. 'I hoped you might come. Have you seen your son?'

Christopher nodded.

'Yes.'

'Is he all right? Is he safe?'

281

'Yes, father. He is safe.'

'And the other boy, Dorje Samdup Rinpoche – is he safe too?'

'Yes. I've left them both down in the pass. Chindamani is with them. They're waiting for you.'

The old man smiled.

'I'm pleased they got away. You must leave as well, help them to get as far away as possible.

'Not without you, father. I came to fetch you.'

The abbot shook his head. The smile left his lips and was replaced by a deep seriousness.

'No,' he said. 'I have to remain here. I am the abbot. Whatever Tsarong Rinpoche thinks, I am still abbot of Dorje-la.'

'Tsarong Rinpoche is dead, father. You can remain abbot. But for now it's better for you to leave. Just for a little while, until it's safe for you to return.'

But his father shook his head again, more sadly this time.

'I'm sorry to hear about Tsarong Rinpoche. He was very unhappy. And now he will have to start his journey through his incarnations again. How tired that makes me feel. It's time I laid this body with the others, Christopher. Time I was reborn.'

'You were reborn,' said Christopher quietly. 'When you told me who you were, it was like a rebirth for me. And again tonight. Tsarong Rinpoche told me you were dead, and I believed him. Coming in here like this, watching you at prayer – it was like another rebirth.'

The old man put his hand on Christopher's.

'Do you know what prayer I was reciting?' he asked.

'Yes. The Canticle of Simeon.'

'He knew when it was time to call an end. He had seen what he spent his life waiting to see. I feel the same way. Don't force me to come with you. My place is here, among these tombs. You have another destiny. Don't waste time here. The boys need your protection. Chindamani needs it. And, I think, your love. Don't be too frightened of her: she's not a goddess all the time.'

Leaning on Christopher's arm, the old man eased himself slowly to his feet.

'Is the Russian still alive?' he asked.

'I don't know. I think so.'

'Then it's time you were on your way. I've no concern with

politics. Bolsheviks, Tories, Liberals – they're all the same to me. But the boy must be protected. See that he comes to no harm. And your own son. I'm sorry I had him brought here, I'm sorry I caused you grief. But believe me that I thought it was for the best.'

Christopher squeezed his father's hand.

'Are you sure you won't come with me?' he said.

'Very sure.'

Christopher was silent.

'You are happy?' he asked after a while.

'I am at peace, Christopher. That is more important than happiness. You will see. In the end, you will see. Now, you must go.'

Reluctantly, Christopher let go of his father's hand.

'Goodbye,' he whispered.

'Goodbye, Christopher. Take care.'

Outside, a miserable sunlight was slowly working its way across the sky. One by one, stars faded and the jagged edges of mountain peaks were etched once more against a grey sky. In the air above, a vulture winged its way to Dorje-la Gompa. Its great wings dragged it forward, casting a grey shadow on the snow.

Christopher ran towards the spot where he had left Chindamani and the boys. The thin air scarred his lungs. His chest heaved, filling with pain. Altitude and tiredness were taking their combined toll.

There was a low ridge. He staggered up it and fell at the top, landing in a soft bed of snow. Picking himself up, he looked down into the pass. It was empty.

PART THREE
Parousia

'And what rough beast, its hour come round at last,
Slouches towards Bethlehem to be born?'

W. B. Yeats 'The Second Coming'

The Road to Sining-Fu

41

Christopher's greatest fear was that he would fall asleep in the snow and succumb to the cold. He had already been tired after his journey to Dorje-la, and the previous night's exertions had taken their toll. The weather was bitterly cold, and his only protection was the clothing he wore. Several times when he rested he caught himself dozing off. He knew Zamyatin and the others would be tired too, but not as badly as himself. And they had two tents, a little firewood, and some food. His only hope lay in the tracks that told him which way they had gone. He would keep following them until his strength gave out.

On the first night, he found a small hollow in a cliff-face: not really of a size to be designated a cave, but big enough to give him a little shelter from the biting winds. He had not eaten since the early evening of the day before.

All the next day, he trudged on, moving deeper and deeper into the mountains. There was no point in turning back: whichever way he headed, he knew he would find nothing but snow and ice. The tracks at his feet became the whole world to him, blotting out everything else.

He was troubled by dreams. In its exhaustion, his mind began to paint the blank snow with strange images. Once he saw a line of ruined pyramids stretch away from him towards a dark horizon. And flanking them all the way a parallel line of sphinxes, robed in black silk and crowned with leaves of juniper. The need for sleep was overwhelming. All he wanted was to lie down and let the dreams take him. Every step became a struggle, every moment he remained awake a victory.

He kept awake on the second night by aiming the pistol at himself and holding his thumb on the trigger so that, if he pitched forward too far, it would fire. He sang to the darkness and carried out exercises in mental arithmetic.

On the third morning, he found another shelter in the rock, a deep one this time. He crawled inside it and collapsed at once into a deep sleep. It was daylight when he woke, still groggy, but he guessed he must have slept through all that day and night, so stiff were his limbs and so hungry did he feel on waking.

When he scrambled out of the little cave, he found himself in a changed world. There had been a blizzard. Try as he might, he could not find any trace of the tracks he had been following. He almost gave up then. It would have taken only a single bullet to make it quick. Instead, he decided to keep on, following the easiest path in the general direction Zamyatin had taken: due north.

He found Chindamani about five hours later, on a low saddle of rock at the edge of a glacier. She had been there since the previous day. When Christopher found her, she was seated outside a small tent chanting a mantra gently to herself, over and over again. He was reminded of his father reciting the Canticle of Simeon.

He sat down beside her quietly, not wanting to startle her. At first she continued chanting, immersed in the mantra to the exclusion of all distractions. Then she became aware of his presence and became silent.

'Go on,' he said, 'I didn't meant to disturb you.'

She turned and looked at him without speaking. He had only seen her before in the yellow light of butter lamps or in stark moonlight, silhouetted. In the watery light of day she seemed drawn and pallid, bereft of warmth.

'How long have you been here?' he asked.

'I don't know,' she said. 'A long time.' She paused. 'Have you come to take me home?' she asked.

He shook his head.

'I don't know the way. There was a blizzard: all the tracks are blotted out. Even if I wanted to, I couldn't take you back there.'

She looked hard at him, with sad eyes.

'You're tired, Ka-ris To-feh. Why are you so tired?'

'I haven't eaten for three or four days. I've scarcely slept. What happened? How did Zamyatin find you?'

She told him. Someone had told the Russian about the stairs of Yama, and he had gone out to the pass by a side entrance. About half an hour after Christopher left to find his father, Zamyatin had found Chindamani and the boys. He had tied them together with a long rope and forced them to start walking.

290

'Where is he headed?'

'North. To Mongolia. He left me behind here because he said I was holding them up. He let me keep one of the tents and enough food for a week.'

'Are the boys all right?'

She nodded.

'They're a little tired and frightened, but he has not harmed them.'

'What about . . .?'

She reached out a gloved hand and stroked his cheek.

'No more questions,' she said. 'I have food inside the tent. It's time for you to eat.'

They moved on that afternoon through a light snowfall, two blurs of white in a white landscape, heading north. That night they pitched the tent in the lee of a tall rockface, out of reach of the constant winds. For the first time since leaving Dorje-la, Christopher felt warmth creep back into his body.

The next day was like the one before, and the next. To make even a few miles in a day called for superhuman effort. Christopher could not begin to contemplate the sheer scale of a journey all the way to Mongolia. They were prisoners of the mountains: for all they knew, they were heading the wrong way. Though they eked it out, there was only enough food for a few days more. If they did not find a pass out of the mountains soon, they would be trapped in them forever. Christopher kept the gun a secret from her: if he had to use it, he would do so while she was asleep.

They slept together for the first time on the third night. Until then, she had kept separate from him, sleeping at her own end of their small tent, dreaming her own dreams, waking to her own loneliness. But that night she came, not simply to his bed, but to his world. It was not that she left her own existence entirely behind; but from that moment it became paler than it had been, less substantial.

She came to him while he was sleeping, as though she were a part of a dream, silent and unnoticed. He did not wake at first. A lonely wind rattled through the gully in which they were camped, but inside the little yak-hair tent it was warm. She lifted the heavy blanket that covered him, her body on the hard ground, shivering,

291

fully awake, more awake than she had ever been. Carefully, like a child who has crept into bed beside her father for comfort, but is afraid to wake him, she lay against his back, awkward and tense.

He woke to her out of a dream of carnage. His sleep was still troubled and filled with dim shapes he could not remember when he woke. Hooded figures slipped away from him down narrow, deserted streets. Vultures descended on angels' wings, their sharp beaks poised to tear his flesh.

He sensed her in the darkness close to him. As sleep left him and consciousness returned, he heard her breathing, felt her breath warm against his neck. He slept in all but his heavy outer clothes and boots. Through his thick garments, he could hardly feel her press against him.

For a long time he lay in the darkness like that, listening to the wind dance beyond the thin walls of the tent, listening to her breathe softly against the exposed skin of his neck. Then, wordlessly, as though still in a dream, he turned and lay face to face with her.

With one arm he pulled her to him until she was close against him. His fingers caressed her quietly, sadly, in a dream. She stiffened at his first clumsy embrace, then let herself be held by him.

Neither spoke. As she moved to him, she felt the dark and the loneliness grow around and within her. Her very nearness to him seemed to intensify whatever distance still rested in her mind.

He laid his voice on her like an anxious hand.

'Why did you come?' he asked.

'Does it matter?'

He stroked her back.

'Are you afraid?' he asked.

She said nothing, then put one hand behind his head and drew herself closer to him. Then, in a very quiet voice, she said 'yes'.

'Of me?'

'Not of you,' she answered. 'Of wanting you. Of wanting to lie with you like this. To become flesh with you.'

'To become flesh?'

Not 'one flesh', she had said, but 'flesh'.

'All my life I have been a vehicle for the spirit,' she said. 'I pretended my body was a mirror, that the image was what counted, not the glass.' She paused. 'I'm tired of pretending. I am what I am. Even if the glass breaks, I want to be more than the mirror.'

He kissed her gently on the forehead, then over her entire face, small kisses, delicate as flakes of falling snow. She trembled and pressed herself against him.

He caressed her back now with longer, softer strokes. She was wearing her indoor clothes from the monastery: a silk tunic and trousers. His hand touched the rising curve of her small buttocks and he felt desire begin in him. 'Desire is greedy. It will devour you,' his father had said. But what if one were already being devoured? By loneliness. By incapacity to love. By simple bereavement of the flesh.

With shaking hands, he undressed her. Her body felt young and supple and quiet as silk. Outside, the wind had fallen and snow fell in unresisted profusion, softening, whitening everything it touched. He bent over her and kissed her forehead again, then her eyes, in equal proportion. She shivered and moaned gently. His lips felt hot against her skin. She thought that, deep inside her, the goddess shivered too.

'I love you,' she said. It was the second time she had told him, but the words still seemed strange to her, a phrase from a liturgy she had heard spoken often but never until now seen enacted.

She felt desire for him grow, suffusing her as a light suffuses a hitherto-darkened room. His fingers moved across her flesh slowly and quietly, like the wings of pigeons stroking the bright air. His mouth found hers in the darkness, without speech or sound, and she opened her lips to his, her breath mingling with his breath, her heart beating alongside his. She reached up a hand to touch his cheek. He felt strange to her: her fingers strayed blindly among the thick hairs of his beard.

As desire grew in both of them, it blotted out everything else. The world shrank to a tiny point, then vanished. Only their bodies remained, floating in the void. They had become a single universe into which no light or sound or good or evil entered.

She helped him undress with fingers made clumsy by passion. Why had no-one told her this, that a man's body was more beautiful than a god's, the awkwardness of desire more satisfying than the most perfect ritual, a moment's fulfilment worth more than a lifetime of righteous virginity? Even the gods cohabited with their celestial consorts: the rhythms of their bodies in the act of love cast shadows over the world of men.

His hands moved over her now with the ease of love that has become whole. Out of his past, memories came to inform and guide his fingers along the uncharted waters of her flesh. He sensed her uncertainty and her hesitation in this strange novitiate. She had no memories to guide her, only instinct and the patterns set by her impassioned deities.

And yet, as he moved into her and they gave themselves up wholly to the dance, they discovered a fierce harmony, a single rhythm that possessed their bodies and their hearts entirely. She moved beneath him, easily, softly, without guilt or shame, in slow, erotic measures no art or artifice could match. And he moved in her perfectly, matching his actions to hers, seeking her in the dark with a dream-like intensity. And so the memories fell away and there was only this moment, only love for her, transcending the past, driving it out, remaking it in her image.

And finally there was silence. And darkness that seemed to stretch into eternity. They lay together, only their fingers touching. Neither spoke.

By morning, the snow had stopped. They were the only living things in a white immensity that seemed to have no end.

42

At noon on the same day, they found a pass leading into the Tsangpo valley region. Beyond the pass, they came upon a hut inhabited by two hunters. The men were sullen at first, but when Chindamani told them who she was, the frowns left their faces and food and drink appeared as if from nowhere. Christopher realized how little he really knew of her. Here, she was a sort of queen, a holy person whom others would obey without question or hesitation. He kept his distance from her while they remained at the hut.

The hunters gave them directions to Gharoling, the monastery to which Tobchen Geshe had tried to take Samdup for refuge. They arrived there two days later. The monastery was situated to the north of the mountain range through which they had passed, in a secluded valley through which ran a tributary of the Yarlong Tsangpo, the northern section of the Brahmaputra. Shigatse, the capital of Tsang province, was only a few days away to the north-east.

An early spring had come to the valley. Grass grew on the banks of the river, riveted to the earth by small blue flowers that neither of them could name. There were trees, and birds to sing in them, and green buds forming on their branches. A small village nestled beneath the gompa, which stood on a low hill near the head of the valley. White prayer-flags fluttered everywhere, filling the air with a soft flapping sound.

They stood at the entrance to the valley, dressed in their travel-worn clothes, pinched and hungry, gazing at the scene in front of them like damned souls gazing into paradise. Chindamani's eyes were wide with amazement: she had never known a world that was not bound by winter. The seasons meant nothing to her. She touched the grass with unbelieving fingers, smelled the warm air, and watched the birds collect twigs for their nests.

Christopher picked a flower for her and placed it in her hair.

'I'll keep it always, Ka-ris To-feh,' she said.

He shook his head.

'No,' he said. 'It will die soon. If you put it in water, it will last a few days more. But then it will die.'

She looked crestfallen for a moment, then smiled.

'Perhaps that is why it is so beautiful,' she said.

He looked at her, at the flower on her temple.

'Yes,' he said. And he thought she was beautiful. And that she would die.

She spent most of the day following their arrival closeted with the abbot, Khyongla Rinpoche. When she emerged that evening, her face was serious, and Christopher's best efforts could not secure a smile. She would not tell him what the abbot had said.

They slept in separate rooms, and that night she did not come to him. He waited for her until dawn, but in the end resigned himself to her absence and slept fitfully through the morning.

A week passed, during which they ate and rested and gained strength for the journey ahead. Each day they left the monastery and walked together in the green valley, or sat on the banks of the river. Dorje-la seemed worlds away, a place of horrors unimaginable here. They were lovers in a world made for love. The rest was a nightmare or an illusion. But when she came from her talks with the abbot her eyes were clouded with sadness neither the sunshine nor his words of endearment could dispel.

'Do you love me truly, Ka-ris To-feh?' she asked.

'Yes, little Drölma,' he said.

'Please. I've asked you not to call me that.' Her face grew troubled.

'Why not?'

'Because.'

He frowned.

'Does she still live in you?' he asked.

She nodded. A shadow passed over the water.

'Yes,' she said. 'No matter what happens, she lives in me.'

'I see. Very well, I promise not to call you Drölma if you promise to call me what my friends call me.'

'What's that?'

'Chris,' he said.

296

'Ka-ris.' She laughed. 'That's all right. I'll call you Ka-ris from now on.'

He smiled at her.

'And you,' he said. 'Do you love me truly?'

She bent forward and kissed him. In the sky a lammergeyer plunged.

They talked of his life: India, England, the war. It was all fresh to her, all beyond imagining. When he talked of cities, she could see nothing but gigantic monasteries, seething with people. When he told her of ships sailing the sea between India and home, she thought only of a vast expanse of rippling snow. The river beside which they walked was the first flowing water she had seen: the ocean was beyond all thought. When he spoke of tanks and aeroplanes, she shook her head in disbelief and closed her eyes.

Once, an early butterfly passed over their heads, bright-winged and doomed to die by nightfall. He watched it go and thought of Puccini's opera, of Butterfly waiting year after year for the return of Pinkerton, of Oriental fidelity and Western treachery.

'My Butterfly,' he murmured, caressing her cheek with a thoughtful hand.

She smiled and looked at him, thinking of the painted wings that had passed her a moment ago. He looked away, remembering a painted stage and a woman in a kimono, dying for love, waiting for smoke to appear on a distant horizon.

In a cave above the monastery lived an old hermit, a *gomchen* who had been immured there at the age of twenty, forty years earlier. The cave had neither window nor door, but inside a spring rose up and flowed through a small opening in the wall before running down to join the river below. Every morning, the villagers would leave food in the opening; every evening they would collect the empty bowl. Otherwise, nothing passed in or out of the cave: no light, no sound, no fragrance. If six days passed without the food being touched, they would break down the wall and take the old man's body for burial.

They went up the hill to visit the cave.

'What does he think about?' Christopher asked.

'If I knew, I would be walled up like him.'

'Don't you know? Doesn't the Lady Tara tell you?'

She shook her head, irritated.

'I've told you. She tells me nothing. I'm just the vehicle. But it's different anyhow. I have no choice about being a *trulku*. He chose to enter his cave. He will escape rebirth through his own efforts. The Lady Tara will go on being reborn, in me, in others after me.'

'We have holy men,' he said. 'But they don't wall themselves up like this. They pray, but not incessantly. They fast, but not to excess.'

'Then they cannot be very holy men,' she replied. 'Perhaps they may have the fortune to be reborn as *gomchens*.'

'I think it's horrible,' he said, 'to be walled up like that. To have no light or company or fresh air, year after year for forty years. It's worse than prison. A man might go mad in there.'

'This world is a prison,' she answered. 'He is seeking to escape. Light and fresh air and conversation are nothing but bars and walls. We are doomed to be reborn to them. In his cave, he is already free.'

He took her hand and held it tightly.

'Do you believe that?' he asked. 'Do you believe that when we make love, when I lie with you? Do you believe that now, here with me in the sunlight?'

She looked away, at the cave, at the little stream running from it, at the hillside.

'I don't know what to believe any more,' she answered. She could hear nothing from the cave, not even the sound of the old hermit's voice reciting prayers.

In front of them, the valley stretched out of sight. Smoke rose from the chimneys of the huts that made up the village. In a field, yaks were grazing. At their feet, the monastery glistened with gilded cupolas.

'I remember,' she said, 'paintings on the walls of the Chöje's room.' She paused.

'Yes. Go on,' he said.

'They were bright paintings. I used to think they showed scenes from the next world, from hell. In one of them, a man was being held by a band of monks. His arms and legs were tied, and they were lifting him.'

She paused again. Beyond the valley, stark peaks rose into a sky of ice. She shivered.

'Yes,' he said. 'Go on.'

298

'There was a hole. They were lifting him to lower him into the hole.'

'I see.'

'And in the next picture, he had been lowered through the hole and was standing in a dark room. I think . . .' She shuddered. 'I think he was held there by a spider's web.'

'I understand. And was there more? Were there any more pictures?'

She nodded.

'Yes. Another one,' she said. 'In it the man was lying down. Perhaps he was not a man, but a boy. He seemed very small. And demons with several arms were attacking him. I tell you, I thought it was hell.'

'Yes,' he said. 'It was hell.'

But he thought – though he could not be sure why – of the photographs he had found in Cormac's desk. 'Simon, Dorje-la?, 1916', 'Matthew, Dorje-la?, 1918', 'Gordon, Dorje-la?, 1919'.

'I think they must have lowered the victims into the room a few days before it was time to go down to the first chamber to bring up the Chöje's things. The rest of the time, there would be some guardians to watch over the treasure; but while the treasure was needed, they would all be feasting at the other end of the tunnel.'

He shuddered. Had his father known what went on? Had Carpenter known to what uses the boys he sold were put?

'When was the last time the Oracle appeared in public?' he asked.

She thought briefly.

'About . . . a week before you arrived at Dorje-la,' she said.

He remained silent. It fitted. The fresh body. No traces of spiders in the treasure-chamber.

'I think we'd better go back down to the river,' he said.

On the fourth day, the abbot called for him. Chindamani took him there, then left them alone. The abbot was old and stern, but Christopher sensed that some at least of the lines that creased the skin round his eyes were laughter lines; he guessed that, at another time and under other circumstances, the old man might have shown himself less severe.

'You are the son of the Dorje Lama? Is that correct?' the abbot asked after tea had been served.

'I am the son of a man who was called Arthur Wylam,' Christopher answered. 'In my world he died. In yours, he became the abbot of a monastery. I don't understand it. I can't explain it. I don't even seek for an explanation any longer.'

'That's very sensible of you. There are no explanations that you would understand. You say you thought your father died. Perhaps it is best if you continue to think of things that way.'

The abbot paused, then looked up at Christopher.

'Tell me about Zam-ya-ting, the Buriat.'

'What do you want to know?'

'The truth. As you understand it. Who he is. What he wants with Dorje Samdup and your son.'

Christopher told him what he could. Each time he was about to let his personal feelings about Zamyatin interfere with the facts, a look in Khyongla Rinpoche's eyes stopped him. It was not a conscious thing, but afterwards he realized it had happened throughout the interview.

When he had finished, the abbot nodded and poured tea into Christopher's cup. For the first time, Christopher noticed that the cups they used were *t'o-t'ai*, identical to those he had drunk from in Dorje-la.

'And the woman, Jebtsumna Chindamani,' the abbot said. 'Do you love her?'

'Has she told you that I do?'

'Yes. She has told me so. And that she loves you. Is that true?'

Christopher felt like someone walking on an ice-covered lake, who hears the ice groaning beneath his feet. He was sure he had contravened a fundamental law of this ritual-obsessed society. What did they do to mortals who ravished their goddesses?

'Have you slept with her?'

Christopher could not keep himself from nodding. Perhaps whatever death they chose to inflict would be quick.

'You don't have to conceal it from me. She herself has told me. I am glad.'

'Glad?' Christopher was sure he had misheard.

'Of course. Did you think I would be angry? We value chastity – this is a monastery, after all. All Buddhist monks and nuns are celibate. But Jebtsumna Chindamani is not a nun. She is not bound to the Sangha by vows. It is merely a convention that the Tara *trulku* at Dorje-la remains unmarried.'

'But I'm not . . .'

'Divine? Neither is she. Not exactly. But I expect she has already tried to explain that to you and failed. I am not sure that I approve of her choice of a *pee-ling* for a lover. That may be unwise. But the Lady Tara dwells in her. And you are the son of the Dorje Lama. I cannot criticize her. If she has chosen you, then the Lady Tara has chosen you.'

Christopher began to wonder if he had any choice in this at all. He had never felt more like a puppet. And he knew exactly whose hands held the strings.

'Go back to her now,' said the abbot, 'and tell her I wish to speak with her again. Do not ask her to tell you what she and I talk about – there are things it is better for you not to know. But do not resent that. You have an important task. You have been chosen for it, see that you fulfil it.'

43

On their last night at Gharoling, she came to his room, wearing a Chinese gown of white silk and small stitched shoes of Indian brocade. She brought tea and barley cakes and purple incense that smelled of honey and musk and wild roses. As they sat and sipped from their tiny cups, coils of smoke wreathed their heads, filling their nostrils with a heavy, intoxicating fragrance. The smell reminded him of his childhood: of church on high holy days, of spring evenings crammed with the sweet smell of holiness, of the white hands of the priest turning bread to flesh and wine to blood.

But there was no priest, no altar, no life-renouncing god to stand between him and his senses. He feasted on her hair and eyes and lips, on the simple miracle that she was there. He had grown to need her, and he wondered how he had lived before he knew her.

'Do men love women where you come from, Ka-ris?' she asked.

He smiled.

'Of course. And women love men.'

'And do they marry?'

'Yes.'

'The person they love?'

He shook his head.

'No, not always. Perhaps very seldom. They marry for money or land or to please their parents.'

'And may a woman have more than one husband?'

He laughed.

'No,' he said. 'One is enough.'

'In Tibet, a woman may marry several brothers at one time. When the oldest brother is away, she has to sleep with the next. She is never lonely.'

'What if she does not like her husbands?'

She shrugged.

'She may like one. What if an English wife does not like her one husband? Can she choose another?'

'Sometimes. If she is wealthy.'

'And if she is poor?'

'Then she will have to stay with him.'

'Even if he beats her?'

He nodded.

'Even if he beats her.'

She paused.

'I think your people may be very unhappy,' she said.

'Yes,' he said. 'Sometimes I think they are.'

Chindamani sighed.

'I don't understand why such a simple thing should cause such unhappiness.' She paused. 'Do I make you happy? Are you happy when you lie with me?'

He nodded. She was beautiful.

'How could I not be happy? I wish for nothing else.'

'But if I ceased to please you?'

'You will never cease to please me.'

'Never is very long.'

'Even so.'

She sat, watching him, lifting her lower lip with little white teeth, breathing the perfumed air.

'Does my body please you?' she asked. 'I never slept with a man before you. I find everything about you wonderful. But you have known other women. Does my body please you in bed?'

'Yes,' he said. 'Very much.'

She stood and unbuttoned the white gown and let it fall to her feet. She was naked. Only coils of incense smoke veiled her. It was the first time he had seen her naked: each time they had made love on their journey, it had been in the darkness of their unlit tent.

'Does this please you?' she asked.

'Yes,' he answered. 'Yes.'

Afterwards she seemed sad and a little withdrawn. She had grown serious again, just as he had seen her before, after her talks with the abbot.

She stood and went to a door that led on to a small terrace. Opening it, she stepped outside. She wore her white gown: the night air was cold. He joined her and took her hand.

She looked out at the darkness. The stars seemed so far away, the darkness so near, so immediate.

'Don't think I can be yours forever,' she said. 'You must not think that.'

He said nothing. Below them, he could see lights in the valley, little lights that twinkled as if the sky had fallen.

'What must I think, then?' he finally asked.

She turned, and he saw tears in her eyes.

'That I am dying, that I am dead, that I have been reborn where nothing can ever come to me – not you, not the Lady Tara, not even the darkness.'

'Please,' he said. 'Don't speak to me in riddles. You know I don't understand. When you speak like this, you frighten me.' He paused and shivered. 'You say we're all reborn. Very well, if you're planning on dying and coming back, why can't I do the same? What's to stop me?'

Her cheeks flushed angrily.

'What do you know of it?' she snapped. 'Do you think it's easy? In places like this, men spend their whole lives preparing for death. They study it like a text that has to be memorized. They know its face as if it were the face of a loved one; the sound of its voice, the feel of its breath, the touch of its fingers. And still, at the very last moment, their thoughts are corrupted and they fail. Do you think you can make death so easy?'

He took her face in his hands. The tears on her cheeks were cold and frosted.

'Yes,' he said. 'I love you. That's enough. Wherever you go, I'll follow you. I swear.'

She bowed her head and put her arms around his waist. In the darkness outside, an owl swooped low across a frosted field in search of mice.

They set off the next day on ponies supplied by the abbot of Gharoling. He had wanted to send a monk with them as guide, but Chindamani had vetoed his suggestion for reasons not altogether clear to Christopher. He, for his part, was entirely happy to be alone with her. Her downcast mood of the previous evening had passed, and she smiled at him often while they packed the ponies with the provisions they would need.

304

The abbot accompanied them to the gates of the monastery, Christopher sensed in his manner a calmness and a self-possession he had not encountered previously in a lama. It was as if every gesture he made, every word he spoke was intended to convey the simplest of messages: that everything is transient, and even the greatest concerns will soon pass into insignificance.

'Travel in easy stages,' he advised them. 'Rest when you are tired. Do not drive your animals hard. Be easy with yourselves and the road will be easy with you.'

They thanked him and turned to leave. As they passed through the gates and started down the hill, a small processions of monks wound its way past them, carrying what seemed to be a human figure wrapped in a white sheet.

'What's happening?' Christopher asked. 'Is it a burial?'

Chindamani nodded, sober again.

'It's the hermit,' she said. 'They found him dead last night. He had not taken the food they left him for six days.' She paused. 'He died on the day after we arrived.'

The monks passed by reciting a slow dirge, heading towards a secluded area high on the hillside, where the *gomchen*'s emaciated remains would be cut into food for vultures. A cloud passed over the sky and threw a shadow across the valley of Gharoling.

44

Tibet moved past beneath their feet, a carpet of grass and barren soil and rock that sometimes erupted in patterns of broken ice or bright mountain rivulets. At times they rode, at others they walked, leading their ponies by their bridles. They had named the animals Pip and Squeak, after the little dog and penguin whose adventures William followed every day in the *Daily Mirror*. To Chindamani, who had never seen a cartoon or a newspaper, much less a penguin, the names were little more than *pee-ling* eccentricities. The ponies were indifferent to names, English or Tibetan, and simply got on with the job of plodding along the road. That was what life was about, after all: plodding and eating and sleeping.

It was not all that different for the two humans, except that they at least could choose when to move and when to halt, when to eat and when to sleep. They avoided all major towns, preferring not to draw official attention to Christopher's presence. The abbot of Gharoling had given Chindamani a letter bearing his seal, and this they used from time to time to secure them lodging. They stayed in tasam houses – caravanserais where they could find fodder for their animals and shelter for themselves – or in small monasteries where Chindamani's letter secured them more than just a bed for the night.

Wherever she went, Chindamani was received with respect, even reverence. Christopher was an appendage to her holiness as the incarnation of Tara – and a lifetime's inexperience of the world outside Dorje-la made it impossible for her to act as though she were an ordinary mortal. With Christopher she could be herself – or at least, that part of herself that she reserved from others – but to everyone else she showed only her incarnational face.

They travelled ever northwards and a little to the east, heading for the Great Wall and the border with Inner Mongolia. They passed to the west of Shigatse, following the course of the Tsangpo.

On their right, at the foot of Mount Dromari lay the red walls and golden roofs of Tashilhunpo Monastery, the seat of the Panchen Lama. On Chindamani's instructions, they hurried past, eager to leave Tashilhunpo behind.

Six days later, they passed through Yanbanchen, where a road struck east for Lhasa and Peak Potala. Just outside the town, an official stopped them and began to question Christopher. But Chindamani interrupted him sharply. The abbot's letter was again produced and the official wilted visibly. They did not stop again until Pip and Squeak were about to drop and Yanbanchen was far behind.

After Shigatse, the going was hard: steep ridges, dark ravines and furious mountain streams blocked their path again and again. They found numerous villages and monasteries, but the mountains through which they rode were bare and forbidding, cleft by narrow gorges whose walls towered above them, blotting out the sunlight.

Each day the world was reborn for Chindamani. The simplest things held her attention as though they were miracles. And in their fashion they were, for her at least. She had come from a world of unmelting snow and ice into a land of changes, where sun and shadows played complicated games with grass and rocks and shimmering lakes, and where sudden openings in the hills revealed clear vistas stretching for mile after unexpected mile. She had never seen so clearly or so far.

She saw men and women as though for the first time. So many faces, so many styles of dress, so many occupations: she had never guessed that such variety existed.

'Is the whole world like this, Ka-ris?' she asked.

He shook his head.

'Every part of it is different. This is only a little part.'

Her eyes grew large.

'And where you came from . . . is it not like this?'

He shook his head again. How could he explain? He thought of the London underground, of motor cars and trains and the tall chimneys of factories. Of the multitudes on the streets and in the omnibuses, tumbling like bees in a hive after a thousand different honeys, each without taste or savour. Of churches hung with military flags and cluttered with dead soldiers' monuments. Of polluted streams and scarred hillsides and black palls of smoke choking the sky. She would consider all those a lurid kind of madness. And yet beneath them there lay a deeper malaise that he thought she would be unable to understand. But when he thought again, he suspected she would understand it only too well.

'There's a place called Scotland,' he said. 'I went there once for a holiday with my aunt Tabitha. To a place called the Kyle of Lochalsh. This is very like it.'

She smiled.

'Perhaps we can go there together some day,' she said.

'Yes,' he replied. 'Perhaps.'

Several times a whole day would pass when they rode together in silence, neither speaking, each wrapped in thought. Spring winds blew across empty plains almost without respite, forcing them to bend across the necks of the ponies, blinded and chilled to the bone. They passed frozen lakes and rivers in which patches of ice still lay, thick and scarred by the winds.

There were mists, white and cold and clinging, through which they and their ponies passed like ghosts. Chindamani's black hair gleamed with bright droplets of half-frozen air. Christopher watched her ride ahead of him, a dim figure passing from visibility to invisibility and back again. The edges of their world were blurred. Nothing was defined: not speech, not thought, not memory. They walked or rode in a silence of their own making, apart from the world, travellers without a destination, voyagers through a timeless, formless space.

Everywhere they saw signs of faith, reminders of the presence of the gods: prayer-flags and *chörtens*, long *mani-walls*, and once, two pilgrims making their way across the freezing ground, prostrating themselves full length time after time.

'Where are they going?' Christopher asked.

'To the *Jokhang*,' she said. 'The great temple at Lhasa. They are going there to pay respect to Jovo Rinpoche.'

Christopher looked puzzled.

'It's a great statue of the Lord Buddha when he was a child,' she explained. 'It's the holiest image in the whole of Tibet. People come from all parts of the world to visit it. Some travel hundreds of miles, measuring the ground by their own bodies – just like these two. It takes months, even years. Sometimes they die before they reach the holy city. It's a very good way to die.'

'Why do they do it?' he asked.

'To wipe out bad *karma* they have acquired in previous lives. To acquire good *karma* for their next life. So that they may be reborn in a condition nearer to the Buddha state. That is all any of us can do.'

He looked at her.

'Is our journey worth any merit?' he asked.

She nodded, serious.

'Yes,' she replied. 'He is the Maidari Buddha. Our aim is to find him and bring him to his people. We are his tools: you will see.'

'Do you really think we'll find him again?'

She looked at him a long time before replying.

'What do you think?' she said finally.

Christopher said nothing. But as they rode on, he wondered what sort of *karma* he would acquire if he rescued the boy from Zamyatin only to put him on the throne of Mongolia as a British puppet.

They caught their first whiff of Zamyatin at a small village near Nagchu Dzong, about one hundred and sixty miles from Lhasa. The *nemo* at their rest-house there remembered a man and two boys who had come through about ten days before. They had been travelling by pony, hard. Zamyatin had been forced to risk visiting the rest-house in order to obtain much-needed provisions and fresh ponies.

'They came here with three of the scraggiest animals I've ever seen,' the woman said. 'All but dead they were. They'd driven them into the ground, riding them hell for leather, I could tell. It was the Mongol's doing, I could see that. He was desperate to move on. Nervous he was, jittery, but I could tell he wasn't the sort to argue with. The children were worn out, poor things. I said they should rest, but he swore at me and said he'd have none of it. They had to be up and going; not even time to take tea.'

She scowled at the memory of such impoliteness.

'I sold them new ponies, but I wouldn't give much for the ones they left. They'll fatten up in time, no doubt; but one's no use for riding any longer – he's broken-winded and fit for the butcher. I asked five hundred *trangkas* for the two I sold them, and he paid it over without so much as a whimper. That's forty *liang* in Chinese money. I said to my husband he must be up to no good. I was half of a mind to send someone after them, to see were the little boys all right. But my husband said we'd best not interfere, and maybe he was right.'

'Did either of the boys try to get your attention at all?' asked Chindamani.

'Well, now you mention it, I think one of them did. I think he wanted to speak to me. But the man would have none of it and whisked him out of the room as quick as a flash.'

'Didn't you try to do something? Protest to him?'

The *nemo* looked at Chindamani hard.

'If you'd seen him you'd understand. I'd no wish to cross him. Perhaps I should have done, I don't rightly know. But if you'd been in my shoes, if you'd seen him ... But then, perhaps you have, my lady.'

Chindamani said nothing.

'Were the ponies you sold them healthy? Strong enough to take them far?'

The old *nemo* looked offended.

'Of course they were. Do you think I would sell anything but a sound animal? Would I cheat, would I pass off a sprained horse as fit for the road?'

He fancied she would, and for an inflated price as well.

'I meant no offence,' he apologized. 'But you had seen what happened to the beasts they came on. Perhaps you were reluctant to let your best animals into his hands.'

Somewhat mollified – but only somewhat – she snorted.

'I might have thought that,' she said. 'But he looked over all the ponies I had and chose three for himself. They were the best in my stable and worth a pretty penny too. He'll do for them what he did for the others. But they'll get him a distance. They'll be twenty *shasas* or more away by now.'

A *shasa* was a full day's march, between ten and twenty miles. At Zamyatin's rate of progress, they'd very likely be thirty full *shasas* ahead of them.

'They're beyond our reach now, Ka-ris,' said Chindamani in a crestfallen voice.

310

'They'll get to Urga before we do, that's all,' he said. But he felt disadvantaged by his rival's easy lead. 'We'll catch up with them there, not before. Slow and steady does it. They still have a long way to go. There won't always be fresh ponies when they need them. And they have to face the Gobi desert – or go round it.'

'And so have we,' she said.

Dispirited at first, they continued their journey. They rode a little faster, rested less often, rose earlier to set off before dawn each morning. At least, Christopher reasoned, they were thus far on the right track. Zamyatin and the boys had passed this way; however much they deviated from the road, they would ultimately return to it – there was only one destination for all of them.

They travelled across the broad steppe regions to the east of Chang Tang, the great central plateau of Tibet. Beyond the northern reaches of the Yangtse River, they passed into Amdo. Always north-east, always towards Mongolia.

Each day, they passed small nomad encampments – low black tents quite distinct from the round Mongol yurts of the north. Shepherds grazed small herds of yaks in the valleys: they watched Christopher and Chindamani ride by, then turned back to their endless vigil.

Ten days after leaving Nagchu Dzong, they reached the southern shores of Koko Nor, the great lake that stands guard over the north-east border of Tibet. A few miles further and they would enter China's Kansu province.

Christopher was nervous. The Chinese were on edge, feeling the pinch in Mongolia and toying with Tibet as a possible recompense should the former territory slip out of their hands again. If he were caught by Chinese guards and identified as an Englishman crossing into Kansu, he doubted very much if his captors would observe the diplomatic niceties. In all probability, his head would soon adorn a sharp, pointed stick on the battlements of Sining-fu.

These were the days of the great war-lords. China was torn by civil war, and no central authority was capable of returning the country to normal. The Manchus had gone, the Republic was little more than a name, and in the provinces chaos and bloodshed reigned. Armies of peasants marched and fought and were wiped out. And in their place, new armies were raised up. It was one of Death's finest hours.

311

The steppe sloped down gently to the dark waters of the lake. Thin waves moved across its surface, making Christopher think of home and the sea. To the north, the mountains of the Tsun-ula range stretched east and west out of sight. On several peaks, white caps of snow nestled against the sky.

In the centre of the lake lay a rocky island on which a small temple stood, cut off from the world now that the winter ice had melted. Chindamani sat still in her saddle for a long time, gazing out at the little temple, watching the dark waters tremble against the rock on which it stood, listening to the waves falling lifeless to the shore. A stiff breeze came down from the mountains suddenly and flattened the waves. Clouds scudded across the sky.

'Let's ride on,' said Christopher.

But still she sat, unmoving, gazing out at the island. The breeze moved her hair, raising it like a dark prayer-flag, then lowering it again. She did not seem to notice. Then, abruptly, she shivered and looked round at him.

'I have been here before,' she said. She looked out at the temple once more. 'And I shall come here again.'

45

That afternoon, they stumbled across Zamyatin's trail again. Leaving the lake behind them, they turned east towards Sining-fu. In spite of the risks, Christopher had decided to head for the town in order to obtain provisions and a guide to cross the Gobi: any other course of action would be suicide. A little before the Hadda-ulan Pass, they came upon a small encampment of black yak-hair tents.

It was strangely quiet. No dogs rushed out to snarl and snap about their heels, as was normal at nomad camps. No smoke rose from a dung fire. No children squealed. Nothing moved. Christopher took his revolver from his belt and cocked it. Bandits were a common feature of life here. Bandits and sudden death.

He saw the first body – or what remained of it – just outside the nearest of the four tents. The vultures had picked it clean, leaving white bones and strips of tattered clothing. A black rifle – one of the long, forked variety carried by all Tanguts and Mongols in the region – lay near the bones.

A second skeleton stood out stark and white against the earth a few yards away, and beside it a third, that of a child of perhaps five or six. The breeze played with the hair on their skulls, lifting and dropping it nervously. A thin cloud of dust blew forlornly between the silent tents and disappeared.

There was a sudden flapping sound, loud and terrifying in the stillness. Christopher swung round and saw a single vulture lift itself up awkwardly from the ground and stumble into the air. There was an indistinct bundle of clothing where it had been feeding. The banquet had not yet ended. As at any meal, there were late arrivals.

They found half a dozen skeletons outside the tents and almost twenty cadavers inside. The ones under cover had not been picked clean, and the cold Tibetan air had so far kept decomposition at bay. The bodies were mainly those of women and children, but

313

several men lay among them. It was immediately apparent how they had died – a single bullet, usually in the forehead or temple. Why would bandits have done this? Christopher wondered. Had China's civil war spilled over into Amdo?

The girl was hiding behind a large chest in the fourth tent. They found her by chance, when Christopher went to pick up a piece of cloth with which to cover one of the bodies. She was ten or eleven years old, shivering with cold, dirty, hungry, and terrified.

Since his presence seemed only to exacerbate the child's terror, Christopher left her with Chindamani and went outside. Even in the clean air, a stench of death seemed to hang over everything. He wondered if his nostrils would ever be free of the smell.

He found the remains of several ponies just beyond the tents. They had clearly been tethered together and most had died of hunger only a day or two earlier. One was still alive: he put it out of its misery with a single shot. When that was done, he walked away from the tents for a while.

At the head of the valley, there was a cairn built from loosely piled flat slates. It was an *obo*, built to propitiate the local gods. Pieces of cloth fluttered from it, the offerings of travellers. The slates themselves were inscribed in Tibetan characters and propped against one another at all angles, with four laid flat across the top as a sort of roof. Christopher made out the mantric formula of *om mani padme hum* inscribed again and again across the dark green stone. He had an urge to tear down the stones, to smash the *obo* and scatter the pieces. What use were gods if they slept?

When he got back to the little camp, Chindamani had succeeded in calming the girl. She was still distressed, but outright terror had begun to give way to grief, an unstaunchable torrent that filled the tiny tent. This time, she did not react to Christopher, so he sat by Chindamani while she soothed and comforted the child.

A little later, the girl fell into a heavy sleep, the first she had known for days. They decided it would be better for her if she did not waken in the camp or near it. Christopher lifted her carefully and put her on Pip, flat across the panniers the pony carried. A nomad child, she would be accustomed from birth to sleeping on the move.

Before leaving, they brought the remaining corpses out of the tents and exposed them for the vultures. Chindamani recited prayers in a quiet voice, then they rode on before the girl should awaken and have her grief renewed or redoubled by the sight of the open burial.

They spent that night in the broad valley just beyond the pass. The child woke briefly once. She ate a little, then returned to sleep. They took turns to stand guard over their tiny camp. It was a cold night, and the stars kept watch with them until dawn.

In the morning, over breakfast, the girl told them what had happened. Her name was Chödrön and she thought she was ten years old. The victims at the camp-site had been her family – father, mother, brothers, sisters, grandmother and grandfather, two uncles, two aunts, and six cousins.

Several days earlier – Christopher guessed about a week – a Mongol had come riding into their camp. He had been accompanied by two boys – a Tangut or Tibetan and one that she said looked like Christopher. The boys wore fine clothes that had been caked in mud and dirt, but they looked unhappy. She had come out of her tent with her mother to see the strangers.

The man had demanded a change of ponies, offering to exchange those on which he and the boys rode for better mounts, along with a sum in cash. Her uncle had refused the offer – with the coming of spring, the men all needed their ponies and could ill afford to be left with two worn-out animals. In any case, the man's manner had been brusque and peremptory, and she had sensed that her uncle had refused out of dislike for the stranger as much as anything.

There had been angry words, she remembered, then someone had fired a shot. She could not be sure whether her uncle or the Mongol had fired first. But the stranger's rapid-firing pistol had made light work of men armed with single-shot muskets.

She could neither explain nor remember with any clarity the massacre that had followed; nor had Chindamani or Christopher any wish to make her relive those insane moments. Her mother had somehow contrived to hide her in the chest behind which they had found her hiding, and she had escaped the notice of the Mongol. There had been no room in the chest for her mother, no room for anyone but her.

Christopher described Zamyatin to her, though he knew what

315

her answer would be. She shivered and said it was the same man, no other. He asked about the boys, and she said they had seemed pale and unhappy, but unhurt.

On the following day, they continued east towards Sining-fu. At Tsagan-tokko, a small village of clay houses, they enquired about Zamyatin. Neither he nor the boys had been seen there.

They had just passed out of sight of the village when they heard the sound of hoofbeats behind them. A Mongol horseman came cantering towards them and drew up alongside. He was a big man, dressed in furs and equipped with a breech-loading rifle slung across his shoulders.

'They tell me you are looking for a Buriat riding with two boys,' he said.

Christopher nodded.

'I saw them five days ago,' the horseman said. 'I was riding in the Tsun-ula, the mountains north of Koko-nor. We spoke briefly. I asked the man where they were headed. "We must be in Kanchow ten days from now," he told me. When I asked him why, he said he had to meet someone there. That's all. The Tibetan boy tried to say something to me, but the man told him to be quiet.'

'Is it possible,' Christopher asked, 'to make it to Kanchow that quickly? Won't they have to go through the Nan-shan mountains?'

The Mongol nodded.

'Yes,' he said. 'But they can make it if there are no delays. All the passes are open. I told him the best route to take.'

He shifted awkwardly in his saddle.

'The Tibetan boy,' he said. 'He was pale, frightened. I dreamed of him that night. He came to me smiling. He wore the robes of a buddha. There was light all round him.' He paused. 'Who is he?' he asked.

Chindamani answered in a low voice, with an authority Christopher had never heard in it before.

'He is the Maidri Buddha,' she said.

The horseman looked at her intently, but said nothing. Half a minute passed like that, then he smiled broadly, wheeled his horse round, and set off at a gallop in the direction of Tsagan-tokko.

They crossed into China quietly on a long afternoon in April, like cattle thieves or scouts sent ahead by an invader, unseen, unsus-

316

pected, unchallenged. There was no true border here, no moment when one might say 'This is Tibet' and then, in an instant, 'This is China'. Just a gradual shift, a change of tone, a series of dimly perceived modulations in the landscape and the faces. The nomadic world of Amdo began to fade, and in its place a new terrain slowly asserted itself: a world of valleys and high, fortified villages, of narrow gorges and fast waterways, of gilded temples, ornamental gates, and narrow, fluted pagodas that rose above dull walls of beaten clay.

The people of the margins and the salt-lakes of the Tsaidam basin – fur-clad and dirty and scarred by constant winds – gradually made way for the inhabitants of the settled regions that lay within the confines of the Great Wall. Traders and artisans, peasant farmers and *hong*-merchants eager to return to Canton or Peking. The chief difference – or so it seemed to Christopher – lay in their eyes. The nomads and the men who came with the long camel-trains down from the Mongolian steppes or the regions beyond Urumchi had a far-away look: they saw vast distances and open horizons unencumbered by city walls – a world that was never the same from one day to the next. But the Han Chinese of Kansu dwelt in a world of narrower horizons, and in their eyes Christopher could see the walls and doors and mental bars that hemmed them in.

Mandarins with sallow faces and tired eyes, many still wearing their hair in the Manchu style, with long pigtails behind and their foreheads uncovered in front, rode past in the company of Hui Muslim soldiers on their way to Sining-fu and, beyond it, the provincial capital of Lanchow. But none of them challenged Christopher or his companions. To the casual eye, Christopher seemed of no interest – merely a nomad who had travelled far with his wife and child for reasons that could be of no possible interest to Chinese officials. His face had grown dirty and his hair unkempt, and all traces of foreignness had been burned out of him by the wind and ice and snow.

Sining-fu received them with indifference. Three travellers more or less meant nothing to the town or its inhabitants. All along the top of the square wall that enclosed the city, soldiers walked on a narrow street, keeping watch over the countryside around and across the mosaic of roofs below, a jumble of red pantiles and

317

dragon arabesques. But no-one noticed the three newcomers among so many.

They walked down the main street that lay through the centre of the town, passing on right and left the *yamens* of local officialdom, small painted houses guarded by stone lions and dragons, each bearing a sign in Chinese lettering to indicate its function. At every step they were jostled by passers-by: Mongols leading hairy Bactrian camels as they went from shop to shop trading yak-hair or fur for pots and pans and kitchen knives; mules with huge blocks of Shansi coal; carts carrying Chinese girls in bright red coats, their hair well greased and their tiny feet crippled forever by a lifetime's binding.

In a side-street, near one of the large trading houses, they found a small *deng* where they could stay for the night. The inn was dirtier and more cramped than most, but it was out of the way and attracted the sort of clientele who knew better than to show too much interest in their fellow guests. They cajoled the *nemo*, a small, reserved woman in her mid-forties, to provide them with a room to themselves. She was reluctant at first, but Chödrön seemed so tired and sad that she gave them the room for her sake.

It was early evening by the time they settled down. The *nemo* provided food and a tripod brazier on which to cook it – all at a price. Chödrön fell asleep soon after they had eaten. Chindamani and Christopher stayed awake a little longer, talking. They would have made love, but with Chödrön around they felt inhibited. At last they slept, in one another's arms, not safe, but alone.

Christopher was wakened in the middle of the night by the sound of knocking on the door. At first he thought he had been mistaken, but the knock came again, a little louder this time. Chindamani stirred but did not waken.

He got up and walked to the door. The wooden floor was cold against his bare feet. In the distance, someone coughed. And coughed and coughed again and fell silent, breathless. It was utterly dark.

He opened the door and squinted. A man was standing in the doorway holding a lantern.

46

The stranger's arm got in the way of the light and cast a shadow over his face.

'Yes?' said Christopher sleepily. 'What do you want?' He spoke in Tibetan, hoping the man would understand.

'Hello, Christopher,' said the stranger. The words were English, the voice icily familiar.

The stranger moved his arm and the light fell on his face. Simon Winterpole had travelled a long way. But he had not changed a bit.

Christopher stepped into the passage and closed the door behind him. Winterpole was dressed in European clothes, dapper as ever, a vision from a world Christopher had thought he had left behind for good.

'Don't stand there staring at me, Christopher. For God's sake, I'm not a ghost.'

'I'm sorry,' said Christopher. 'I hadn't ... You're the last person I expected to see. How on earth did you get here? How did you find me?'

'Good Lord, you don't imagine you're invisible do you?' The light wobbled as Winterpole moved his arm, shadows scuttled with crab-like dexterity across his face. 'You were seen near Lhasa a few weeks ago. After that, we had tabs kept on you all the way here. You wouldn't believe the things we can do. I came up from Peking last week in order to be here when you came. I knew you'd have to pass through Sining-fu. You and I have things to talk about; things to do.'

'You're mistaken. We don't have anything to talk about. Not any more. Enough is enough. I'm not working for you any longer. I'm not working for anyone.'

'Don't be tiresome, Christopher. We went through all this before. When I came up to Hexham. Surely you haven't forgotten.'

'No,' said Christoper in a tight voice. 'I haven't forgotten. I told you then I no longer belonged to you. You helped me get on the track of my son, and I'm grateful. But I came here to find him, that's all. I don't want you meddling in things that don't concern you. Stay out of this, Winterpole. It has nothing to do with you.'

Down the corridor, the coughing recommenced.

'But I'm afraid it does,' Winterpole objected. 'Listen, we can't talk here. There's a room we can use downstairs. Come and hear me out. I've travelled a long way to speak with you. Do me that favour. Please.'

It was useless to resist, just as it had been useless that night in Hexham. The dark current that had reached out for him then surged beneath Christopher once more, drawing him out further into the depths of a cold and lightless ocean.

The room to which Winterpole took Christopher was low-ceilinged and lit by tallow candles. Two groups of four men sat at low tables playing *mah-jong* for small stakes. The small ivory tiles stood in neatly assembled ranks in front of each player – wind tiles and dragon tiles, flower tiles and character tiles. A few other men were smoking opium through long-stemmed pipes tipped with old silver. The soft brown sap melted and bubbled as they applied hot coals held in long iron tongs. They glanced up as the two strangers entered, eyeing them with the air of men who live by suspicion.

It took Winterpole less than a minute to clear the room of them. He had come equipped with a letter bearing the chop of Ma Ch'i, the Dao T'ai of Sining-fu, a Hui Muslim whose cousin, Ma Hung-k'uei, was the warlord currently in control of Kansu province. Christopher knew that Winterpole was not above using his influence to have a man flogged or tortured or even beheaded if it suited his purpose. And tonight it might just suit.

'I know you found Zamyatin,' Winterpole commenced once the door of the room had closed on them. 'And I know about the Tibetan boy he is spiriting away to Urga.'

'You knew before you sent me, didn't you?' said Christopher.

Winterpole nodded.

'Yes. Not everything. But a little, yes. We had to be sure: our sources weren't reliable. We thought it would be a mistake to tell you too much – in case it made you look for the wrong things.

'Of course, we probably wouldn't have done anything much

320

about the reports we had received if it hadn't been for Zamyatin kidnapping your boy. I still don't understand what the point of that was. Were you able to find out anything?'

Christopher stared at him. Not 'Did you find your son?' Not 'Is he well?' But 'Were you able to find out anything?' Information – that was all that interested Winterpole. Anything else was superfluous.

'Yes,' said Christopher, 'I found out something.' But how could he begin to explain it to a man like Winterpole.

'Well? What was he up to? How did your boy come into his schemes?'

'As a pawn – that's all you need to know. William was part of a deal Zamyatin made. What he really wanted was the Tibetan boy. His name is Samdup. Dorje Samdup Rinpoche.'

'And who is he precisely? Some sort of incarnation, is he? Is that what Zamyatin's up to?'

'Yes.' Christopher sighed. 'The boy is the Maidari Buddha. That means he can be proclaimed ruler of Mongolia in place of the present Khutukhtu. That's what Zamyatin's gone to Mongolia for. To make the boy a god.'

Winterpole was silent. He seemed to be weighing up what Christopher had told him, fitting it into some scheme of his own.

'I see,' he said. 'It all makes sense now. All we have to do is find Zamyatin.'

'That's easier said than done. I've lost them – Zamyatin, William, Samdup. They're half-way to Urga by now. Before anyone can catch up with them, Zamyatin will have a cordon of Red soldiers round Samdup and a ringside ticket for the coronation in his own pocket.'

'I wouldn't bank on it.'

'No? Listen. I lost them at Hadda-ulan, all three of them. Zamyatin had made a rendezvous with someone in Kanchow about three days ago. He's well on his way to Urga by now. Or . . .' He hesitated.

'Yes,' prompted Winterpole casually.

'Or he's on his way to Moscow.'

'Oh, I'm sure,' said Winterpole. 'I'd already heard about Zamyatin's rendezvous. He's made contact with a man called Udinskii – a Russian and a fellow-Bolshevik who was until recently involved in the fur and wool trade at Urga. He worked for a Danish-American company called Andersen and Myer. Udinskii was waiting for him in Kanchow for over a month. He's to be Zamyatin's courier to Urga. He has a motor-truck, a strong one capable of making the journey across the Gobi in a matter of days. They'll be in Urga any day now, I expect. Or at least . . .'

Winterpole paused, as though the well of his omniscience had suddenly dried up.

'At least?' repeated Christopher.

'He'll probably not try to go straight to the city. Things have changed in Mongolia since all this started. The Chinese have been pushed out. The man in charge now is a White Russian general called von Ungern Sternberg. Baron Roman von Ungern Sternberg, to be precise. Now, there's a mouthful for you.

'Ungern was pushed out of Siberia last year by the Bolsheviks. He and his men were almost the last of the Whites. They made for Mongolia, picking up reinforcements on the way. At the start of February, they took control of Urga. Ungern rescued the Living Buddha from the Chinese and put him back on the throne. But the real ruler is Ungern himself.

'So, you see, Zamyatin can't just turn up in Urga, with or without some incarnation. Von Ungern Sternberg isn't the sort of man to make a deal with the Bolsheviks. And Mongolia is turning into the sort of place sensible people steer clear of. If Zamyatin has any sense, he'll go somewhere else. What do you think? Has he got any sense?'

Christopher leaned across the table.

'For God's sake, this isn't a game of chess! Zamyatin thinks he can conquer Asia with this child. Don't you see? Sense doesn't enter into any of it. The stakes are too high.'

'Then he'll go to Urga. In that case, he'll have to be bloody careful. Ungern's busy killing everyone in sight: Russians, Jews, runaway Chinese. And now any White armies that are left in Siberia are moving south to join him. Kazagrandi is in Uliassutai; Kazantzev has taken Kobdo; Kaigorodov has been reported in Altai; and in the West Bakitch has joined up with Dutov and Annenkov. It's a madhouse, Christopher. Ungern Sternberg believes he's a reincarnation of the Mongolian god of war. He's

322

convinced half the population of the country of that fact. That means he's answerable to no-one.'

Winterpole paused to take a cigarette-box from his coat pocket. He opened it and offered a cigarette to Christopher.

'No thank you.'

Winterpole took one for himself and lit it.

'So, you see,' he continued, 'that with Ungern in control of Urga, neither Zamyatin nor Udinskii can risk heading there directly. So I think they'll make for somewhere outside the city to dump the motor and Udinskii. That'll leave Zamyatin free to do the rest of the journey with just the two boys for company.'

Christopher felt a chill go through him. Wouldn't it be even more convenient for the Russian to dump William as well?

'Why are you here, Winterpole?'

'To keep an eye on you, of course.'

'That's very touching. And I suppose you intend keeping an eye on Zamyatin as well, while you're at it.'

Winterpole blew out a thin jet of smoke.

'Yes, of course. He has to be stopped. And you, I imagine, would still like to find your son. You've done very well so far, but it's time to get a move on. I want to get to Urga before Zamyatin does.'

'And exactly how do you propose to do that?'

'The same way as Zamyatin. By motor car. I have one waiting at the Dao T'ai's. I bought it from some Danes in Kalgan. It's a Fiat, specially built for country like this. We can do the journey to Urga faster than Udinskii and his truck.'

'And when we get there? What then?'

'We sit tight and wait for Zamyatin to make his move. Ungern will co-operate with us. Zamyatin in exchange for your son. And the Tibetan boy, of course. Ungern's position is precarious: a promise of British help isn't something he can turn down. I'll send him an official telegraph tomorrow, through the normal diplomatic channels. He'll be told to expect us, to offer us protection. Zamyatin's been outfoxed, Christopher. He's walking straight into a trap.'

Christopher looked at Winterpole as though he were far, far away. His dress, his cigarettes, his self-importance were all products of another world. He was a schemer, but he knew precious little of the world his schemes were made for.

'I wouldn't bank on it,' said Christopher.

323

47

True to his word, Winterpole sent a telegram early the next morning. It was a complicated procedure – the message had to be routed to Peking through Lanchow, then forwarded to Urga, where it would be received at Ungern Sternberg's splendid new telegraph office. Even at the best of times, there were unavoidable delays, errors in transmission, and, as often as not, cut lines. And these were not the best of times – not in China, not in Mongolia.

If Winterpole had waited another day, he would have been told that the telegraph lines between Yenan and Peking had been cut by rebel troops and that his message would be delayed 'indefinitely'. But less than an hour after dispatching the telegram, he was back with Christopher, urging that they be up and going. They sat in the downstairs room of the rest-house as before.

'I'm not certain that I want to come with you,' said Christopher.

'Why not?'

'Because I don't trust you. Zamyatin doesn't interest you. As you say, he's walking into a trap. All you had to do was send your telegram to this man Ungern Sternberg and go home. But you want to go to Urga in person. You want the boy for yourself. You want to turn him to your advantage.'

Winterpole took a white linen handkerchief from his pocket and blew his nose carefully. With equal care, he folded the handkerchief as before and replaced it in his pocket.

'To *our* advantage, Christopher.'

'Not to mine.'

'You want to find your son, don't you? You want to take him home?'

Christopher said nothing.

'Yes, of course you do. Then come to Urga with me. And bring the Tibetan girl. You can't leave her here.'

Christopher guessed what Winterpole had in mind. With Chindamani on his side, he could hope to exert the necessary influence

324

over Samdup. But he was right, of course. Christopher was not going to give up his last chance to save William.

'Who is von Ungern Sternberg?' Christopher asked.

Winterpole shrugged.

'That's not an easy question to answer. I've had men working on him for over a year now, and all I get are conflicting reports in triplicate. One for me, one for "C", and one for some nameless clerk in archives who makes fifty more of them for half the files in Whitehall. But we still know next to nothing about him.'

He halted, thinking, his expression serious.

'What we do know, however . . .' He paused. 'Well, let's just say it's far from pleasant. Von Ungern Sternberg is what I believe the psychologists call a psychopath. He appears to have no notion of right and wrong.

'But . . .' He paused again. 'He is the man of the moment. The right man in the right place. God knows, we don't always choose our friends well. But as often as not we have no choice.

'Ungern is the sort of man who could only rise to the top at a time like this. He was bred for it; it's in his blood – and bad enough blood it is. His family are one of the four leading clans on the Baltic coast – the Uxkulls, the Tiesenhausens, the Rosens, and the Ungern Sternbergs: "The Four of the Fist."

'The Ungerns are descended from an old line of Otsei knights who went on some sort of crusade against the Russians in the twelfth century. They made Riga their stronghold. A rough lot: always picking a fight with someone, always coming home with their pockets stuffed with loot. Bullies, pirates, raiders, robber barons: they made toughness into an art. And now the last of the line – a madman who thinks he's the Mongolian god of war and acts accordingly.'

'How old a man is he?' asked Christopher.

'About your age. He was born in 1887. He started out in the Russian navy – graduated from the naval cadet school at St Petersburg. But he doesn't seem to have liked naval life a lot, in spite of having pirates for ancestors. Either that or the navy didn't like him. Anyway, he resigned his commission, went east, and ended up with the Argun Cossacks in Transbaikalia. Had a great time, so they say – falconing, duelling, hunting. But in the end, even the Cossacks chucked him out: too many brawls, too much insubordination.

'After that he became a bandit for a while. Then the war broke out and he saw his chance for some action. He wrote to the Tzar personally, asking to be allowed to re-enlist. Back came the go-ahead, and off he went to join up with the Nerchinsk Cossacks under Wrangel. He wasn't popular, though. By all accounts his fellow officers kept their distance. Still, Ungern could fight, there was never any question of that. He got all the decorations going, all the way up to the St George's Cross. He was so heavily decorated, they had to make him a major-general. Then the revolution broke out.'

Winterpole paused and licked his lips. His fingers played idly with ivory mah-jong tiles that had been left on the table, arranging them in little groups of two and three. They made tiny clicking sounds, faintly irritating.

'As soon as Ungern saw which way the wind was blowing, he cleared off from the German front and made his way to Transbaikalia, where he joined up under Ataman Semenov. It wasn't long before he was made a full general and put in charge of the region round Dauria.'

Winterpole's eyes had grown deeply serious. The small movements of his fingers ceased. The tiles sat untouched on the table.

'I visited Dauria once,' he said. 'Did you know that?'

Christopher shook his head. Just a fraction.

'It was in the winter of early 1920. Our troops had pulled out of Siberia. The White generals were finished. Kolchak, Wrangel, Kornilov: all dead or in exile. Only the Japanese had stayed behind, in Vladivostock. They were backing Semenov, sending him arms and money and sweet promises of political recognition.

'I was sent to visit him at his headquarters in Chita, to see if I could discover just where his loyalties lay. That was the easiest mission of my life. It took me no time at all to discover that Semenov was loyal to Semenov. And Semenov's men were loyal to themselves.

'I've never seen men more brutalized. Perhaps they thought they were already dead and had no more care to be human, I don't know. They whored and gambled and drank – not the way soldiers do on leave or before a battle, but constantly, feverishly. And the officers were worse than the men. More vicious, in the true sense. They didn't just stick to beer or spirits. Most of the time, it was morphine or cocaine or opium. And they couldn't stop killing. I think the drugs drove them to it. It had become a habit with them. No-one stopped them, no-one invoked penalties. They had become a law to themselves. They killed anyone they liked, it didn't matter. As long as they didn't kill one of their own kind, no-one would interfere.'

He paused once more, and the fingers of one hand began again to play with a tile. His eyes seemed haunted by memories still not remote enough in time to have lost their shadows.

'As you're aware, the International Express from Siberia to Manchuria runs through Transbaikalia. I was taken for a journey along the railway, to see how Semenov was keeping communications open in the region under his control. The whole country along the Transbaikalian sector was dotted with what Semenov called his "Killing Stations". People would be plucked off trains – Jews, suspected Bolsheviks, commissars, rich merchants. They were taken straight to one of these stations. None of them ever returned to finish their journeys. If ever an enquiry were made, the official answer would always be: "Missing en route." And in those days, who asked such questions anyway?'

He hesitated briefly, then began again.

'Once . . .' – and here his eyes grew large with memory – 'Once I saw the strangest, most awful thing on the horizon. It seemed to go on forever: an endless line of trains, all jammed together. Miles of them, miles and miles of carriages and locomotives, all joined together like a giant serpent. A sea monster, but long enough to swallow a navy.

'The first locomotive had run out of fuel and water and then frozen to the tracks. The metal had been soldered together by the cold. Then a second train had come up behind and tried to push the first, but without success. And it had frozen too. And all this time, no-one was getting word through about what was going on, so they kept on sending trains. Train after train.

'We went up close. It was freezing, I remember; everything was frost, bleak white frost that lay hard on the metal of the trains, turning them white. They were full of bodies, the bodies of all the passengers who'd frozen to death there, afraid to leave the security

327

of their compartments, not knowing what had happened, waiting for help to be sent out from Moscow. They told me that forty-five thousand people froze to death in those carriages. I don't know if that's true. But I saw a lot of bodies. All preserved, all beautifully preserved.'

He stammered.

'I . . . I saw a beautiful woman in one carriage, dressed in sable, with frost clinging to her hair like lace. She hadn't changed, not really. She'd grown pale as ice and stiff with frost, but her features were still perfect. Beautiful – she'd become a sort of doll, white and sad and untouchable, like Pierrot in a mask. I wanted to break a window and go inside to look at her more closely. I wanted to kiss her, just to taste the ice on her lips. I thought I could thaw her, I thought my warmth could bring her back to life. She was so still, so very still.'

He grew silent, lost in the pain of memory, walking alongside the frozen tracks of the Trans-Siberian Express, watching pale faces in the gathering dusk, and wooden cattle-trucks crammed with the dead.

Christopher left him like that, brooding, and returned to the room upstairs. It would soon be time to leave. He had no choice. He had never had a choice.

Mongolia

48

They left later that morning. Chödrön stayed in Sining-fu with the family who ran the rest-house in which they had lodged: the *nemo* had taken a fancy to her and, on hearing her story, expressed a wish to take her in. For her part, the child had been overjoyed: the excitement of Sining-fu, the first town of any size she had ever seen, and the luxury of living in a house instead of a tent were, for the moment, compensations of a sort for the losses she had sustained. She readily agreed to stay, and neither Chindamani nor Christopher could recommend a better solution.

But Chindamani had found it hard to part from the little girl. Apart from her old nurse Sönam, she had never known female companionship; and Chödrön's loneliness had reminded her acutely of her own as a child. Perhaps the laws dictating that a child be taken from its parents at an early age merely to live out another phase in the cycle of incarnation were in their way as brutal as the violence that had made Chödrön an orphan.

The car was a sturdy little Fiat which Winterpole had obtained at a price from the Dao T'ai. It had been modified for the desert and used up until then by the Dao T'ai for brief hunting expeditions into the Gobi. There were enough cans of petrol for a journey to Siberia and back, water, food, and tents. Winterpole was to drive while Christopher navigated with the help of charts that came courtesy of the British Embassy in Peking.

They skirted the eastern fringes of the Nan Shan mountains, travelling north from Sining-fu, then veering slightly east. Late that afternoon they passed through the Great Wall near Wuwei. Here, the Wall was little more than a symbol: low mud ramparts, broken and eroded by man and time alike. But for all the insignificance of mud and cracked stone, Christopher felt they had passed more than a token barrier.

Once, they passed a long train of astonished camels. For a moment, the air held a smell of spices, then they were past and the

331

desert was all about them again. Ahead of them, the Ala Shan stretched out into a blue haze on the horizon. Beyond it, the Gobi proper shifted beneath a shimmering sun. Inside the car, it was unbearably hot.

'You were telling me about Dauria,' Christopher reminded Winterpole. 'About Ungern Sternberg and Dauria.' He was sitting in the rear with Chindamani, who had taken much coaxing to ride in the machine. She was still torn between terror and wonder at the speed with which the motor car travelled.

Winterpole glanced up, like a man suddenly woken from a deep sleep.

'Dauria? Why yes, of course. Dauria.' He looked out of the window, at the desert rushing past, at the sand piling up on all sides, pale and sterile.

'I want you to understand what it was like, Christopher. I want you to know what you'll be going into. Believe me, if I thought we had any choice, I'd see Ungern in hell before I made a deal with him. But it's him or Zamyatin now.'

He paused. Something was making him reluctant to say more about what he had seen.

'I went there afterwards,' he said. 'After I'd seen Semenov, I went to visit von Ungern Sternberg in Dauria. Semenov suggested it himself; he thought I might be impressed. I don't know what he expected really. They didn't understand us. Still don't.

'I arrived late one afternoon, just as the sun was setting. We came down into a vast plain through a narrow circle of sandy hills. The plain was devoid of life as far as we could see. Nothing grew, nothing moved – there was just a collection of dirty huts, like a leper colony in the middle of nowhere. I've never felt so great a loss of the sense of place, of definition, boundaries. It was as though we were nowhere at all, as if we were at the centre of a great emptiness.

'There was a little Russian church with a spire, more in the western than the Byzantine style. It might have been quite pretty once, I don't know; but it had lost all its tiles and paint . . . and something else. Whatever it is that makes a church a church – how can I explain? And down in the middle of the plain was Ungern's headquarters. A small fortress built from red bricks. From where I first saw it, it looked very much like a slaughterhouse – a slaughterhouse someone had daubed all over with blood. And there was wind blowing through it all, an empty sort of wind.'

He paused briefly, seeing the red walls of Dauria again, hearing the empty wind whistle across the plain. Outside the car, the sands of the desert swayed past, faded, hazy, a waterless mirage shimmering in the late afternoon light.

'That was where I first met Ungern. I won't forget it. The way he looked at me when I walked in . . . The way he waited for me.'

He shuddered.

'Ordinarily, I'd hit a man who looked at me like that. But I didn't hit him. I knew better than that. I tried to stare him out, but . . . Anyway, you'll meet him soon enough. Be very careful when you do. He can shift from complete affability to the purest sadism or rage in a matter of seconds. I saw it myself.

'He always carries a sort of riding crop made of bamboo. Extremely thin and flexible, but with rough edges. One of his staff officers came in. A youngish man, probably not long out of military academy, but already showing marked signs of the dissipation I'd already seen in Chita. He reported something Ungern obviously didn't like to hear. The baron flew into a rage and hit him full across the face with the cane. It cut the man's cheek open, right along the bone. He almost fainted, but Ungern made him stand and finish his report. He was quivering with rage – Ungern, I mean. But the second the boy left, he began talking to me as though nothing out of the ordinary had occurred. From what I know now, I suppose nothing had.'

Winterpole looked out of the window to his left. In the west, the sun was setting, blood-red in a haze of sand. Behind them, the dust laid a long plume across the desert.

'Something else happened while I was there,' he went on. 'They brought in an old man, a Jew. His son had been executed on Ungern's orders the day before, for no reason I was able to ascertain. The old man had come to ask for the body. That's all. He wanted to give his son a Jewish burial, not leave him to be eaten by the dogs the way they do in those parts. He made no complaint. He didn't criticize. But whether it was his face or his manner or his being Jewish or something else, he infuriated the baron.

'Ungern called two of his aides and had them take the old man outside. He told me to come out and watch, to see how he punished traitors. I saw I would have to obey: being a foreigner was no guarantee of immunity there.

333

'They took the old man and put him in a tall wooden box. There was a hole in the side of it, and they had the old man put his arm through it. It was freezing, well below zero: we were all dressed in warm furs, but it still felt cold, bitterly cold.

'They tied the old man's arm so he couldn't get it back inside the box. Then they poured water over it until it was soaking. It didn't take long to freeze. Three hours later, they came back. The arm had frozen solid, like a lump of ice. Ungern just walked up and snapped it off. I watched him do it. As if he were snapping off a rotten twig. It made a cracking sound, like an old branch. It didn't even bleed.'

He paused. It was growing dark suddenly. He switched on the headlights of the car, long white cones that stabbed into the darkness far ahead, catching insects in their beams, creating narrow worlds in which small creatures stirred for brief moments before being swept away again into the blackness.

'The old man died, of course. He died that night in great pain, and by morning the dogs had eaten what was left of him, along with his son.'

Winterpole looked up. All the aplomb, all the casual affectation had drained away to leave him empty and bereft, like a shell far away from the heart of the sea.

'So now you know,' he said. 'Now you know who we're dealing with. Who our friends are.' His eyes filled with a sense of horror.

'He's all we have here, Christopher. He's all that stands between us and the Bolsheviks.'

There was silence. The car drove on through the dark waste, a brightly lit warning of times yet to come. The desert was coming awake. Between them, Winterpole and Ungern Sternberg and Zamyatin would bring the benefits of their cold civilization into the wilderness. If it did not blossom, they would not despair: they had time: they would water it with blood.

'Do we need friends like that?' asked Christopher. He failed to see the necessity. He failed to understand how such a frail barrier could stand between two philosophies.

'It's hard for you to understand, Christopher. You weren't in Europe during the war. You didn't see what we did to one another. We lost our heads. We became animals. When the war ended, it was the general opinion that the beastliness had ended with it. As if that could ever be. "The war to end wars" – that's what we called it. But how can war end? It's part of us, it's in our blood.

'If the Bolsheviks spread their creed any further, there'll be another war, one worse than the last. My job is to prevent that, at any cost. Our people back home have just won a war, and peace has never seemed so good to them. They want it to go on forever: poppies in the fields, photographs of Uncle Arthur wearing his medals on the mantelpiece, the flag unfurling day after day in a stiff breeze, the home fires burning all winter long. And I'm afraid for them. They're about to be overtaken by Zamyatin and History, and they don't even know it. That's why Ungern Sternberg is necessary. Regrettable, but necessary, I assure you.'

He cleared his throat.

'He won't last long, don't worry. Men like him serve a purpose in times like these. He cleared the Chinese out of the way – and did a good job of it. There would have been an incident if we'd done the same. Diplomatic rows. Reparations.

'He'll hold off the Bolsheviks until we can organize something better, something more permanent. Then we'll put our own man on the throne in his place. The Tibetan boy, perhaps. We'll supply arms and advisers, monetary reserves. We'll put up telegraphs and open banks and start trade flowing. It'll all work out in the end – you'll see. Believe me, people in very high places have discussed this thing. Very high places indeed. Discussed it inside and out. It's for the best. You'll see. All for the best.'

The roaring of the engines filled the world. In front, the darkness was forced aside only to fall in again behind them, thick and unappeased.

Chindamani turned and spoke to Christopher.

'It's like magic,' she said. 'Lamps that can turn the darkness to daylight. Boxes that can run faster than wind-stallions. You never told me about any of this, that your people could do such wonderful things.'

'No,' said Christopher, staring into the darkness. 'I didn't tell you. Everything we do is magic. One day we'll turn the whole world into fairyland. Wait and see.'

335

49

They halted that night in the centre of a vast depression one hundred and eighty miles north of Sining-fu. A large moon gave them light out of a cloistered sky, turning the sand to silver and the hollow in which they rested to a giant, polished bowl. Without the sun, the sands had given up their heat. They lit a fire with charcoal bought in Sining-fu and ate in silence, shivering.

Christopher was unable to explain his worries properly to Chindamani. He told her they would be in Urga in a matter of days. Brought up to believe in miracles, and entranced by the magical pulse of the motor vehicle that had already carried her so far into this iceless and snowless land, she believed him.

He told her what he knew of Ungern Sternberg, not to frighten, but to warn her. He said the Russian had kept a pack of wolves in Dauria – so Winterpole had told him – and that he had fed his victims to them on occasion. But she had never seen a wolf or even heard one calling in the stillness of the night, and thought he was telling her tales like those she had once delighted Samdup with in his *labrang* when winter was at its height.

She missed the boy terribly and was afraid for him, the more so now that the distance between them was growing shorter every day. Some superstitious fear had been aroused in her that she might somehow cause his death. More realistically, she had seen what Zamyatin was capable of, that the killing of children was not beyond the bounds of possibility for such a man.

Her relationship with Christopher gave her growing cause for uncertainty. She had found she loved him in ways that constantly surprised and delighted her. His eyes, his hands, the foreign roughness of his beard, the odd ways he used Tibetan words, the tenderness of his fingers, the lightness of his breath against her wet skin – all filled her at different times with alien and undefinable pleasure and a simple contentment at being with him. When she shared his bed, she experienced an intensity of joy that nothing in

336

her experience had prepared her for. She had always regarded sensual pleasure as a thing reserved for ordinary mortals or for gods: since she was neither, it had been remote from her until now.

For the first time, she understood the meaning of temptation: its power, its subtlety, its intimacy. She would have given lifetimes to have him enter her just one more time or to feel his lips on her breasts or even merely to lie naked with him in the darkness. On their first night in the desert, he came to her urgently, with a desperation she had never known in him before. At the moment when she felt him enter her, she understood something vital: love did not diminish. It increased daily until nothing could contain it except itself.

And she wondered again how she would manage when the moment came for her to leave him and go back to the shadows where she belonged.

It took them another two days to complete the crossing of the Gobi and a low range of mountains just beyond. The car broke down five times, and each time Winterpole swore it was the end. But he cursed and tinkered, tinkered and cursed until something happened, the car bowed to the inevitable, and they were on their way again. Christopher was astonished by this display of manual dexterity in a man of Winterpole's apparent indolence. Cars, it appeared, were Winterpole's passion. He said he preferred them to people, and Christopher believed him.

At last the desert was behind them and they were driving on the open plains. Grass stretched ahead of them as far as the eye could see. This was nomad country, a world of white felt *yurts* and prancing horses, of gently sloping meadows and winding streams where vast herds of sheep and goats and cows grazed in a tranquil silence. They passed a small herd of white horses wearing talismans wrapped in bags of felt across their broad chests – sacred animals belonging to a nearby monastery. Dogs rushed out to bark at the car as they passed small encampments, then they were out of reach, gliding into the blue horizon in top gear. Their spirits lifted.

'Urga's only about one hundred and fifty miles away now,' said Winterpole. 'We'll be there tomorrow with any luck.'

*

That afternoon, they came upon masses of purple and white pasque-flowers in a vast expanse of waving grass. Suddenly, winter seemed impossibly far away, and the deep snows of Tibet nothing but a mirage. Wherever they looked, a coloured carpet stretched to the horizon. At Christopher's request, Winterpole stopped the car and they got out.

He watched as Chindamani bent down in wonder and cupped her hands about the head of a purple flower.

'Smell it,' he said.

But the smell was already everywhere, filling the air all about them, rich and strange and unbearably fragrant, like a woman's perfume, warmed by the bright sun.

'I told you there were flowers in Mongolia,' she whispered. A thin breeze came down from the north and lifted her hair. The grass and the pasque-flowers waved: it was a great ocean, shoreless and moving to unseen music.

'Are they worth your coming here?' he asked.

She stood up and smiled, ravished by the sight of so much greenery. It was ordinary to him, just a meadow filled with flowers. But to her it was the world turned upside down.

She laughed suddenly and began to run, weaving among the scattered flowers like a child on its first picnic. Christopher tried to picture her at home in Northumberland, in an English summer, running down to the river at Carfax across trim, delicate lawns: but her moving form called for something else, something that would tear that prim and tidy world to pieces.

Suddenly she stopped running. She did not scream or cry out, but Christopher knew at once that something was wrong, badly wrong. She was standing stock-still, her body rigid, her hands clenched, staring at something just out of his range of vision.

'Stay here,' Christopher ordered Winterpole, taking command at once. 'Get your revolver from the car. It may be nothing, but we can't afford to take chances. Keep the engine running.'

He ran towards her, praying she was all right, that it was only something startling she had seen, something unexpected, like a running fawn. But her silence alarmed him more than a cry or call for help would have done.

He could not make out what the objects were at first. Chinda-mani was standing at the top of a gentle slope that ran down towards a small river. In either direction, as far as the eye could see, the slope was covered by round objects that looked at first sight like the stems of plants topped by gourds or small melons.

But as he drew alongside Chindamani, he saw what she saw. Stakes had been cut from a nearby forest and planted all along the banks of the river and as high as the slopes on either side. On each stake, like a grotesque offering of some sort, a human head had been impaled.

Christopher guessed the heads had been there for perhaps a month. Some were little more than bone, others had shrivelled like the heads of mummies, parched and old and leathery. On several, he could see the caps of Chinese soldiers. It was impossible to guess how many there were. He imagined them stretching on for mile after mile until the river reached the sea. As it was, he could not see the end of them, whichever way he looked.

He took Chindamani by the shoulders and led her away from the river. As they turned, his eyes caught sight of a stake at the top of the slope. It was one of several to which a board had been nailed. Christopher went across and examined it.

It bore writing in Chinese and Russian characters. He read the Russian, but it made no sense to him:

One hundred and thirty days yet and it is finished. I am Death. I am the Destroyer of Worlds. Roman von Ungern Sternberg.

He recognized the last two sentences as quotations from the Hindu religious text, the *Bhagavad Gita*. But the first sentence remained mysterious. It read like something from the Apocalypse. But he was sure he had never read it in St John's Revelation.

He looked back again at the grim trophies, at the tokens of Ungern's carnage. Then he glanced at the river. It was peaceful and unsullied now, free of its winter ice and flowing once more to the sea. But he imagined it a month ago, filled with the headless corpses of ten thousand Chinese soldiers slaughtered by von Ungern Sternberg and his men.

The Saviour of Mongolia had come at last and was at work among men.

50

They heard the first shots about an hour before sunset. It was the day after their discovery of the field of heads. Each time they passed by clumps of flowers after that, Chindamani turned her face away. 'O Rose, thou art sick,' Christopher whispered beneath his breath; but the worm that had entered the bud of Chindamani's life was far from invisible.

'Stop the car!' he cried. Another shot rang out, somewhere in the distance, carried to them by a slight echo.

Winterpole braked hard, slewing the car round on its tracks, and killed the engine. A profound silence rushed into the world. Somewhere a bird sang, a quirky, warbling note. Then there was a sharp crack, followed by a second, then silence again.

'What the devil's going on?' demanded Winterpole.

'Shut up,' said Christopher. He was trying to guess the direction from which the shots had come. They were gunshots, he could not have mistaken them.

Two more reports sounded nearby. There was something careful, something methodical about the shooting that Christopher did not like. It was not the seasons for woodcocks, and Mongols did not hunt birds with guns.

'Winterpole,' he said, 'stay in the car with Chindamani. Keep your pistol ready and use it if you have to — if anyone comes, frighten him off. Even if he looks harmless. We can't afford to take chances. I'm going to check out those shots.'

'Why don't we just drive on?' queried Winterpole.

'Drive on into what?' Christopher retorted. 'Before I go any further, I want to know just what they're shooting out there — birds or people. I doubt very much if it's the first, and if it's the second I want to know who's doing the shooting and who's being shot at. I'm relying on you to keep Chindamani safe. You're a man of action now, Winterpole. It's time you got your lily-white hands a little dirty.'

'At least call me Simon, old boy. Do me that courtesy.'

Christopher said nothing. He reached down and found his pistol, the one he had brought from Dorje-la, Tsarong Rinpoche's pistol.

They had been driving along the edge of a vast pine forest, which lay to their right. Christopher was sure the shots had come from there. His suspicion was confirmed when another two rang out in quick succession as he got out of the car. Making allowance for the trees, he guessed they had come from a spot about half a mile away.

'Be careful, Ka-ris To-feh,' Chindamani said in her quietest voice, addressing herself to him alone, in their private universe. 'I'm frightened for you – please take care.'

He bent and kissed her cheek.

The trees swallowed him up instantly. He was like a diver entering the sea, plunging out of the sunshine into a green world fingered by narrow shafts of broken light that struggled past murky shadows. His footsteps died away into a thick carpet of pine needles.

Everywhere, fallen cones lay in profusion. Silence reigned like a mad king over an unpeopled kingdom, determined and murderous, eager to lay waste. His breathing was the only sound, raw and melancholy, vexed by the heavy scent of pine resin and dead undergrowth. If there were birds here, they were hidden away, voiceless and wingless, watching from secret branches. If there were other animals, they licked their teeth in dark burrows deep beneath the earth.

The forest went on, breeding itself with a green intensity on every side. He was enveloped in a lacework of boughs and low-hanging branches. He cocked his pistol nervously. This must be near the spot from which the shots had come.

Nearby, a man's voice sounded, barking out what seemed to be words of command. A brief silence followed, then two more shots shook the trees. He thought they came from a clump of trees to his left. A murmur of voices came indistinctly from that direction, but he could not make out what they were saying, or even what language they spoke.

He slipped into the close-set thicket and made for the voices. The trees concealed him – but they also concealed whoever was

341

responsible for the shooting. Perhaps it was rabbits. Perhaps they were shooting rabbits. But nothing ran through the undergrowth.

If he had been a rabbit, Christopher might have bolted at the next shot and run straight into the clearing. But he froze and pressed himself against the trunk of a tree. Out in the clearing just beyond where he stood, night was being summoned into the world.

The last sunlight was being drained from the sky. It clung hopelessly to the branches of the trees, thinning, loosening, breaking apart. Soon it would be dark. It would have been better if it had been dark.

In a ring that stretched all round the clearing, stood about twenty men in dirty white uniforms. On their head they wore scarlet forage caps bearing a death's-head symbol above crossed shin-bones: the uniform of Annenkov's now-defunct Siberian units. In their hands, they held 8mm Mannlicher rifles pointed inwards to the centre of the clearing. They had come a long way from home, and the road back was closed. They were living their apocalypse here in the Mongolian wilderness. Some of them had been fighting since 1914. Seven years, and it still had not ended.

In the centre of the clearing, along a low depression from which undergrowth had been meticulously cleared, about forty bodies lay tumbled in a ragged heap. They were dressed in grey uniforms with red triangles on their sleeves; most had astrakhan caps bearing red stars; a few wore helmet-shaped felt caps with a hammer and sickle device. Near the bodies stood another dozen men, dressed in the same basic uniform and lined up for the same fate.

But Christopher's eyes were focused on one man alone. By the side of the heap of victims stood a small White officer. He was dressed in a tattered grey Mongol overcoat and an old green Cossack cap with a visor. His right hand was held in a black sling that looked as though it had been there since the man's childhood – if he had ever had a childhood. But on his shoulder he sported a general's epaulet. And in his left hand he held a heavy service revolver. As Christopher watched, he turned and faced the next prisoner in line.

'*Kak vasha familia?* What's your family name?' he asked. His voice carried in the stillness, hoarse and menacing.

The condemned man shivered in the departing sunlight. In his

342

eyes Christopher saw only an utter hopelessness of the spirit, as though life had drained away long before the bullet entered him. He was young, a mere boy.

'Arakcheyev,' the boy replied. How old was he? Fifteen? Sixteen? His voice was toneless; for him, identity meant nothing any longer.

'*Imya i otchestvo?* Christian name and patronymic?'

'Yuri Nikolayevitch.'

The general turned his head a fraction and barked a command at a second officer standing nearby. This third man was dressed in a soiled white uniform, a lieutenant fresh out of military academy. In his hand, he held a large book in which he was writing.

'Write them down!' ordered the general.

The lieutenant wrote the names in the book, in their proper order, all according to form. No court, no tribunal, no sentence but death, but a record must be kept of the dead. When the new Tzar sat on his throne and thrilled his people with the glamour of his return, he would find all in order. A million dead. Two million. Twenty million. But all in order: a graveyard with numbered plots and arrows pointing to the exit.

'From?'

'Gorki.'

'Rank?'

'Corporal.'

'Unit?'

'Second Squadron of the Communist Interior Defence.'

'Age?'

The boy hesitated.

'Eighteen,' he said. But it was a lie. They both knew that.

'You admit to being a Bolshevik?'

The boy paused again. For a moment, he saw something like hope. Would a denial not be enough? Then he looked into the general's eyes and all hope faded.

'Yes.'

'And a traitor to the Tzar and Holy Russia?'

'Not a traitor,' protested the boy. 'I have been loyal to Russia. I have served the Russian people.'

'Write "Traitor".' The general paused and looked at the boy.

'Have you anything further to say?'

The boy remained silent. He was shaking, trying to control

343

himself. The light was going out of the world. In just another moment he would see the day ending. Suddenly he wanted very much to see the last of the light. It was unbearable to have it snatched away from him by an executioner's bullet. But he could not bring himself to say anything, not even to ask for another minute of light.

'Very well,' the general said. Some made last speeches, others remained silent. It made no difference. He and his men were impervious to both.

'In the name of the princess Anastasia, Tzarina of all the Russias; in the name of the blessed Tikhon, Patriarch of our Holy Mother Church; in the name of Baron Roman von Ungern Sternberg, Protector of Khalka and Supreme Commander of Russian forces in the East: I sentence you, Yuri Nikolayevitch Arakcheyev, to death. May your soul find mercy with God.'

He raised the pistol to the boy's trembling head. His victim's eyes were open, staring, lusting after the dying light. He fired and the boy jerked and toppled backwards on to the heap of corpses. The general bent down, saw he was still moving, and fired again. The boy became still. It was growing dark.

'Light torches!' shouted the general.

In a matter of moments, lights flared in the circle round the clearing. Every other man held a torch high in the air. The red flames flickered against white uniforms and long bayonets, and in the centre of the clearing, arms and legs and heads would be singled out momentarily before slipping back into a merciful darkness.

Christopher watched transfixed. Who was his enemy? That was what he wanted to know.

The killings went on. One by one, the prisoners would be led up, questioned, and inevitably shot, usually twice in quick succession. It was a nightmare that repeated and repeated itself.

The last prisoner to be questioned was a thin, stooping man with iron-rimmed glasses, a commissar of the Cheka who had been caught with the military unit whose surviving members had just been executed. The others had been soldiers, but here, thought Christopher, was a real revolutionary. His face was white and drawn, plainly visible in the light of a nearby torch.

Even before the general had a chance to pronounce his death

344

sentence, the man stretched out a hand. With his eyes, he held his executioner fixed, willing him to pass over the gun. A minute passed, two minutes, during which neither man spoke. It was clear what the prisoner wanted. And at last the general gave way.

Using his single hand, he emptied the chamber of his revolver of all but a single bullet, reclosed it, and handed it to the commissar. Even at such an ideological distance, they understood one another. All round the clearing, rifles were raised and pointed directly at the prisoner.

But he had no intention of attempting a clumsy escape. He raised the pistol to his head, slowly and deliberately, while all the time his eyes held those of the little general. There was a look of terrible disdain on his face, disdain less for what the general and his men were doing than for what they were, or what they had become.

Watching from the trees, Christopher felt it like an icy blast, the power of this man's contempt. In a moral sense, he had already escaped his captors. He made no speech, he called down no retribution. It was enough, watching him, to know that the whites were defeated. It was only a matter of time. He held the gun firm against his temple, so that it would not slip. A single motion and all would be well again. He pulled the trigger, and the gun fell to the ground.

The silence that followed was terrible. Whatever pleasure these men had had in their day's work, whatever triumph they had felt meting out death in such measured handfuls – all had been wiped out in a moment by one man's gesture. The general bent down and picked up his pistol from the ground. His hand shook as he retrieved it and replaced it in its holster.

Christopher stood up slowly, eyes still fixed on the clearing, on the white uniforms of the living, the blood-stained forms of the dead. He turned to go, worried that he might not be able to find his way back through the trees in the dark.

A voice came out of the night, a soft voice speaking in Russian.

'Just drop your gun, tovarisch. We have you covered from all sides.'

He did as he was told. His gun made almost no sound as it fell to the floor of the dark forest.

51

Behind them, the sky was reddening, as though dawn were breaking in the south. From edge to edge of the horizon, hell was creeping on silent feet across a black sky. It was midnight. The little general – Rezukhin was his name – had ordered his men to set fire to the forest with their torches. The previous day, he and his unit of forty men had been ambushed passing through the forest on their way back to Urga from a six-day reconnaissance. Half of them had been killed before they succeeded in luring their attackers out into the open and gaining the upper hand.

Now, Rezukhin had decided that the forest represented a danger to any White troops passing its edge: his solution was to burn it to the ground. But it seemed to Christopher that the general's reasons for setting mile after mile of trees alight were not military at all. The general and his men were no longer soldiers fighting a war. They had lost their war long ago. Now they were actors in an apocalyptic drama, half out of their minds with drugs and alcohol and disease, half-crazed by bloodshed and destruction.

Here in Mongolia, they dragged out a phantom existence, banished forever from wives and family and sweethearts. They thought of themselves as the damned and lived accordingly. They had no fear and no morality, no expectations, no hopes, no reason to do anything but kill and loot and wreak a sort of vengeance on a world that had turned its back on them. They were the men of the brave new age now dawning. And they would spawn a brood vaster and more mysterious in its savagery than any that had ridden these same steppes with Genghis or Hulagu Khan.

Christopher rode with Chindamani. Winterpole was just behind. They were at the head of Rezukhin's column, near the general himself. Their car had been commandeered and driven off at speed to Urga by a Russian mechanic.

At first, Winterpole had argued with Rezukhin that he and Christopher were British agents sent to assist von Ungern Sternberg. But the general had only laughed and, when Winterpole persisted, told him sharply to shut up or be shot. Even Winterpole had known when to pipe down. But now he fumed and brooded, believing desperately that Ungern needed him and that he would discipline Rezukhin for discourtesy towards a representative of a friendly power.

Winterpole was a man of the world, but his worldliness, though vast, was of the wrong sort. The sins and vices of polite society, however interesting, are not those of the barracks or the open steppe. Where Winterpole came from, there were rules and conventions, even for the darkest of crimes; how otherwise could men of consequence be distinguished from common criminals? But here no code existed at all: here, desperation swept aside all the niceties and made brutish insanity of everything it touched. It was a fire raging in a doomed forest, out of control and consuming all it touched.

They camped late that night, well away from the blazing forest. A wall of fire shimmered on the horizon still, creeping with the prevailing wind across an unassuming backdrop of night sky. The three prisoners were kept together in a single tent under heavy guard. They slept fitfully or lay awake listening to the sounds of the darkness: birds calling, remote and tuneless; men calling out in their sleep; the crackling of camp fires lit to stave off the penetrating cold. The guards discouraged them from talking together when they woke, though they refrained from using any real violence against them. All that night, Christopher held Chindamani without speaking. She was silent in his arms, preoccupied with some private sadness, sleepless and dreamless.

Throughout the next day they rode on in gloomy silence, strung out across the empty plain like a broken necklace of cheap glass. One man died of wounds sustained in the skirmish at the forest. They left him on the grass, naked and pitifully pale. His horse came with them now, bearing an empty saddle.

By the second night, the men had started to grow restless. Suffused with killing and the infant joy of setting alight a forest merely to lay black ashes on the scene of their crimes, they had ridden until then in a state of morbid contentment, their flagging spirits buoyed up by an infusion of vanity.

347

But during the second day's riding, and certainly after the death of the wounded man, a terrible ennui had begun to fix its grip on them. They shifted in their saddles mile after mile, itching to be back in Urga or off on another hunt for Bolshevik infiltrators. Someone rode out from the road to a nomad encampment and returned with a plentiful supply of *hanchi*, a local drink.

That evening, *hanchi* was passed round after supper and the men's mood changed. They sang old songs, Russian songs about girls with flaxen hair and birches waving in the mists of autumn, and as they sang they grew sentimental and even maudlin.

The older men regaled their juniors with pathetic tales of valour that had grown tarnished from overmuch recounting. As the night progressed, stories of bravery gave way to accounts of bawdy excess. New songs replaced those of the early evening. In a spot set apart from the rest of the camp, Rezukhin sat by a solitary fire, his black sling invisible against the night, smoking hashish from a private supply kept in his saddlebag.

It was just after midnight when they decided to come for Chindamani. The fires had died down and clouds had come up from the south to cover the moon. Perhaps the *hanchi* rendered them incautious, perhaps the darkness gave them a sense of security in what they planned. Rezukhin had ordered the woman off limits – in spite of everything, he knew enough to cover himself against the possibility that the Englishmen might indeed prove of value to Ungern Sternberg. But he had gone to sleep in his tent and would be oblivious to anything that went on.

Some of the men had been watching her furtively all that day, but no-one had approached her or tried to speak to her. It had been years since any of them had had anything to do with a woman who was not a prostitute or the near equivalent. But, coarsened as they had become, in some part of them they retained memories, however dim, of the social conventions that had formed their upbringing. Some of them still had wives or sweethearts at home. And Chindamani, unconsciously perhaps, but with unmistakable clarity, set up a barrier between herself and the men around her which, however imperceptible, served to restrict their activities to sidelong glances.

That had all changed with the onset of night and the powerful effects of the *hanchi*. From sentimentality they passed to self-pity

348

and from self-pity to regret. It was not long before regret had wakened in them feelings of resentment against Germans, Bolsheviks, and anyone else responsible for the loss of Russia and its privileges. And out of resentment was born a curious and unreasonable lust, not merely physical but shaped out of the greed and bitterness that lay in the depths of wounded psyches.

Chindamani was to be their victim, not merely because she was the only woman there, but because she represented too many conflicting opposites for them to cope with. She reminded them at once of the women they had left behind in their homes in Moscow or St Petersburg and of the eastern women they had known since then. She was physically attractive in a way that only their lost sweethearts had been, yet untouchable, a Madonna-like figure who inflamed them while making them feel like children or priests, castrated, pure, yet seething with impurities. They could not bear the contradictions.

Four of them came to the tent where she and the others had at last fallen into an uneasy sleep. Only a single guard was left, half-asleep himself and a little drunk on *hanchi* that some friends had brought for him.

They kicked Chindamani awake, and before she had time to protest, hauled her roughly to her feet. She could tell at once that they were in no mood to be reasoned with, and at once gave up the attempt to struggle. Christopher woke at once, but one of the men grabbed him, holding a gun at his head.

'One word out of you, tovarisch, and I'll send your brains to Urga before the rest of you. *Ponimaete?*'

Christopher nodded and sank back. He had not understood much, but he got the general idea. Behind the man with the gun, the guard was watching him, his rifle poised. Winterpole came awake, unable at first to comprehend what was happening.

Chindamani turned as they dragged her to the entrance and spoke rapidly to Christopher in Tibetan.

'Ka-ris To-feh! Find him! Tell him I love him! If you can, hide him! It's not time yet! Tell him it isn't time!'

One of the men clamped a heavy hand over her mouth. They wanted her out of the tent, away from the light of the oil-lamp. They did not want light for what they were going to do. The fourth

349

man let go of Christopher, holstered the gun, and followed the others. The guard remained, intently watching his charges.

A terrible silence formed round them. They knew what was happening, what would happen when the men had finished with her. They heard coarse shouts, then a laugh, raucous and prolonged. Then the laugh was cut short and a group of men cheered. Someone began to sing a song, not a melancholy dirge about maidens or birches, but a coarse drinking song of German origin – *ich liebe* something-or-other, but transposed into Russian, witless, brash, more sordid than usual out here in the wilderness. It was a song that needed a tavern and the smell of sour beer.

Christopher threw his bedclothes back and made as if to stand. The guard levelled his rifle at him nervously. A hand grabbed his arm and pulled him back down to the ground.

'For God's sake, Christopher, don't be such a bloody fool!' It was Winterpole's voice, hissing in the semi-darkness like a snake.

'They're raping her!' Christopher shouted back. 'Don't you understand? Those bastards are raping her!'

'It doesn't matter, Christopher, really it doesn't. She's just a darkie. Don't get things out of proportion. She isn't important, you know that. Don't get yourself killed for her sake.'

Christopher sat up again, but Winterpole got in front of him and fastened his hand on his arm even more tightly.

'There are plenty like her, Christopher, plenty. They breed like rabbits, these Asiatics. You can have as many as you like once this is all over. The best, the very best, I swear. Lovely women, I guarantee it. Just don't let this one get to you. Try to behave like a professional for once. It's part of their way of life here, they expect it. You can't stop it. They'll kill you if you try to interfere. So just stay out of it.'

Christopher hit him harder than he had ever hit anyone. The blow caught Winterpole full on the jaw and sent him sprawling back on to the floor. Christopher started to get to his feet, but Winterpole, groaning from the blow, somehow managed to twist round and make a grab for Christopher's legs, toppling him.

That was when the guard made his mistake. He moved across to separate the struggling men, using his right hand while he held his rifle awkwardly in the other. Perhaps he thought he was invulnerable since he carried the gun. Perhaps he imagined the combatants were more interested in one another than in him. On both counts, he was wrong.

As the guard reached for Winterpole, Christopher lunged for his left arm, swinging it back hard against the shoulder. He heard a bone give with a snap and the guard scream in pain. The rifle dropped from paralysed fingers. The guard had sufficient presence of mind to throw himself round on Christopher as he scrabbled on the floor for the weapon. But Christopher was impatient now and out of control.

As the guard rounded on him, he heard a scream outside, a woman's scream. Instinctively, he recoiled from his opponent's grip, straightened, and lunged upwards with his knee, catching the man hard in the groin.

Christopher reached for the abandoned Mannlicher. It had been rendered clumsy by the long bayonet at its end. He heard Chindamani cry out again, a tight scream followed by a sob. They were hurting her. Without pausing, he turned and made for the entrance.

'Christopher!'

It was Winterpole, shouting urgently.

'He's got a pistol, Christopher! I can't get to him!'

The guard had struggled to his feet in spite of the pain and was fumbling with a pistol in his side-holster.

Christopher swung round. The man held the pistol in his right hand, trembling. He was swaying, dizzy with pain, unable to take aim. Christopher did not want to fire – it would bring attention in his direction too soon. He swung the rifle round, feeling it move like a spear in his hand. Men had fought a war with weapons like this, in cold trenches, over rusted wire, yet he had never so much as handled one before. He felt primitive, a sort of god, cold metal in his hands. The man had steadied and was pointing the pistol at his chest. It was heavy, black and diabolical.

Christopher lunged, images of parade grounds in his mind. He had seen men stabbing bags of straw, shouting as they did so. The revolver fired, a sudden light, and a sound of roaring filling the world. He felt the rifle grow heavy, felt something cumbrous move at the end of the long spike, felt the rifle jerk in his hands, heard the revolver fire again, felt himself fall forward into the heaviness.

The bayonet twisted and there was a sound of screaming. Christopher realized he had closed his eyes. He opened them and saw the guard beside him, vomiting blood, rearing against the long spike in his stomach like a fish made passionate against death on the angler's gaff. He closed his eyes again and turned the blade once more, drawing away, empty, entranced, striving to escape the tearing of flesh. There was a softer cry and a silence and a pulling away, and suddenly he was adrift in the supremacy of life over death.

'There is no death. There is no death,' he kept repeating, but he opened his eyes and saw the guard on the floor, entering another world. The bullets had not touched Christopher. He was unhurt, but blood from the guard had splashed on his hands and the bayonet he held was dark and wet.

'You bloody fool!' screeched Winterpole from his corner of the tent. 'You've ruined us!'

Christopher ignored him and ran out, clutching the rifle.

A fire had been brought back to life about twenty yards away, a red fire that threw tremendous sparks out to tease the darkness. A semicircle of men stood near it, their faces lit like carnival masks, inflamed and bestial. They were cheering as though watching a cockfight. They seemed not to have heard the gunshots, or perhaps they had decided mutually to ignore them in order to concentrate on more immediate concerns.

Christopher raced towards them, pulling back the bolt on the rifle, gauging the distance and the positions of the men round the fire. Coming from the darkness across soft ground, he was at an advantage. There was a cry and the circle parted a fraction. Through the gap, Christopher could see one of the four men who had come for Chindamani. He crouched above her, half-naked, pawing her breasts, breathing heavily. Christopher stooped, took aim, and fired a single shot that left the man with only half a head. The camp filled instantly with silence. Only Chindamani's sobbing could be heard, and the voice of a hunting owl drifting on the darkness.

'Chindamani,' said Christopher calmly. Hysteria would not help them now. A cool head and a steady hand were what was needed.

'Push him aside, stand up, and come here to me,' he told her,

352

praying they had not disabled her or that fear had not frozen her into immobility.

For what seemed an age, she lay there, sobs racking her, the dead man's blood wet on her naked skin like a baptism into all that life was really about. The men were unarmed, uncertain of how many guns their former prisoners might have trained on them. They could not see into the darkness and knew they presented good targets against the light of the fire. Someone shouted in a harsh voice.

'Put that bloody fire out before he shoots somebody else!'

But nobody stirred. No-one wanted to be the one to move and be singled out for the next shot.

She lifted herself slowly, thrusting the dead assailant away from her with loathing.

'Ignore them,' Christopher said. 'They won't hurt you. Walk towards me slowly.'

She began to move, arranging her torn clothes about her to conceal her nakedness. He willed her to him, steadying her faltering footsteps with words of encouragement. She reached the circle of men and started to walk through.

One man reached out to snatch at her, intending to use her body as a shield for his own escape. Christopher shot him through the throat, a single shot. The others fell back warily. The way lay open for her.

She was at his side, trembling as she touched him. Her hand clutched at his arm fiercely, hurting him, her fingers digging into his flesh. She said nothing. He felt a rage in him that neither the darkness nor the lust of killing could stifle. He would feel it always, from that moment: it would never leave him, though it would lessen in magnitude.

'We're leaving,' he said. 'The horses are behind us. I'm going to keep these bastards pinned down here: can you get to the horses?'

She nodded, choking back the last of the sobs.

They inched back slowly across the rough ground, heading for the area behind the tents where the horses had been hitched for the night to tent-pegs. The sound of the animals came to them out of the darkness, whinnying softly and stamping their feet, restless on account of the shooting.

'Find two horses you think we can handle,' Christopher

353

instructed her. 'Untie them. Don't worry about saddles, we'll have to go bareback. Untie the others as well, but leave one for Winterpole, in case he makes it.'

She slipped away from him, her confidence returning. Someone had thrown water on the fire and he could no longer see clearly what was happening in the camp.

A voice came out of the darkness, soft and familiar.

'The rifle, Mr Wylam. Throw it away from you as far as you are able. I am aiming at your back and the range is negligible, so please behave like a reasonable man.'

52

Christopher stiffened. He recognized the voice: Rezukhin. A long sigh escaped him. He had forgotten that the general's tent was next to the temporary paddock. With a groan, he threw his rifle down as ordered, several yards away.

'Christopher! What is it?' Chindamani called from the darkness.

'Stay back!' he shouted. 'Take the nearest horse and ride. Don't wait for me. Don't wait for anyone! Just ride as fast as you can!'

'Keep quiet, Mr Wylam,' Rezukhin's voice came again. 'But first tell the girl that if she so much as moves a muscle I'll shoot her where she stands. Is that understood? I can see her perfectly clearly from where I'm standing. And I see very well in the dark, I assure you.'

Christopher called again.

'Stay where you are, Chindamani. Don't move. He says he'll shoot you, and I believe he means it. But get ready for a chance to make a break for it.'

He would have to make a chance for her, distract Rezukhin long enough to let her make it to the horse.

'I can't go without you, Christopher!' she called back. 'I won't leave you here!'

'You've got to! For his sake. For my sake. When the moment comes,' he pleaded.

'Stop babbling!' Rezukhin barked. He was frightened and unsure of what was happening. Was the camp under attack? Had his prisoners allowed a band of Red infiltrators to slip past his guards?

Christopher wondered how good Rezukhin's aim was at this distance. The range was short, but he sensed that the general had originally been right-handed and that there were limits to how well he could use his left.

'Your men raped her, Rezukhin!' he called out. 'You promised us a safe passage to Urga. You told your boys to keep their hands off us – but see what happened when your back was turned.'

'I told you to keep quiet. If my men need a woman, I don't interfere. They endure enough privations. You have no privileges here, no rights – as far as I'm concerned, you and the other man with you are nothing but spies. Which means I can have you taken out and shot.'

'The way you shot those poor bastards in the forest? Without a trial? Judge, jury and executioner all rolled into one? I thought you were a soldier. I thought we were on the same side. But I appear to have been mistaken.'

'This is Mongolia, Mr Wylam, this is a world apart. We are under martial law here. That law empowers me to condemn a man to death and to have him executed on the spot if the situation demands it. In this place, it is situations that compel us to our actions, not men or their morality.'

Rezukhin steadied the pistol, holding it firmly in line with Christopher's chest. It was heavy, but his hand did not waver.

'And frankly, Mr Wylam,' he went on, 'I think the present situation calls for action. For condemnation and execution. You have killed at least one of my men, possibly more. You have endangered the lives of my entire unit. You are attempting to escape from military custody. It will be a pleasure to deal with you as you deserve. Come closer. I want to see you.'

'Ka-ris To-feh!'

Chindamani had found the right horse, a small gelding she had ridden since leaving the forest. She slipped its rope and pulled herself on to its smooth back.

'Run!' she cried. 'It's too dark, he'll miss you!'

It took Christopher less than a second to decide. He turned and broke into a run, praying he was right about Rezukhin's aim.

The general swung the barrel of his gun round, panning after Christopher's running figure. He saw the girl on the horse, anticipated the direction in which the Englishman would run.

Christopher had forgotten the rifle. It lay where he had tossed it, half-hidden by grass, invisible in the darkness. His foot caught on it, twisting his ankle and pitching him forward heavily on to his face.

Rezukhin saw the Englishman fall. He smiled with satisfaction: Wylam would never make it to the horse now. He glanced forward at the girl sitting on its back, calling desperately to the man on the ground. She would be better out of the way: women only bred discontent, their presence invariably led to brawls and breaches of discipline. Witness tonight's episode.

He raised the pistol, aimed at her, and fired.

Chindamani dropped from the horse with a startled cry, like a bird plummeting wingless out of the night sky. Rezukhin smiled and walked forward. He might as well finish the Englishman off as well.

Christopher scrabbled for the rifle, but he had lost it again in the darkness. He heard a gun being cocked, a soft click like a small door closing. He looked up to see Rezukhin standing over him, a stunted shadow etched against the sky.

Rezukhin's finger tightened on the trigger. Christopher caught his breath. He would call her name whatever happened, not even a bullet would deny him that. He closed his eyes. There was a roar and a second roar that followed instantly, like doors slamming in a great temple. He let his breath go urgently, calling into the blackness, against the roaring, calling her name.

There was no pain. He found that strange. Someone was shouting at him. He found that stranger.

'Get up for God's sake, Christopher! The whole camp will be on our backs in a minute!'

It was Winterpole, leaning over him, helping him to his feet.

'I'm . . .'

'You're all right, man. The first shot you heard was mine. Rezukhin's was aimed somewhere in the direction of Jupiter.'

'Chindamani!'

'She's all right too. Rezukhin's shot grazed her arm and made her lose her balance. She's not much of a horsewoman. Come on, we've no time to lose.'

Christopher heards shouts from the direction of the main camp. Someone fired wildly in their direction. It would still be touch and go.

He dashed with Winterpole to the horses. Chindamani had remounted her pony and sat clutching its mane. In one hand, she held the leading ropes of two medium-sized mounts.

'Be careful,' she said. 'The shooting has made the horses restless.'

357

'Let's get those other horses loose first,' Christopher suggested, uprooting the peg holding the animal next to him. Winterpole followed suit. Closer now, the shouting had grown in volume and violence. A shot rang out and they heard a bullet whistle past.

'Hurry!' Christopher shouted.

Suddenly, a figure appeared out of the darkness, brandishing a sabre and shouting incoherently. Winterpole turned, drew his pistol and fired. The man crumpled, choking loudly.

'Get on with it!' creid Christopher.

The animals were loose now.

'Let's go!' shouted Winterpole.

But Rezukhin's soldiers were already on them. A burst of indiscriminate firing came out of the darkness, narrowly missing them, the bullets passing audibly just over their heads.

They took a horse each and mounted. Winterpole raised his pistol and fired four times in quick succession over the heads of the remaining animals. There was a frenzied whinnying and snorting, then they bolted. Their own horses rushed off along with the rest in a thunder of hoofs. Behind them, inarticulate shouts and loud gunfire chased them into the darkness. Someone started firing from their flank.

'Keep your heads down!' shouted Winterpole. But they were racing now, holding desperately to the naked backs of their mounts, feeling the darkness rush past in a roar of horses' hoofs and frightened snorting.

Slowly, the unridden horses outdistanced them, and bit by bit their own mounts slowed as the panic left them.

'Are we all together?' shouted Christopher as soon as the pace of their flight had steadied to a canter.

'Chindamani! Are you all right?'

Her voice came back to him, frightened but controlled.

'I'm here, Ka-ris To-feh. I'm all right, don't worry about me.'

He rode across to her.

'Hold on,' he called to Winterpole. 'I want to move Chindamani to my horse.' He needed to be beside her, after what had happened.

They stopped and he helped her mount in front of him. They led her horse behind, its rope held in Christopher's hand.

'Winterpole! What about you?' he shouted once they had got under way again.

Winterpole was fine. He had done his bit. There was no need to apologize now for anything: they were quits.

They rode on at a steady pace. Rezukhin's men could not catch them now, without horses, in the darkness. But Christopher wished there was more light, that the moon would put in an appearance, however briefly. The sky was thick with clouds, through which not even the faintest glimmer of light escaped. They had no conception of the direction in which they were headed, nor could they easily measure how far they travelled. Time seemed to pass to a different measure, desperately slow and unrelenting. Only the horses were indifferent.

From time to time, one or another would fall into a fitful sleep, only to waken soon after, jolted by a change in the horse's rhythm or a cry out of the darkness.

For a long time Chindamani did not sleep. Christopher held her about the waist, steadying her against the swaying of the horse, but he sensed that she did not wish to talk. Perhaps she would never be able to discuss the events of that night; but he wanted her to know that he would be there if she wanted to. A few times he felt her body quivering, not from cold – though the night was icy – but from unwanted memories suddenly crowding in on her.

A little before dawn, he felt her grow more relaxed and realized she had finally fallen into an exhausted sleep. Though desperately fatigued himself, he struggled to keep awake in order to prevent her slipping. The horses were walking now.

Dawn, when it finally came, was torn between splendour and drabness. On the edge of the horizon, directly ahead of them, a pale and insignificant light suddenly erupted in jets of red and gold only to be swallowed up lazily by sordid banks of tattered cloud. It was not a dawn in which to look for auguries. It promised neither peace nor war, but something infinitely more grotesque than either.

With the light, it was possible to make out the sort of country they were in, a barren scrubland, devoid of any interesting features or signs of life. It seemed to stretch behind and ahead of them forever. They were strung out across it, Winterpole far in front, followed by Christopher and Chindamani with their two horses.

Christopher called at the top of his voice to Winterpole, telling him to stop. It was time they halted and rested properly. At first Winterpole paid no need, then he raised a tired hand to show he had heard, reined in his horse, and slipped awkwardly to the ground. He waited for them to catch up with him, his arms folded across his chest, relaxed and apparently unflustered by their adventures. They did not hurry to reach him nor, when they did, did Christopher find anything to say to him. He dismounted and helped Chindamani to the ground. She yawned and held on to him tightly, shivering in the dawn breeze.

'Where are we?' she asked.

'I don't know,' said Christopher. He turned and spoke to Winterpole in English. 'Do you know where we are?'

Winterpole smiled.

'As a matter of fact, I do,' he said. 'I overheard some of them talking last night, before all the trouble started. I got a rough idea which way we were travelling.'

He turned and pointed.

'Do you see those mountains ahead of us?'

Christopher nodded.

'That's the Bogdo Ula range. Urga is on the other side.'

53

'I'm tired.'

They had been walking for days now, but Zamyatin showed no signs of slacking off. Samdup had begun to wonder if he was human at all.

'Won't you have another chocolate?' the Buriat said, holding out a large beribboned box to the boy. God knows where or how the man obtained the thing, but it had appeared one evening at Uliassutai, a burning temptation to a child who had scarcely tasted sugar in his life. The box bore the legend 'Debauve & Gallais', and had clearly originated in their little shop near the top of the Rue des Saints-Pères, whence it had travelled to St Petersburg in the halcyon days before crowns and chocolates were together interdicted. But by what circuitous route the box – now in far from pristine condition – had come to the steppes of western Mongolia or how it had in the end fallen into Zamyatin's egalitarian hands as an offering for his little god-prince, it was impossible to know.

Samdup shook his head and walked on in silence. He was not to be drawn so easily from his tiredness. It had not been petulance that led him to complain. The boy really was tired and needed more than battered chocolates to fortify his spirits or his body against the rigours of another day. He hated Zamyatin with a raw and pitiless loathing, and longed to be rid of him. Yet a mutual dependence had grown up between man and boy, such that Samdup had little comfort in the thought of their parting.

Zamyatin fell back a little to where William was trailing along behind on his pony. They had agreed that he should have the remaining pony since he was in such poor shape. The bite he had received in the tunnels beneath Dorje-la had swollen out of all proportion. In the past week, it had become red and angry, the skin over it drawn taut like the skin of a drum. The boy suffered constant pain from it now and could scarcely sleep at night. At each of their recent halts, he had been examined by Mongol

361

doctors, but all they had been able to do was to prepare herbal concoctions, which William drank without effect.

'Have a chocolate, William,' Zamyatin urged, holding the box up to him. But the boy did not even look down or show that he had heard. He was not eating properly, and Zamyatin was growing worried.

Strictly speaking, he should have dumped the English boy weeks ago. Tibet was still a long way in the future, and he was not sure how useful William would prove anyway. But something in the boy's situation had awakened what little conscience there was in Zamyatin. He identified with him and in some respects regretted having taken him from his home. All the more now that he was sure the boy would not survive much longer unless he received proper medical attention.

The two boys had formed a strangely intense friendship in spite of their inability to understand one another's language. William had taught Samdup a little English and learned some Tibetan in return, but they had only words without grammar or syntax. They communicated in some manner that transcended or side-stepped language. William would let only Samdup tend to him when his neck was particularly bad. And Samdup would go nowhere unless William was by his side. They had become like brothers.

Zamyatin tried without success to win the favour of one or the other. He knew that, if William accepted him, Samdup would come round in time. Without Samdup, Zamyatin would lose all purpose in being here. True, there were communist cells at Urga and elsewhere now, with which he could liaise. But he knew that another Comintern agent, Sorokovikov, was already in the country and that he had organized the existing revolutionary group into the Mongol People's Party under the leadership of a man called Sukebator. Udinskii had told him that a delegation from the MPP had visited the head of the People's Section of the East for the Party's Siberian Bureau in Irkutsk. That had been last August. After that, a Mongol-Tibetan section of Comintern had been founded. The first Mongolian Party Congress had been held in Russian Khiakhta in March. Puzorin, commander of the Soviet of the Fifth Army, was already mobilizing his men.

So events had overtaken Zamyatin while he had been tucked away in his little monastery in the Himalayas. He could feel the

362

reins of power slipping out of his grasp before he had even learned to move them through his fingers with any real dexterity. More than ever, everything hinged on the boy. Ungern's defeat, the Khutukhtu's overthrow, and Zamyatin's elevation to the vice-regency of the East. Others might move cells and parties and armies, but what could they achieve in the end without the underpinning only a Saviour-child could give them?

Already his expedition had met with success, as he had anticipated. The riot at Uliassutai had been a mere beginning. He had met with the Sain Noyon Khan and one of the princes from his *aimak*, a man called Damdinsuren, and had presented them to the boy. It had gone exactly as planned – both men, together with the lamas in their entourage had recognized Samdup as the new Khutukhtu and promised their support, moral and military both. They had given him letters to other princes, to the Tushetu and Setsen Khans, and to the heads of several key monasteries.

Somehow – he could not explain it, did not wholly admire or admit it even to himself – the boy exerted some sort of charm over everyone he met. He played the part, but there was more to it than that. Perhaps it was simply that Samdup had throughout his life been little else but a god, so that he behaved as a god might be expected. And the boy did not have to act: he really believed he was the Maidari Buddha. But the Mongols, like the Tibetans, were accustomed to little boys who deported themselves as godlings; yet they responded to Samdup with genuine respect.

Mongolia then was divided into several large provinces or *aimaks*, each of which was further divided into several *hoshun*. Zamyatin calculated that he had already perhaps ten *hoshun* solidly behind him – or, to be precise, behind the boy, which was the same thing as far as he was concerned. There would be more riots, and next time he would see to it that the participants were armed.

The main thing was to keep the boys on the move. Word would be out by now, and if what he had heard about Ungern Sternberg was even partly true, the baron would stop at nothing to crush the rebellion breeding beneath his nose. Every night, Zamyatin and the boys stayed at the *yurts* of a different clan, moving in a broken pattern across the country, never keeping to a straight line, never staying in one place long enough to make tracing them easy.

Tomorrow they would start for Urga. The Sain Noyon Khan

would organize a series of uprisings in the west and north while Zamyatin and his young Pretender took horses to the capital. By the time they arrived there, Ungern's attention would be focused elsewhere. They would make their way into the city with the assistance of a few sympathizers. Zamyatin would make contact with Sukebator and the other revolutionaries, explain what was happening, and put himself in charge.

Up ahead, Samdup had stopped and sat down by the side of the track. Zamyatin went up to him slowly, holding the rein of William's pony.

'What's wrong?' he asked.

'My feet hurt,' Samdup said.

'What do you want me to do about it?' snapped Zamyatin. His own feet hurt. 'We've still got miles to go. Do you want to spend the night out here with the wolves?'

But he liked the boy. He really did. He liked both of them. It was just that he did not know how to show it. He had never known. No-one had ever told him.

Urga

54

Urga lay in the sunshine uneasily, trapped in a hollow between dark hills. Sunlight had entered it in proper measure, scattered from a cloudless and smiling sky, but no sooner did it touch its narrow lanes and fetid alleyways than it lost whatever lustre it had possessed and became a grey and sickly thing. The city's rooftops were golden and the spires on its temple tipped with sunlight and precious stones, but shadows hung over them and the sound of great trumpets echoed round them with a mournful and desperate flatness.

Mountains enclosed a melancholy plain across which the city stretched for mile after mile, in three separate sections: Mai-mai-ch'eng, the Chinese trading city, to the east, its stores and warehouses deserted and empty; Gandan, the grey city of the lamas, with its temples and colleges for the study of theology and medicine, to the west; and in the centre, Ta Khure, where the Living Buddha dwelt behind thick walls of dull red and white, among rooms full of holy relics and a thousand ticking clocks, each set to a different hour and minute. Time passed in those chambers to a morbid creeping sound, like ice moving down a mountain-slope.

In slow procession, pilgrims walked or crawled in circles about their god, while trumpets played and gongs shivered and the voices of ten thousand dreaming priests shimmered and echoed in the hollow air. All was as it had been, nothing was changed, nothing was altered – except for the actors and their faces. They wore ancient robes and spoke ancient lines, turning and bowing and lighting the proper incense in the proper places, as generations of actors had done before them, as they themselves had no doubt done in former lifetimes. Precise, mannered, without a syllable altered or a gesture changed. And in the Buddha's chambers, clocks ticked and rang out in the stillness.

In the centre, brooding, dressed in scarlet, his eyes heavy from sleepless nights, Roman von Ungern Sternberg sat among the warm tents of his troops, planning the stages of a small apocalypse. He drank small cups of Chinese tea and smoked dark-scented cigarettes, but all the time his mind was on other things.

He stood up and went to the door of his *yurt*. It was situated in the courtyard of an abandoned *hong* that had once belonged to the great Shansi house of Ta Sheng K'uei. The Buriat regiment under Sukharev was stationed here by Ungern's choice; nearby were the Chahar and Tatar regiments commanded by Bair Gur and Rezukhin. But Rezukhin had gone south with a Russian detachment two weeks ago and still had not returned.

The city filled his nostrils with its peculiar smell, a rich, sour smell that was a blend of holiness and corruption, sanctity mixed with greed and simple, raw humanity. He had not chosen Urga – a malign Fate had chosen him for it and sent him there to serve its purposes.

Stubbing out a half-finished cigarette on the door-post, he lit another. His nicotine-stained fingers trembled slightly. It was late afternoon, time to receive the reports that had come in at lunchtime. The combined sounds of men and horses conveyed to him a sense of ease and normality. They did not know what burdens he carried on their behalf, what worries and anxieties he bore for their sake. But when the time came, they would ride out of Urga in his train, like a host of riders out of hell, destroying all that lay in their path. He could already see the dust rising above their horses' fetlocks and hear the sound of their galloping. He had come to long for that moment as a lover for his wedding-night. Mongolia was to be his bride: he would tear her to pieces in order to possess her.

He turned and went back into the *yurt*. Colonel Sepailov had just finished his third glass of *hanchi*.

'Have some more, Colonel.'

Ungern poured another measure into the colonel's empty glass and watched him throw back the powerful drink as if it were milk. If the colonel drank much more of this stuff, he would cease to be of much use, and that would be a pity. Ungern could only really trust two of his staff now – Sepailov was one and the other was Burdokovskii, whom the men had nicknamed the Teapot. They were his eyes and ears – and when there was dirty work to do, his hands as well. There was often dirty work to be done. Sepailov would have to cut down.

'Start at the beginning again,' Ungern said, 'and tell me the story just as you had it from Jahantsi.' He lit another cigarette, blowing smoke carelessly in Sepailov's eyes.

The Khutukhtu Jahantsi was Chairman of the Mongolian Council of Ministers. A sinecure really, but Jahantsi was astute enough to make his position count for something even in these times. He had spoken to Sepailov that morning and asked him to pass on information to the Baron. It gave an impression of intermediacy, even though all concerned knew such things were mere formalities: the Baron was in control for the moment.

'Jahantsi says something is going on at Uliassutai. Two riders came yesterday using *tzaras* with your name. They were given horses at every staging-post.'

'Who gave authority for the *tzaras* to be written?'

'Kazantsev, or so they said.'

'Very well, Kazantsev. And?'

'There was a riot.'

'A riot? You're sure? Not just . . . a disturbance?'

Sepailov shook his head. His skull was curiously shaped, flattened on top, a little like a saddle: in a deformed world, he was a prince.

'People were killed, General. A group of about ninety Mongols attacked a detachment from the Uliassutai garrison. They had to be beaten back.'

'Were they carrying weapons?'

'No. No, that's the curious thing. They were all unarmed. One of the riders . . .'

He hesitated.

Ungern sucked on his cigarette. Smoke hung around him like a noxious halo.

'Yes?' he prompted. 'Go on.'

'He . . . he told Jahantsi they chose to be unarmed. They had access to arms but chose not to carry them. They believed they were immune to bullets. So they rushed a group of armed soldiers, waving talismans and chanting slogans of some sort.'

'Slogans? Bolshevik slogans?'

Sepailov shook his head.

'No, religious slogans. That sort of thing's more in your line of

369

country than mine, sir. But I expect they were the sort of chants I hear them mumbling when I go past the temples here. Mumbo-jumbo, sir.'

Ungern nodded, a little impatiently. He believed in the chanting. It wasn't mumbo-jumbo. Nervously, he drew on his cigarette. He was up to eighty a day now. What would happen when his supplies dried up?

'No doubt,' he said. 'You say some people were killed. Were any shots fired?'

'Yes, sir, a few. It seems young Schwitters was the officer in charge. Do you remember him? He . . .'

'Yes, I remember. Get on with it!'

'Sorry, sir. As I was saying, Lieutenant Schwitters was commanding officer. It seems he panicked and ordered a volley over their heads. When that didn't work, he had his men shoot into the crowd. They killed about twenty of them, no-one's really sure how many. Then they charged in, using their rifle butts. That did the trick. They cleared off double quick. But . . .'

'Yes? Yes?'

'Jahantsi thinks . . . He thinks it's just a start, sir.'

'A start? What makes him think that? Has he any reason to think that?'

'The rioters were shouting about some child, sir. Some sort of Buddha, Jahantsi said. I didn't really understand what he was talking about – it's all gobbledegook to me, begging your pardon, sir. But it seems they expected this child to be some sort of leader. So Jahantsi says, and he should know, I suppose.

'The child, well, he's supposed to be some sort of Saviour they've been expecting. You know how it is. Jahantsi says there have been rumours about this child from other parts of the country. I asked him if . . .'

Sepailov's voice trailed away into silence. Von Ungern Sternberg had grown rigid in his seat, his hands feverishly tight against the arms of his leather-upholstered chair. He wore a red Mongolian coat of silk above black Russian breeches and leather boots: a general learning to be a god. His face made Sepailov think of icons he had worshipped as a child. It was a thin, ascetic face, arid and Byzantine, waiting for ochre and crimson and gold leaf to transubstantiate it. All the fine, exhausted tensions of saintliness, yet

370

without so much as a trace of anything holy. He had always been untidy, but recently Sepailov had noticed a greater disorder in him, less physical than mental. Ungern was breaking down. He was full of prophecies and dreams and undercurrents of a mad divinity. But basically, he was breaking down.

'Where does this child come from?' He snapped out the question angrily.

'Jahantsi thinks . . .'

'Yes?' Ungern stubbed out his cigarette, half-finished, and lit another.

'He thinks he may have come from Tibet. In fact, he's almost certain. I think he knows more than he's saying. Someone told him there's a man with him, with the boy.'

'A man? A Tibetan?'

Sepailov shook his head.

'Jahantsi thinks he may be Mongolian or . . .'

He hesitated.

'Yes?'

'Or Russian. A Buriat. So Jahantsi says.

'And there may be a second boy. A European child, so the rumours go. There's talk that he's some sort of incarnation as well.'

'The first boy, the Tibetan – did Jahantsi say who he thought he was? Who he claims to be?'

'Only some sort of Saviour, sir. A Buddha. You'd have to ask Jahantsi himself.'

Ungern Sternberg's features were set hard. A long vein in his forehead throbbed, pulse by pulse. Sepailov could not look him in the eyes.

'What sort of Buddha? Didn't Jahantsi say? Come on, man! What did he say?'

'I . . . I . . .' Sepailov stammered. How many men he had killed with his bare hands, but Ungern could make him stammer like a schoolboy still.

'Well?'

'I can't remember, sir. Something . . . something beginning with "M", I think.'

'Maidari? Was that it? The Maidari Buddha? Come on!'

'Yes. Yes, I think that's it, sir. I'm sure it is. But you'll have to ask Jahantsi. He knows.'

371

'Very well. Tell Jahantsi I want to see him. Right away. Make sure he understands. I don't care if he's in Council or what he's doing, just get him here. And tell him I want to see the Bogdo Khan tonight.'

'The Khutukhtu?'

'Yes, the Khutukhtu. In private. In his palace. Tonight.'

'Very well.' Sepailov rose to go.

'Sit down,' snapped Ungern. 'I haven't finished yet.'

Sepailov sat hurriedly.

'I'm sorry, I . . .'

'Send a message to Kazantsev. Go to the radio station yourself and send the message in person. Make sure they bring Kazantsev to the other end.'

'Yes, sir.'

'Tell him to initiate a search for these boys and the man with them. He's to put every man on it he can spare. Make sure he understands. Good men. Mongols, Tibetans, Buriats. No Russians. Understand?'

'Yes, sir. Is that the whole message, sir?'

'No. Tell him I want the boys killed. Keep the man alive if possible. But kill the boys. I don't care if he has to kill every youngster between here and Uliassutai, just as long as he makes sure the boys are dead. The Tibetan child above all. Make your instructions clear. You can go.'

Sepailov rose again, saluted, and turned.

'And Sepailov . . .'

'Yes, sir?'

'Tell Kazantsev I want the head. He's to send the boy's head to me. Be sure about that. He can stuff it with straw or anything he likes. But I want the head.'

'Yes, sir. The head. Very good, sir. I'll tell him.' This was more like it. Heads he could understand. Heads he could relate to. All this other mumbo-jumbo just made him bilious. He would tell Kazantsev about the head.

Sepailov lifted the flap of the *yurt* and went outside. His hands were shaking. He hadn't seen Ungern as angry in months. He took a deep breath and walked away. The thought of heads had made him restless. He hoped there would be an execution before bed-time.

55

'Will he come?'

'Yes,' said Chindamani. 'He will come.'

'Why?'

'Because I have asked him to. He cannot refuse me.'

Christopher got up from his seat and went to the window. He and Chindamani were sitting in a faded downstairs room belonging to Urga's old Russian consulate building, roughly midway between Ta Khure and Mai-mai-ch'eng. The consulate consisted of a large, two-storey building built from wood and plaster, topped by an iron roof. Immediately beside it stood the house chapel, with a small cupola.

The consul and his staff had fled months ago, leaving behind a priest, two dogs, a caretaker, and the old Russian cemetery – a wasteland of rubble, unmarked graves, and inconstant weeds.

They had met the priest, Father Anton, on their way to the city. Winterpole had engaged him in conversation, regaling him with stories of his meetings with Father John Sergiev of Kronstadt, the famed spiritual healer at the naval base guarding St Petersburg. They found that they had friends and books in common, although Christopher suspected that much of Winterpole's familiarity with Russian Orthodoxy was little more than bluff. Bluff or not, it was enough to secure them the friendship of the old priest.

He brought them to share his rather primitive quarters at the consulate. He himself lived in an icon-lined room in the west wing of the ground floor, but he gave them rooms on the first floor, more luxurious apartments that had belonged to the departed diplomats.

The building had been looted shortly after the consul and his people left, and the rooms were all but devoid of furniture or trappings. But Father Anton had access to meagre stores in a little cellar. He brought them a battered samovar and plates, musty bedding, and lamps with oil. For all its roughness, their situation seemed a special comfort to them, luxury after so much hardship.

There was black tea for the samovar and charcoal to burn in an iron stove at night when it grew cold, and in the mornings sunlight would lie like warm oil on their sheets.

Winterpole was upstairs writing some sort of report, though God knows how he intended to transmit it to anyone. Christopher and Chindamani were waiting for a man to arrive from the city, a monk to whom Chindamani had sent a message via the caretaker on the previous day. Tsering had originally been a *trapa* at Dorje-la, but a few years earlier he had travelled to Urga to study at the *mampa tatsang*, the medical college of Urga.

'Can he be trusted?' Christopher asked.

'Yes, Ka-ris To-feh, he can be trusted. More than Wan Ta-po upstairs.' She still found the name 'Winterpole' unpronounceable.

'What is his name?'

'Tsering. Tsering Gyaltsen. There were two brothers at Dorje-la, Tsering and Tsewong. Tsewong was at Dorje-la until a little time before you came.'

Christopher looked round at her. In the yard outside, yellow dust was blowing in all directions.

'I've heard of Tsewong before,' he said. 'At Kalimpong, in India.'

Gently, he explained to her what he knew of the circumstances of Tsewong's death. But he did not mention the silver cross that Martin Cormac had found hidden on him.

Just as he finished, there was a knock on the door. Christopher opened it to find the caretaker waiting for him.

'The man you ask for here,' he said in stilted Tibetan. 'He ask you come outside. Not come in.'

Chindamani joined Christopher and together they stepped out of the room. In the passage, crows flew in and out through broken windows. One of the two dogs, a great fawn creature with a spotted back, ran backwards and forwards, growling aimlessly. In his palace of icons, Father Anton sang in a cracked voice, antiphonal refrains to a Palestinian virgin.

A young lama was standing awkwardly by the outer door. Dust blew in through a window and swirled around his feet. He moved from one leg to the other restlessly, unable to keep still. Tsering

374

was narrow-faced and intellectual looking, thin and ascetic like all monks, yet honed to it by more than prayer or fasting.

Chindamani greeted him formally. He flushed and bowed deeply, then advanced and presented her with a *khata* scarf, which she accepted with a smile.

'I have no scarf to give you in return,' she said.

'It is enough for me to be in your presence again,' he said, keeping his head bowed.

'And I am very pleased to see you,' she replied. 'Do you have a scarf to give my friend Ka-ris To-feh? He is the son of the Dorje Lama. You must treat him with respect.'

The young man lifted his head and produced a second scarf, which he proceeded to place in Christopher's outstretched arms. Chindamani passed the scarf she had just been given to Christopher, and he laid it in his turn on Tsering's wrists. The monk bowed even more deeply and remained standing, waiting for permission to move.

'Please come inside and talk with us,' said Chindamani.

'I would prefer to stay here,' Tsering said.

'Very well. Let us stay here. Have you done what I asked you to do?'

The lama nodded. His head moved on a stalk of a neck like a bird snapping for seeds. He was dressed in the usual drab weeds of a lama, but lacked the downtrodden, resigned look so many of them presented to the world. Whatever the source of his asceticism, it had little to do with disgust for life.

A yellow robe is no guarantee against humanity. The words came unbidden into Christopher's head. Hadn't that been what Martin Cormac said, referring to this man's brother?

'What have you discovered?' she asked.

'First, I have something to show you, with your permission,' the monk said.

He indicated something lying on the ground a few yards from his feet. It was a small leather bag stitched roughly with cord. He picked it up and handed it to Christopher without saying a word. He felt it in his hand, slightly spherical, somewhat uneven, and quite heavy.

'Open it,' he said. Christopher did as asked, unfastening the clumsy knots tying the neck. The leather fell away, revealing the

375

small head of a child, the face twisted and smeared with blood. Mercifully, the eyes were closed, but Christopher almost dropped the gruesome object in shock.

Chindamani came to Christopher's side and looked.

'Is it Samdup?' Christopher asked, uncertain whether or not he recognized the dead face.

Chindamani shook her head.

'No,' she whispered. 'It is not Samdup.'

She turned to Tsering.

'Where did you get this?'

'The Russian general Ungern Sternberg has filled a room with heads like this. All boys of Dorje Samdup Rinpoche's age. He knows he is here. He is looking for him.'

Christopher replaced the head in the bag and retied the cords that held it. He wondered where to put it. For a moment, he felt more absurd than horrified.

'Can you help us find him before he does?' she asked.

'I think so. One of my friends at the *mampa tatsang* belongs to a revolutionary club started a few years ago by a man called Sukebator. This friend confides in me because I am a Tibetan and because he thinks I hold more liberal views than most. For several days now, he has been excited about something, although he won't say exactly what it is.

'However, he did tell me something that seemed important. "Ungern is collecting heads," he said. "He's looking for a boy, a *khubilgan*, but he won't find him. The boy is safe, but Ungern won't know until it's too late." He told me where the heads had been thrown, and I managed to take the one I showed you. There was no guard, they had just been thrown into the room to rot. I brought it to you as proof that my friend's story is true.'

'What is a *khubilgan*?' asked Christopher.

'It's the Mongol term for a *trulku*,' Tsering said. His voice had a fresh quality to it, its rhythms less stilted than those Christopher had observed in other Tibetan monks. 'There's no difference really. But my friend said "*khubilgan gegen*", meaning an enlightened incarnation, so I knew he was referring to someone of very high rank. Someone like the Maidari Buddha.'

'And did your friend tell you where this boy is being kept?'

Tsering shook his head.

'No. But I believe I know where this revolutionary club meets. There is a large *yurt* just off one of the smaller alleyways in Ta Khure. I've seen my friend near there several times. If that is their centre, they may be holding the Lord Samdup there.'

Christopher pondered. It sounded as if Tsering was right and that the boy was here in Urga, waiting for Zamyatin to make his move.

'Did your friend say anything about another child, another incarnation? A *pee-ling* incarnation?'

'I do not understand. Do you mean a *trulku* like the Dorje Lama?'

'Yes. He is the Dorje Lama's grandson. He is my son.'

The lama shook his head again.

'No,' he said. 'He mentioned only a *khubilgan*. I think he meant a Tibetan. He said nothing about a *pee-ling trulku*. I'm sorry.'

Chindamani took his hand and held it tightly.

'He will be there, Ka-ris, I'm sure of it. Please don't worry.'

He pressed her hand in return.

'I know,' he said. 'But I'm becoming anxious now that we're so close.'

He turned to Tsering.

'When can we take a look at what's going on in this *yurt*?'

'It must be soon. We don't have much time.'

'Why not?'

'The Lady Chindamani will explain.'

Christopher looked at her, puzzled.

Chindamani's face grew serious. She bit her lip gently.

'It's a prophecy, Ka-ris. The Maidari Buddha must appear on the Festival of Parinirvana.'

'Parinirvana?'

'The final entry of the Lord Buddha into *nirvana*, the state of heavenly bliss. The festival commemorates the day of his earthly death.'

'What does this prophecy say?'

She looked at Tsering, then back at Christopher.

'It says that the Buddha of the new age must appear on the day the last Buddha passed out of this world. They are one person. The Buddha who entered nirvana must now return from bliss for the salvation of men. It says that he will return to earth in the Maidari Temple at Urga.'

'And if he fails to appear there on that day?'

She hesitated.

'He will have to die in order to be reborn yet again,' she said. 'If he is not proclaimed, he will return to the state of *nirvana*, where he will choose a new human vehicle for his next incarnation.'

'But if Samdup doesn't appear this year, why can't he do so next year? Or the year after?'

She shook her head. A crow flew past her in a cloud of dust, its wings black and tattered.

'It must be this year,' she said. Her voice was low, almost a whisper. 'Do you remember,' she continued, 'when you were in Dorje-la, your father told you of another prophecy? "When Dorje-la is ruled by a *pee-ling*, the world shall be ruled from Dorje-la."'

He nodded. He remembered.

'Did your father tell you of another verse?'

Christopher thought.

'Yes,' he said. 'It referred to the son of a *pee-ling*'s son. He thought it referred to William.'

She smiled at him.

'I think he was right,' she said. 'The verse reads: "In the year that the son of a *pee-ling*'s son comes to the Land of Snows, in that year shall Maidari appear. He shall be the last abbot of Dorje-la, and the greatest." Now do you understand? Now do you see why it must be this year?'

Christopher was silent. He stared at her, at a long bar of dust-flecked sunlight that straddled her face, at a wisp of hair that fell, black as an omen, across her cheek. Behind her, the thin monk stood among the shadows, his eyes fixed on Christopher. He felt like a plaything, passed from hand to hand, chased hither and thither by forces beyond his reckoning.

'When is this Festival?' he asked. 'You said it would be soon. Are we in time?'

Her eyes held his. At the end of the passage, a crow cawed and flapped its wings.

'Tomorrow,' she said. 'It begins at dawn tomorrow.'

56

It was dark when they reached Ta Khure. An uneasy darkness, edged with fear. In the streets, corpses lay exposed for the dogs, pillows beneath their heads, prayer-books in their cold hands, waiting. It was the custom.

On Tsering's advice, they had walked from the consulate rather than draw attention to themselves by riding. Winterpole had not wanted to come at first, but Christopher had insisted he accompany them. He did not trust him on his own.

Gradually, the walls of the sacred city had enfolded them as they made their way through the tangled maze of silent alleyways towards the centre. The temples were full of chanting and the flickering of lamps. Everywhere, monks were preparing themselves for tomorrow's festival. In the larger streets, pilgrims still walked or hobbled or crawled towards the Khutukhtu's winter palace.

It was not clear to them how Tsering found his way through the dark lanes of the Khure without a light; but he seemed not to falter, as though possessed of eyes akin to those of an owl or a cat. The festival moon had not yet risen, and the faint light of the stars made little impression in the cramped and narrow alleys down which they wound their slow and uncertain way.

Tsering and Christopher went in front, with Chindamani and Winterpole watching their rear. On their way to Ta Khure, Christopher explained to the monk the circumstances of his brother's death. He kept from him the fact that Tsewong had been a Christian convert, that he had died wearing a silver crucifix that had once belonged to Christopher's father. *Not to the abbot of Dorje-la*, thought Christopher, *but to my father, who really died all those years ago in the snows beyond the Nathu-la.*

'I don't know why he killed himself,' Christopher admitted. 'He left no message, no clues. Perhaps the missionary with whom he stayed would know. But he denied all knowledge of your brother.'

379

'Yes,' said Tsering. 'That is what I expected: that he would deny him in the end.'

'I don't understand. You speak as if you knew him. As if you knew Carpenter.'

Tsering nodded, a dim shape in the gathering dusk.

'I knew him, yes. He once came to Dorje-la. Didn't you know that? About six years ago, a year or so before I left Tibet to study here. Perhaps he came again – the Lady Chindamani would know.'

'I've never spoken about him to her. Why did he come to Dorje-la?'

The monk paused, slackening his pace.

'He had heard – I do not know where – that the abbot of Dorje-la was a *pee-ling*, that he had once been a Christian. Perhaps he thought the abbot was still a Christian, that he was some sort of missionary like himself – I don't know. Anyway, he came to us at the height of summer, asking to be granted admission to the *gompa*. He stayed for several weeks: his journey had been bitter, and he was tired and feverish. When he had rested and taken herbs, he was allowed to visit the Dorje Lama. They were together for a day. Then Kah-pin-teh returned and said he wished to leave. The abbot appointed my brother as a guide, to lead him back through the passes to Sikkim.'

He walked more slowly now, watching the darkness form gently about his words, calm nightfall envelop his memories of his brother.

'When he returned,' he resumed, 'Tsewong and I were together a long time, talking. He said that the *pee-ling* teacher had converted him to his faith, that he had become a Christian.' He paused and looked at Christopher. 'After that, he was never easy in his mind. It was always a burden to him, this foreign faith, this thing of a dying god and a world redeemed in blood. He had never been happy with the life of a monk, but his new beliefs did not seem to bring him happiness either. He struggled with them, as though the pity of it all devoured him from outside. Once, I think he told the abbot of his dilemma, but he would never tell me what passed between them.'

Christopher felt the silver crucifix against his chest. He guessed how deeply his father must have understood Tsewong's position.

They walked on into the thickening darkness. Winterpole

changed places with Christopher, allowing him to walk behind with Chindamani.

Chindamani kept close to Christopher, her hand in his, seeking security or warmth or something he, in his present nervousness, felt scarcely able to give. Once her lips found his briefly in the darkness as they stopped at a narrow intersection redolent with the scent of some hidden blossom. He did not know whether she had explained the nature of their relationship to Tsering; but before it grew dark he had seen that the monk still observed all the proper tokens of respect for the Tara-*trulku* with whom he walked.

For his own part, Christopher was finding it easier to treat Chindamani as an ordinary woman. He thought of her now with less awe than previously. Away from Dorje-la, the goddess in her was stifled somewhat. Or perhaps that is the wrong expression. The open plains and nervous vistas of Mongolia seemed to have swept away something of the air of naïve self-sufficiency that had been nourished in her by the narrow walls and shadowy, painted chambers of the monastery.

They found the enclosure with little difficulty, though Christopher could not see how it differed externally from any of the others. Urga was in reality little more than a nomad settlement that had grown huge and permanent. Many of its temples were tent-temples that could be dismantled and moved when occasion demanded. And the majority of dwellings were *gers*, circular *yurts* of thick felt erected on thin birch lattices.

The wall was not difficult to climb: it had been designed for privacy rather than as a protection against robbers. Even in troubled times like these, theft was uncommon. They slipped over, clinging to the shadows, watching and listening for a sign of life. Christopher carried a pistol he had found at the consulate. He held it ready, but prayed that he would not have to use it. He wanted to find Samdup and, if he was there, William, and take them out quietly, with the minimum of fuss. Zamyatin could wait. Without Samdup, Christopher suspected, he was nothing.

In front of them, barely visible, were two *gers*, one small and one larger than average. They loomed out of the darkness, white, dome-shaped structures that seemed somehow confined by the walls around them.

'Which one?' Christopher whispered to Tsering.

'The large one. The smaller *ger* will be used for storing fuel and provisions. The boy may be in the large *ger* or the wooden house to the rear, I've no way of telling. Let's try the *ger* first.'

They started forward, bending low and moving on tip-toe towards the *ger*. The ground was hard-packed clay, firm and resilient, smothering their footsteps. No sounds came from the tent. In the distance, dogs were barking madly as they circled the city in search of food: there was no shortage.

Suddenly, Tsering stiffened and halted, crouching lower than before. He motioned to Christopher and Chindamani to get down. At the south-east corner of the tent, where the door was situated, they could make out the dim figure of a man. He was leaning on something that could have been a rifle, and seemed to be keeping watch.

'Go round the back,' Tsering hissed. 'Wait for me there.'

He moved off into the darkness without a sound.

'You two go,' whispered Winterpole. 'I'll go with the monk, keep him covered while he carries out a reconnaissance.'

Winterpole vanished after Tsering. Christopher and Chindamani slipped round the curved side of the tent. It was even darker here. They crouched down, listening intently.

No more than five minutes passed before Tsering returned, although it seemed much longer.

'There's only one guard,' he whispered. 'We can get in through the bottom of the *yurt*: it's only held down by blocks of wood for the winter.'

He bent down and began to remove pieces of wood from the *khayaa*, the bottom layer of thick felt that formed the rim of the *yurt*. Christopher started to help him.

'Where's Winterpole?' he asked.

Tsering looked at him.

'Isn't he here?' he asked.

'No, he went with you, to keep you covered.'

Tsering put the block of wood he had been holding to the ground.

'He didn't come with me,' he said. 'I thought he stayed with you.'

They looked round, but Winterpole was nowhere to be seen.

382

'I don't like it,' Christopher said to Chindamani. 'I knew he wasn't to be trusted. Where do you think he has gone?'

'He could be anywhere. But I think we should be quick here.'

She bent down and helped them remove the last of the wooden blocks. It was the work of moments to lift a section of the *khayaa*. A dim light came from inside the *yurt*.

Christopher went in first, holding his pistol ready. Tsering and Chindamani followed. Neither of them was armed.

The interior of the *yurt* was conventional in design, with a central hearth in which a large fire was lit. In front of the fire lay carpets and a triangular arrangement of cushions. Cabinets and chests stood along the walls, and to the right of the door was an elaborate Buddhist altar, stacked with images and other ornaments. Only a few lights provided any illumination.

Christopher crept forward on hands and knees. At first the *yurt* seemed empty, then he made out the shape of two small figures seated on cushions near the door. His heart gave a leap as he recognized William and, beside him, Samdup. A Mongol guard had been placed to watch over the two children. His back was towards Christopher, and he appeared to have dozed off. The barrel of a rifle jutted out above his left shoulder.

Christopher continued to creep forward. Suddenly, he froze. William had caught sight of him. Desperately, Christopher motioned to the boy to keep still. But William could not contain his excitement. He reached a hand out to Samdup and pointed eagerly in Christopher's direction.

What Christopher feared happened. The guard's attention was drawn by the boy's sudden activity. He stood and, turning, caught sight of Christopher and his companions.

The guard shouted and raised his rifle. He fired too hastily, without taking proper aim. The shot missed Christopher by inches, giving him time to move into a crouching position. As the guard aimed for his second shot, Christopher fired. The man staggered, dropped his rifle, and fell back on to the altar, sending its contents crashing in all directions.

The door-flap opened suddenly and the guard who had been keeping watch at the entrance came running in. Christopher fired before the newcomer's eyes had time to adjust to the light inside the *yurt*.

'Quickly!' he shouted, running towards the boys. 'We've got to get out of here before someone comes.'

But in spite of his sense of urgency, he had to stop to hold William and assure himself that his son was still alive. Chindamani came running up behind him, taking Samdup into her arms and lifting him into the air.

There was a sound of voices outside. Christopher put William down and ran to the doorway.

'Come on,' he said, reaching for William's hand. 'Let's go!'

But William looked up at him, tears in his eyes.

'I can't!' he cried. 'Look!'

Christopher looked down at the spot to which William was pointing. There was an iron shackle on the boy's ankle, to which a chain had been attached. The chain was pegged fast to a heavy chest a few feet away. Samdup had been chained in the same way.

Christopher let out a cry of rage. He bent down and picked up the guard's rifle, lifting it as a hammer to break the chain away from the chest.

At that moment, there was a sound of running feet outside. The door-flap was raised and several men came in. They were all armed. The last one held the flap up. A moment later, Nikolai Zamyatin stepped into the *yurt*.

Christopher dropped the rifle and his pistol. Zamyatin smiled.

'You're just in time for the party,' he said. 'The festival begins in a few hours' time. I have a celebration planned.'

57

He had coughed up blood so many times recently, the sight of yet more in the bowl scarcely frightened him. It made him angry more than anything, angry yet impotent, for it was his own body that was in a state of rebellion, and he could hardly order himself taken out and shot. He intended to die on the battlefield, even if he had to drag himself there on his hands and knees; but each time he expectorated blood now, a tiny stab of doubt entered his mind. Perhaps the thing that was eating his lungs away would finally cheat him of the hero's death he craved. There was no glory in spitting this pink fluid into a steel bowl.

The boy had slipped through his net. From reports now being received, it was clear that he and the man with whom he was travelling had made their way clear across the vast plains between Uliassutai and Urga, and that, in all probability, they were already here, within the city, indistinguishable among its multitudes, secret, hidden, walking down darkened alleyways in the dead of night.

He had been sent heads, dozens of tiny heads, enough to fill ten copper chests and more, but still the boy had escaped him. The heads had arrived daily, sewn up in sacks of leather or hessian, the blood on them dried and sticky, and on their heels reports had come of sightings further east or talk of the boy's presence in scattered *yurts* far from the beaten track. The boy had eluded his best efforts to hunt him down, and now he was making ready to challenge him here, at the heart of his kingdom. It was time he saw the Khutukhtu again. Time he warned him of the consequences if the boy could not be found in the next forty-eight hours.

He hastily covered the bowl with a cloth as the sound of feet approached the door of his *yurt*. He heard the guard come to attention, then a voice tell him to stand at ease. The door-flap opened and two men entered: Sepailov and a European in a white suit. Why couldn't Sepailov deal with these men on his own? He knew he needed no permission to have a man flogged, or for that matter, hanged.

Sepailov saluted – rather sloppily, Ungern thought. The colonel's uniform was soiled and torn in places. For that alone he should be shot, Ungern decided. He hated the Russians, above all the military men. All he wanted was to wage war with his Buriats and Chahars, his Tartars and Kalmaks. The rest could go to hell for all he cared. They were just passengers, and some of them weren't even paying their fare.

'Yes, Colonel Sepailov?' he said. 'Who is this man? Why are you bringing him to me?'

Sepailov swallowed hard. He noticed the bowl on the table, near a pile of papers he had given the baron earlier for his signature. Ungern thought no-one but himself and the camp physician knew of his ailment. But Sepailov knew. And he also knew that when Ungern had been coughing blood his behaviour became even more erratic than normal.

Winterpole did not wait for the colonel to make his introduction.

'My name is Major Simon Winterpole of British Military Intelligence. You may remember that we met rather more than a year ago, General, when I visited you at Dauria. I was on an official mission to Ataman Semenov at the time. We were providing assistance to your people in our mutual struggle against the Bolsheviks.'

'You will have to forgive me, Major, but I do not remember you. Life was very busy at Dauria. I saw dozens of people every day. There were representatives from several foreign powers. Now, perhaps you could explain to me just what an agent of British Military Intelligence is doing in Urga. Without permission.'

'But I sent a telegram to you almost two weeks ago. You must have known to expect me.'

Ungern shook his head.

'No, sir, I have received no telegram from you or from anyone else associated with British Intelligence.'

He reached inside his tunic and drew out a silver cigarette case. The family monogram had worn down badly, he noticed. Perhaps it was just as well; he would certainly have no children. He took out a cigarette and lit it quickly, seeking to disguise the tremor in his hand.

'I see.' Winterpole began to wonder if he had done the right thing in coming to Ungern directly.

'Well? I'm waiting for your explanation. I am a busy man, Major. At present, all I know about you is that you are a self-confessed spy who has been operating in an area under my jurisdiction for an unspecified period. I think you have some explaining to do.'

'I assure you, General, that I am not here on an espionage mission. My own position within Military Intelligence is entirely administrative.'

Ungern exhaled a snake of scented grey smoke.

'Meaning that you get others to do your dirty work for you.'

'Meaning that I am authorized to enter into negotiations with representatives of foreign powers. Meaning that I have come to Mongolia with the express purpose of making you an offer of financial and military assistance on behalf of the British Crown.'

The general half raised an eyebrow.

'Indeed? I take it you carry with you credentials.'

'Of course.' Winterpole started to reach inside his jacket.

'They will not be necessary for the moment, Major. Now, I would like to know how you come to pay me a visit in such a hasty manner. This is not normal procedure, as I am sure you are aware.'

Winterpole gave what he hoped looked like a smile.

'I came here tonight in order to bring you information. Information that I believe is important to you. Concerning a boy. Two boys to be precise.'

He saw he had hit the mark. Ungern's flimsy composure visibly cracked. He started as though the Englishman had raised a hand to strike him.

'Go on,' he said. With a shaking hand, he stubbed out his cigarette and lit another.

'I know where you may find the boys . . . if you are quick. I can lead you to them tonight. If you are lucky, you will also be able to lay your hands on Comintern's principal agent in this region. And perhaps more than a few of his Mongol confederates.'

Ungern held his breath very still. If the Englishman was telling the truth . . .

'And you,' he said, 'what would you want in return for this information?'

'Your co-operation. In return for military and financial help. Great Britain will recognize you or anyone you choose to appoint as the Mongolian head of state. We are willing to establish you here on the borders of Russia in readiness for the day when you are ready to go back to claim your own. Tonight's information is merely a start, a token of intent, no more. Take it or leave it, it's your choice.'

'Where are these boys?'

'In Ta Khure. They're being kept in a compound two streets away from the Tokchin temple. There's a large *yurt*, what I believe the Mongols call a "twelve-*khana*". And a summer-house behind it.'

Ungern looked past Winterpole.

'Do you know it, Sepailov?'

'Yes, sir. We've been keeping an eye on it for a little while now. It sounds very likely to me.'

'Good. Send a detachment of men round there straight away. They're to take everyone alive if possible, except for the two boys. Have them shot on the spot, I don't want anyone having second thoughts. You'd best send Russians for this job.'

'Very good, sir. I'll see to it at once.' He saluted and turned to go.

'Colonel.'

Sepailov turned back again.

'Before you leave, have this man taken out and shot. Do it yourself if you have time.'

Winterpole spluttered, then drew himself erect.

'May I ask what is the meaning of this? I'm a representative of His Majesty's government. I have diplomatic immunity. Your behaviour is most improper, General.'

Ungern stood up and leaned across the desk. Winterpole blustered to a halt. He had joined his army of glass, and found himself as brittle and vulgar at heart as any of them. When glass breaks, it shatters, it does not splinter like wood.

'You are not a diplomat, Major. You are, by your own admission, an intelligence agent. Whether you are a spy or an administrator of spies, it is not for me to judge. My task here is to eliminate three groups: Bolsheviks, Jews, and foreign agents.'

'For God's sake, General. We're on the same side!'

'Not any longer,' Ungern told him.

'What do you mean "not any longer"?'

'Just that. Your government has just entered into a trade agreement with the Soviets: it was signed in March. Surely you cannot pretend you did not know.'

'I assure you, I . . .'

'Your Mr Lloyd George signed it alongside Krasin, the Soviet representative, on the sixteenth of March. The Russian Trade Delegation has already been granted permanent status in London. The next step will be diplomatic recognition. Do you tell me you were ignorant of this?'

'I left London long before that. No-one thought to tell me. There must be some mistake.'

'There is no mistake. You are, are you not, one of the two men responsible for the deaths of General Rezukhin and seven of his unit at a camp five days south of here? Were you not originally arrested by the General for spying on the execution of a party of Bolshevik infiltrators?'

Winterpole tried to stand, but his legs had lost their strength. He felt Sepailov's powerful hands on his shoulders, pinning him down. He was beginning to break. In a moment he would shatter and be gone.

Ungern stepped out from behind the desk.

'Please don't take too long, Colonel. I want that boy dead by midnight.'

He went to the door and stepped outside. Sepailov put one hand on Winterpole's windpipe.

'Relax, Major,' he said in a whisper. 'It won't hurt if you don't fight against it.'

58

Sometimes the ticking of the clocks soothed him. At others, it depressed him, and he sought out the silent chambers of his palace, where time seemed to stand still. Tonight, it brought him neither pain nor pleasure, and he realized that he was growing old. He was fifty-one, but he felt older and sadder than that.

Tomorrow, he would have to play the god again for the multitudes already assembling outside in the darkness to receive his festal benediction. A long cord of red silk stretched from his throne through the length of the palace, across the perimeter wall, and into the wide street outside. For the entire morning, he would have to sit holding the cord in one hand while pilgrims gathered in the mud and refuse to touch its other end. They believed that a blessing would pass down the cord from him to them, wiping away their sins, cancelling all the bad *karma* they had accumulated. It was a farce; but it was the only farce he knew.

He had been blind for seven years now. The doctors said it was because he drank so much, but he set little store by their dictums and went on drinking regardless. At least it consoled him in his blindness. He loved *maygolo*, a sweet aniseed brandy that the Chinese traders had sold in small round bottles; and French cognac, whenever Ungern could get a shipment through, which wasn't often; and above all the *boro-darasu* wine that they used to send him from Peking. They gave him a kind of sight, or at least a shimmering in the blackness.

For all that, he resented his blindness. It meant he could no longer enjoy all the beautiful things he had gathered about him over the years. The world was such a place, he thought, such a place; and he had seen so little of it. Locked up in monasteries and palaces all his life, he could not go to the world; but he had brought the world to himself.

His secretaries were in bed. His wife was amusing herself with a new lover, in her own palace outside the walls of Ta Khure: he would cover her breasts with oil and her thighs with essence of sandalwood. His monk-attendants were busy praying in readiness for the Festival tomorrow. Alone, he walked through the silent rooms and corridors of his private residence, touching his past with regretful fingers.

It was all here: plate after plate of Sèvres porcelain, from which he had never eaten, silvered with a fine patina of dust; pianos that he had never learnt to play, cracked and out of tune now; clocks of every description, their hands set at every conceivable hour; albums of ivory and malachite, of mother-of-pearl and silver, of onyx, agate, jade, and ornately tooled Russian leather, of blue and red and purple velvet, crammed with fading photographs of the dead and the living; liqueur stands, champagne tweezers, gold and silver and glass candlesticks for which there had been no candles in years; cigar-cases, card-cases, spectacle-cases of tortoise-shell and gold and silver filigree; telescopes through which he had once gazed at the stars, abandoned and dust-covered now. Dreams and fancies to keep a god happy and a man possessed. He ran a stubby finger over a set of Japanese wind-chimes. They tinkled in the still air like flakes of falling ice.

As the sound faded, it was replaced by another. Footsteps, heavy footsteps. He had expected no-one at this hour. Least of all here, in his private quarters, which no-one entered without his permission. The footsteps grew in volume, muffled by the thick kincob carpet that covered every inch of floor. His visitors were not pilgrims seeking a private audience: pilgrims would have come on silent feet or on their hands and knees. The footsteps halted, still several feet away from him. He turned to face them.

'Your holiness,' a voice said, 'I beg your pardon for this intrusion, but I have brought someone to speak to you. Please listen to what he has to say.'

He recognized the voice. It was Bodo, a high-ranking lama who had once served briefly as one of his secretaries. What on earth could he be doing here? Before he had time to respond, someone else spoke. He could not be certain, but he thought he had heard this voice before as well.

'You are the *khubilgan* of the Jebtsundamba Khutukhtu, the Bogdo Khan, known by the reign-title "Exalted by All"?'

He nodded. He was sure the voice was familiar.

391

'Who else did you think I would be?' he asked.

'Then I am authorized to tell you, on behalf of the Provisional Government of the Mongolian People and the Central Committee of the Mongolian People's Revolutionary Party, that you are hereby placed under house arrest and will be confined to these quarters until such time as it has been decided what is to become of you. Do you understand?'

He nodded again.

'Yes,' he replied. 'I understand perfectly. I recognize your voice, but I cannot remember your name. Who are you?' He thought the man had sounded nervous, as though something was wrong.

'My name is Nikolai Zamyatin, a Buriat representative of Comintern. We met last year when I came here to negotiate with you concerning your possible role in the coming revolution. You denied me then. You shall not deny me this time.'

'Yes,' he said. 'I remember you. You talked about giving power to the people. But then I had no power to give: the Chinese held it all. And now you have taken away whatever power I might have gained. Who will be the new ruler here? You?'

'The people will rule themselves,' Zamyatin said.

'Yes,' he replied. 'But who will rule the people?'

'We're wasting time! I've already instructed your secretaries to prepare your study. There are papers you must sign.'

He did not move.

'You are early,' he said. 'I was not expecting you until tomorrow. I understood you intended to have me arrested after the ceremonies in the Tsokchin. Has something happened to make you change your plans?'

There was perfect silence. He imagined the Buriat staring at him. There was a note of increased nervousness in the voice when it resumed.

'How did you obtain that information?'

'I know everything,' he answered. 'Didn't anyone tell you?' He smiled evenly. Strangely, he was not afraid. After all, this had happened before. And this time at least his captors were Mongols. It was a pity they had come tonight, though. That had rather upset his plans.

Someone stepped up to him and took his arm.

'Come with me, my Lord.' It was Bodo. He could sense the

392

embarrassment in his voice. Bodo would not last long, he thought. He would be one of the first to fall when they brought out the guillotines. A pity, he mused; I should like to have seen a guillotine in operation. He loved mechanical things. And he had heard that guillotines were particularly efficient. Perhaps he could purchase one and have it sent out. It might entertain him for a while. And then he remembered he was blind.

They began to walk, arm in arm, down the corridor. He could hear the footsteps of more than one person in front. When the strangers had first entered, he had guessed there were about eight of them. One was a woman, he thought. And two of them children.

In less than a minute, they reached his study. Bodo helped him find his chair, though he could have done so perfectly well without assistance. Someone else opened his drinks cupboard and took out a glass and bottle.

'I would prefer some port,' he said. 'The decanter on the top shelf.'

He had first been introduced to the drink twelve years earlier by an English explorer called Barnaby or Farnaby or something. Barnaby had sent him several cases of what he called 'vintage tawny' through the Chinese *amban*, who had kept a couple for himself. He was down to his last case or two now, but with care they should last some time. In fact, it was quite likely that they would outlast him.

The port arrived on his desk and he took a tiny sip. He kept it for special occasions. This, he fancied, was as special an occasion as he was likely to experience for some time. The problem was, how to get Ungern here to share it. He had planned everything for tomorrow, and now here they were already, stamping over his carpets, opening his bottles, sampling his wine, and, for all he knew, redistributing his wealth.

'What exactly is it you wish me to sign?' First the Chinese, then Ungern, a saviour turned monster, and now a home-grown menace. They all wanted him to sign something. Two years ago, Hsü Shu-tseng had given him thirty-six hours in which to sign a list of eight articles relinquishing sovereignty to the Republican government in Peking. He had refused; and his ministers had been forced to sign instead. In the end, it amounted to the same thing: he had no real power, only what others chose to give him.

The Buriat answered him.

'This is a document in which you acknowledge the sins you have committed during your reign as Khutukhtu. In it, you state that, as a result of these sins, you have ceased to be a *khubilgan* and that the Jebtsundamba Khutukhtu has incarnated in another body. You accept that this is so and freely permit the reins of power to pass into the hands of the true incarnation, who is to rule in your stead, assisted by the people's government led by Sukebator. The new Jebtsundamba Khutukhtu and the people's government in their turn acknowledge the help rendered to them by the People's Soviet of Russia and seek to establish a special relationship with that country. You yourself shall become a private citizen, living in your summer residence and relinquishing your other properties and your Shabi fiefdom.

'We shall deprive you of nothing but your title and your power. You may continue to drink. You may have as many women and boys as you like. You may keep all your toys and baubles, although you may not add to them. The state will repossess them on your death.'

And how soon would that be? he wondered. There must be a way to get Ungern here. Let them sort it out among themselves. What had all this to do with him? He knew now who one of the children must be, of course. He had expected as much. But who was the second child?

'And if I refuse to sign?'

'You have no choice, you know that. But if you co-operate, it will make life considerably easier for you: a comfortable home, a generous allowance, gratification of worldly desire. In a way, I envy you.'

'Do you?' he said. 'Perhaps you will change places with me, then. Your eyesight for my blindness, your power for my comfort, your humanity for my divinity and my drunkenness.'

The Buriat said nothing. He had not expected him to.

'So,' he said, 'what else do you want me to do? What other papers are there for me to sign?'

'You can help us prevent bloodshed,' said the stranger. 'Your soldiers are still loyal to you. Most of them are disaffected with von Ungern Sternberg – the Khalkha Mongols, some of the Buriats, the Tibetans, the Chinese you gave an amnesty to. He tries to buy

394

them with booty, but they owe an allegiance of faith to you. Tell them to lay down their arms or to join the People's Army. The baron will have nothing left but his Russians and the handful of Japanese he brought to Urga in February. I have a decree here in your name, instructing all Buddhist troops to stand down and await further instructions from you or one of your representatives. It only wants your signature and your seal.'

And if there is bloodshed, he thought, *whose body will be first on the gibbet?*

'You have a *khubilgan* of your own,' he said. 'Let him sign the decree. Let him rally the faithful.'

'You know that will take time. We don't have time. We must act now if lives are to be saved.'

Whose lives? he asked himself. *Mongol lives? Or the lives of Soviet troops?* He knew Red forces were already moving into the north of the country.

'That is none of my concern. But if you will permit me, I want to speak to my Minister of War.'

He reached out a hand and lifted the telephone. Dandinsuren would understand. He would send Ungern. And then he could sit and listen as they bickered for power.

The receiver was dead. He should have guessed.

'I'm sorry,' said the Buriat. 'Your telephone has been temporarily disconnected. You'll have to make your own decisions tonight.'

He leaned back in his chair, defeated for the moment.

'Bring the boy to me,' he said. 'I want to speak with him. I want to touch him.'

There was a pause, then Zamyatin spoke quickly in bad Tibetan. A woman answered him, but he overrode her objections. There was a shuffling sound. Someone was standing by his chair. He reached out a hand and touched a face, a child's face.

'Come closer, boy,' he said, speaking in Tibetan. 'I can't feel you properly. I can't see you, so I must touch you. Don't worry, I won't hurt you.'

But the boy remained rigid, standing just within reach, yet holding back from him.

'What's the matter?' he asked. 'Are you afraid of me? Is that it?' He could feel his own heart racing. It was curious, but now they were so close, he realized with a start that he himself was afraid of the boy. It seemed a sort of blasphemy for them to be here together, two bodies incarnating a single godhead. In the recesses of his mind, an image formed and became clear: an endless row of shining mirrors, repeating a single figure until it grew quite dim in the distance. He understood himself better than he had ever done before: he was a mirror, and he suddenly felt fragile, like glass bending in candlelight. With the slightest touch he would shatter and fall into tiny silver pieces.

'Yes,' said the boy. His voice trembled, but it was a finely-modulated voice. He was sure the boy was pretty and that his cheeks would be soft to the touch. What if they should sleep together? Would that hold the mirrors firm?

'What is there to be afraid of?' he asked.

'I don't know,' said the boy. 'But . . .'

'Yes?'

'But Tobchen told me you would try to have me killed. If you knew of me.'

He moved a finger along the slanting ridge of the boy's cheek. It always cheered him to hear Tibetan spoken.

'Who is this Tobchen?'

'He was my tutor. And my best friend. Except for Chindamani. He was an old man. He died while we were trying to get to Gharoling. That was a long time ago.'

'I see,' he said. 'I'm sorry. And I'm sorry he told you I would try to kill you. Why would he want to say that?'

'Because you are my other body. Because only one of us can be Khutukhtu. They want to make me Khutukhtu in your place.'

Such soft down on the child's face. Old Tobchen had been right, of course. He would have the boy killed if it helped him keep his throne. But the thought frightened him. If he smashed one mirror, what would happen to the images in all the others?

'Perhaps,' he murmured, 'I could be your tutor. And we could become friends. I have a palace full of toys. You could stay here: you would never grow bored or tired.' Or old, he thought.

The boy ventured a little closer.

'What's your name?' he asked.

'They say I am now called the Jebtsundamba Khutukhtu. But I find it hard to say.'

396

He snatched his hand away. How perverse to be caressing his own cheeks! His hand felt cold and empty.

'Do you have another name? A Tibetan name?'

'Dorje Samdup Rinpoche.'

'Dorje Samdup Rinpoche? When I was brought here first, many years ago, my name was Losang Shedub Tenpi Donme. That's a mouthful, isn't it? I was ten years old. How old are you, Samdup?'

'Ten, sir.'

His heart froze. Perhaps it was true, after all. Perhaps a death of some sort had occurred, perhaps he had truly been reborn while still in the flesh.

'Who is the other child with you? I heard the footsteps of a second child.'

'He is a *pee-ling*,' replied the boy. 'His name is Wil-yam. His grandfather is the abbot of Dorje-la. One of the men with us is his father.'

'His father is a Bolshevik?'

'No. They've taken him prisoner. He came to rescue Wil-yam and me tonight.'

'I see. And who is the woman you were talking with?'

'Her name is Chindamani. She used to be with me in Dorje-la Gompa, where I lived.'

'Was she your maid?'

'No,' the boy said. 'She is the Tara *trulku* of Dorje-la. She's my closest friend.'

He reached out an unseeing hand. The boy had long hair that made his fingers blush to touch it.

'Do you think she would speak with me?' he asked.

The boy was silent. Then the woman's voice answered, quite near. She had been standing beside the boy.

'Yes,' she said. 'What do you want to say to me?'

'I want your advice,' he said.

'My advice? Or the advice of the Lady Tara?'

'The Lady Tara's help,' he said. 'I want to know what I should do. Should I sign these papers? What is the right thing?'

She did not answer straight away.

'I think,' she said at last, 'that the Lady Tara would tell you not to sign. You are still Khutukhtu. It is not for these people to decide who shall and who shall not be an incarnation.'

'Do you believe I am an incarnation?'

'No,' she replied.

'Was I ever one?'

'Perhaps,' she answered. 'Before the child was born.'

'Then what would you advise me to do?'

She was silent.

'I cannot advise. I am only a woman.'

He shrugged.

'And I am only a man. You have said so yourself. Advise me what to do. As one human being to another.'

She was long in answering. When she spoke, her voice was dull and flat with defeat.

'You must sign the papers. You have no choice. If you don't, they will kill you. They already have the boy. They have all they need.'

He said nothing. She was right. They would kill him, and what would that achieve? He turned and faced the Buriat.

'Are you still here, Za-abughai?' he asked. He meant Zamyatin.

'Yes. I'm waiting for your decision.'

'Very well,' he said. 'Give me my pen. I'll sign your papers. Then you can get out.'

59

Christopher wondered when the nightmare was going to end. They had shot Tsering seconds after entering the *yurt*. Then he and Chindamani had been tightly bound and taken outside with William and Samdup. There had been a long wait while Zamyatin got his men ready for their move against the Khutukhtu's palace. Christopher had somehow managed to get close enough to William to talk to the boy, reassuring him, telling him his ordeal would soon be over. They had set off about an hour after Zamyatin first discovered them.

He remembered a maze of crooked alleyways and streets smelling of ordure and decomposition, hands holding him, pinching him, guiding him, voices whispering and whimpering in the troubled darkness, the darkness itself struggling to become flesh as faces swam in and out of view.

Then the moon had glided out from behind the clouds, copper and stained in a turbid sky, and the alleyways had become silent streets of silver filled with dogs and the dim, shrouded bodies of the newly dead. Above them, the towers of the Maidari Temple, eighty feet high, made bold pillars against the sky; on the Tower of Astrology, a single light burned in readiness for tomorrow's Festival.

It had been a simple matter for Zamyatin and his men to effect an entry to the palace. There were fewer guards on duty than usual, with half of them preparing for the festival. Those that remained had put up little resistance, and the revolutionaries had rounded them up in a matter of minutes.

William sat on his knee, the way he had once sat when he had been a much younger child, many years ago, before all this began. He was telling his father the details of his journey to Dorje-la. Christopher let him talk, urging the boy to get everything off his chest. He wondered if William would ever recover properly from his ordeal – assuming, that was, that they ever got out of this place and made it back to England alive.

Samdup had told them that the swelling on William's neck had started to go black about a week ago. Zamyatin had been too preoccupied making the arrangement for his coup to waste time getting a doctor for the boy.

'How does your neck feel now, son?' Christopher asked.

'It's no better. I think it's going to burst all the time. It feels as though things are crawling round and round inside. If I touch it, it hurts terribly. Sometimes I want to scratch it off, it gets so bad. Samdup had to tie my hands behind my back two nights ago. I'm frightened. You'll make it get better now you're here, won't you?'

The boy's trust was almost unbearable. Christopher felt more helpless than at any time in the past months. The Khutukhtu had sent instructions for his personal physician to come. Now all they could do was wait.

The Khutukhtu was growing drunk on his port. He sat on a long sofa in one corner of the room, smoking long Turkish cigarettes with the peculiar affectation of the blind. Chindamani and Samdup sat beside him. For all the differences between them, they understood one another. They were all *trulkus*, they all suffered from the same deformity.

Samdup was tired, but he could not even think of sleep. Chindamani was with him again, and the *pee-ling* who had helped to rescue them from Dorje-la that night, Wil-yam's father. He felt uncontrollably excited: perhaps something would happen now, perhaps he and Wil-yam could escape from Zamyatin at last.

He did not like his other body. The Khutukhtu drank alcohol as though he were an ordinary person, and he appeared to be quite drunk. Samdup disliked the way the fat old man stroked and frotted him with smooth, clammy fingers. The vacant expression in those blind white eyes unnerved him. Unaccustomed to either vice or sensuality, the boy had no capacity for sympathy. He was too young to understand that sin was just as much a part of life as prayer, or that holiness, like water, would grow stagnant if it were allowed to lie too long without being stirred.

'Come here,' the Khutukhtu said, standing and taking Samdup's

400

hand. Samdup followed him across to a huge table on which stood a huge machine with a wooden horn. It reminded Samdup of the great trumpets on the terraces of Dorje-la. The Khutukhtu bent down and cranked a handle in the side of the machine, then, with blind fingers that shook from a combination of port and nervousness, dropped the needle heavily on to a spinning black disc. Instantly, a raucous voice blared from the horn, accompanied by rapid, jumping music.

> *I would say such – wonderful things to you*
> *There would be such – wonderful things to do*
> *If you were the only girl in the world*
> *And I were the on-ly boy.*

'That's a gramophone,' said the Khutukhtu. 'It makes music, as though someone were inside, singing.'

'Turn that infernal thing off!' Zamyatin was sitting at a little table at the far end of the room, sorting out the various papers he would need to legitimize his coup.

'Until my Lord Samdup is installed as my successor tomorrow,' said the Khutukhtu, 'this is still my palace. If you want silence, there are plenty of other rooms to go to.'

'The boy should not be listening to music. He should be sleeping. Tomorrow will be a long day. He is about to have responsibilities thrust upon him.'

The Khutukhtu snorted loudly.

'The boy should not be sleeping. He should be in my private chapel, praying, meditating, and generally preparing himself for his proclamation. The formalities must be observed. The boy must not go cold to his destiny.'

He paused and inhaled a stream of smoke. He remembered the days before his own enthronement as Khutukhtu: the vigils, the offerings, the fasts, the long, dull hours of liturgical recitals. Such a terrible waste of time. But he wanted the boy away from here before trouble started.

'This no longer concerns you.' Zamyatin creased his brows, more in irritation than anger. Tonight, he would not be angry. Mongolia was his. Next month, he would sit in a gilded room at the Kremlin and dine with Lenin and Zinoviev as their equal.

401

'I am the boy's tutor now,' said the Khutukhtu. 'Who better than I to train him? I mean to teach him everything I know. Don't worry – I'll spare him my vices, if you spare him yours. He won't need them. But he will need my experience; and my memories. I tell you that he will need prayer more than sleep tonight. And meditation more than prayer. Or do you intend to act as spiritual director to your new ruler? I hardly think you're qualified.'

Zamyatin said nothing. Whether the boy slept or prayed meant nothing to him. So long as the child was pliable. So long as he was fit to be paraded in the proper regalia and knew how to make the right gestures tomorrow. He already had men scouring the store-rooms of the palace for the clothes the Khutukhtus wore as children.

From somewhere in the distance, the sound of shouting came, followed by silence. A door slammed, heavy and muffled. Then, quite distinct, between the ticks of a clock, a series of shots rang out, clear and perfect in the stillness of the night.

Zamyatin ordered two of the guards to the door.

'See what's happening,' he said, 'and get back to me as quickly as possible. I'll stay here with our prisoners. Hurry.' He took a revolver from his pocket and checked it.

The guards hurried through the door, taking their rifles with them. No-one spoke. The counter-attack had come sooner than expected, and Zamyatin's men were thin on the ground.

Less than a minute later, the guards returned looking visibly frightened.

'An attack. Von Ungern Sternberg. He has the palace surrounded.'

'How many men?'

'Impossible to say, but the men at the gate think we're outnumbered.'

'Any news of Sukebator and his men?'

'They're tied up at the radio station. Ungern's Chahar units have them pinned down.'

Zamyatin turned to Bodo.

'Think, man! Is there another way out of here? A secret passage? This place must be riddled with them.'

The lama shook his head.

'They were blocked up by the Chinese when they held the

402

Khutukhtu prisoner. They've not been opened up again. Except . . .'

'Yes?'

'Except for one, I think. Behind the treasure rooms. It's better hidden than the others. There's a tunnel behind it leading to the Tsokchin. Once we're there I can arrange for horses.'

Zamyatin thought quickly. If they could make it to Altan Bulak, where the provisional government was located, there was still a chance that they might join up with the Bolshevik forces moving in from the north. He had the Khutukhtu and the boy. All the aces were still in his hands.

'Quickly then,' he shouted. 'Lead the way. You and you' – he pointed at the two guards – 'keep our rear covered. Hurry up.'

The sound of shooting was growing louder. Ungern could be here in a matter of minutes.

The little group was assembled quickly, Bodo in front, then the prisoners, followed by Zamyatin and his guards.

The corridor outside the Khutukhtu's study took them directly into his treasure rooms. They were like Aladdin's cave, crammed from end to end with bric-a-brac of every description, the product of a lifetime's obsession.

Chandeliers hung everywhere like patterns of webbed and shattered ice. Vases from China, rugs from Persia, peacock feathers from India, two dozen samovars of every size and style from Russia, pearl necklaces from Japan – all jostled each other in cosmopolitan disorder. The Khutukhtu had ordered goods in multiples: a dozen of these, a score of those, sometimes the entire contents of a trading house during a visit to Mai-mai-ch'eng. It was a vast jumble sale to which no buyers ever came.

In one room, there were long rows of guns in glass cases: rook rifles, sniders, Remington repeaters, breech-loading pistols, carbines – some purely ornamental, others quite deadly, all of them unfired. In the next was the Khutukhtu's vast collection of mechanical inventions. There were dolls at a small piano that could play Strauss waltzes one after the other without ever tiring; a monkey that could climb a pole and another that could spin round and round a horizontal bar; tin soldiers that marched, motor cars that rolled on painted wheels, ships that bobbed on metal seas, birds that sang and flapped their wings or hopped along branches of gold tipped with leaves of emerald – all still and silent and rusting now.

Zamyatin hurried them along too quickly to see anything very clearly. They could hear loud explosions from the front of the building now, and shooting had opened up on both sides. Chindamani slipped and fell against one of the cases. At first, Christopher thought she had hurt herself. But after a few moments, she picked herself up and took Christopher's hand. He thought she had picked up something from the case, but it was too late for him to see what its contents had been.

William kept falling behind. He was tired and sick, and running exhausted him; but he would not let Christopher pick him up and carry him. Zamyatin pushed and prodded the boy, urging him to make haste. When Christopher made to defend him, the Russian just waved his pistol at him and told him to keep going. Christopher knew the only reason Zamyatin kept him alive was the thought that he might come in useful as a bargaining counter.

They reached the last room. It was a plain room panelled in dark wood and hung with rich Tibetan tapestries. Zamyatin hustled everyone inside and shut the door.

'Where's the way out?' he shouted.

Bodo scrambled over a pile of cushions at the rear of the room and pulled back one of the tapestries. The entrance to the tunnel had been concealed with very great skill, having been set into the panelling without any obvious join. It was opened by means of a small lever in the floor. Bodo pulled the lever and the panels slid back with a low grinding sound.

'What are you waiting for?' cried Zamyatin. 'Let's go!'

Bodo stepped into the entrance. Chindamani stepped up, followed by the Khutukhtu and Samdup. Suddenly, there was a cry from near the main door.

'I'm not going into another tunnel! Please, father, don't let him make me!'

It was William. The sight of the dark opening had awakened in him memories of the tunnels beneath Dorje-la. He hung back, clinging to Christopher.

'What does he say?' demanded Zamyatin. 'What's wrong with him?' The man was growing terrified now. He was so close to victory, yet the sounds of defeat were all about him: guns, high explosives, the child whimpering.

'He says he's frightened. He won't go into your blasted tunnel. You know what happened at Dorje-la. For God's sake, let him stay here with me. He's no danger to you.'

'And let you show Ungern straight to our exit? No-one stays. If he won't come, I'll shoot him here and be done with it!'

Zamyatin reached out a hand and grabbed for the boy. William struggled, twisting away from the grasping fingers. The Russian lunged and found the boy's shoulder, but as he did so his hand slipped and struck his neck.

William screamed with pain. Zamyatin's hand had struck the swelling, breaking the skin. The boy collapsed, falling into Christopher's outstretched arms. Zamyatin reeled back, horror-struck.

They expected blood or poisoned matter. But there was no blood. It made no sense at first, there was just a seething, something black moving on the child's neck. And then the blackness broke and became multiple.

The spiders had been on the verge of hatching. Now, suddenly released from the body of their host, they tumbled into the light, tiny legs unfolding and quivering across William's neck and on to his shoulder. There were hundreds of them, each one no bigger than a very small ant.

Christopher cried out in horror and disgust. The tiny spiders were running everywhere now, masses of them, in search of food. Chindamani ran across to Christoper and helped him brush the last of the brood from William's neck. As though transfixed, Zamyatin stood staring at the boy. Spiders ran across his feet and vanished.

Christopher looked up at the Russian. His face was expressionless, his eyes empty of any emotion.

'He's dead,' he whispered.

Zamyatin looked at him blankly. He did not understand.

'He's dead,' Christopher repeated in Tibetan. 'My son is dead.'

60

What happened next was a blur. There was a sound of shouting outside, followed almost immediately by a crash as the door was smashed open. The two guards inside the room panicked and opened fire. Two seconds later, the barrel of a heavy pistol appeared from behind the door-jamb. The guards had forgotten to take cover before firing and presented easy targets. Three shots rang out in quick succession, taking the guards and Bodo.

As that happened, Zamyatin whipped out his own pistol and waved it at the Khutukhtu, who was sitting beside Christopher alongside William's body. Chindamani grabbed Samdup and made for a door at the rear of the room, leading into the tunnel.

The man at the door stepped across the bodies of the guards into the room. He held his pistol high, pointed at Zamyatin's head. It was Sepailov.

'Drop your gun, Mister Zamyatin,' he said in Russian. 'Otherwise, I will be forced to shoot.'

'One step closer,' Zamyatin replied without looking round, 'and your Living Buddha is a dead one.'

'Be my guest.' It was a different voice this time. Von Ungern Sternberg eased himself past Sepailov into the room. He cast a quick glance at William's body, unable to make out what lay behind the small tragedy. His men were in control of the palace. Sukebator's forces had pulled back to the outskirts of the city. The remaining revolutionaries had been rounded up and were already being executed or interrogated. There was just this little matter to clear up.

'The Khutukhtu is a traitor,' he went on. 'I have in my pocket a document signed by him, instructing his forces to transfer their allegiance to the revolutionary army. I have already issued instructions for his execution. You're wasting your time, Zamyatin. Go ahead and shoot him if you want: you'll only be doing my job for me.'

Zamyatin glanced round. Ungern and Sepailov were in the room now. Only Sepailov held a gun; the baron was too much in control to feel he needed one. Zamyatin looked back at the Khutukhtu, then at Christopher. He needed another card to play, one that would force the baron to bargain. He turned and caught sight of Chindamani and Samdup at the rear door, still hesitating.

'For God's sake, Chindamani!' shouted Christopher. 'Get out of here! Take Samdup and run!'

'I can't go Ka-ris To-feh, not without you. Don't ask me to leave you.' She had the boy and she knew she ought to make a run for it. His life was at stake: it was her duty to save him. But she could not move. With William dead, Christopher needed her more than ever. Her love for him tore at her love for the boy, like a trapped beast with its claws.

Zamyatin lifted his pistol and pointed it at Samdup.

'You!' he shouted in Tibetan. 'Come over here and bring the boy with you!' He knew Ungern would need the boy now, if he intended to execute the Khutukhtu. Ungern would not let Sepailov fire as long as he was aiming at the boy.

'Ka-ris To-feh!' cried Chindamani. 'Tell him to put his gun down or I'll have to kill him. Please tell him!'

At the main door, Ungern and Sepailov hesitated. Zamyatin had realized they needed the boy. But why didn't the woman take the child and run? And what did she mean, that she would kill him?

'There's no point, Zamyatin,' Ungern said. 'You're finished. Sukebator has retreated. The members of your cell in Urga are either dead or in prison awaiting my orders. If you kill the boy, the Khutukhtu lives. If you kill the Khutukhtu, the boy will serve me as he has been serving you. And in either case, Sepailov will kill you. Better just to drop your gun and make the best of it.'

Zamyatin's hand was shaking. He could scarcely control the gun. He turned from the boy to the Khutukhtu and back again. Sepailov took a step forward. Zamyatin raised the gun and pointed it at Samdup.

Ungern nodded. Sepailov took aim and fired, hitting Zamyatin in the left shoulder. Zamyatin's hand jerked, firing his pistol, then he dropped it. It fell like a stone to the heavily carpeted floor.

Sepailov motioned with the gun, directing Zamyatin to join

Christopher, and the Khutukhtu. Clutching his bleeding shoulder, the Buriat complied.

At first, no-one noticed what had happened at the rear of the room. But when Zamyatin moved, Christopher saw Chindamani bending over Samdup, who was lying on the floor. Her long black hair fell over the boy like a curtain, concealing his face. But from the edge of the curtain, like the petals of a tiny flower pushing themselves out above the black soil, fine drops of blood appeared, spread, and combined into a gently moving pool.

No-one spoke. Sepailov continued to cover Zamyatin with his pistol. Ungern turned his attention to the woman and the boy. When she raised her face at last, it was smeared with blood, and blood clung in fantastic drops to her hair. She said nothing. All her eloquence was in her face, in the blood that had fastened to her cheeks and lips, in her eyes, staring past her matted hair into the still room.

Christopher rose from his seat. He felt a great numbness come over him, striking his limbs into immobility. He remembered Chindamani's words, speaking of the prophecy: he will have to die in order to be reborn yet again. Her blood-streaked face chilled him. He knew that some terrible doom had taken hold of them and was harrying them towards an end of sorts. Or a beginning: it was all the same now.

'Let me go to her,' he said in English, addressing Sepailov. The Russian did not move. He held his pistol pointed at Zamyatin, ready to fire again. Christopher stepped towards him, but Sepailov did not alter his position. He let Christopher pass.

Ungern watched as though fascinated as Christopher walked up to Chindamani and raised her. Samdup's head had been shattered by the bullet: there was no question of saving him. He held her against his chest, feeling the futility of everything.

They stood like figures of wax, separate, immobile, dreaming individual dreams. There were no prayers to take away the blood or the spiders, no gestures to bring life back to the dead. No-one saw Chindamani move, or if they did, they ignored her.

From the folds of her jacket, she took out a gun, a small Remington she had somehow managed to palm and hide during the tour of the Khutukhtu's treasures. She had no certain idea how it worked, or whether it was loaded, or whether it worked at all.

408

She had picked it up without any notion of what she intended to do with it. Now she knew.

The first shot found Sepailov's back. He dropped without a murmur, dead or paralysed. Zamyatin saw his chance. He ran forward, fingers clutching for the gun that had fallen from Sepailov's hand. As he picked it up, she fired again. And twice more.

Zamyatin clutched the air. He tried to breathe and swallowed blood. He tried harder and blood came gushing out of his mouth and throat. Suddenly, his legs felt like lead and his head was spinning through space, divorced from his surroundings. He heard himself coughing, choking, drowning in his own blood. The red flag fluttered in front of his eyes against a velvet sky. Then it was blood, smothering the world. And at last he was one with History and the sky was empty and as black as night.

Chindamani dropped the gun. With a moan, she bent forward, burying her face in her hands, sobbing without control. With Samdup, the last vestige of her world had vanished. Her love for Christopher had destroyed the boy and the world he had symbolized.

Christopher picked up the gun. He had guessed who the baron was, guessed what he had to do if they were to get out of here alive. Von Ungern Sternberg carried a pistol in a leather holster strapped to the belt around his waist, but still he had not drawn it. He had watched everything without emotion, a spectator rather than a participant. Now, he looked at Christopher and the gun in his hand as if it were a flower he held out to him.

The precision of death, its absoluteness, its finality – these had been the things that had commended it to him and made him linger over it in the long days and nights at Urga. How simple it was, he thought, how plain, how lacking in affectation. It was all that he admired, the ultimate statement of man's innate simplicity. There was a perfection in it such that he had never found in anything else, and he loved to see that perfection renewed, that bold simplicity restated time after time in his presence.

And now his own death. It had come sooner than expected, but it was welcome all the same. It seemed like a good enough time to die.

Christopher raised the pistol. There were still a few bullets left, but he would need only one. He stepped up close to the baron, looking him directly in the eye. Yes, he could understand the stories he had heard. It would be better for everyone if von Ungern Sternberg were removed. He put the pistol to the baron's head and felt the trigger start to give to the pressure of his finger. The baron did not move or flinch. He stared into Christopher's eyes patiently, without reproach.

It was no good. Christopher could not be an executioner. Not even of this man. He lowered the gun and threw it away from him, into a corner.

There was a sound of running feet outside.

'Why didn't you shoot?' Ungern asked.

'You would never understand,' Christopher replied, turning away and putting his arm round Chindamani. She was trembling.

The door opened and a group of armed men ran into the room. They stopped dead, slowly taking in the scene before them. Two of them stepped past Ungern and took hold of Christopher and Chindamani, dragging them apart.

'Let them go.' Ungern's voice was sharp.

The soldiers looked puzzled, but the baron's tone had been unmistakable. Their hands dropped, leaving Christopher and Chindamani free. Christopher bent down and picked up Samdup's body. He was still warm. Blood ran unimpeded over Christopher's hands. He cradled the small body against his own for a moment, then passed him to Chindamani. Ungern watched as Christopher crossed the room to where his own son lay and picked him up carefully.

They said nothing as they left. Ungern sent a man with them, to see that they got through. They left the Khutukhtu behind, sitting on a heap of cushions, kneading his soft robes with nervous fingers. His hands still held traces of scent from the boy's skin. By dawn, even that faint perfume would have faded forever. He closed his eyes as though something had crept into his darkness, and he dreamed of freedom.

61

They carried the bodies to the Maidari Temple and left them there, at the foot of the giant statue of the Maidari Buddha. There was no resemblance between the statue and Samdup, except that neither lived nor breathed. Chindamani tidied Samdup's clothes and hair, but otherwise did nothing to disguise the fact that he was dead. Christopher took the small teddy-bear and put it in William's hands as he had done in England when he was asleep. There were no words.

It was dawn when they left the temple. The first rays of the sun were striking its towers, and everywhere pilgrims were rising to pray the first prayers of the Festival. They prayed for paradise and an easy death to take them there, for the removal of the weight of their sins and enough food for the journey home. Today, nothing would be refused them.

Christopher and Chindamani walked out of the city without any very clear idea of where they were headed. Their clothes and hair were covered with blood, but they walked on without stopping to wash or refresh themselves.

It was well after noon before they halted. They had long since lost anything that looked like a road or a track, but had gone on as though they had found a path of their own to follow. They went north into the Chingiltu Ula mountains, making their way by guesswork. The sides of the steep hills through which they passed were heavily forested with dark conifers. They passed no-one. They could hear birdsong, but saw no birds or any other form of wildlife.

The place they stopped in was a small temple, abandoned and partly ruined. They spent that night there, huddled against one another for warmth. The following morning, Christopher went into the forest to find food. There were berries on low bushes and small mushrooms that he gathered in his shirt. He found a small stream close to the temple and carried water back in an abandoned bowl he discovered in an inner room.

411

They spent the rest of that day in the temple, resting, and decided to spend the next night there too, lighting a fire with wood Christopher collected from the forest floor. By now, they could talk about what had happened.

There was no point at which they decided to stay in the temple. But gradually, they made themselves more comfortable there, and soon they regarded it as home. No-one came there. Nothing disturbed them. Christopher found abundant game deeper in the forest and made small traps for deer and rabbits; but Chindamani would eat no flesh and subsisted on what they could gather from the trees and bushes.

She suffered badly from a sense of guilt. She was convinced that her illicit passion for Christopher had in some way been responsible for Samdup's death. Her hesitation at the entrance to the tunnel had, she was certain, cost Samdup his life. No amount of reasoning could convince her otherwise.

She was a *trulku*, she said, a vehicle for the Lady Tara. She had not been born to love or marry or have children. That was for mortals; but the goddess in her was not mortal. He used the arguments that she had used with him before, that she herself was a woman, that she was not a goddess, that their love was its own justification; but she would not listen, or if she did, she chose not to accept his reasoning.

For the first two months, she would not sleep with him. He, for his part, neither pressed her nor made her feel unwelcome. But when they walked in the forest together, she would sometimes hold his hand, and at those times he would feel she still loved him in spite of herself. And one day towards the end of June – he kept a rough calendar on the trunk of a tree outside the temple – she came to his bed as she had done the first time, without explanation.

The summer passed in shadows and bars of sunlight slanting through the trees, restless and delicate. Chindamani prayed each day in a small shrine that formed part of the temple, and together they restored the building as best they could. They never spoke of leaving or finding a place for the winter, although they both knew they could not stay where they were much longer.

At the beginning of September, a traveller passed near the temple. A lama, he spoke adequate Tibetan, and was able to explain to them what had happened since they left Urga. At the

412

end of May, von Ungern Sternberg had taken his forces out of Urga for a last engagement with the Soviet troops now entering the country in large numbers. He had been defeated, captured, and, it was rumoured, executed – exactly one hundred and thirty days from the time of his visit to the Shrine of Prophecies in Urga, when the words recorded on the placard to the south had been whispered to him. Sukebator and his partisans had taken Urga at the beginning of June, assisted by Bolshevik troops, and a People's Republic had been proclaimed. A sense of normality was beginning to return to the country.

The lama was on his way to a monastery north of the mountains, a place called Amur-bayasqulangtu, situated on Mount Bürün-khan, of which both Christopher and Chindamani had heard. It was the site of the tomb of Ondür Gegen, the first of the Jebtsundamba Khukukhtus.

They persuaded the lama to stay with them for a day or two. He explained to them that the temple in which they now lived was known as Maidariin süme and that it had been dedicated to the Maidari Buddha. When it was time for their visitor to leave, he asked if they would accompany him to Amur-bayasqulangtu, and they agreed. The nights were growing cold and before long food would become scarce. But they had another reason for leaving. Chindamani was one month pregnant.

Amur-bayasqulangtu was a vast establishment that amounted to a small town, with some two thousand lamas in permanent residence. The abbot, known as the Khambo Lama, was happy to receive them and provided them with quarters where they could spend the winter. During the coming months, Christopher and Chindamani lived together as man and wife. Once, a deputation from the new government paid a visit to the monastery to assess it for taxes; but the lamas hid their guests until the officials had gone. Once winter set in hard, they were not troubled by further visits. But Christopher knew the monks would not be left in peace for ever. There would be fields to dig and roads to build and armies to train. There would be a price to pay for independence.

Years later, Christopher thought he was never so happy as during that winter and spring. All his time was spent with

Chindamani or doing things for her. And he believed she too was happy.

'If I left you, Ka-ris To-feh, could you bear it?' she once asked him while they lay in bed together listening to the wind flapping against the walls of their *yurt*.

'No,' he said, and held her hand beneath the rough blanket.

The wind blew and snow fell and ice lay packed against their door. It was a bad winter, during which many of the monastery's livestock died. But in the end spring came and the ice melted and turned to water. At the beginning of May, Chindamani's baby was born. It was a boy. They called him William Samdup.

Christopher woke one morning a week later to find both Chindamani and the baby gone. He looked everywhere, but could not find them. Then, on the table where they had eaten supper the night before, he found a note in Tibetan. It was not easy for him to read, but he persevered, and in the end he understood it.

Ka-ris To-feh, it read, I am sorry that I could not leave you in any other way. Forgive me if this causes you pain, but it is hurting me too, more than I can bear. If I could choose, I would stay with you forever. Even if it meant endless lifetimes, I would willingly stay with you. I love you. I have always loved you. I shall continue to love you until I die.

But I cannot stay with you. You already know that, I am sure. Our child cannot stay here, he will always be in danger. We cannot go to your country, for you have told me there are no gompas there. I think you know who the child is, who he is destined to be. I will tell him about you. Every night when the sun goes down and the monks leave us alone, I shall talk to him about you. I will never forget you. Please remember me.

He remembered the last evening at Gharoling, when she had gone out to the terrace to gaze at the darkness. *Don't think I can be yours forever*, she had said. *You must not think that.* But he had thought it and he had wanted it.

He left the monastery two days later. He knew where she had gone, of course. In his mind, he could see the little lake on the borders of Tibet and the rocky island in the centre, with the tiny temple. And he heard her voice, speaking into the wind: *I have been here before. And I shall come here again.* More than anything, he wanted

414

to go there, to see her just once more. But of all the places in the world, he knew it was the one place he could not go.

He headed for Urga. For the first time that year, there were no clouds in the sky. England was a long way away.

Thanks to everyone who helped with this book, especially my agent, Jeffrey Simmons, John Boothe and Patricia Parkin at Grafton, Patrick Filley and Jennifer Brehl at Doubleday; Frs. John Breene and Tony Battle for their patience; Dr Dermot Killingley for his rendering of the Bengali song on pages 44 and 96; and Beth, for everything.